SOLANGE'S H
MAN – BUT HER BODY BETRAYED HER
TIME AND TIME AGAIN . . .

'Let me make love to you, *querida*. Only an older man knows how to cherish beauty. It isn't too late for you to belong to me.'

'Let me go!' I choked, kicking his legs. He cradled my neck in the hollow of his hands as I twisted violently, trying to free myself.

I felt weak, realising that as I pushed and pummelled his broad chest, even the feel of his body caused my pulse to beat faster. I could not mistake his look of deep passion. It enveloped me like a quivering screen of heat. He sensed my hesitation and covered my mouth with his own. My knees buckled weakly and we collapsed together, sprawled on the grass . . .

Love's Raging Torment

ALMA ASHLEY

SPHERE BOOKS LIMITED
30–32 Gray's Inn Road, London WC1X 8JL

First published in Great Britain by
Sphere Books Ltd 1982

Published in America by Tower Publications Inc., 1978

TRADE
MARK

Printed and bound in Great Britain by
Cox & Wyman Ltd, Reading

Book One

Chapter 1

Little did I guess, as I lay awake in bed, that my entire life was to change in a matter of hours. The January night was freezing in our small cottage and I hugged myself desperately in my undershift. The winter of 1701 had no more mercy on a girl of sixteen than on old Grandmère, coughing and spluttering on her pallet of straw at the side of our precious fire of peat and twigs. Our wretched hovel was tightly shuttered, but the wind howled and blew furiously down the stone chimney. The fire alone was unable to cope with the chill air in the bleak room and we were thankful for the body heat from the livestock huddled at the other end of the room. Only yesterday a ragged beggar had been found stiff and dead by the church wall, and the winter vegetables that we had worked so hard to plant were frozen into the rock-hard ground. For weeks we had lived on thin stew made of the few remaining scraps from the pig we had killed in October, and now the goat was going dry. I wondered how we were going to keep from starving. Never had I known such a winter.

I wrapped the rough blanket over my shoulders, pushing my feet into my list slippers, and crept to the kettle over the fire.

"Grandmère," I whispered, pouring the hot posset of honey and wine into the pannikin, "You must drink this to soothe your chest."

But even as I spoke the coughing continued, and I could see that she was exhausted.

I gently pushed the tendrils of damp, grey hair from her gaunt face and spooned a little of the liquid down her parched throat. She lay back, breathing in rasps, and a thin, gnarled hand clutched at my arm. The lips moved, but I could make no sense of what she was trying to say. I leaned closer and she whispered my name.

"Listen, Solange . . ."

"Grandmère, be still. Save your strength. Try to get some sleep."

"No, listen, child. I must speak with you."

"It can wait till morning. You must not tire yourself needlessly."

"Solange, please be still and hear me out."

I could tell she would not rest and drew the wooden stool to her side. Her breathing was labored and her voice faint.

"Listen well, Solange, and take heed of what I tell you. When the fire is out, you must remove the brick from the hearthstone."

"You mean the loose brick where you keep the papers and your marriage lines?"

"Yes, child. Be patient." She closed her eyes as if to regain some strength. Then the whispery voice continued.

"The yellow Venetian lace is there."

"Yes, I know the old lace is there, but what of it? I will get it for you in the morning when the fire is out."

"But wait, that is not all." She began to speak more quickly, and the words became jumbled. I wondered if she was just rambling.

"There is a diamond wrapped inside the lace, child—a gem of such great worth that I dared not try to sell it for fear of tricksters and rogues."

Now I knew the fever had her. Two golden louis would have bought the entire cottage, plus its miserable contents.

"Yes, Grandmère. Now try to rest."

"Wait, Solange. Listen! Perhaps I've been wrong to keep the truth from you all these years."

"Truth? What truth? I wish you would try to sleep, Grandmère."

She didn't seem to hear me, and stretched out a scrawny hand again, the prominent bluish veins raised under the dry skin, and stroked my hair without changing expression. Staring through watery eyes, she went on with renewed strength.

"Now that you are sixteen I think you should know."

"Know what? What are you trying to tell me?"

"My daughter Wilhemina was very much in love as a girl. I told her no good would come of it, going with the gentry, but she knew better. Laughed at me, she did. I can see her now, throwing back her hair, her curls dancing in the sun. 'He loves me, *Maman*. Don't worry, my gentleman loves me. Look what he gave me—this diamond.' And off she'd go to meet him, never saying where. Secrets, always secrets. I'd never seen a diamond before—it just looked like a shiny piece of glass—but I knew I'd better hide it, made her let me hide it under the hearthstone. But when you came along, I lost her." The watery greyish eyes blinked and turned toward me. "Do you understand what I'm telling you, Solange?" Her breathing seemed a little easier now.

I heaved a sigh of exasperation. "Are you trying to tell me that my mother didn't die from the pox, but giving me life?"

"I've been meaning to tell you all these years, but I waited till I thought you'd be old enough to understand. Then the years seemed to go so quickly . . . I meant to tell you."

"I'm sorry you lost your daughter for me, Grandmère." I didn't believe a word.

"You are my little girl all over again. You have my Wilhemina's eyes, sea-green changing to the color of winter grass when you're angry."

"I don't understand why you bothered to lie to me, though."

"Because I didn't want you to think it was your fault,

Solange. Your mother died happy, do you understand? She named you Solange, and smiled before she went."

Grandmère was asleep at last. I crawled into the bed beside her. At least we could share the heat of our bodies. I lay there thinking about my mother's death. No, I told myself, sick old women were apt to say anything. My stomach ached at the thought of the posset, but I decided to save it for her and keep the old life flickering.

I must have dozed, for when I opened my eyes the light of day was throwing shadows on the bare walls. Grandmère felt ice-cold beside me. My heart pounding, I put my hand in front of her mouth. There was nothing—Grandmère was gone. Perhaps it was a mercy, as there was nothing left in the house to eat.

I pushed my feet into my sabots, stuffed with straw to keep out the cold. I had to send for the village women to lay her out, and the priest had to be called. But first I must remove the papers from the hearthstone, for I would have to beg for work at one of the inns. All the little farms were too poor to keep themselves properly fed this brutal year, and few had any beasts left.

The hearthstone came away as I pushed it, revealing a large space containing an old wooden box. I lifted it out with the old poker, forced open its creaking hinges, and gathered together the scraps of paper. There was the yellow ochre lace that poor Grandmère had prized so highly. Perhaps I could sell it to the inn wife in exchange for food and lodging,

I pushed the hearthstone back into place and opened the box. I gasped, forgetting the freezing room, forgetting the cold, stiff body on the straw. My fingers trembled as they reached out to touch the enormous, cushion-shaped diamond resting regally in its golden setting on the delicate lace.

Then the unbelievable was true. Grandmère had been speaking the truth. Could that be her voice which now whispered, "Put it on, Solange. Put on the diamond that was meant for your mother from the great gentleman."

I became conscious of my patched shift and stood up. I removed the string from the hook on the door and ran it through the ring of the setting, and then hung it around my neck. Our only pewter dish had been polished with sand till it shone like silver, and I held it to see my reflection. The diamond sent blazing colors onto the bare walls when I brought the candle nearer to admire my magnificent heirloom. Never had I imagined, when I listened to the travelers on their way from Paris to Normandie, or to the village gossip about the great balls at the chateaux, that anything comparable to the stones which clustered and glittered from fingers and ears could ever be mine. Only my hair was fit to wear this ornament that shone brighter than the summer sun.

I dressed quickly and removed the shawl from the dead body of my only relative. It would partly shield me from the icy winds as I ran for the women and the priest.

He was far from pleased to be called out on this sharp, bitter morning, and muttered under his breath, "There's a venison stew waiting good and hot for me at home. We must be quick." His small nose was red with cold. He chanted and with the utmost haste as the women placed the yellow tallow candles at the head and foot of the bed. But the ground was too hard to take the dead, and I left her with the good village women. I had to give them the last of the corn for the animals in the pen.

I took one last look at the only home I had ever known, this barren cottage outside the village of Clagny, and left. The blanket of snow stretched as far as the eye could see. My small bundle of effects served as a muff, and I kept my hands tucked inside it. The wind was icy on my face, and I tried to pull the shawl tighter around my head. My feet became numb with cold and the snow reached my knees. There was never a soul in sight, for who but a starving dog or beggar would be abroad on such a godless day? Tears stung my eyes as I realized one of my sabots had fallen off. I would never find it now.

I grew weary from hunger and the extreme cold and wanted only to lie down and sleep. I must have lost my way—how much longer could I push myself forward? But, as I was about to give up hope, I spied smoke curling from a chimney ahead. Just a little further, I told myself with heartfelt relief. I managed to crawl as far as the great black door and fell against it. The thud must have been heard from inside, for I was lifted by a fat, bloodshot-eyed giant.

"What have we here, my pretty? A babe from the storm, it seems."

I looked up at a pock-marked, bulbous nose and a mouth with but two teeth, both black as night.

"Bring her over to the fire, Pierre. The poor mite is soaked to the skin."

I caught sight of a round-faced *commere,* with the look of a russet apple, tending the fire as she spoke. I tried to smile to show how grateful I was, not only for the fire roaring up the chimneypiece, but for the friendly presence that would protect me from the evil-smelling innkeeper.

"Run and fetch me a blanket and a dish of stew, you lazy good-for-nothing, and be quick about it!"

My soaking shawl and woolen shift were beginning to steam. She removed them and rubbed my hair till I thought I would faint. My innards clutched at the good fare she poured gently through my chapped lips.

"There we are now. Isn't that better, my child?" And so saying, she wrapped me in a huge green shift like her own, tied by a drawstring. I remembered to keep my hand over the diamond, for what would a penniless wanderer be doing with such a treasure if it had not been stolen? I must keep my newfound knowledge to myself, lest I be thought of as halfwitted. "Daughter of a gentleman!" I could hardly believe it myself, and would guard my secret well, biding my time.

"You are too kind, mistress. How will I repay you? I have some precious lace I could exchange for shelter if the innkeeper will allow."

"I am the inn wife, my child. The innkeeper, my husband,

has been gone three long years. Pierre is but my bedwarmer, for he is good for little more."

I felt the color rise from my neck to my face. She was plain-spoken if nothing else.

"Lift your skirts and follow me. What is your given name? If you are with child, do not fear, for I will not turn you out."

"Oh, no, mistress. I am most certainly not with child, and my name is Solange."

I followed her up the winding staircase, as Pierre eyed me from his stool, lazily rubbing his legs. I hated the hot, hungry look in his eyes. She left me in a tiny attic with a sloping roof. I lay down, exhausted and thankful for a full stomach and a place to rest. I undid my bundle and removed the lace.

"Please take this, mistress, with my thanks."

She wiped her hands on her soiled apron and bustled over.

"That's a fine piece of stuff and no mistake. Did your sweetheart bring you this? Are you sure you are not with child? For I will help you."

"Oh, no, mistress. I speak the truth and I have no sweetheart."

"Well, if you don't want to tell me, we won't speak of it. But I will keep the lace—it must be worth a pretty penny. Now I'll leave you the candle and will wake you sharp at six. There's plenty to do, although the inn is very quiet. No travelers, this wretched winter."

"Good night, mistress, and thank you."

"You call me Clothilde and I will call you Solange. I'll look proud and no mistake with this tied over my bun of a Sunday."

As soon as the door was shut, I brought the diamond out of my bodice. I was enthralled by the glistening lights that danced this way and that. I recalled some of the tales I'd heard of Madame de Maintenon, who, it was said, wore diamond buckles on her shoes, and the great ladies with diamond coronets on their gleaming curls. The light from the candle made the flashing colors dance around the garret. I was so absorbed that I only became aware of the stench of sweat, garlic and horses emanating from Pierre when he jumped at me from the door.

"Just a little kiss, my pretty. And what's that you're holding?"

"Get away," I croaked.

"I could get us a King's ransom for that! Give it here! I've got connections. I'll get plenty of gold for that."

I thrust it out of sight. My fingers turned into claws and scratched with all my strength the lascivious visage that loomed so close to mine. His big fat hands grasped me painfully as he pressed his gross body against me. I was like a piece of driftwood swept by the storm, and fell back across the bed, powerless. I felt his fumbling paws tear my shift with his urgency.

"I'll get the diamond as well," he laughed roughly.

I writhed and fought as I screamed, "Clothilde! Clothilde!"

The weight was lifted as I heard Clothilde shrieking, "Get out, you fat swine!" She boxed his ears with her sabot till she drew blood. He wiped the trickling mess with his torn sleeve.

"I should have warned you to lock your door, my child. The pig is going out this night, and may the devil himself take him!"

She had no mercy as she swung the stool over his head, and I watched it crash into pieces at their feet. He was only just conscious as his eyes rolled and his knees buckled under him.

"You're just jealous 'cos you're old and look like a witch on All Hallows Eve!" he bellowed.

She kicked him out of the door, and I heard a roar as of an animal being slaughtered as his body landed at the bottom of the stairs. Then there was only a dragging sound, and the opening and closing of a door. The bolts were put in place, and I breathed a sigh of relief.

A panting and puffing Clothilde returned and collapsed onto my pallet and fell into a snoring sleep as if drugged. In spite of the weight of her buxom frame I, too, dozed off, and knew no more until it was morning.

"I cannot remember a winter as wicked as this," Clothilde muttered as she bustled about the kitchen taking the hot bread from the oven. I loved the warm aroma that greeted me each morning.

We sat at the table drinking warm wine mixed with water. Frou-Frou, the black cat, waited expectantly for his saucer of milk. Nothing else would budge him from his spot at the fireside. I poured him his breakfast from the leather jack.

"There you are, *mon ami*. You enjoy your meal and then sit on my lap to warm me."

I had been at the inn five weeks. Clothilde needed a serving maid for the travelers she expected soon, and I was indeed grateful to be wanted.

"I will not forget your kindness to me. One day I will be able to repay you in full."

"What a dreamer you are, child. Drink your warm wine. There will be enough to do for you to repay me when the coaches start to arrive."

How right she proved to be, for spring in all its wonder was just around the corner. One morning, suddenly it seemed, I woke to the trilling of birds and padded to my window, flinging it wide, breathing deeply of the sweet-scented air. The walnut and olive trees were in bud. I laughed as a little brown rabbit raced from his burrow, blissfully unaware of my curious eyes. I sang as I ran down the stairs to my chores.

"'Tis indeed a good morning, Solange," Jacques, the stable boy, grinned, wiping his mouth on his cuff.

"'Tis more than good, Jacques! It is a joy to be alive this lovely day! I thought the winter would never end."

He stood in the yard, gawking at me like a dolt.

"But there's work to do," and I hurried about my tasks, in haste to be rid of his playful dallying.

That very morning brought two cloth salesmen on their

way to Normandie.

"'Tis a fine wench we have to serve us, friend, as innocent as the spring itself, I'll be bound." He slapped his fat thigh in merriment, no doubt thinking himself a great wit.

I held my head high as I banged the jug of wine on the table and set the venison at their places.

"These buxom damsels are not so innocent," replied the thin one, with a face like a goat, eyeing me up and down knowingly. I turned on my heel, but he was too practiced for me. I felt his heavy hand pinch me through my bodice, and I crimsoned with embarrassment and rage. I lifted the jug and, much to the fat one's delight, poured the good wine slowly over his head. Spluttering curses, he leaped to his feet but I ran to safety behind Clothilde's skirts in the kitchen. Frou-Frou scurried for shelter under the table.

Clothilde waited at table until they were gone.

"They say the king is on his way to Paris with Madame de Maintenon, child. I hear it said they will be on this very road."

My heart leapt to hear such news. "How could they be sure? Those salesmen would say anything to gain attention."

"They didn't know I was listening. It's surprising what they let slip when they're in their cups."

"Then it must be true," I reasoned. "Oh, Clothilde, I would dearly love to see the royal coaches and wave as they go by!"

"Indeed you shall, child, but run to the cottages first and bring that Flavie to lend a hand. I would not miss such a sight myself, but the inn is my livelihood. I'll want to hear of the ladies' jewels and manners, if you catch sight of them. Remember everything if you should spy the royalty."

I ran all the way to and from the cottages, deposited the frizzy-haired, churlish Flavie at the kitchen door, and skipped by the hedgerows of peeping buds. The sky was a clear blue with only a puff of cloud here and there, and I stopped under a vine to munch the bread and cheese Clothilde had insisted I take for my midday meal. It seemed more flavorful than ever in the fresh air. I brushed the crumbs onto the grass and stretched my arms wide. What an exciting day this was for me—an adventure to be sure! I gossiped merrily with the peasants as I hurried on my way.

"We're to see the King along the road this day and no mistake," a fat-faced shepherd shouted as he stopped with his cart of hay. "Climb on the back with me, my fancy, if you be coming too."

"Thank you, but I will see all from here," I replied.

Before long I saw that the bourgeoisie had clustered down the road. The outriders of the entourage could be seen and heard in the distance, bright plumes of white and red blazing and flowing in the breeze, thundering hooves coming nearer every second.

The rumbling became deafening as I spied the gentlemen-at-arms. They sat erect and proud, ignoring the deeply rutted road as if, by magic, the crevices had disappeared for them. I realized they would be gone in a flash and pushed myself to the front of the crowd, my legs weakening with fear and excitement. I lifted my hand, but it refused to wave. I opened my mouth to shout and cheer, but only a very faint noise emerged, rather like a cat mewing.

When the huge white horses in their shining accouterments were almost upon us I was seized by a sudden impulse and flung myself in front of the magnificent coach with the coat-of-arms of France emblazoned on it.

The coach drew up sharply, and I felt a grip of steel.

"You stupid girl, you could have been killed!" A man's hand grasped my free one roughly. I noticed that my rescuer wore a dark red signet ring with a castle design cut in it. I turned my mud-spattered face up to the scowling horseman and felt my mouth drop open at the sight of his fine attire and very dark brown eyes. This must surely be a nobleman, not a mere servant! He let go of my hands and I threw my bunch of dog roses into the coach and heard for the first time the voice I later learned was that of Madame de Maintenon.

"Oh, throw them back, your Majesty! You never know where they've been."

To delay them a little longer I tried to sing a village song,

"When we were locked in the cow shed," but could only croak the first few bars.

A voice that could only belong to the King laughed deeply and the famous head appeared at the window. His small black eyes were mocking as the thin lips curved into a smile.

"So, you are holding us up, are you? There are some bonny girls in this part of the world." He lifted my chin. "None too clean, mind you. Here's something for your sweet face." He pressed a gold louis into my numb fingers. An elegant, beringed hand flashed as it delicately touched the black crimped periwig thoughtfully: "I think I remember a golden girl," and the lines that ran from nostril to mouth were creased the more. "But that was long ago."

The bouquet was lifted to the long aristocratic nose.

"We've wasted enough time, your Majesty," Madame interrupted impatiently.

With a flick of the lace-clad wrist he signaled for the journey to continue.

I closed my mouth and tasted the salt of my tears. I had missed my chance to declare myself the daughter of a gentleman, and they were already disappearing from view. The soft, brown eyes of the nobleman were imprinted on my mind. I had never seen a more handsome man. I felt my arm where his hand had gripped me and held it out to see the imprint of his long fingers turning red.

As the crowd began to disperse I ran blindly toward the inn. They had seen their bit of fun for the day and I knew they were pointing fingers at me, guffawing. But that was as nothing compared with the thought that I had not spoken what was in my heart. When would I get another chance to be face to face with the great Louis? I would give much to meet the handsome nobleman again—my heart lurched at the thought of him. I ran, the coin clutched in my hand, and did not feel the fine rain that had begun to fall. The sky had turned grey by the time I collapsed into the warm arms of Clothilde.

"You're soaking, child, and flushed like a newborn babe. Did you see them? Was it too much for you?"

Excitement had turned to despair and words failed me. "I saw them, yes," was all I managed to whisper. Clothilde led me to the kitchen where she rubbed me down and left me to dry in a blanket with my clothes laid out. Later I sat forlornly sipping the watered wine and answering the exasperating questions. Flavie and Clothilde stood gawking, the travelers forgotten for the moment.

"Did you see the King? What did he wear? How many rings did he have on his fingers? Did he look old? What did the ladies wear? Are they beautiful?" they chorused.

"The King is a handsome man, although his skin is pockmarked. He was very kind, and spoke to me." (I did not mention the coin I still had clenched in my fist.)

"What did he say?" Clothilde gasped.

"He said I was a comely brat, but dirty." I bawled, "I'm not dirty!" and put one bare foot behind my leg to rub it, hoping in vain that Royalty hadn't noticed the dirt on my feet.

I would not be pressed any further, and was promptly bundled up and hurried off to bed by a clucking Clothilde.

"To be honored by his Majesty and all you can do is cry! It must be the shock."

By the time she shut the door I was already half asleep, fingering my diamond and my gold louis. I now had two things that had belonged to the gentry, I realized—one to royalty in fact! My thoughts turned to the young gentleman who had held my arm so tightly. I rubbed the spot where he had gripped it and didn't mind the soreness. Sleep overcame me, and I dreamed he was astride a fine black horse and calling me to join him, beckoning me as through a fog. I called back to him, telling him that my father was a gentleman, but he just laughed louder and louder as the fog enveloped him.

"Ever since she was addressed by Royalty all she has done is mope, can't do anything with her, walks around like a half-wit," Clothilde could be heard to say many times after that memorable day. And no doubt it was true. I went about my work, but always in the front of my mind were the great King and his party, the splendid coaches, and the finely clad, dark-haired nobleman. Each night I tried to dream again of him calling to me, and wondered what it would feel like for him to hold me in his arms. I would close my eyes and imagine him kissing me and whispering words of love. I would hug myself into my blankets, and see especially his velvet-brown eyes. I had never felt this lurching in my heart before.

Sleep would not come as I relived our brief meeting; I wouldn't let myself doubt that we would meet again.

The days dragged on. I would know what to do in time, I told myself. I lay abed planning to buy a bolt of good cloth for a gown from one of the traveling men with my gold louis.

Spring turned into summer, and one day Clothilde ran into the kitchen.

"A grand coach has just arrived with ladies and gentlemen, and one of the ladies has asked for the serving maid with the golden curls and green eyes! She wants you, Solange! Quick, child, she's waiting! Oh, dear, mercy me," Clothilde muttered, sending a jug clattering to the floor. "If only an outrider had come to prepare me, I would have had flowers arranged and a table laid with the best pewter. What an honor is bestowed upon me this day!" Her face was flushed with agitation. "Move yourself, Solange! Don't stand there like the village idiot! Put that blue ribbon in your hair that you bought last market day. Shoo! Shoo!" She bustled me out of the kitchen and up the stairs.

I turned and faced her. "What use will a blue ribbon be with this miserable skirt and apron? And I don't know any ladies. She must be mistaken."

I walked slowly to the front of the inn and was greeted by a small, thin woman with an aquiline nose. She held a lace handkerchief to it as if she were shutting out a noxious odor.

"That's the girl. Come here, child, you've been summoned. Follow me."

"Summoned?" I stammered. "What do you mean?" I wondered hopefully if the brown-coated nobleman had summoned me.

The tight little mouth tutted with impatience, and the square-toed shoe tapped.

"What I say. You have been summoned by his Majesty and must come at once. What name have you?"

"My name is Solange, Madame, my Lady, your honor."

"Solange! Hmm. You're not my idea of a sun angel!"

I thought I was dreaming and just stood there, staring at the two spots of rouge and wondering why she still looked sallow in spite of the powder and paint.

I felt a push from behind. "Hurry up, Solange, and wash your face!" It was the good Clothilde.

"There's no time for that, the king is waiting. You must hurry, I say. Come along." And with that, she turned on her heel, impatient to be off.

"Wait, please, my Lady, your honor," for the truth had finally dawned. I really *had* been sent for. My heart leapt in my throat. "I will get my things."

"Your things!" She turned as she answered, her swirling brown skirts swishing. "And what use do you think there will be for your rags at the Chateau? Come along, I say! Make haste!"

I followed her into the grand coach, trying to emulate her arrogant walk and holding my head high. I threw Clothilde a kiss, and she whispered, "Don't forget us, child. We'll be thinking of you."

"No fear of that! I'll be back."

I left my sabots at the side of the road—I would not need those things where I was going—and entered a fairytale world. I wriggled my toes in the fur carpet, luxuriating in the silky feel of it.

"You may address me as Madame de l'Eglise," the pinched nostrils sniffed as if still perceiving an odor. She moved to the corner of the coach.

I looked out at the gentlemen-at-arms who were accompanying us and felt a glow of happiness. At last I was entering the world to which I really belonged. A coffer encrusted with gold appeared and a delicious comfit was popped into my mouth. I pushed it from one side to the other, and sat like a lady sucking on the delicacy.

I would be sure to see my handsome nobleman at Court, I told myself. There had been a twinkle in his knowing eyes, even if his words had been harsh. I stared at the countryside racing by and was brought back to the present with a jolt.

"Are you a virgin, child?"

I gazed at the gold feather in Madame's hat bobbing as we rode along.

"Oh, yes, your Ladyship, Madame de l'Eglise!"

"Are you sure? For we will soon know if you lie."

"I do not lie, Madame de l'Eglise. I have not known a man."

She seemed satisfied, for she nodded her head and continued to ignore me from the opposite side of the carriage.

"I am one of the ladies of Madame de Maintenon. Why she thinks you would amuse his Majesty in these troubled times, I cannot imagine. Your speech is atrocious. We shall have to do something about that at once." A delicate wisp of white lace was held to the proud nose and held there until she spoke again.

"His Majesty suffers with the gout, and his digestion leaves a lot to be desired. If gossip about his health reaches your ears, you will show suitable respect, and not encourage such prattlings."

"Yes, m'lady." I nearly lost the comfit as I replied, but slurped it back to the side of my mouth just in time, much to the disgust of Madame de l'Eglise. She tut-tutted with downcast eyes and an exaggerated sigh, seeming to suggest that there was no hope of dealing with me.

"Can I . . . may I ask you something, Madame, my Lady?"

"What is it?"

"Who was the gentleman traveling with the King, the day his Majesty noticed me?"

"What gentleman? There are hundreds of gentlemen at Court."

"Oh," I felt foolish. "He was very dark-eyed and had curly black hair with a velvety brown skin."

"You didn't miss much, did you!" she shot at me slyly.

I blushed and looked down. "I noticed he wore a ring with a seal that looked like a castle."

"Hmm, that would be Don Fernando of Spain. From a most noble Spanish line."

I gulped. "I knew he was a nobleman, Madame, my Lady."

"It is I who should be questioning you. Kindly remain silent, you insolent girl, and remember your place. And stop saying 'Madame, my Lady'—'my Lady' is sufficient."

"Certainly, my Lady . . . Madame . . ." I said with downcast eyes.

"Oh, dear, never mind!"

Although a little dismayed at being treated thus, I determined to do my best not to disappoint Madame de Maintenon or, indeed, the King. I would do as they wished. He had been kind to me; Pinched-nose was only a servant. I shot her a quick glance out of the corner of my eye, but she seemed to have dozed off, her chin resting on her chest. I was much relieved and put out my tongue as far as possible in her direction, but my laughter awoke her and I was horrified to think she might have seen my impudent action through her half-closed lids.

It was all too much for me to understand. So he was Don Fernando of Spain—I knew he could not have been an outrider. He'd be shocked to see me at Court. My heart leapt at the thought. But perhaps he had a sweetheart already. What a fool I was to imagine he'd be interested in me. Madame had said I spoke very badly. Supposing he were married. I gasped aloud and stole a quick glance in her direction, but she slept again, the feather in her hat bobbing in time to the motion of the coach. He couldn't be married, I reasoned. I felt sure that my instincts were right.

"What's the matter? What was that noise?" Madame shrilly inquired of me.

"I didn't hear anything, m'Lady. Only a horse, perhaps."

"Humph! I'm stiff from this carriage. The sooner we arrive at Versailles, the better. Of course, the Court isn't what it was, with the wars still going on in this year of Our Lord 1702! His Majesty is still fighting for peace, and there is much unhappiness. Of course, the King does not lose an ounce of dignity. He behaves as if nothing is amiss at the Court, but a person in my position hears things." She lifted the sharp nose even higher as I was dismissed once more. She resumed her nap, and her head slid to one side, her hat slanted at a rakish angle.

I felt my own eyes grow heavy, and my head slipped sideways, though I tried to keep awake. That I could sleep with the bumping of the coach and so much to see was a bitter disappointment to me. I rubbed my eyes and stretched my arms wide, blinking. Perhaps I was dreaming, I thought, but reality came flooding back with a quick glance at the crab-apple face of Madame, straightening her hat while she held something in front of her face to catch the reflection.

"Hold this still for me, child. No, no, lower down and hold it steady!" She applied two blobs of rouge and now resembled a jester from the fair I had seen last summer in the village. I covered my smile behind my free hand. I did not wish to be in her bad graces if I could help it.

I pressed my nose to the window as if in a trance. I could see an immense building illuminated with light, a vision of beauty in pink, red and white that must surely be the Palace. I blinked at the wrought-iron balconies. Its chimneypots seemed to be made of gold. It was a huge gilded casket with sparkling silver slate roofs against the velvet blue sky. It seemed to be a heaven on earth—surely heaven could be no more perfect than this!

"Oh, m'Lady! Madame de l'Eglise! This is the Chateau! No one has ever managed to convey how truly magnificent it really is," I gasped.

"And not before time. What an interminable journey this has been! We should have gone by way of Saint Cloud. It may take a little longer, but at least the road is not as muddy and bumpy. These horses are like tortoises," Madame whined in her high-pitched nasal twang. "And not a wink of sleep have I had this entire journey!"

I shot her a surprised glance but held my tongue in check. I was learning fast—one did not contradict one's betters if one did not wish one's ears boxed, I mused.

I watched the bustle as our coach slowed its pace.

"Oh, but Madame, how the Chateau glows with splendor! We're here at last, at Versailles!"

Chapter 2

The journey to Versailles had made me dizzy with excitement, and now I gazed about me wide-eyed. As we passed asses and cows, I could not help but remark to Madame, "Look! All those people and animals scurrying to and fro!"

How Madame sniffed!

"Oh, they are on their way to provide milk for the little Princes, Louis Augusta, Prince de Dombes, and the cheeky Prince Louis, Duc d'Orleans, and the two little Princesses, Louise Adelaide and her cousin, Charlotte Aglee."

"Oh, how lovely!"

"Some courtiers just stop to chat or are hurrying from one ceremony to the next," Madame explained. "Of course, a country girl would know nothing of all this." I was too excited to care that she was being rude to me.

I spied a man being carried in a sedan chair. "Excuse me, m'Lady, but who is that gentleman?"

"Don't point, child. That is his Majesty's Minister, and the people walking about aimlessly are just common folk come to gawk. How hideous is their attire! You will, of course, have to be educated to discern foreign visitors."

"It's so crowded, Madame, my Lady de l'Eglise."

"There are 10,000 people living here, you know."

"That seems an enormous number."

There must have been at least 200 fiacres waiting as we passed by. At last our carriage slowly drew to a halt. The door was flung open and Madame was helped down. I followed as best I could in my bare feet, gasping at the sights that met my eyes. I was stupefied at the finery of the men's coats, some royal blue with gold trimming, and at the beautiful ladies with their hair piled high and covered with delicate arrangements of silks and laces.

We entered the nobles' wing where guards stood beside the huge double doors emblazoned in gold.

"Only Royalty use the Cour de Marbre," Madame complained. "The clutter here is impossible. Come along," she threw at me, stiff-lipped, "before someone inquires what a kitchen maid is doing in the north wing."

We came to the end of the corridors and I was met by several women who eyed me suspiciously from head to toe.

"So this is the rose that has been culled from the dung heap, is it!" a tall, thin matron drawled. She held a languid hand in front of her face. "I can smell the farmyard."

Flushing, I looked down.

"Follow me and we will try to get rid of that unfortunate odor," snapped Madame de l'Eglise.

I was mortified at being addressed in such a manner, but meekly obeyed, averting my eyes, with my head held low. The opulence of my surroundings rendered me dumb. There seemed to be brightly colored silks hanging and covering everything possible.

Madame de l'Eglise led the way into a large, heated chamber and instructed two footmen to bring a hip bath, and maids brought jugs of hot water and vials of scent.

Madame pulled a strand of my hair. "Lice, I think."

How horrified I was! "We might have been poor, but nevertheless clean!"

"We will need at least three changes of water," the thin maid sighed.

"Now get undressed, child."

"What? Take my clothes off in front of all these people!"

"Come along, come along!"

I began to undo the strings of my blouse, but was pushed aside as their impatient hands began to fumble at the fastenings. I twisted and put my hand around the diamond, gathering it secretly so no one would catch a glimpse of its glory, and bundled it up quickly under a nearby stool with my folded clothes.

"Come back here at once, child," and they pushed me into the warm bath. "That hair resembles a bird's nest!"

I was eyed and remarked upon to the most embarrassing degree.

"The breasts are white, at least, and just the right size for a man's hand," the fat one added.

My face colored with embarrassment.

"You stay here until you are told what to do. Try to be helpful at least. What a mess you are, to be sure!"

"I didn't ask to come here. It wasn't my idea," I mumbled, as I was scrubbed and prodded from head to foot.

"More hot water at once," Madame shouted to the little maid. "And a vial of scent, too."

"But I have already had two baths, Madame, I beg you!"

"You need at least another one, you're so dirty," she replied, as she handed the maid the empty jugs. "Quickly, girl!"

The ladies drew their skirts away from me, not to be contaminated, it seemed.

"Please don't pull my hair," I cried, as they combed and tugged until I thought there could not be a hair left on my head.

"It's full of knots. I've never seen anything like it!"

"I'm sorry," I whimpered.

Another cut-glass bottle was produced, and yet more scent flung into yet another change of water, and I was doused with perfume. It seemed as if whole gardens of roses and lilies were floating around me. Through a scented steam I kept an anxious eye on my bundle under the stool. At any other time I would have enjoyed the luxury of silky, fine soapy water.

At long last, Madame de l'Eglise said, "I suppose that will have to do."

As I stepped out of the bath I felt myself crimson under their close scrutiny. They were discussing me as if I were a prize cow at market-time. I was grateful for the large towel they quickly wrapped around me.

"Clear this away now," Madame instructed. "Your hair will need to be rubbed with scented oil and washed regularly with soft soap and rainwater."

The little maid smoothed something onto my eyelashes and brows.

"What is that you are using now?" I questioned.

"'Tis but almond oil, Mam'selle, and now a little unguent to moisten your lips."

"Ouch! That lemon juice stings! My hands are sore!"

"Hands!" they echoed. "More like little horse's hooves!"

"My hands are fine, even if I have done rough work! Thank goodness I never got chilblains like some of the country girls, whose hands swelled up like sausages," I proudly told the women.

"You'll have to sleep with creams and gloves on to get them as soft as a lady's," they assured me.

They led me to a bed and Madame commanded, "Open your legs."

"What!" I yelled.

"Open your legs, girl."

"No! I won't!" I screamed, holding the fine coverlet closely around me. "What are you going to do to me?"

"We're going to make sure you're a virgin. Now be still or we'll have to hold you down."

"Of course I'm a virgin! And I'm not having any people touching me!" I slapped the lady as she put her hands forward, and she gasped, horrified. Then I kicked at another maid and began to scream. Somebody sat on my legs while another held my wrists.

"Don't worry, it won't hurt," a plump, kind-faced woman

said. "I'm Berthe, the midwife."

"Oh, my God," I wailed. "What are they going to do to me now? What's coming next!"

She gently opened my legs while Madame de l'Eglise and the others looked on. Shame came over me as I felt myself being prodded.

"She's a virgin, all right," the plump one announced, dropping a cover over me.

"Hmm..." Murmurs of surprise and malicious disappointment went round the room. "A girl so pretty..."

A fine peignoir of pink silk was slipped over my shoulders and I was lifted to my feet, feeling more confident.

"What now, Madame de l'Eglise?"

"Are you hungry, child?"

"I'm as hungry as a peasant at Candlemas!"

She took me by the hand to a table with a bewildering display of glass and silverware and pushed me into a gilded chair. "Keep your back straight." She stiffly walked around the table as footmen entered with silver trays. One of them set a gilded, porcelain plate in front of me. Madame told me it contained saltwater fish. A steaming tureen with a silver ladle was set to one side. I looked and wondered which cutlery to use.

Madame broke in on my thoughts. "You will raise the spoon in the right hand daintily, so." But my appetite had gone at the sight of so many people watching me.

"This is sole, served in almond milk—very delicate." It tasted delicious, as if flavored with rosewater, and I realized again how hungry I was, but was rapped on the knuckles with a fan.

"Slower, if you please. We're not in the farmyard now. Madame de Maintenon does not wish for a piglet to be presented to his Majesty."

"Then why did she send for me!" I cried. Tears welled up behind my eyes. I had been through too much for one day. "I've never eaten out of a silver bowl. It isn't my fault."

Madame heaved a sigh. "Dry your eyes with this." She handed me a lace handkerchief and I did as I was told.

"No, keep it." She refused to take it back and yawned daintily behind her hand. I quickly tucked her handkerchief into my sleeve, wishing to please.

"Thank you, m'Lady." And I wiped my runny nose on the pink silk sleeve, having a good sniff.

Madame lifted her eyes despairingly. "Oh, what a hopeless task it has been my misfortune to be saddled with. Isn't it enough, dear God, that my only daughter, Thérèse, defies me?"

"Your daughter defies you, Madame?" I could not believe that anyone defied this iron-willed woman.

She snapped her fingers. "Ah, she's a silly child. I have picked out a most suitable husband for her, but she's got some silly ideas..."

Madame was taking me into her confidence, telling me about her daughter's infatuation for a penniless young blade, when the Count Bissot had already shown his interest in Thérèse, but pulled herself up abruptly. I had not, as yet, met Madame's daughter, but felt a growing sympathy for her as Madame gathered her thoughts back from the ingratitude of children and came smartly back to the business of teaching me to eat like a lady.

I had never tasted such a tender slice of meat. Each course was followed by another. I sipped, as Madame advised me, a goblet of wine, and soon felt fit to burst. A contented drowsiness overcame me and I leaned back in my little gold chair and sighed. "I am so weary, Madame, and would love to sleep for a while."

"Sleep! Is that all you can think of?"

I had not seen the door open, but now heard the rustle of silk and looked up into the brilliant eyes of a most attractive middle-aged woman. A large cross of the utmost quality, encrusted with diamonds, hung around her plump neck on a chain of pearls. Madame de l'Eglise rose and curtsied, and I whispered, "Madame de Maintenon!"

"I see you have already set to work, Madame de l'Eglise. You may sit, Madamoiselle Solange." What a beautiful voice she had! She sent a page for a comfit for the little dog that was dancing merrily around her skirts.

"I have brought Tienne, the page who is to attend you."

I had not noticed the little boy, resplendent in an apple-green velvet suit, a miniature angel with a crown of ash-blond hair shaped like a pudding basin over large brown eyes. I had never seen such a mischievous grin. "Your servant, Mam'selle." He bowed appealingly, his innocent eyes never leaving mine.

Madame de Maintenon took my hand and drew me to a sofa by the window, settling her silken skirts. In the rosy glow of the sunset that touched her face I could see that her chin was creased and sagging onto her chest and her face fat and pasty.

"The King seemed to know your face the day you interrupted our journey at Clagny, but of course I told him that that was impossible. He seemed curious, however, and asked me to have you brought here to sing for us."

"Oh, dear!" I was terrified.

"A very pretty sight. You must always look bright and happy to lighten the King's heart. He is full of aches and pains today. Perhaps you will be able to soothe his troubled spirit."

"But Madame, how will I do that?"

"A pretty little thing like you will have no trouble, I'm sure." Madame pulled her lips slyly and I could not help but notice how much older she appeared than I had first thought. There were noticeable lines at the side of her eyes.

"Can you play the mandolin?"

"I do sing. I always sang at the village fêtes, but I cannot play any instrument, and I am afraid of the courtiers I have seen," I confided.

"Zut!" Madame admonished.

"They are so beautiful and rich and turn their noses up at me. One of the ladies even has a monkey for a pet—I've never seen one before. It was wearing a red satin coat and she was feeding it grapes."

"If the King likes you, they will compete for your smiles. He is bored with them and dying of ennui. I was once young and pretty," Madame sighed. She fluffed out the French point lace above and below the elbows of her mulberry gown and a waft of perfume caught my nose, delicate yet heavenly, as of roses in summer.

"But I grow tired and must keep his Majesty amused and free from care." She fed her little dog absently as she spoke.

I let my hands feel my new peignoir, smooth and satiny, and smelling of springtime.

"I pray for his soul, but that is not enough," she sighed yet again as she fingered the cross at her throat. "He spoke to me again only yesterday of 'the golden girl with the dog roses'."

"I hope I will not disappoint his Majesty," I said, trembling.

The little dog danced close to her skirts and she popped another cake into his mouth. He ran around her adoringly.

"I don't think you will do that—I wish you to amuse his Majesty. You are a most fortunate girl, are you not?"

"Indeed I am, my Lady, Madame de Maintenon," I whispered.

"Stand up, child," she said. "Tell my ladies to come in," she said to the page, and she lifted a strand of my hair. "Yes, soft and silky—the King will love this. It is like pure gold, but it needs to be dressed fashionably after you're gowned."

The ladies came forward, including the one with the monkey. A dandified man accompanied them.

"My own hairdresser, André."

A small, moustached, bewigged person bowed low. "Enchanté, Mam'selle."

"I would like you to dress the hair with ribbons, André. Wait in the anteroom," Madame instructed.

"As you wish, Madame. I will create a masterpiece." His hands seemed to be creating his masterpiece already as he minced away in a trance.

I was quickly surrounded by scurrying maids."

"Prepare Mam'selle Solange to be presented to the King," the maids were told.

She turned to me. "You will be brought to my apartments when it is done."

She turned to go with a swish of her skirts and paused at the door. "Be as helpful as you can," she threw at me, and disappeared, followed by her yapping dog.

"How many undergarments must I wear?" I asked the maids.

I picked up a pair of high-heeled shoes and then dropped them onto the thick carpet. "I'll never be able to walk in those heels. I've mostly gone barefoot. I'll fall over and everyone will laugh."

"Keep that wagging tongue still and hold on to the bedpost while we lace your stays."

"But I can hardly breathe now!" I felt the carving on the bedpost as I gingerly obeyed. They pulled and pulled at the laces until I was sure I would break in two.

I cried out for them to stop. "Please!" I begged, as I felt the whalebones nip into me.

"There, that's very fine, a hand's-span waist. You'll be the envy of the whole Court."

"Oh, I'd sooner not, if you don't mind. I'm frightened. I don't wish to be envied." I should have saved my gasping breath, for no one was listening. "I've never worn a corset in my life!"

"Hmm. Not surprising from the sight of you when you arrived," the pale one sniffed.

I panted and struggled to get air into my compressed lungs. "I'll surely die from lack of breath!"

"Don't be ridiculous, child. Sit down!"

White silk stockings were pulled onto my legs and fastened at the knee with garters of yellow satin. Standing, I stepped into a green silk gown as glassy as the sea. It fell around my hips, wide and shimmering, to meet matching satin slippers with silver buckles. The skirt was embroidered in real silver thread. The gilt-edged mirror, adorned with its ribbons and flowers and encircled with cupids, was no less ornamented than I.

"Oh, yes, very nice. You will certainly do." The women stood back, admiring their work. I was pushed down onto a dressing stool and a page was sent for Monsieur André.

"Ah, Mam'selle." He twirled a comb and leaned backwards with pursed lips. "I think ringlets, entwined with ribbons, pulled forward on either side of the face. Madame de Maintenon suggested ribbons for the coiffure, and I think perhaps a few rosebuds on the crown." He pulled his black moustache in deep thought and then began weaving a twist of hair here and a plait of ribbon there, as if his work were a true vocation.

"Madame de Montespan's 'thousand ringlets,'" he half whispered to himself. "Just right, I think."

He leaned backwards again some time later, admiring his arrangement, arms akimbo. *"Trés magnifique,"* he murmured. "A most charming coiffure!"

He took his leave kissing the thumb and first finger of his left hand theatrically, and glided out of the room, convinced of his genius.

The women gathered round me again, exclaiming ecstatically, "André had worked wonders... Madame de Maintenon will be most pleased... A man does seem to do hair very well... How times do change..."

"Now, hold still and tilt your face up a little. A touch of color, I think." A hare's foot dipped in rouge was dabbed onto my cheeks and upthrust breasts, pushed up by the whalebones till they formed pink half-globes. A "Coquette" beauty spot was pressed close to my lips. "Make a kissing mouth." They painted my lips rose red. "Now, stand up and walk into the middle of the room."

I wobbled in the unaccustomed high heels.

"Now turn around."

I twirled slowly, glorying in the silk in spite of the tightness around my middle. I suddenly remembered my diamond under the stool and was wondering how to get it without drawing attention to myself, when a maid entered with a carafe of wine on a silver tray.

Without warning, the monkey leapt from its mistress's arms and grabbed the maid's hair. The little claws dragged off the mob cap, covering her eyes and causing the poor girl to stumble and spill the wine down the gown of one of the ladies. She shouted in horror, and the enraged lady slapped her face repeatedly on either side.

"You've ruined my dress, you clumsy creature!"

The ringing slaps left red marks on the sorry girl's face. All the women clustered round the spoiled dress, exclaiming, and no one noticed as I bent down, in agony as the whalebones gripped me, and retrieved my precious jewel from under the stool. I forced it down my bodice, gasping with relief.

As the commotion died down, I regained my composure and stared at my reflection in the ornate mirror. André had created a coiffure fit for any princess. The curls danced, shimmering under the bright chandeliers. What a miracle had been performed with water, paint and powder! No one would guess that I had recently arrived from the dung heap, as the ladies had remarked. I now resembled a princess of the blood, I was certain.

But I was reckoning without the eagle-trained eyes and ears of the critical people who surrounded the king.

Chapter 3

Madame de l'Eglise grudgingly gave her approval. I was led, trembling with fear and excitement, by Tienne, up a staircase of unbelievable beauty to the apartments I was to come to know as the Queen's. I grasped the page's little hand and my own felt cold and clammy as we walked on the thick carpets, passing footmen in powdered wigs who stood like statues of stone. Madame de Maintenon was not as fashionably dressed as the courtiers, I was later to realize, but the richness and embroidery of her gowns were equal to those of any of the most gorgeous coquettes.

At least half an hour later, after walking down many corridors, we entered a sumptuous apartment. All about me was furnished with the utmost elegance. I gasped at its richness.

"Down, girl," someone whispered.

I felt myself pushed into a curtsy. I lost my balance and fell clumsily amid titters. I had no idea how I could attain an upright position without falling. I was momentarily paralyzed with fear and stared down, memorizing the blue-and-gold flower design of the Savonnerie carpet, when I felt slender fingers cup my chin. I saw what could only be the

King's beautifully turned legs, encased in the finest red silk hose, and exquisite shoes of the same red, adorned with diamond buckles.

I felt a rude prod on my derriere and Madame hissed, "Get up as his Majesty addresses you."

I pushed a wobbly knee forward, but fell on the floor to much amusement on all sides. At the second attempt I managed to regain a little composure and stood with beating heart and trembling hands.

Then I knew why they called him *le Roi Soleil*—he dazzled my gaze. I saw again the large square face and the surprisingly kindly eyes looking reassuringly into mine, and I caught a whiff of musky perfume that scented his clothing.

The King wore a gold and blue coat, heavily embroidered with precious stones. White satin showed six inches from the sleeves and the cuffs were trimmed with double falls of white lace and red ribbons, which also adorned his neck in a jabot. His breeches had diamond buckles. I could see a blue ribbon across his chest where the coat was unfastened. On his head he wore a gorgeous tricorn hat of black beaver with a cascade of red ostrich plumes.

"So this is our golden country girl. Congratulations, Madame, you have certainly wrought a transformation." Madame smirked, because indeed she had.

"I remember you sang a little."

I huskily answered, "I'm afraid my songs are only country songs, your Majesty."

"No matter."

I blinked at the sheen of his satin coat and the glittering jewels. I felt drained of strength, a lost soul, as I pinched my silk dress into tiny damp pleats, my fingers trembling. The twinkling eyes looked down into mine.

With a wave of his well-kept hand, he bade the courtiers be settled, and they rustled to obey him. I swallowed and sank gratefully onto the chair he offered me. Tienne stood at my side, strumming the mandolin. "What do you know, Mam'selle?" he whispered.

I gulped with a dry throat, "I could try 'The Cock and the Hen.'"

"If you'll hum a little, I'll try to pick it up."

I hummed a few bars and Tienne cocked a fair eyebrow and smiled. He tried a few chords.

"I think I have it."

"Hmm. She has a common voice, to be sure," I heard a whisper from a corner of the room.

"What can you expect from the farmyard, my dears!"

I blushed scarlet with embarrassment. They had not even heard me sing yet. In fact, I had hardly spoken a dozen words.

The room was illuminated by a myriad of candles and it seemed to have become crowded without my noticing it. And then I caught sight of the Spanish nobleman, and wanted to die.

I turned my eyes to the King. He frowned and motioned me to begin.

Taking my courage in both hands, I embarked on the rollicking tune that I had sung at harvesting and haymaking. At first there were titters, then they fell silent. The presence of the King was felt as the ladies, some seated on tabourets and others standing with their cavaliers, yawned. They were impatient to be finished with this bore and on to the gaming tables, no doubt, to play Louis' favorite, *reversi,* or the new game, *bassette.*

His Majesty lifted a jewelled hand as a sign to go on. My voice was small and husky to my ears—I was never a songbird—but it began to strengthen as Tienne strummed louder and I threw into it all my acting ability, remembering the fairs at Clagy. Presently I heard laughter, and before I was halfway through the company threw back their heads delightedly and choked with mirth into their handkerchiefs. Even the King was slapping his silk-clad thigh and throwing back his head with glee. Guffaws were coming from all sides, and I could go on no longer. Tears pricked my eyes, and I wished that I could disappear.

"They do not laugh at you, but with you." A girl a little older than myself was standing at my side, an arm on the back of my chair. Her red curls glinted under the crystal chandelier, complementing her russet-colored dress. I drew a shuddering breath and glanced into her clear, hazel eyes.

"Are you sure?" I asked hopefully. But even as I questioned her I realized that she spoke the truth.

"I am Madame de l'Eglise's daughter, Thérèse," she said.

"Oh, what a *drôle* she is—mercy me..." A handkerchief was dabbed at an eye.

"Go on, Mam'selle, the country song is most entertaining and so bawdy. What a little dark horse you are..."

"Am I? What do you mean?"

"I think you know well enough, Mam'selle." I gasped and felt my cheeks burn. Don Fernando was gazing at me through amused eyes, and walking lazily in my direction.

"So sweet and funny..." the courtiers twittered. "Where did you learn such a lewd ballad?"

"Another verse, Mam'selle, we beg of you," they chorused. Some were clapping their hands and stamping their silk slippers.

"Continue," his Majesty commanded, with a twinkle in his eye. "You are indeed the star of the evening. Madame did well to suggest you brighten our Court. Do you agree, Don Fernando?"

"I find Mam'selle enchanting, like a breath of country air." Was Don Fernando insulting me? He'd raised a fine eyebrow and seemed to be mocking. As I looked around, I felt jealous eyes, mingled with admiration, but the King's pleasure gave me courage. The King had given me his accolade. The lady to my left was nodding respectfully to me. How could she breathe with her bosom laced so tightly? She must surely have been short of breath in that crimson bodice.

"I assure you," I ventured, "I do not know what 'lewd' means." They fell about shrieking with laughter again, but I revelled in my new-found popularity and decided to play on it. The King was holding his sides and threw back his head at my naïveté.

"It was just a song that we would sing at the fair. I remembered it from my childhood."

Tienne was strumming again and Don Fernando leaned over and gently took the mandolin out of his grasp. As his dark curls brushed mine, he whispered huskily, "Sing again, Mam'selle."

I smiled gratefully at him. His strong face was wreathed in admiration and for a moment I forgot where I was. I closed my eyes, dreaming of his kiss.

"Well?" he prompted. I flushed and continued with the ballad, 'The Man with Two Wives.' I heard the King whisper to Madame de Maintenon, "My taste exactly! But where have I seen that face before?"

I finished to the roar of wild clapping and stamping.

"More, Mam'selle, we beg you!"

But my face was prickling with sweat and I was gasping deeply for breath and praying that I would not faint. Madame de Maintenon must have seen that I had grown pale, for she beckoned one of the ladies.

"The child is clearly exhausted. Give her a glass of wine. She will continue later, after she has rested."

The King held out his hand to raise me from my chair and said, "Well, dear little Solange, we mustn't overtire you now."

I stumbled into the curtsy once again and kissed his hand. As I rose, I felt a steady pressure on my arm from the girl in russet. She assisted me to walk safely to the doorway. I was aware all the while of Don Fernando's gaze following me at every turn, causing me to warm inwardly.

"Ah . . ." Sighs of disappointment went around the room, but I gratefully departed after bobbing a curtsey to Madame.

A plump lady in a grey gown followed us to the door. "You are to stay in the apartments of Madame de Maintenon for a while. She has ordered me to report everything to her."

"Could Mam'selle Thérèse stay with me, please?"

The girl dismissed the plump woman, and then she turned to me and said, "I hope we will be great friends."

"Oh, yes!"

Tienne's tiny hand squeezed mine. I looked into his small face shining with the enthusiasm and hope of the very young.

"I expect you find this place bewildering. I will explain everything," Thérèse promised.

"Why do they call this staircase the Queen's?" I whispered to Thérèse. "After all, the Queen is dead."

"You will soon realize that Madame de Maintenon is Queen of the Court. Why do you think she has been installed in the Queen's apartments? The widow Scarron has done very well for herself."

"Is she a widow?"

"Yes, and she gave the King the vapors when she first came here."

"I've seen some beautiful ladies, but she's not as beautiful as they. Why did he choose her?"

"I think she knows how to soothe him and listen to his troubles. Even the greatest King in the world has troubles, my dear."

I looked at her wide-eyed. "I always thought that everything was perfect for our King."

"My mother told me she was brought here by the King's mistress, Athenais de Montespan, to be governess to their children, but Madame de Maintenon knew how to get round the King. The little Duc de Maine was her weapon, the King's favorite son. She talked each day to him about that extension of himself. That way the dullest woman can hold a man, particularly if he is not very young."

"She is clever," I marvelled.

"I heard that when she met Athenais de Montespan on the Queen's staircase, she snidely remarked, 'Going down, Madame? I am going up!'"

"Do you think she meant to be cruel?"

"I am sure she did, because Montespan was out and Maintenon was in after that." Therese laughed and looked at me fondly as we turned a corner.

We passed golden urns filled with sweet-smelling flowers, arranged on either side of the grey, black and brown marble staircase. Nearly everything seemed to be accented with gold. At last we reached the bedroom. The furniture, I later learned, had been made by Monsieur Boulle, and it glowed with marquetry and gilded bronze. I could smell the jasmine and tulips that the King had had brought to Versailles from Holland during more peaceful times.

The grey-clothed, somber woman had arrived before us. Thérèse turned to her. "You did say you could arrange for me to stay with Mam'selle?"

"I have asked Madame de Maintenon, who has agreed as you are in favor with the King," she said. I flung my arms around the neck of my new friend. "Oh, Thérèse, thank you!" I sank exhausted onto the bed. "I couldn't bear the thought of sleeping in this huge bed alone, to spend the night here."

"You're lucky," one of the little maids remarked. "There isn't much privacy at Versailles. You have a whole room for only the two of you, and a window. Only royalty have a room to themselves. Most of the courtiers haven't even got a cupboard to hang their clothes in, and sleep in the recesses in the corridors."

"But it's big enough to hold an entire village," I gasped.

"We have to burn tallow candles and put our legs into bags filled with straw to keep warm. Only in the royal apartments are there wax candles and wood to keep fires alight," the maid added.

Thérèse said, "I'll help you with your dress."

She laughed as I held the bedpost and I scratched where the unaccustomed corset bones had gripped my flesh. "Oh, what a relief!"

Presently we were ready for bed, and a maid was sent scurrying for a warming pan. Tienne brought me a nightrobe. Then there was a knock on the door as another little maid followed with a ewer of hot water. The warming pan was put between the sheets and the curtains drawn.

I scratched with pleasure and Thérèse did the same. "I'll *never* get used to wearing those corsets, Thérèse."

"Oh, you will, everybody does. *La mode* is *la mode*. When I was a little girl my mother gradually laced me tighter and tighter. This is the price you have to pay for fashion," she smiled as she continued scratching.

I sighed with relief as the fine, white shift was slipped over my head and I was helped onto the cushiony softness of the goosedown comforter. The silkiness of the covers caressed my exhausted limbs, and my legs and feet tingled at the touch of the delicate, luxurious bedclothes.

"There are so many things I want to talk to you about and ask you, Thérèse. But my eyes are so heavy I can hardly keep them open."

Despite my weariness, Thérèse and I gossiped most of the night. I was so excited and was eager to know who everyone was, but most of all I wanted to know all about Don Fernando, and decided to pump Thérèse.

"Who was the man standing next to the King, looking me up and down so insolently?"

"Oh," Thérèse laughed. "The blond? That's Raoul. He has a wife in the country. He's a real ladies' man. Watch out for him," she advised, running her fingers through her hair. "He'll tell you anything to suit himself. He likes his girls young—and his boys, come to think of it.

"Oh, no, not the fair one with the slanty eyes—the tall, dark one that he was always sidling up to, with the crinkly curls and very dark eyes. He was wearing blue velvet."

"Oh, that's Don Fernando of Spain, just back from England on a mission for his Majesty."

"I thought him very handsome indeed. He has such a noble look and an excellent figure. I felt his eyes riveted on mine, but I did not dare look straight at him."

"Would you like to get to know him properly?"

"I would indeed! Could you arrange it?"

"Well, you country girls don't believe in playing hard to get, do you?" I could have bitten my tongue off for sounding too eager. "He's a wonderful horseman. Do you ride, Solange?"

"No, why?"

"Well, we have a riding school here. I will ask Madame de Maintenon if you can learn and then perhaps you will ride with Don Fernando and my sweetheart, Charles. We can go hunting together."

"How long will that take?"

I saw Thérèse was laughing at me. "You are keen, aren't you?"

"Well," I admitted, "I do think he's rather . . . er . . . Spanish, if you know what I mean."

"Yes," Thérèse teased, "I think I really do know what you mean, even if you don't. I wish my mother would agree to my marrying Charles. You will adore him, Solange. He is as fair as the moonlight that shines through that window, but, alas, he has no fortune. My mother has promised me to the crotchety old Count Bissot."

"Thérèse, I am sorry." I sat up in the bed.

"Bissot is a widower with seven children, all older than I am. I want to please my mother," Thérèse confided. "It would make her fortune, for he is very rich and owns much land, but I cannot marry him. You must not speak of this to anyone, Solange."

"I swear, Thérèse, I'll tell no one."

"And now, dear friend, it is nearly morning," Thérèse pecked me on the cheek as she bade me goodnight. "Our faces will be sunken if we do not sleep a little."

"I do not know how I would have got through this evening without you, but I cannot sleep on this soft bed," and with that, I slipped onto the floor, dragging a single cover with me. "I am not used to such luxury. I will be much more comfortable here."

Thérèse giggled as she turned and snuggled into the goosedown, and soon we were both lost in sleep.

Chapter 4

And so the days passed. Life at Court was indeed delightful, in spite of not being 'what it had been before,' as Madame de l'Eglise was often muttering. There did not seem a day, or indeed a moment, not given to pleasure.

I spent so much time having lessons in manners or deportment that there seemed little time for Thérèse's suggestion, but one morning at the beginning of June, while we were walking in the garden, they told me we were to go out riding. Madame de Maintenon sent for me to be taken to her apartments where she informed me, in her precise voice, "It is high time you were taught to ride, Mam'selle Solange."

Her maid was rubbing her feet as she rustled her black skirts about her.

"Oh, yes. I'd love that!"

"Thérèse seemed to think Don Fernando should be your tutor."

I felt myself blushing at the mention of his name, for I had thought of him a great deal, and on many occasions had felt his eyes on mine as we exchanged glances across the room at *appartement,* the gala festivities held in the King's chambers.

"I must admit he wasn't overanxious to take on the task,"

she added, "but we have managed to persuade him."

I felt my heart sink at this news. Had my instincts played me false? Did he dislike me?

"I am most grateful, Madame."

"He is not a Frenchman, of course, but he is an excellent horseman."

"Thank you, my Lady."

"You could have no better tutor."

I hardly dared to trust my voice. Although Thérèse had already been improving my speech, I was very conscious of my country accent compared with the refinements of the Court. Love was very much the mode at Versailles, and all seemed to have made their choices. What chance had I with Don Fernando? He was just to tutor me, much against his will, it seemed. I must not hope for more . . . at this point.

Madame brought me back to the present with a start. "We've had a riding habit made. The ladies will dress you at once. I am pleased with you. You may go, child."

I smiled gratefully at her and rushed with flushing cheeks along the dark corridors to be attired for my lesson. At one of the windows an elegant figure put out a hand and grabbed my arm.

"Who is that?" I gasped, knowing full well who it was, of course.

"Have no fear! It is Raoul, come to court the fairest flower."

"I am not one of your Court butterflies. I can't stay. I have orders from Madame de Maintenon."

"Orders? Poof! Do you run every time she calls you, like her little dog?" He pulled me round to face him. "Do you know your eyelashes are nearly black?"

"This is not the time or the place, Sir."

He tried to kiss me, but I twisted my head away, remembering what Thérèse had told me. I was trembling, but tried to steady myself.

"I am going riding." I attempted to pull away, but he held me fast and laughed into my face, revealing wolfish white teeth.

"You have startled and bewildered me, and I know you for a libertine." I snatched my hand away when he insolently drew it to his lips and, lifting my silken skirts, I fled down the corridor to my room, his laughter echoing in my ears. I was gasping as I fell across the bed.

"Where have you been, Solange? I have been ready this half hour."

"Oh, are you to accompany me, Thérèse? I am glad. Forgive me, please. It was Raoul. He waylaid me in the dark corridor and gave me quite a turn. I'm sorry for his poor wife."

"Oh, I shouldn't be. She's probably grateful to be left in peace from such a conceited peacock."

I pushed Raoul from my mind. "How lovely you look in that light brown habit, Thérèse. Am I to wear the red?"

The maid helped me into a long skirt trimmed with black at the hem. The coat fell from my waist in long folds, and was caught at the neck and wrists with the same black braid. A jabot of white flounced at my throat and white lace fell at my wrists. My hair was tied back with a black bow. I felt aflutter at the thought of meeting my noble Spaniard.

We hurried to the stables and across the cobbled yard where pigeons pecked fearlessly around the horse's feet. I saw the rows of horse boxes and young tutors with their royal charges. The groom helped me to mount correctly and instructed me on how to dismount. Then Don Fernando appeared, his dark hair glinting in the sunlight, slapping leather gloves against his muscled thigh. He seemed to look at me rather insolently and frowned, eyeing my figure slowly from my head down to my hem. I felt myself turn red and became flustered. Then I forced myself to look straight back at him.

"Don't you want to teach me to ride?" I ventured.

"I have far more important things to do than to teach young ladies to manage a horse."

"I'm sorry, Monsieur, but Madame de Maintenon decided you should tutor me. If you like, I'll ask her to have someone else undertake the task."

He smiled and put out a staying hand. "I think I'll survive. You seem intelligent for one so young. I've seen you at *appartement*. You're new at Court, aren't you?"

"I've lived in the country." I was glad he had noticed me, but relieved that he hadn't remembered our first meeting.

"I see they've given you a quiet, fat horse. That's fine to start with."

I stammered some remark, blushing whenever his eyes met mine.

"We will stay in the riding school today."

"Now keep your back straight, Mam'selle," he advised, as the horse started to walk. I sat as upright as I could, but bobbed up and down, completely out of rhythm with his gait.

"Mam'selle will never learn to ride like that. We'll start again."

There were several ladies and gentlemen clustered among the grooms, but I had eyes only for Don Fernando, resplendent in his tight coat of dark brown cloth, his boots gleaming in the sun.

"Try to move *with* the animal, Mam'selle Solange."

What a rich voice he had, and how beautiful my name sounded when spoken by him!

"Hold the reins so."

I swallowed and nodded, unable to speak with him so near. How I wished that I were knowledgeable in the arts of love, as the gorgeous ladies in our group so obviously were, lowering eyes under long lashes so beguilingly. Time went quickly, but I memorized every flirtatious gesture I had seen and tried to emulate them.

"I think you've done well for the first lesson. You'll make a horsewoman yet."

"Thank you," I stammered.

"You're very beautiful, Mam'selle. You could twist a man's heart," he chaffed me.

I blushed with pride as I was helped down and accompanied back to my room. I would have to remember not to take too much notice of courtiers' pretty speeches, although I wanted to believe that this one meant every word.

Thérèse told me there was soon to be a picnic. "Do you think you'll be riding well enough by then, Solange?"

"Oh, I do hope so. Don Fernando said I'm doing very well."

We had lessons each day in the riding school. I had become very fond of my little fat horse and always carried a carrot which Tienne would acquire from the kitchens for his pleasure. Occasionally I would feel Don Fernando's strong arms around me, and I copied the meaningful looks of the other ladies and brushed against him at every opportunity. At last the day came when I heard Don Fernando say, "I think you're ready to ride abroad with us, Mam'selle. I'll look for you at the picnic tomorrow."

"Will you?"

"For sure. I'll have to keep an eye on my pupil!"

"So it seems you are reconciled to teaching me to ride."

"It seems I am." Then he gave me a dark look which made my heart beat faster and my stomach lurch.

"You are being very kind to give me so much of your time when you have many more important matters to attend to." I glanced at him from beneath lowered lashes.

"Now you are being facetious, Mam'selle!" But I could see he was playing with me.

The June day dawned bright and clear. There was much laughter and merriment as we joined the gay company, the ladies colorful in bright habits as they assembled for the ride. The horses were frisky and ready to be off. The woods were fresh and green around us and I was comfortable on my horse at last.

"That's excellent, Mam'selle."

I beamed with pride as Don Fernando complimented me on my seat. The horses were richly caparisoned, adorned with ostrich plumes and ribbons of red and purple, yellow and bright blue. I was not riding my little fat horse this time. My new mare was jet black, a fine contrast to my red outfit, but I felt far away from the ground on this new, taller mount.

Don Fernando let the others continue and we followed at a leisurely pace. The sun warmed us and the rustling branches of the old trees towered above us. As we rode, Don Fernando sang softly. His voice was strong yet soothing. I felt a closeness to him.

I glanced into his face. "What does that mean, Don Fernando?"

"It is a very old song, in the antique Spanish tongue. It means 'In writing these words I have attained all my object, . . . I have achieved what, with your help, has been all I desired.'"

I felt flustered and knew that if I was not careful I would look foolish. I tried to keep my voice steady. "How beautiful—and how melodious your voice is!" But I really wanted to shout, "I love you, Fernando! Why don't you tell me that you love me and take me in your arms and kiss me!" I could tell he had no idea what I was thinking. Instead of declaring passionate love for me, he taught me the tune and we hummed it together, laughing and brushing branches from our path. We soon caught up with the rest of the party.

"We are to have the picnic soon, Mam'selle. I hope you are hungry."

I felt my stomach growl at the mention of food.

"Just a little," I answered demurely, smiling up at him. In the village at Clagny I would have answered quite differently, saying that I was half-starved. The country air had given me an appetite, but I must remember not to eat too much. I did not wish to seem unladylike.

I dropped my yellow glove and was disappointed that it was Monsieur Raoul who rushed to pluck it from the grass. He drew it to his lips and kissed it. I leaned forward and snatched the glove from him, turning my head away. I was glad when Don Fernando lifted me down, and I flounced my red dress prettily around me.

The pages ran hither and thither, unpacking the rush baskets in the shelter of the leafy trees, preparing the picnic. They spread a white damask cloth edged with lace and set out dishes of salad, meats, and game pies, and succulent portions of sparrow grass. The gentlemen served the ladies with wine and fruit cordials. How my mouth watered, but I tried to pick up a chicken leg daintily like the other ladies. Fruit tarts were served on silver trays and I licked my lips at the thought of the sweet-tasting confections.

Suddenly my appetite vanished. I had caught sight of Don Fernando laughing with a voluptuous, bright-faced woman in a very tight blue dress. She was tilting a goblet of wine to his lips so that it dribbled down his chin and she stuck out a dainty tongue and licked it from his face greedily. Her ample body was thrust against his, and he was clearly not averse to her advances. Her flashing eyes held his and I could plainly see the promise in them. I knew the tortures of jealousy for the first time.

"Why are you looking so angry?" Thérèse put an arm around my waist.

"Just look at that disgusting spectacle." I nodded toward them.

"Pretend not to notice," she smiled and spoke to me softly so no one would realize whom we were discussing.

"Who is she?" I snapped. "I've seen her before. She was with him at the Ball."

"She is the wife of Count de Villette. He is rich and ancient. She flirts with anyone."

"She's far too fat," I sulked, and would not look at them again.

Soon the pages came to help us to our feet and brought the horses around. Other servants were clearing the food away. As we readied ourselves for the ride home, the plump woman did not leave Don Fernando's side. I had to think quickly; I was blazing with anger.

"I wish there was something I could do, Thérèse. Men are so fickle, it seems."

"I'm sure he'll tire of her soon, Solange. Don't worry."

But I was not so sure. "The hussy!" I hissed. "Look how she flaunts her bosom. One deep sigh and she'll be naked to the waist!"

There was half a gooseberry pie forgotten on the grass

near a clump of trees. I sauntered up to it casually, and kicked at the juicy morsel until the fruit spilled out. The ever-present wasps began to circle it at once. As one settled on a gooseberry, I swooped and picked it up by its wings, carefully between finger and thumb, just as we used to do at Clagny, and concealed it behind my back.

I walked disdainfully over to the overblown de Villette, meaning to distract her attention. I opened my eyes wide and innocently inquired, "Isn't that your husband over there?" As she turned to look, I dropped the wasp between the pale, swelling orbs of her breasts with a sleight of hand that would have done justice to a conjuror.

"Wasps! Wasps!" I then screamed, flapping my arms about, and Thérèse soon took up the cry, "Wasps!"

There was a real to-do, with everyone rushing around. De Villette clapped her hands to her bosom and let out a piercing shriek. "I'm stung! I'm stung!" She pulled the bodice of her dress down but she was stung again. "Oh! *Mon dieu!*"

I gleefully slapped her face to stop her hysteria. "Calm down, Madame," I said. "You will be stung more if you don't keep still."

Everyone was keeping well away by this time, but Don Fernando was fussing around and held a vial of cloves under her puggish nose. Red, ugly lumps swelled up on that hated flesh. She wouldn't wear low-cut gowns for quite a while. I began to edge away as she moaned, "*Mon dieu!* Help me! *Mon dieu!* I'm in agony, I tell you!"

The curvacious de Villette was very flushed indeed. Thérèse shot me an amused look, but I wasn't satisfied. Don Fernando was still with her, the fool.

A voice behind me spoke amusedly. "You wicked little vixen!"

I swung around to face Monsieur Raoul.

"I saw your little performance. You can buy my silence for a mating in the shade of that big tree," he leered. He suddenly drew me to him and kissed me hard on the lips before I could stop him.

"Get away from me! I am in a hurry," I mumbled through

lips still half attached to his wet mouth. He just laughed again and lifted amused eyebrows as Don Fernando walked over to me, showing more interest now that Monsieur Raoul had kissed me.

The de Villette woman clung to his arm with both hands as if her very life depended on him. Order was already being restored and Don Fernando was still dancing attendance on the unhappy woman! The idiot! I was raging and scrambled astride onto my mare in a most unladylike fashion, forgetting in my haste that I was supposed to pretend I could not mount without assistance. I dug my heels into the mare's sides and she cut the turf with her hooves.

"Don't drag on her mouth, you silly little fool!" a man's voice shouted.

The mare snorted and cavorted, but I was not afraid even when she broke into a furious gallop.

Voices shouted, "Hold on, don't let go!"

"She will be killed!"

"Mam'selle, I'm after you!" At last, the voice I wanted to hear!

A woman's cry followed, "Let the little fool kill herself!" I knew who that was.

The only thought that worried me was that my dear Tienne would be in trouble, for I remembered Don Fernando warning him never to let go of the bridle. Surely they would realize that he had not had a chance to stop me, but I knew Madame would be furious. I tried desperately to slow down. My hat was snatched off by a hanging branch and my hair fell about my shoulders. My mare was galloping fast now. The trees rushed past, and fear began to clutch at my heart as I tried yet again to make her check her pace. I was breathing in gasps. What if I was injured and they found my diamond! It was a stupid chance to have taken on the spur of the moment. All I had done was to provide a little sport and entertainment for the others. Don Fernando would be angry, I felt sure, because I was in his charge.

We were galloping now along the rise of a hill, and I tried to guide the mare as best I could among the dark trees and under the gnarled, leafy branches. The forest seemed deeper and more tangled here, and I was more than a little afraid of the pungent smell of the fungus and rotting leaves. I remembered poor Grandmère fleetingly and wondered if Don Fernando would believe the inevitable guesses that would be put forward as to my diamond's origin if I were found dead. Would he think I had sold my virtue? And would the rumors eventually be spoken of as fact?

I kept my head down, but the branches tore at my hair. Suddenly the mare swerved, the ground swung up to meet me, and I felt stones batter me. I put my hands up to my head instinctively, and shut my eyes for a moment. Then I could hear hoofbeats, so I ignored my throbbing head and played dead, praying it was Don Fernando. My hands felt sweaty as I anxiously waited to know who it was. I heard a snorting horse and footsteps which hurried to me. I felt a hand under my head and softly whimpered. It *was* Don Fernando.

"Solange," he whispered, and I let my eyes flutter open. "You wicked child! You could have been killed." I felt his hands on my arms and legs to see if they were broken. He put an arm around me and I leaned against him and looked up languidly. "The mare was specially picked for you—it was quiet. I ought to have let you break your foolish neck!"

"I'm sorry. It was the only way I could think of of parting you from that dark-eyed flirt," I said, in all honesty.

"I'm flattered that you risked your pretty neck for me. There was really no need, you know. You are lucky to have no broken bones. What a way to tease a man!" He smiled, melting my heart. I sighed and hunched my shoulder toward him and was delighted to see the gesture had not gone unnoticed. A shadow passed over his eyes as he became aware of my bosom. I wondered how long it would be before he'd make a move. Afraid that he would suddenly jump up and insist we return to the others, I brushed an imaginary stain on his thigh.

"Oh!" I said innocently, "Did you spill your wine? Here, let me remove the mark for you." I stuck out my tongue and wet my lace handkerchief, taking plenty of time, darting my tongue in and out as I'd seen some of the other ladies doing.

At last his arms slid around me gently and he kissed me for the first time. An exquisite pain clutched me somewhere below my stomach when he traced a nipple through my thin bodice with his forefinger. We lay a long time embracing in the peaceful rustic glade, surrounded by a screen of trees that led down to a gentle slope. I'd never known such happiness as there in that grassy valley. Through the trees I could see the weak sun slowly sinking, the approach of twilight thickening the landscape. I had won the first round against my rival. One learned quickly at Court.

I felt my clothes being loosened and removed. A strange and delicious sensation was running through my body. I remembered the talk I had heard of men liking you to open your legs and quickly did so, but he smiled quizzically and gently pushed them together again. It was like a dream when he took my hand in his and placed it between his own legs. He crushed me to him, kneading my breast between his long fingers. I wanted my life to stop then and there, to hold him in my arms forever. Innocent though I was, I felt my legs open of their own accord. I gasped as his hand met the bare flesh of my inner thigh.

He continued to kiss me, forcing my lips apart. His tongue found mine and I clung to him, forcing myself to believe that this was actually happening. I could barely comprehend that at last my beloved cared for me enough to kiss me with such emotion. I could feel his warm breath on my face and hear him panting more quickly as I stroked his silky hot manhood. I felt his hand exploring between my legs and a long, gently probing finger. I cried out at the trembling sensations this caused and became frantic when he removed it.

"Don't stop," I heard myself moan. "Quickly, please Fernando!"

I was going to be a woman. I would be knowledgeable at last.

A delicious feeling pushed the pain to the background as he entered me, and I felt my body move in motion with his.

Strong legs were astride mine, and I was melting into the ground.

"Oh, Fernando, I love you. Don't let go of me!"

"Never, dearest. Am I hurting you?"

"No, no, don't stop—go on."

Suddenly our movements quickened and together we plunged into an ecstacy that I hadn't known existed. I couldn't bear for it to end. He lay gasping and rolled away from me on his back with his eyes closed.

I crept to his side and covered his limp manhood with my hand, not daring to look down, stroking very gently. He opened his eyes and grinned at me. "It isn't only riding horses that you learn quickly, my Solange!"

I slapped him hard across his satisfied face, and he grabbed me to him, laughing, and so we began again. But this time I was in charge—or so I thought.

Chapter 5

When at last we returned to the chateau, a hot bath took some of the stiffness from my legs and the burning from between them. Berthe fussed around me with dabs of witch hazel. I held a hand mirror to examine the bruises, but they were faint and a dust of powder would cover them.

"Not another new dress!" I exclaimed with excitement at the lemon taffeta creation held up for me by the maid. It was trimmed with gold lace at the neckline and down the front of the bodice.

"Madame de Maintenon is so good to me. Why does she spend so much money on me?" I asked Madame de l'Eglise. She shot me a knowing look. "You'll find out soon enough," she said, and refused to be drawn further. She continued her lessons on etiquette till my head was reeling.

As Madame adjusted my coiffure, Thérèse gave me a peculiar glance, but I could not tell what she meant. I would ask her later. I stepped into the yellow slippers, scattered with seed pearls.

"This bodice is so low, I dare not breathe, Madame, or bend," and I tried to pull it up, but my breasts had been pushed so high and my middle so tightly laced I could only breathe in gasps.

"You'll get used to it," she replied, without a glance in my direction.

My hair was entwined with ropes of pearls. Nosegays of buttercups were embroidered on my skirt and sleeves, held with pearls at the elbow.

That night in the *Salon d' Appolon* we celebrated my escape from death, but I could dance little because they clamored for me to sing again. Every bone in my body seemed to ache and I excused myself as soon as I had given them "She Was Only the Farmer's Daughter, but Her Corn Was the Ripest by Far." With one exception, everyone clapped their pleasure. I no longer cared about that buxom woman, sidling up to Fernando once more and sending me glances of hate. I bet she hadn't had what I'd had earlier in the day; I could still feel the delicious soreness where he'd thrust into me.

When I considered it decent to leave I was glad of Tienne's arm, but Fernando interrupted and claimed me for a dance. Suddenly, as if by magic, my limbs seemed to lose their stiffness as I gazed up at my handsome Spaniard. His charm passed all credence and his dark complexion was as lustrous as the deep brown velvet coat he wore, set off by cream ruffles at his throat.

We danced under the sparkling chandeliers, our reflections repeated a hundred times in the walls of mirrors. It was a brilliant Ball, but tension seemed more evident than pleasure. Although I knew myself to be in love, I was not such a bumpkin as not to realize there was treachery in every corner.

"Did you enjoy our little assignation?" he whispered in my ear. "I think you did, my not-so-innocent young maid!"

I didn't like him referring to my wild lovemaking in so light a vein and was about to tell him so, but Raoul, bowing low, chose me for the gavotte. I was chagrined to see de Villette, her rose-garlanded hair dressed too youthfully for her mature years, in the arms of my love. I could gladly have thrust her through with a bodkin, but I dared not make a scene and had to continue smiling. We were all trapped in the tinsel charade of the Court and forced to play our parts. I kept my head averted and would not look into Raoul's eyes, with their unnatural luster. All eyes seemed to be upon us.

"What a fine pair they make, to be sure...." someone remarked as we glided by. "Two golden gods—their hair is like the sun..."

Raoul's lips curled into a leer as he heard this. "Listen to what they're saying about us—made for each other."

"Why don't you go to the country to your wife and babes?"

"Aha! So that's what's upsetting you, my sweet daffodil."

"I'm not upset, but I should be obliged if you would leave me alone." He greeted this with laughter, and the courtiers smiled in our direction, no doubt thinking we were having a marvelous time.

"You've not yet become accustomed to the flirtations of the Chateau, my flower."

"I'm in no hurry."

"You will learn to be intrigued with pleasure and excited by passions in time. The bud has yet to be plucked."

"But not by you, M'sieur," I tossed at him, and beckoned Fernando to my side as the music stopped. I felt ill-equipped to deal with Raoul. His conversation was too bold for me. I smiled to myself, knowing that the bud he spoke of had been plucked already.

The musicians struck up a minuet and I flushed with pleasure as I put my trembling hand in Fernando's. We joined the others on the floor, and I heard someone whisper as they glanced our way, "They're at the stage where they can't stop looking at each other."

They were right. We kept our eyes locked and his seemed to say to me, "Soon I will make love to you again, slowly this time, indoors by a warm fire on a soft bed." My own answered, "Why not now, my beloved, my legs feel weak for want of you."

At the end of the dance his warm lips kissed my hand and I felt my heart flutter and had to fan myself to hide my blushing face.

"Are you a little warm, Mam'selle?" he asked me solicitously. "Shall we take a stroll on the terrace?" I realized he had to speak to me in this cold manner, as there were inquisitive ears all around.

Just as I was about to answer him he was tapped on the shoulder by a grotesque creature, standing hand on hip. I was startled to see it was a man wearing woman's makeup, bejewelled and beribboned, who fluttered long lashes and opened rouged lips to simper, "Fernando, you never dance with your little Philippe." He lowered his eyelids and pouted, lifting a limply hanging hand to be kissed. I caught many people smiling knowingly.

Fernando stiffened and said coldly, "May I introduce Mademoiselle Solange to his Majesty's brother, Philippe, the Duc d'Orleans?"

Philippe made a moue and through half-closed eyes he seemed to compare my figure with that of his own overindulged body, then brushed his lips near my hand.

He twisted his chin to one side, glancing askew at me as he did so, then flounced onto a chaise longue and drew Fernando down beside him. I stood before them awkwardly.

"What do you think of my new gown?" Philippe leaned slightly backwards to let us appreciate the whole picture.

"It is . . . very grand, I'm sure, and I've never seen so many diamonds," I stammered, for I was stunned that this creature should be the brother of the great Louis. He seemed pleased with my answer and nodded slightly. He switched his gaze to Fernando and smiled and sidled against him, pressing hip to hip. Everyone was watching maliciously.

"That shade of blue suits Monsieur admirably," Fernando spoke graciously, without a trace of sarcasm.

"But what say you to my new wig? Is it not most becoming?" Philippe prompted sullenly.

"Most becoming," Fernando agreed.

Philippe's thick, sensual lips slowly parted into a smile, his dark eyes trying to convey a deeper meaning, it seemed. His hand rested on Fernando's velvet-clad thigh, lingering as if by accident. He looked down his long nose as he absentmindedly caressed the strong, hard muscles beneath his fingers. I could feel rather than see the ogling eyes of the courtiers upon them. Fernando stood up hastily and coughed behind a hand.

"Such a wonderfully pure gem you wear on your doublet, Monsieur. I think it is a new treasure?"

Philippe beamed his delight as he lifted both hands to his face. "Oh, you noticed! It was brought to my attention only this morning by my dear wife, Liselotte, Elizabeth-Charlotte, you know. She showers gems upon me, and doesn't seem to care for them herself. Isn't it fine?" He fingered the huge sapphire as he rose to his feet and pirouetted away. Hips swishing, smiling slightly to left and right, to the veiled amusement of the company, he went to join Raoul by the windows.

I turned to Fernando. "Tell me all about him, please. I have never known such a strange person."

Fernando looked after Monsieur with a frown. "Ah, some say his mother, Anne of Austria, dressed him as a girl for years and treated him as one, so her own darling Louis should have no rival. Monsieur's collection of jewels is said to be fabulous and he certainly shines at Court. There is no one better at arranging a party. I hear that when his son, the Duc de Chartres, was a child, someone asked him if he liked dressing up."

"And what did he answer?"

"He said, 'I like it better than my mother, but not as much as my father!'"

"What an amusing child he must have been."

"He's grown up into a very—unusual young man. But let us forget about him and have some supper, Solange. Come."

In the supper room, hundreds of courtiers were milling about. I felt light-hearted as we followed Tienne. I saw Thérèse and nodded to the company as we took our places by her for the meal. The table, a trestle the length of the side of the room, was covered with an embroidered cloth. The royal servants in their splendid livery served whole sides of meat, enormous salvers of savories and fish, fowls roasted and broiled, cream sweets and ices in the most amazing shapes. The royal kitchens were famous for their patisseries and sweetmeats, displayed in abundance, and of course, wine aplenty. The room was hung with the richest tapestries depicting scenes of the hunt in brilliant reds, blues and greens, and we ate from gold plates. I was still not accustomed, however, to the intense heat from the candles in the enormous chandeliers. They dripped hot wax onto the company, as I had found out to my cost!

The strawberries looked delicious and Elizabeth-Charlotte was gobbling them greedily.

"The poor woman is finding more pleasure in food than in her joyless marriage," someone cattily remarked.

"Oh, no," Thérèse was quick to reply. "They adore each other."

I couldn't help but remark to Thérèse, "Little Monsieur looks more like his wife's wife. She is so big."

Thérèse giggled and confided, "I overheard him telling someone once that he didn't think he'd be able to manage. However, by dint of hanging holy medals in a certain place, rather impeding any pleasure Madame might have felt, he did manage to have three children by her!"

"You heard him say that?" I gasped.

"Oh, yes. He's very *drôle,* is Philippe."

"He certainly is!"

"Their marriage seems to work very well. She is out riding most of the time, and they say she is in love with the King."

Elizabeth-Charlotte looked pale, from overeating I thought. Suddenly she put her hand on her stomach and I saw her ladies hurriedly help her out.

"She's been making a pig of herself again!" Philippe tossed after her. "She's probably got stomach pains. Not poisoned, I hope, like my first wife Henrietta. Liselotte is such fun," he laughed. "Her German accent is so amusing."

After the meal Fernando claimed me again as his partner as soon as his duty dances were over. His tender eyes told me all I needed to know. He loved me, I was sure, and we danced while the music flowed around us. I thought I must move like a cow in a barn compared with the other ladies, and said as much to my partner.

"Certainly not. You have a natural grace, *ma cherie,* and look more lovely tonight than ever I remember, like a flower kissed by the sun. Your hair shines with a hundred sparkles."

His hand felt hot and I trembled at his touch. I could feel my knees weakening as we held glances, oblivious to all around. When, all too soon, the music came to an end, I curtsied and waved to Thérèse and her Charles, who joined us.

"What is that awful smell, Thérèse?" As I said it, I looked round and was shocked to see a nobleman relieving himself against the Gobelin tapestry in a corner. The stench was strong, and soon he was followed by others.

"I suppose it is the royal privy," I giggled and we fell about laughing into our hands and could not stop until Madame de l'Eglise came up behind me and rapped me on my shoulder with her fan.

"Manners and etiquette, if you please."

"Manners and etiquette, indeed. Why, even the village peasants don't do that!"

"Kindly do not address me in that manner. You should be ashamed after the care that I have bestowed on you."

"Yes, my Lady."

"Oui, Maman."

We both stifled a last giggle and curtsied to Madame as she began a serious conversation with Madame la Duchesse de Berri about her health. "I am so glad your temperature is down," she sympathized. "And I do hope Madame la Prenson de Condé recovers soon."

Tienne appeared at my side. "His Majesty desires you to take wine with him."

The people nearby heard, and soon there were impressed "oohs" and "aahs" from all sides at this piece of news. The whole ballroom was twittering.

"When?" I gasped.

"At once, Mam'selle. 'Tis a great honor."

"Don Fernando, you must accompany me," I begged. "I couldn't possibly go alone."

"When the King commands, one obeys. It is *you,* Mam'selle, who has been given the accolade, not I."

"Oh, I can't!"

"I think I know why he honors you," Fernando scowled. "You had better go alone."

"What do you mean?"

"I think you know." And with this he turned his back on me. I wondered what he could mean.

"His Majesty will not eat you," Tienne laughed, leading me, my heart beating, to the Grande Appartements. I was not so sure. However, we were holding hands as we entered the anteroom.

"I will be waiting outside," Tienne whispered as he pulled his small paw away, those trusting eyes gazing into mine. His cap of silky ash hair swung about as he darted out, and the great doors were shut behind me.

"Your Majesty," I whispered, and fell into a deep curtsey. The King's clothes were solid with pearls and diamonds, which followed the pattern of the Spanish needlepoint lace with which his coat was trimmed.

To my dismay, he dismissed his entourage with a flick of the hand. We were left to sup *á deux*. I gulped and sat on the edge of the little red and gilt chair which his Majesty indicated, in front of a table laid with gold and crystal. He poured wine for us with his own hands and lifted a goblet to his old lips, bidding me to do the same. The cool wine slid down my fevered throat and steadied my trembling hands. I could not force myself to partake of anything, but watched fascinated as his Majesty nibbled at sugared confections. He held out a candied almond and I bit it to please him, but it stuck in my throat as his beautiful hand caressed my shoulder.

"Your face is not unfamiliar to me. Was your mother at Court?"

"Er . . . no, Sire."

"Such a white little neck," he smiled. "I hope you are happy here, my sweet angel?"

"Indeed I am, your Majesty," I choked, for he had cupped my breast and squeezed a little.

I pressed back in my chair. "Your Majesty, there is something I would like to ask you."

"All in good time, my little country flower."

"It is of the utmost urgency."

"Do not tremble so. Here, take another sip of wine. It is a red wine of Burgundy. I no longer take the white wines of Champagne, for the red is better for my health. So Fagin, my physician, tells me."

He held the glass to my lips and I was forced to sip.

"You have always seemed so clever and amusing to me. Now what is this urgent question you wish to ask me?" he prompted, as his free hand groped among my many petticoats.

"Your Majesty," I gasped, for to my horror the feelings he aroused in me were not unpleasant. "My father was a gentleman," I choked.

"You don't say." His Majesty didn't seem at all surprised, in fact not in the least bit interested.

His flushed face was close to mine and I opened my mouth to protest, but his old, dry lips met mine, and I was appalled to find that I did not find the sensation distasteful, or even wrong. They were not Fernando's lips, but nevertheless exciting. It had never occurred to me that you could love a man deeply and still find the kisses of another amusing.

He tickled me under the chin, and I thought he was admiring the beads of my necklace when he said, "They're charming, quite charming."

"Oh, they're only little things Thérèse gave me."

He eyed my bosom skittishly. "Not so little, I think, my sweet!" causing me to blush crimson.

"You do like me, don't you, my dear?"

"Oh, your Majesty, indeed I do," for it was true enough. He was about to hold me closer, but the doors were flung open wide and a lackey appeared.

His Majesty was obviously astounded. "What is the meaning of this intrusion? I will not have it!"

"Forgive me, your Majesty, but your brother, Monsieur, insists on speaking to you at once."

I quickly rearranged my skirts and jumped away from the King, thankful for the interruption. Even as the lackey spoke, Philippe pushed past him and stood in the doorway, his face as mottled as the wattles of a turkeycock.

"What the devil, Philippe! Go and amuse yourself elsewhere!" The King motioned his dismissal with a flick of the elegant hand.

"I'll tell you what the devil!" His evil face was screwed up with spite toward his Majesty. "What right have you to treat my son, the Duc de Chartres, in so disgraceful a manner? I must protest, Monsieur!"

Fancy calling the King "Monsieur," even if he was his brother, I marveled!

"You must protest!" the King echoed, standing calmly, arms akimbo.

I felt my jaw drop, terrified that I might hear something awful, but I was glued to the spot.

"You, whose hands are always in unexpected places," the King continued.

Philippe seemed to color more as his Majesty indicated to the lackey to leave, but he was already retreating discreetly from sight. Philippe strutted around the room screeching, his voice raised high as a woman's and his head darting forward like a chicken being strangled.

"I won't stand for it any longer," he shrilled.

The King lifted an eyebrow quizzically and held the back of his hand to his mouth, yawning leisurely while Philippe stood and fumed.

"I will leave you, your Majesty," I offered, finding my voice at last. He put out his hand and gripped my elbow, drawing me back to the chair.

The King was controlling himself with effort. He twisted his fingers into hard knuckles. "*Mon Frère,* a glass of wine?"

Philippe sucked in his breath and took a step back.

"Thank you, no. You treat me too lightly," and folded his little arms in front of him, leaning backwards.

The King waved his hand to silence his brother. "On the contrary, it is your son who is at fault."

"At fault!" Philippe shrieked, turning puce. His small feet almost left the ground and his voice nearly disappeared into a high-pitched squeak.

The King sat opposite me, one beautiful leg outstretched, and sipped at his wine, boredom showing in the downward drag of his mouth and sleepy eyes.

"Of course, you would say that," Philippe continued, half dancing around the King in agitation.

The King now looked extremely angry and leapt from the chair. He crashed his crystal goblet onto the table, spilling some wine. It began to turn slowly from a spot of red to a bloodlike stain on the lace cloth. He was beside himself with rage and grabbed hold of the front of his brother's jewel-bedecked coat, causing it to jangle and tinkle wildly, and stared hard into the eyes below his.

"Chartres was having a wild love affair with one of Liselotte's ladies in front of the whole Court, and his wife, my daughter Princess Francoise Marie, pregnant at the very same time as another of his paramours!" Philippe's eyes looked about to pop out of his head as he tried to answer. He resembled a pomeranian yapping at a lion. The King held fast to his brother's clothes as Philippe slapped in agitation at the exquisite hands.

His Majesty continued, "And he even went to Paris to visit the two young mothers-to-be at the same time! Madame de Maintenon told me herself."

"Well," Monsieur answered boldly, having managed to fall back into a chair as the King towered over him. "What did you expect? Naturally a virile young man would be restless with nothing to do but kick his heels at Versailles. You have behaved dishonestly with him. You lured him with many a specious promise, none of which has ever been kept, into a wretched marriage."

He was screaming now and his molelike hands fluttered

about. He continued, "You treat him no better than you treated your Queen, Marie-Thérèse!"

The King paled. I gasped, fearing he would strike Philippe, but he loomed over his brother, trapping him in the chair, his knuckles white as he gripped its arms. He spoke quietly, almost touching the face tilted upwards and cringing under his. "Very well. I will do something for you. I am obliged to make economies, and I will begin by cutting off your allowance."

The quarrel was well under way. Neither of the men noticed as I slipped out of the room and joined Tienne, who stood with several servants, ears flapping, clustered in the anteroom.

My heart was pounding, my head in a whirl, as I ran to my room, where I undressed, strewing my fine clothes about the room. I lay tossing on my bed and presently fell into a troubled slumber.

Some hours later I was awakened by a fresh and wide-eyed Thérèse, all agog with the news. "I hear there was a real to-do while you were with the King."

"Oh, Thérèse, my head is fuzzy. Why did you wake me?" I snapped, dragging my hair upwards and out as I scratched my head and turned over, pulling the covers tighter and snuggling down in the bed.

"The whole Court is buzzing with the news, and we all want to know how the King treated you." She pulled down the covers from my neck and smiled, eyeing me for the love bites I had seen on the other ladies. "My mother thinks Madame de Maintenon had you brought to Court to do more than 'amuse' his Majesty."

I pushed her hands away. "I'm sure that can't be true. Leave me alone. I am tired."

I rubbed my eyes, yawning and irritable. Thérèse, put out, flounced in her night shift across to the window and drew the heavy blue curtains letting in the daylight. I covered my eyes with my hands and begged her to close them. She turned to me and made a mouth of bored impatience. Then, realizing that I was beaten, I thrust back the bedclothes and padded bare-footed to join her and put my arms around my dear friend.

"Come back and sit on the bed. I am sorry I was grumpy. To tell the truth I am tired."

She allowed me to pull her onto the bed, but sat with her lower lip pouting and sighed, "Well, what happened?"

"Nothing happened."

"Nothing happened! They say Philippe was raving. And you, Solange, what about you and the King?"

I shivered, for it was still very early. Seeing that I was chilled, she covered us both with a fur.

"I wonder why Don Fernando was annoyed that the King sent for me? I do hope he isn't still angry."

"Oh, men!" Thérèse laughed. "He was probably jealous!" I felt a surge of power. Perhaps he was! "I tried hard to stay awake last night to hear all your news and now you say there is little to tell."

"I took a glass of wine with his Majesty, and I think he was about to seduce me, but Philippe forced his way in and started shrieking about how the King terrified his son."

Thérèse turned to face me, her huge eyes a little surprised.

"But that is all?" And then she broke into peals of laughter and hugged me to her. "The rest of the quarrel is all over the Palace, but I do believe you."

And then she was off, chattering about the happenings of the Ball. "Did you notice the Duchesse de Seasti is letting her corsets out? How fat she is looking. I can't imagine there is a babe nestled in her at such an age."

"Yes," I agreed, for I had come to adore gossip of late. "She did look a sight, with all that white lead on her face and breasts. She's letting her age show, it seems."

Thérèse had forgotten her disappointment at my lack of news.

"They say the Duchesse de Ventadour is warming the bed of the Compte de Toulouse, but he is so ill with stone I doubt if it is true."

"Oh, yes, I doubt it too."

"I was waiting to tell you all last night. Did you notice

how dashing my Charles was looking? He claimed me for many dances. We are to meet in the Summerhouse soon. You'll aid me, won't you, Solange?" her sweet face begged.

"If you will do something for me, dear."

"What is it?"

"I have a little money that Madame de Maintenon gave me and I would like to buy a bolt of good cloth to send to the inn wife who sheltered me. I have thought of Clothilde many times."

"Oh, that's easy. Leave it to me, dear. I'll have a basket packed with sweetmeats as well."

"That would be lovely, Thérèse. Thank you."

"Now will you say yes?"

I was about to agree when there was a bustling in the anteroom and our serving maid entered with Tienne.

"Ah . . ." The bed curtains were pushed completely aside. She grinned and put down our breakfast of peaches and sage and angelica tea.

Tienne was bursting with news as he waited for her to depart, his little face quite flushed. "The most shocking news, Mam'selle. The Court is in a turmoil!"

"What's the matter? What's happened?" we chorused.

"Monsieur—the quarrel was too much for his heart—the King is greatly upset—he collapsed at supper."

"The King did?"

"No, no!"

"Collapsed?" I gasped.

"No, no, *not* the King! *Monsieur*. He's dead!"

"Dead? He can't be!"

"He died of a stroke in the night, they say. The quarrel finished him off."

I felt faint at this news. "But he was in good health when I left. That's terrible, Tienne."

"They say they ate their late evening meal together after they had calmed down, so Monsieur went back to St. Cloud as usual. Dr. Fagin rushed to his home as soon as he received a note by courier from the Duc de Chartres to say his father was ill."

"Oh, how awful! Then what happened?"

"The King was still in a temper, so he took no notice of the message that Chartres had received and went to bed instead of rushing to be with his brother."

"I know he was always worrying if Philippe's little finger ached," Thérèse intervened.

"Come and sit here, Tienne, and tell us the rest." I patted the chair next to mine, and he plopped down and took a deep breath before continuing.

"Well, he was assured there was nothing more to be done. When he heard some hours later from Dr. Fagin that Philippe was dead, he was full of remorse. They say he told Chartres that now that he is the Duc d' Orleans, he must think of the King as his father, and is going to shower him with riches."

"Poor Madame," Thérèse sighed. "She had grown quite fond of him of late, it is said. Dr. Fagin did warn him not to eat such huge suppers, you know."

"On your way, *mon petit*. Thank you for bringing us this sad news." I mussed his blond halo and he skipped out.

We began to dress and the maids gossiped, throwing in a line or two about Philippe's pretty boys and what a scandal they had been.

So the colorful, malignant Monsieur was no more. And all agreed that the parties at Court would never be quite the same after his death. He had been so gay, Monsieur—a carnival of one that brought such merriment.

I heard afterwards that his wife, Liselotte, spent hours burning letters from his paramours, the Duc de Nevers and the beautiful Chevalier de Lorraine, even that nuisance Raoul. She missed him and did all she could to erase the sordid evidence of his sodomy so that his memory should not be tarnished.

Chapter 6

Thérèse and I were sipping hot chocolate after our afternoon nap when Tienne burst into our room yet again.

"There's an ugly rogue at the royal stables, Mam'selle," he gasped. He seemed to have been running, and his rosy cheeks were glowing as he blurted on, "And he told one of the cooks to ask you to visit him this day."

"No! Visit a stableman? What impudence! Who told you, anyway, my little rascal?"

His eyes widened. "You don't understand, Mam'selle."

"Let him talk," Thérèse admonished, putting her cup down on the table. "What kind of a rogue, Tienne?"

"The kitchen boy said he's a villain, if ever he saw one, fat and shifty eyed, with two black teeth.

Fear clutched at my heart. I knew who it must be. Pierre, come to try to get the diamond he had remembered from so long ago. My old life seemed an eternity away.

"I'd better see him, I suppose," I faltered.

"Mam'selle, he said it would be the worse for you if you didn't."

"He must *not* see you," broke in Thérèse. "Shall I run to Don Fernando at once and inform him?"

"No, I don't want anyone to know."

"You will not go!" Thérèse shouted. "I think I know who he is. You've told me of that swine at the inn. He means trouble, for sure."

"I must go," I whispered. "For who knows what evil tales he will spread. Give me my stockings at once."

The little maid began to dress me as I hastily brushed my own hair. "Perhaps he thinks I can put in a good word for him to the Master of the Household, that is all," I sighed hopefully.

"We shall go with you," Thérèse was already half-dressed herself. A hyacinth blue shift of plain cloth was thrust over her head, covered with a full skirt of blue velvet, dark as the night. A long coat was tied at her slender waist and ended at her knees. Silver lace edged the long hanging cuffs and formed a matching fichu at her throat. Her ensemble was finished with a bow of velvet drawing her hair back from her face.

The rose-pink gown brought out for me to see was pushed aside. "No, I will wear the grey cloth."

The little maid gave a shrug and glances were exchanged. "You become more imperious by the hour, mistress."

I stood back to check my appearance. None would guess the shaking knees and dampness behind my neck in these understated but obviously expensive garments. I covered my hair with a black velvet hood that diminished my youthfulness and gave me a little confidence. My sleeves were trimmed with the same stuff and heavily embroidered with plum-colored braid to match the three layers at the hem of my skirt and train. The front of my coat had the pattern repeated, and I took a black riding crop in my hand.

Without further ado, Tienne led the way to the stables, his sweet face creased with concern.

"What a serious child you are, *mon cher*."

"I do not wish to worry him," I whispered to Thérèse. "He gives me such heart, but I am all of a tremble." She squeezed my hand tightly to show that she understood.

We crossed the sunlit stableyard, disturbing the pigeons picking at the grain in the shadow of the stables. An ungainly body scrambled up from a heap of straw and shambled over. I held my breath. The sounds of the ostler's shouts reached me as if from afar, and the ringing of the horses' hooves and everyday sounds seemed curiously muted.

"Quite the fine lady, aren't we now! 'Tis alone I'd speak with you." He was bloated, and even more foul-smelling that I remembered. I turned my head away from Pierre's stinking breath.

"Oh, no, you don't!" Thérèse stood her ground, arms akimbo, as Tienne clutched my skirts stoutly.

"No, you don't!"

Pierre impudently stretched out a hand and felt the cloth of my coat. I clutched the riding crop in front of me, longing to bring it down across his dirty wrist.

"I think you owe me something," he sneered as the stale wine fumes hit me.

"Indeed I do not."

"You've plenty of pretty trinkets now. My silence means much to you. That diamond will buy it. I don't ask for more. I told you I had need of it."

"I have no 'trinkets,' as you put it, and I don't know what you mean."

Thérèse was looking bewilderedly from me to him.

"As to your silence, who would take notice of anything that came from your toothless mouth?"

"Ah—that's more like the farm-chit I knew."

Tienne doubled his little fists in front of him and I put a gentle hand out to stop him.

"Come, *mon petit.*" I turned to leave.

"I will make sure all hear from whence you came, my grand lady!"

"You're wasting your time," I shouted over my shoulder. "Everyone knows already!"

"Not so fast, my pretty. What about the babe I gave you that dark and frosty night? I wasn't wasting time then, was I?" he leered.

I felt Thérèse's eyes upon me. I could see she was astonished.

My anger flashed and I turned to face him. "You lying

swine! No one would believe you! They knew I was a virgin when I arrived at Court."

"We'll see about that." He wasn't playing with me now. I tried to pull myself back, but he grabbed my arm in a vicelike grip. "What about the diamond then?" and he lunged at my throat. Tienne thrust a little foot under his leg to tumble him in the still-warm horse droppings. He fell in a heap, moaning and cursing.

"I'll not be finished with you," he growled as the three of us fled from him.

As we washed the stable stink from us in our room, Thérèse questioned me.

"He spoke of a diamond?"

"A diamond!"

"And what of the babe? Whose did he mean?"

"You know I was a virgin, Thérèse. How can you ask?"

"But a diamond!"

"Oh, Thérèse, I feel I must confide in you. The diamond I hide in a secret drawer at night and in a linen bag down my bodice by day. It is my only valuable possession and it was bequeathed to me by my Grandmère."

"Oh, let me see."

I removed the diamond from the bag and smiled when Thérèse marveled at its beauty.

"But I thought you were so poor?"

"It's true, we were. I don't think Grandmère could sell it and I didn't know about it till the end."

"You are wise to keep it hidden, dear. Put it away quickly."

"Yes. If I'd been more careful at the inn, that Pierre would never have seen it."

She seemed to be satisfied, so I didn't tell her any more, and Berthe entered the room at that moment. She gasped when she saw the marks on my arm.

"You must look where you're going, dear. I'll get some salve at once to dab on the bruises," she clucked.

"Will you wear your rust-colored gown for the Ball this evening, Thérèse? I do so love you in autumn shades."

"If you think my Charles will like it. I expect a note from him at any moment, but we have to be so careful."

"Can we walk a little, Thérèse? I feel quite agitated."

"That would be a good idea. I'm ready. Just pin this flower in my hair," she commanded the little maid.

I gazed into the mirror and saw that I was quite pale. Grey didn't look right on me today. "Just a moment, Thérèse. I look so pasty-faced. Shall I change my gown?"

"No. Just add more color to your cheeks and lips."

The maid bade me be seated and touched my cheekbones with a hare's foot dipped in rose-tint, and my face didn't look so pallid.

"That's better," Thérèse remarked. "We'll walk now."

In the garden we linked arms as we crossed the closely cropped grassy lawns. A peacock displayed his colorful fan for us and the dull peahens scurried away.

I sank down into an iron chair surrounded by hundreds of tubs in which orange trees were growing. "The park is so beautiful and restful, Thérèse."

"Yes. Monsieur Andre de Notre is a genius."

"Who is he, dear?"

"He designs all the grounds for the King, even the fountains, and his family before him always worked in the Royal Parks."

"Oh, I didn't know."

"He is the only one who has refused a coat of arms. He made the King laugh. He said, 'I already have one.'"

"How could he?"

"It was a joke apparently. He said his coat of arms was a cabbage leaf with three caterpillars over it!"

I couldn't help smiling, even though I was still suffering from shock.

"Let's have some wine. I still feel a little shaky."

Tienne flew to do my bidding.

"I was so worried when that beastly man grabbed your arm, Solange. Can you still feel the pain?"

I rubbed it. "No. That ointment Berthe rubbed in helped and the witch hazel was soothing. But she said I'll have a fine bruise. She thinks it's from Don Fernando!"

The wine was set before us, with little sugar cakes. I pushed my black thoughts to the back of my mind and soon we were lost in girlish gossip. Thérèse was probing, but again I put her off.

"Oh, Thérèse, the effort of recalling all that has gone on tires me so. Believe me, one day you shall hear all, *cherie.* Thank you for being so patient."

She flung her arms around my shoulders, holding her cheek close to mine. "Of course I shall. You look better already. The air is good for you."

Dressing that night, I silently prayed that Fernando would attend the Ball.

A pink gown of shimmering satin was laid on the bed for me. "Yet another new dress! I wonder why Madame is spending so much money on me still?"

Thérèse shot me another of her peculiar glances. "I told you why. To amuse the King," she hissed.

Madame de l'Eglise fussed as she adjusted my cap of rosebuds. "You'll find out soon enough."

My gown was flounced with the finest ecru lace at the hem, revealing matching slippers with heels covered in diamonds.

"This bodice is even lower than the last," I objected.

"It is *à la mode,*" Madame replied in a bored voice.

My bosom was rouged to match my cheeks, and my hair was entwined with ropes of rosebuds at the sides of the cap. Nosegays had been embroidered on my skirt and my sleeves were held at the elbow with buds. It was the grandest gown that I had yet been given, even more beautiful than the yellow.

When Fernando caught sight of me entering the ballroom, his fine black eyebrows lifted approvingly. Or was he mocking me? I could never be sure. He came to me and pushed back the lace of my cuff to kiss my wrist. I looked up from under lowered lashes. My heart missed a beat and my knees went weak just looking into his eyes.

He bowed low and whispered in my ear, "In the Summerhouse, after the Ball."

I spent the rest of the evening in a happy daze of anticipation. I leaned forward and spoke close into Thérèse's ear. "Will you stand guard for me?"

She squeezed my hand. "Of course I will."

I kept a keen eye on Fernando as he danced, first with the pig-faced de Villette, who pushed herself round the floor like a too-heavy pudding. He was so handsome and attentive to her stupid twittering! Then he chose as his partner Madame de l'Eglise, and they danced a pavanne. Madame de l'Eglise held herself ramrod straight, like an old wooden doll. The two spots of rouge were more evident than usual as she grimaced and made sure everyone noticed with whom she was dancing by laughing shrilly at every other word he spoke to her, causing the courtiers to glance in their direction.

"Who is that handsome blond man with the double chin?"

"Where?"

"There!" I pointed. "The one with that revolting woman."

"Oh, he is the Dauphin, Louis' son. Everyone believes he married her in secret. He has a weakness for ugly women. The Dauphine was just as repulsive. She had brown marks on her forehead and big red hands—he especially liked her for them, and they say her legs were like tree trunks."

"How odd!"

"Yes, it does seem strange when his father only worships beauty. And it is said the second Madame was terribly rude to Madame de Maintenon because of her insufficiency of ancestors. German people do take that far more seriously than we do, you know."

"No, I didn't know. What is the name of this second wife?"

"She is called Madame de Choin. Isn't she fat? So squashy!"

"She certainly is plain. I've never seen such an enormous mouth and, oh! Look what the Dauphin's doing!"

We both gaped in astonishment as, much to the amusement of the courtiers, he was beating a tattoo to the music on his wife's huge breasts.

As the dances drew to a close, Thérèse and I walked in the garden arm in arm, laughing, strolling on the close-cropped lawns like any two ladies taking the air, to allay suspicion.

Suddenly she caught her breath and halted. Already leaning against the door to my rendezvous, Fernando was having a conversation with a young man of his own stature but of leaner build. She gave a little cry of pleasure as she ran forward. Charles was an ally to my beloved, it seemed. In an instant, Thérèse was in Charles' arms. How wonderful that we were all in accord.

Fernando held out a hand to me and we left our friends entwined together in the moonlight and drew inside the Summerhouse.

"I thought the dancing would never end," he said, taking my hand.

"Oh, I had a lovely time. I do love the gavotte," I replied flippantly to tease him.

"I hear you didn't stay long with the King."

"No, not long," I whispered, and let my free hand caress his neck. My fingers found his mouth and I gently pushed myself against him.

Hidden from sight, Fernando took me in his arms and at once I was lost in his embrace. I had never dreamed that I could feel so happy. This man could make me forget everything but my love for him. My body arched to meet his and I felt his strong fingers unlace my gown. He carried me to a silk-covered chaise longue. His firm mouth met mine, and I ceased to think. The weight of his muscular body pressed on mine and we wrestled till the sweat from us both made our limbs slippery. His tongue explored my teeth, then thrust into my mouth. I grasped it tightly. My nails scratched his broad back, urging him on. But he was in no hurry.

"Not so fast," he whispered. "You must learn to relax, *ma cherie*... try to make the pleasure last longer."

"I'll try, darling," I agreed, but wrapped my legs around his waist and dug my heels into him, forcing him to enter me.

He gasped, "Ohhh! You've tricked me." He heaved me up and under him, and began to pound in and out of me exactly as I wanted him to.

"You've stopped, Fernando."

"Yes," he grinned down at me. "You're trying to win a race. Slow down."

I wanted to please him, so I forced myself to lie still, and closed my eyes. "But I need you now, darling," I moaned. "I'll burst if..." But he covered my mouth again and we clung together till the explosion shook us both.

"Mon amour," I whispered. "You steal my heart."

"You have already stolen mine, my dearest Solange. I will carry you away with me to my home in Burgos one day soon, when the wars are over."

"Oh, my darling, how wonderful!"

"*Ma chere, ma vie,*" he whispered. The moonlight shone on his tanned, smooth face. I touched his cool cheek with my fingers and tried to think. Could it be right to feel the need to cry because I loved him so dearly? I was afraid that it would carry me away and break my heart. I must try and forget that he was a nobleman and I only a bastard. Thc word, admitted for the first time, shocked me, but I knew I was deeply in love.

"Fernando, we must not stay too long—Madame will miss me." But he silenced me with kisses.

"No, no... I meant..."

He put a finger to his lips and held me close, the warmth of his body caressing me as we lay lost in time. I knew that no one had ever loved as I loved my darling.

My blood pounded through my veins, as his dear hands caressed my breasts, causing the nipples to stiffen. As he pressed his warm lips to my breast, I held it for him so that only the tip would be in his mouth, and the ecstasy was almost morc than I could bear.

The now familiar heat enveloped me and I could feel myself moist and open with longing again. We thrashed about until almost exhausted, and he entered me at last. We came together, unable to resist a moment longer.

Later, with arms around each other, we walked out into the garden between the flowerbeds of roses and in the scent of the flowers.

"Fernando...?"

"Shh..." he silenced me yet again with kisses.

In a shadowy corner our friends were close in an embrace, lost in the oblivion of love. We smiled conspiratorially and tiptoed past. I shivered although the night was warm.

"I am afraid."

"There's nothing to be afraid of, my darling," and he squeezed my waist tightly and kissed my lips. "I am here, Solange, what are you afraid of?"

"That you do not love me as I love you."

He just laughed and kissed me again lightly, and then plucked a bud of velvety red and tucked it into my bodice. I felt myself blush and forgot my fears.

"Truly roses are the scent of love," he whispered hoarsely.

We sat in the moonlight at a little table in the garden and he held a cup of burgundy to my lips. We both drank, and he turned the cup to drink where my lips had touched. He covered me with his cloak, then kissed each finger of my left hand separately. "My little white dove, you have been so short a time at Court," he said softly, as he kissed my wrist. "What did the King want of you? You never told me."

Then I noticed him eyeing the marks that Pierre had made. Half teasingly and half angrily he asked, "Who gave you those?" and his eyes seemed to darken.

"I fell in the garden, that is all." I hastened to explain, but I could see he didn't believe me. "I was brought here to amuse his Majesty by Madame de Maintenon," I said proudly, "To sing and be amusing."

"And did you... amuse him? Were there just the two of you?" he asked, a little angrily I thought.

"I didn't have time. His brother, Monsieur Philippe, broke in on us and I left them to their unfortunate quarrel."

"Ah, yes! That was most unfortunate. Poor Philippe!" He looked down at me. "Since leaving Spain I have known many women, but never one to ensnare my heart or my senses so completely as my Solange."

Silently I rubbed my cheek against his.

"Have I a rival?" he asked. "I cannot believe I am your first love."

I kissed him quickly. "Don't be silly," and entwined my

hair around my fingers, smiling coquettishly.

I stood up and smoothed my dress as I answered. "I have lived in the country and wouldn't let the farm louts near me." I spoke quickly to take his mind off his questions. "How time has flown, dearest. They must not miss us."

He grasped my wrist firmly. I could see his mood had changed. Suddenly alarmed, I tried to draw further away from him. The sweetness had been driven from the evening by my panic. I couldn't tell him the truth about my lowly birth that night. His love was so precious to me that I did not dare to put it to the test. As I drew away from him and he kissed me goodnight I could see a question in his eyes. I hurried away in silence.

In the half-light I groped my way to bed and saw that Thérèse was already asleep, but that she was sighing. I fell on my knees and prayed that no evil would come of my passion. "Dear God, help me to be strong and keep Fernando's love, and help Thérèse find happiness with Charles." I sobbed and prayed that Fernando would not take our love lightly.

Thérèse sighed again.

"Are you not well?" I whispered. But she didn't answer, so I crawled into bed and just lay there, crying into the night until sleep overtook me.

Thérèse wakened me the next morning, holding her stomach and looking pale.

"Are you ill, Thérèse?"

"Yes, I have been sick."

"What is it? Was it the goose? It was greasy."

"Yes. No. Perhaps it was the goose. I don't know. There's nothing you can do." She drew a hand across her puckered brow.

"Is your mother still...?"

"Yes." She was looking down.

"Is it a babe, Thérèse?"

"I daren't tell her—she'll kill me."

"Oh, Thérèse, you must tell her!"

"I can't and I'm too worried to go to the midwife the Court ladies use."

"Many is the reputation that has been saved by a

buttonhook," I answered. "Has he spoken of marriage, Thérèse?"

"No. How could he speak of marriage? What would we live on?"

"I have the same problem as you, it seems. Fernando confessed his love for me last night."

"Oh, Solange, I am so happy for you both. But do not get yourself into the same position that I am in. I don't know what will become of me."

"I would be happy to be in your position. I can't imagine anything more wonderful." I held her close. "We will think of some way, Thérèse, I feel sure. Don't worry dear." But she just sobbed in answer as I patted her shoulder.

Chapter 7

Summer stretched into autumn and the weeks continued happily—at least for me.

"Your stays won't lace very tightly," I remarked to Thérèse one morning. I was short of breath from pulling her laces.

She just shrugged.

"I'll have to let them out again if you don't want anyone else to know that you're putting on so much weight."

"Oh, yes. No one but you must know. Don't let the maids see."

"Phew! It gets harder with each day, dear. Try not to eat so much." I sat, legs spread in front of me, fanning my face with a glove.

As the months passed, I continued to let the stays out even more. On many occasions Thérèse and Charles would slip out into the night while I held Madame de l'Eglise in conversation, asking many questions as to deportment and etiquette, and inquiring of her good taste as to the color of my new sleeves.

"You are wise, child, to emulate your elders. Madame de Maintenon is pleased with you and thanks me for my good advice to you."

"Thank you, Madame de l'Eglise," I replied, smiling up at her.

Thérèse woke one morning feeling more unwell than usual. Pale and drawn, she dragged herself around the room.

"Don't go riding today," I advised. "Have a rest."

"I must. I've made excuses too often. Help me, Solange. Lace me up. And don't let's stay with the others today. Then we can talk."

"Very well, dear, but would you like a quieter horse?"

"No, there are too many eyes watching. Oh, Solange, what a beautiful morning! I shouldn't plague you with my problems. Perhaps things will work out in time."

So we made ready and went out. We laughed and talked of our loves, with only our horses and Tienne to eavesdrop, our hair blowing behind us in the autumn sunlight. Yellow leaves fluttered and slowly danced about us, but I remember thinking to myself that Thérèse looked really sick.

I was just going to ask her if she felt all right when a hare scurried across our path and her skittish stallion gave a snort and reared up on its hind legs, its eyes rolling. Thérèse cried out. Before I could reach her, she fell to the ground, doubled over and clutching her stomach. "Catch my horse," she gasped.

"Never mind that now!" I quickly dismounted and tied my mount's reins to a tree.

"Do you think my time has come?"

"Surely not!" I was panic-stricken.

"Has the fall damaged the child, do you think?" Thérèse's large, frightened eyes met mine.

"You must lie down properly."

"I want Charles with me! Oh, Charles, Charles," she moaned, clutching herself again.

Tienne ran up to us. "What's the matter with her?"

I felt myself sag. "She's poorly. Where can I take her? Help me!"

We were all on the ground by now, Thérèse on her hands and knees with her head down. I stood up and tripped over my skirt. Then it began to rain. I felt so helpless and frightened I didn't know what to do.

Strands of hair were covering Thérèse's face as she looked up from the ground, and her cheeks were wet with the rain and her tears. I pushed the hair away from her eyes.

"Oh, the pain!" she cried.

"I've never known the pains to come so quickly," I said, as I rolled her over and loosened her stays, my fingers trembling. Tienne's worried elfin face looked on.

"Shall I go for help?" he whispered.

"Not yet. I remember we passed a charcoal burner's hut. Look, it's quite close." I pointed back the way we had come. "Help me to drag her there."

The sodden girl groaned and cried as we pulled her to the dirty little hut.

"I can't go in there—it's filthy!" Thérèse was in no pain for a moment, gasping for breath.

"Don't be silly!" I was exhausted, puffing and panting. "You'll be out of the rain at least."

"But I have been delicately brought up!"

"Nonsense, it won't harm you. This is an emergency!"

The charcoal burner stood in his rags among several snotty-nosed brats and a stout woman with a snaggle-toothed grin. Barefoot and ragged, they clustered around us like a family of goblins.

"Out! Out of the way!" I shouted. "My Lady wants privacy. Can't you see her time has come?"

They gawped at me, moving slowly backwards.

"Get some water!"

The man brought an earthenware pot and dipped in a soiled cloth. I took it and wiped Thérèse's forehead and gently tucked some sacking I found to form a pillow under her head. Tienne was frightened to come in; I could see him hovering in the doorway.

"Tienne, quickly, gather some bracken to cover the bed."

He flew to do my bidding, as Thérèse cried, "Get my Charles!"

"Shh . . . All in good time, dear. Try to rest."

Sooty smoke was coming from the feeble fire. I pulled a hand from rubbing my eyes and saw that it was black.

"Shoo!" I cried to the runny-nosed brats, who were

peeping around the door, and they jumped back at my shout, terrified.

The only light came from the door, half open to the daylight. Tienne brought armfuls of bracken, frowning in worry. We covered the bed from side to side, gently moving the moaning Thérèse.

"Just a moment, dear," I began.

"Don't leave me!"

"There, that's better. I won't leave you. My God, you're bleeding!" I must have shouted, for the woman entered eagerly with the children.

"Get those brats out!" I ordered her.

She kicked them smartly and thumped one around the legs. They scurried to obey her, disappointed at missing the sight of more blood.

The woman took it all in her stride. "After seven, you've seen it all before," she boasted, and cut Thérèse's stays with a big, rusty carving knife, which she then put under the bed.

"To cut the pain," she grinned at me, then tied a rope on the head of the crude wooden bed.

"For her to pull," she explained.

"The knife doesn't seem to be working!" Thérèse yelled.

The woman asked, "Is it the first? Oh, it always takes longer with the first. The rest'll be like shelling peas."

As the hours passed, Thérèse's cries grew louder, but the woman seemed unaffected by her agony. I turned my hand away from the loathsome creature when she asked, "Have her waters broken? We don't want a dry birth."

"I don't know." I moved her pretty coat and saw that it was soaking wet.

"Oh, I can see they have," the woman said.

Poor Thérèse was writhing in agony and hauled on the rope. "Oh . . . Ah . . ." she groaned, twisting her head from side to side.

I held a mug of wine to her parched lips, but it dribbled out of the corner of her mouth, and a piercing scream rent the air.

"Bear down," the woman remarked with unconcern,

standing with folded arms. "Push. Put your knees up." She put her head down to look. "It's coming—I can see its head. Thank goodness, not feet first."

A chill ran through me. Tienne clapped his hand to his mouth and rushed out. I shouted after him, "Fetch Charles as quickly as you can!"

Suddenly there was a rush of blood. I was terrified, but the dirty-nailed woman was enjoying every moment. No doubt it was the only subject she knew anything about.

"Give another heave and it'll be out," she instructed as she examined Thérèse's fine shift between thumb and finger with interest.

I gasped as the babe pushed out into her filthy hands and she placed it on the blood-stained bracken. I felt sick as she bit through the cord and tied it with a piece of cotton. Both the woman's arms were stained to the elbows with blood as she picked up the miniature creature by its heels. It was perfectly formed.

"What's the matter?" I cried. It's blue—and it isn't breathing!"

She smacked its bottom. "It's no good," she said. "It's dead."

"Isn't there anything you can do?"

"No—it didn't have a chance. Born too soon. There's nothing we can do."

I began to cry.

Thérèse stretched her arms out. "Where's my baby?"

I whispered gently, "I'm sorry, it didn't live." I took the mug of wine from the woman. "Here, sip this."

I lay down beside Thérèse on the filthy floor and rested for a moment. I was sick at heart for my poor friend, and was relieved to see she had fallen into an exhausted sleep.

I sat up with a start as I heard hoofbeats approaching. But it was Fernando, not Charles, I saw standing in the doorway; his brow like thunder and a handkerchief held to his mouth.

"Oh, Fernando, darling, I'm so glad you're here!"

"So, Raoul is a proud father, is he? I might have known—you dirty little slut!"

I shook my head, horrified at his misconstruction of the scene, as he looked with distaste down his aristocratic nose, pale with anger.

"You don't understand, darling, it isn't mine, and anyway the baby's dead." I wept onto the blood-stained bed. "Oh, help us, Fernando!"

But he flung himself onto his horse and rode away at a furious pace. Tienne looked at me uncomprehendingly.

"Is that the brat's father?" the woman asked, shrugging her shoulders.

"That's no concern of yours," I croaked, weak with unhappiness.

I knelt and prayed as the nightbirds called. The dark was drawing in, and the leaves rustled down.

"You must go for the priest, Tienne."

I felt his arm around me. "I'll go at once, Mam'selle. Try not to cry."

When the dear little soul was gone on his horse, I felt the peace of the night entering my being. I stood shakily and drew a long, shuddering sob.

"We must bury it," I said to the woman.

"Never mind the child. It has no soul." She turned to get a spade from the jumble of odds and ends outside the hut. I followed her out, carrying the still, tiny form wrapped in a piece of fine linen torn from my shift.

"We must find a quiet corner," I told her, and looked around for a shady tree. She shuffled after me, carrying the heavy spade as we walked up the slope toward a tall, old oak tree.

"This will be a peaceful spot," I called to her over my shoulder, and began to push the crisp leaves away with a fallen branch.

"I don't see what difference it'll make, here or there," she grumbled, but nevertheless ambled over and placed the rusty spade in position. She pushed the blade with her foot in its scuffed shoe, and said, "This is too dry. I can't slice the turf, and it must be deep. We don't want the dogs to dig up the body, do we?"

I shuddered at her plain speaking.

She pushed again with all her might, pressing on the spade until the ground gave way. I couldn't look, and turned my back as she lowered the little bundle into the hole. She wiped her sweating brow with the corner of her filthy apron, muttering under her breath, "What a fuss over nothing," and made her way back to the hut.

I picked up a spray of autumn leaves and berries and placed them in the center of the pathetic little grave.

Just then Tienne returned with a little priest astride a mule. He had a fat stomach and peered through suspicious eyes as he climbed down heavily.

"Well, what's this the boy's been telling me? Where's the child that's just been born?"

"I'm afraid it died and we've just buried it," I answered in a low voice, indicating the newly dug grave.

"You shouldn't have brought me out for this." His slack jowls wobbled in irritation as he rubbed his hands in a washing motion.

"Won't you at least say a prayer?" I asked angrily. "Are you trying to tell me a man of God has no respect for a dead child?"

"It'll cost you a piece of money," he replied, slyly, edging his puffy face close to mine.

"You will be paid. I'll take you to the mother. Perhaps you could give her a little comfort."

He turned to follow me, grudgingly, and when he saw the hut he pursed up a disapproving face and exclaimed, "I can't go in that squalid place!"

"Oh, please, it'll only take a moment." I grabbed hold of his arm and he reluctantly allowed me to lead him to my poor friend.

He eyed Thérèse distastefully. "Hmm. Where's the wedding ring? I can't say a burial service over the child of a loose-living woman."

I threw him a gold louis. His mean little eyes glittered as he snatched at it and half ran back to the graveside. I hurriedly followed him, keeping my temper as best I could, wondering how a priest could be so callous and unfeeling for human weakness.

He mumbled a brief prayer and was about to scuttle off as fast as his short legs would carry him.

"Sin, sin," he muttered. "She'll burn in hell, too late to repent, the child was a bastard." I felt my blood turn cold, for the baby wasn't the only one.

"Go then!" I snapped at him. "You obviously care more for gold than the word of God."

I turned back to the hut to find the woman standing beside Thérèse's sleeping form, her face so pale and still, as if she herself were close to death.

"I'm afraid my friend will not recover," I told the woman, as I watched her potter about quite unconcerned.

"No, she's not going to die."

Tienne was in a huddled heap in the corner, his shocked white face turned anxiously up to mine. I put a hand on his tousled head. "It's all right, dear. I'll see if there's some food."

I gave the woman some money and she quickly hid it in her bodice, saying, "There's only bread and goat's milk, but it'll give you strength."

She bustled away and the husband brought a jug of milk and hard bread broken into chunks. I soaked a bit in the liquid and coaxed Thérèse to swallow some, but I could only drink the milk. Tienne managed to gulp the unappetizing fare, though; the child must have been starving.

"We must have a cart, padded with hay," I told the woman. "You can have my cloak, Tienne. I won't need it."

"You can take the cart if you pay. We can't afford to lose it. Follow me, and you'll need a lamp if you're to leave tonight. How much money have you got?"

I handed still more money from my purse and helped to fill the rickety cart with dry hay. Between us we carried Thérèse gently, though she moaned a bit. "Be careful," I warned the charcoal burner.

The offspring clustered around, picking their noses and hopping about. One scruffy red paw stroked my gown as I passed them. The woman brought a stool to help me mount my horse, and Tienne tucked a rough blanket around Thérèse before pulling himself up on the front of the cart.

"Shall I start, Mam'selle?"

"Yes, *mon petit.* Drive as carefully as you can. I will be glad to see the end of this disastrous day," I sighed, wondering desperately how quickly I could find Fernando and assure him he'd been wrong to think I'd had another lover who had given me a child.

Chapter 8

The cart creaked off and we began the weary drag back. The horse picked his own way, and I nearly fainted with the fatigue of riding through the darkness after such a day. The winding road seemed endless on that dark night, and a lonely vixen shrieked nearby, breaking the stillness.

As we came nearer the Chateau, I straightened in my saddle and on reaching a lane near the stables I sent Tienne for Berthe.

"Don't worry, Mam'selle. She'll look after her."

"Be careful to stay in the lanes and dark corridors," I warned him. "We'll have enough trouble as it is, without having to answer awkward questions."

I climbed into the cart and felt Thérèse's brow. She was asleep and her haggard face looked ghostly in the oncoming dawn light. After a weary wait, Berthe arrived with her brawny and strong husband, the pastry chef, carrying a pallet between them.

Berthe put a foot on the hub of the wheel and grasped the side of the cart. She peered in as I moved the blanket from Thérèse's face.

"Oh, my poor little lamb," she moaned. "What's the matter?"

"Thérèse is ill, Berthe, but there's no need to worry," I answered.

"Oh, my God, let me see!" Berthe tried to struggle and almost lifted her ample body into the cart, but I put a restraining hand on her shoulder, pulling her back.

"No, she'll be all right. I'll tell you all about it later. She only needs rest, but no-one must know."

"Why? What's the reason?" Berthe's frantic eyes searched mine for some hidden terror, her pale face ghastly in the semi-darkness.

"She'll need some nursing," my voice was sharp with anxiety. "But not a nurse who'll pry."

"Oh, I know just the one. Don't worry, she'll keep her mouth shut. Let's get Thérèse up to her room."

Her husband took Thérèse by the shoulders and Berthe took her feet, holding the sleeping girl carefully, and after a slow procession through the dimly lit corridors, with Tienne going ahead and keeping a watchful eye, we finally arrived in our room.

Before I collapsed on to a chaise longue, I watched Berthe bustling and tutting around Thérèse. She lifted the blanket carefully. "Oh!" Her plump hands flew to her mouth. "Her petticoats are soaked with blood. What happened?" She swayed with shock, and put her shaking arms about Thérèse's sleeping form, bravely fighting back the tears. "My lamb is gravely ill, I know it."

"No, she isn't ill. I'll tell you in the morning, Berthe. I'm too exhausted now. She just needs rest, I swear it."

Berthe breathed a sigh of relief and choked a sob back. "I know you wouldn't lie about Thérèse, Solange. She's had the baby, then?"

"You know!"

"I guessed. Did she miscarry?"

"It was born dead," I answered, my head hanging leadenly on my chest. "Don't ask me any more."

"Maybe it's as well it died," Berthe grunted.

A damp cloth was being lovingly sponged over my friend's ashen face, and her torn petticoats removed one by one.

"She'll be clean and tidy in a moment," Berthe mumbled

under her breath as she briskly set to work. "I don't know what's to be done about the two of you—you're such a worry to me!"

I knew Thérèse would be all right now and in good hands.

I was half asleep when I felt Berthe shaking me gently. "What is it?"

"Drink this, it will relax you."

"But I was nearly asleep—I don't need it. Whatever it is, give it to Thérèse." I closed my eyes again, but she gently forced the soporific down me and I felt a blanket being tucked about my legs and arms. I remember muttering, "Yes, Berthe, I'll tell you in the morning."

I awoke gummy-eyed and struggled back to consciousness, resolving to put a brave face on as reality came flooding back.

A strange peasant woman, in a brown headscarf, with a weather-beaten face was standing over me.

"Who are you?" I tried to force myself to sit up properly.

"I be the nurse, mistress. I brought 'ee something to eat."

I saw the silver dish she held. "I don't want anything."

"You must. Come on." She sat on a stool and uncovered the dish. "There's good chicken breasts in mushroom sauce. Now go on, taste it," she advised as she held the spoon out.

I looked over to Thérèse and saw my friend's grey, drawn face against the white pillow.

She turned her head slowly. "I've had a tray of slops, too, Solange. Bread crumbled in soup," and she drew her lips away from her teeth in a parody of a smile. But the effort must have been too much for her, and I watched as her head fell back again. Berthe nodded happily from her perch next to her angel.

I pushed the spoon away from the nurse and, swinging my legs off the chaise, padded over to Thérèse. I leaned over her, but she just stared vacantly, as if looking through me.

"It's Solange, Thérèse. You just spoke to me."

Berthe put a finger to her lips and motioned with her other hand for me to go and eat. "Thérèse will sleep," she whispered, and she continued to stroke the hair from the sunken face.

I forced the bland food down my throat, but its glutinous taste nearly made me vomit. "Take it away, please."

The woman was most unhappy. "You girls don't eat nearly enough. No wonder you're so pasty-faced and skinny. Good food'd put fat on those bones. 'Tis a sin to waste good fare," and she proceeded to finish greedily everything that I couldn't stomach, and shovelled it down with relish.

I sat at Thérèse's bedside while Berthe hovered, ever watchful. "You'll stay here for a day or two and you'll feel better."

I pulled the fine coverlet to Thérèse's chin. Her eyes seemed to have grown enormous in the shrunken face. Her voice was only a thread of sound. "Charles..."

"I will see to it that he hears all, dear. Take heart."

A tear crept down her cheek, as she plucked the cover into tiny pleats. "Was it a... boy or a... girl?" she whispered, without looking at me. "A girl," I answered.

"Your mother mustn't hear of this. The nurse that Berthe chose will keep her mouth shut."

Thérèse just sighed and closed her eyes, mumbling incoherently.

As the days passed, Berthe nursed her back to health. Thérèse was out of bed and more cheerful at last; in fact a little color had appeared in her cheeks again.

"Thérèse almost seems herself again," I remarked to Berthe, as my little maid brushed my hair.

"Oh, yes, she's quite excited. She insists on Charles visiting her here, the silly girl. She isn't really better, you know. She must be careful. I'm to smuggle him in."

"Thérèse, you never told me." I pretended to be vexed, sticking my bottom lip out. "Brr... it's so cold this morning. Look at the frost on the window."

Berthe gathered a fur about my shoulders. "You must keep yourself warm, or I'll be nursing you, too."

The fur brought warmth to me at once, and I held it close

as Thérèse slid from her chair to sit on the floor, her arms about my knees, her sweet face upturned to mine.

"Berthe only brought me a note from Charles early this morning. Don't be vexed, dear. I did tell you I wanted to see him here as I haven't been allowed out of doors as yet. Look what I am making for Charles." She pulled a needlework purse of tiny stitches of many colors from the pocket of her gown.

"So that's what's kept you so busy over in the corner. I wondered what you were doing. It's lovely, Thérèse. Charles will treasure it."

"But you look sad, Solange."

I stroked the pink velvet sleeve of her gown and reknotted the ribbon that held it tight at her elbow to make the bow prettier.

"Did Charles say anything of Fernando in his note?" I tried to make my voice sound natural, but felt it was a weak attempt.

Thérèse looked away from me, keeping her eyes on the purse, and moved over to the window seat.

"Well, Thérèse, I'm waiting. I can tell you're hiding something." I ran to her, letting the fur fall to the ground. Suddenly I felt warm and my cheeks were burning. "Please tell me the truth! It's better that I know."

Thérèse spoke quickly and all in one breath. "It is said he is flinging himself into all the wild adventures of the Court."

"Oh. I see."

"I'm sorry, dear. If you were at Court, I'm sure you could win him back," Thérèse advised.

"I shouldn't need to win him back," I replied angrily.

"Well, you know men. As soon as they've got what they want, they no longer desire it."

"I feel so ashamed, Thérèse. Has he said nothing of me?"

"They say he only has eyes for de Villette."

"So he isn't sad. He doesn't miss me."

"He doesn't seem to, dear."

I felt a pang that struck right through, sharp and cold to my very heart. "How could he be so fickle?"

"His name is connected with many ladies, it is said."
"Oh," I answered forlornly.
"Well, men are men, dear."
"If that's the case, I've finished with the lot of them! I am going to walk in the garden where it's quiet. You must see Charles alone. Thank you for telling me the truth. I know it wasn't easy."
She turned a worried face to mine. "How pale you look, Solange. Will you be all right?"
I felt sick and faint to hear such news, and dressed in the drab gray wool dress and cloak with the sombre hood that befitted my somber mood.
"I will be fine, dear." I kissed her affectionately on the cheek and was gone swiftly down the many corridors to the garden where no one promenaded. I wanted to be alone with my thoughts.
How I wished that things had not gone wrong between Fernando and me! It was my own fault, I reasoned, walking dejectedly through the crispness of the day. I pushed my hands deeper into my muff. It was so cold. Burying my face in my muff I sank onto a bench and wept tears of anguish. Presently the fit of weeping passed, leaving me drained and hollow. I must go back to Thérèse. What a fool I'd been to imagine that he'd loved me as much as I'd loved him! He had used me like a professional whore, which was probably what he thought I was. I'd meant no more to him than a servant girl he'd seduced.
I thought back to that terrible moment when he had stood in the doorway of the hut. He'd thought the child was mine. How could he have believed that? He should have known that I would never bear another's child. He knew I'd been a virgin. If the one I loved could think so ill of me, he had really cast me off. Truly I felt my heart was broken.
With shaking limbs I got to my feet and pulled the hood over my head to hide my tear-stained face. Then, when I had forced myself to walk for a while more briskly, past the bare trees, a weak sun began to climb in the winter sky.
Suddenly I became furious and roughly brushed tears of

anger from my eyes. He was stupid! How dare he cast me off so lightly, the conceited Spaniard! I stopped still and stamped my foot on the hard ground. I would show him. I would stiffen my resolve and no one, not even he, would know what was in my heart. I would start at once. I would wear my finest gown. "I'll show you," I muttered to myself as I ran to change my gown. It no longer suited my mood. "I'll make you pay for the heartache you've caused me!"

Thérèse was ready for her promenade, eyes shining, "I'm to have five minutes in the garden, Solange."

"I'll be changed in a moment. Wait for me. I can tell by your face that Charles has been here."

Berthe was fussing around her, as usual. "Make sure your collar is tight and, here, pull the hood closer about your face. I don't want you catching a chill."

"Stop fussing, Berthe. I'm covered in fur."

I wore my favorite day gown and cloak of emerald green velvet, with a large gold cross around my neck, a birthday gift when I was seventeen from Madame de Maintenon. My hat of sable matched the rich fur trimming of my sleeves and muff. I applied an extra dab of rouge with the hare's foot because I wanted to seem robust, not delicate, as if I didn't care a dash about the arrogant Spaniard.

I took a last look at myself in the mirror, and it gave me strength to see that no one could guess the coldness in my heart. I touched the hard knob of my diamond talisman hidden in my bodice for good luck, to give me courage.

"You look lovely, Solange! Come along, dear."

We made our way outside and had been walking only a moment when we spied Tienne running towards us over the lawns, his little green cap clasped in his dimpled hands.

"Ooh," I laughed. "Your nose looks like a cherry on a Christmas cake; it's bright red!"

He grinned impishly as he gasped for breath, puffing little smoky clouds in the freezing air. "Berthe says Thérèse has been out too long and must be taken back to her room at once. She is waiting with one of her steaming brews."

Thérèse pulled a face but blew me a kiss and meekly

followed the ladies who had silently appeared behind us.

"Your face is as fresh as a rose this morning, cherub," I said to Tienne.

"I'm *not* a cherub, and I have orders for you."

"Orders? What orders?"

"Madame de Mainenon calls for you to attend her morning salon."

I braced myself. It had been days since I had mixed with the courtiers. I must remember to smile.

"Very well, dear. Lead the way. Have you got your breath back?"

"I never lost it. Only old people lose their breath. I've seen them looking for it under cushions and chairs!" He grinned up at me—the little imp always knew how to cheer me.

"What a wise little soul you are, *mon petit.* I think you know too much. Perhaps I'll have to box your ears." But he knew I was joking and skipped in front of me to the Grande Appartements.

I stopped in the ante-room to see if I could find out who was there today. I loosened my furs as I looked about me and went through the doorway, my heart in my mouth. My outdoor clothes were removed by a lackey. There were the usual groups of men and women chattering and gesturing. They sounded like bees collecting nectar in a flower garden, buzzing from one topic to another.

I held my head high and, walking slowly, stopped to talk with the bent old Count Bissot, looking more yellow than usual in the unkind light of winter.

"Heh, heh, I am well, thank you, Mam'selle." He imprinted his wet mouth on my hand without his back moving. He had no need to bow, as he was bowed already.

I moved over to another group, who gestured for me to join them.

"Where have you been hiding yourself?" The Duchesse de Seasti simpered through red lips. The white lead was cracked on her face and some of the rouge had run and caked into the corners of her mouth. The December light was indeed cruel.

"I have had a slight chill, that is all. I must speak with

Madame de Maintenon. Excuse me, Duchesse." I turned away from the ugly sight and sauntered over to Madame, seated with her little pet dog. Her stark black dress of velvet trimmed in lace and the cross she inevitably wore made her seem *religieuse* amongst the bright colors of the courtiers. My eyes scanned the room for a sign of Fernando.

"I hear Thérèse is absent, Solange. Where have you both been? Not ill, I hope." Her round face looked unfashionably scrubbed and clean as she eyed me with warm affection.

"Only a slight chill, Madame. We have both been ill. How kind of you to enquire."

We were joined by several ladies and gentlemen and I strolled over to the screening lattice-work and hid behind it. I held on to the screen, taking gulps of breath. I had behaved well, but my heart was pounding.

Suddenly I spied a broad back and thought my legs would give way under me. I could almost have reached out and touched him in his coat of brown. He turned slightly and I felt sick. Fernando was laughing with that tart, de Villette. She looked like a Paris whore in a red satin dress, decolleté as a ball-gown in spite of the cold, and adorned from head to toe in black lace, rouged lips simpering. I caught part of their conversation as I forced my ear closer to the lattice-work. My fingers clutched at the wood and I felt the familiar lurch at the sight of my beloved.

Then I heard his voice, but the only word that I could catch was 'Spain'. Oh God, I still loved him and he was going away to Spain! He had turned and was almost facing me, but I was well hidden. I felt faint as I looked into the remembered eyes of my only love, so knowing and experienced. He whispered in her ear and I thought I would lose consciousness from the pangs of jealousy that clutched at my heart. She squealed with laughter and linked his arm intimately so that their bodies touched.

"So you are to leave us, Don Fernando," she said, wide-eyed. "I trust not for long?" and fluttered her lashes at him.

"As long as His Majesty has no need of me," he answered her respectfully.

I could stand it no longer and wiped my damp palms on

the skirt of my dress as I straightened my back. I dabbed my brow with the scented pomade hidden in my bag and smelt the perfume. My blood was boiling in my veins. I forced myself to seem unconcerned, but my legs felt weak.

I walked over to them feeling like a sleep-walker, or a person in a dream. "I would speak with you a moment," I said to him in a small voice, my back to her.

He looked down at me coldly. "I've nothing to say to you." His eyes were hard and he turned his head away.

The plump de Villette hunched her shoulders, expecting some entertainment, and smirked at me.

"Leave us alone, you old street-walker," I hissed. "At your age you should know better than to fling yourself at a man who is young enough to be your son!"

She narrowed her eyes and forgot to pose for a moment. "You forget yourself, farmer's daughter," she ground out through clenched teeth.

I felt a stabbing pain in my arm and screamed as she stood looking as if surprised, eyes wide with wonder as she deftly stuck a jewelled pin back into her coiffure. One or two people turned enquiringly, but Fernando ignored them.

"You do not understand," I whispered under my breath to him.

"I'm sure I could believe the evidence of my eyes," he answered disdainfully.

"Get rid of that cow and I'll explain."

The cow strained her ears.

"There's no need to show your country manners in front of a lady," he chastised me.

"A lady! Hmm! A tart!"

She pretended shock and swayed as if about to faint, a limp hand on her forehead, fluttering her fan, and was rewarded with Fernando's arm about her waist.

"What a common girl," de Villette lifted her pug nose.

"I'm surprised at you, Solange," he grated. "There's no sense in making a scene."

I looked around and saw that several of the courtiers had formed a half-circle around us.

I smiled sweetly as I naïvely remarked, "Madame la

Duchesse, I am sure you will be grateful to me for drawing your attention to the fact that your *postiche* is falling off." I moved as I spoke, lifting my hands. "Here, allow me to straighten it for you." I gave her false hair one hard tug, and the curls hung grotesquely over one side of her head, as if she had been drinking too much.

People were enjoying the spectacle and pointing fingers at de Villette, who was boiling with rage at their delighted laughter. She tried to put her hair to order, but obviously didn't know how to arrange it without her ladies or her mirror. She had aged ten years as she tried to smile up to Fernando, her face flushed and her mouth a garish slit.

"I will be in the garden later, Don Fernando; I do not care for the low company you keep!" she snapped.

He bowed low and she ignored me, weaving her way out amid bellows of laughter, looking like one of Princess Charlotte Aglaé's battered dolls.

"Oh," I screeched. "She looks so funny, as if her head is falling off!"

Even Fernando half smiled, but suddenly grabbed my arm above the elbow in a vice-like grip and he scowled at me. "You've no right to talk, you little whore!"

"Ow! That's where she stuck me with a pin. Let go!"

"Who stuck a pin in your arm?" he enquired unbelievingly. "What an imagination!" But he loosened his grip, and I gasped as I gently rubbed my arm.

"Come out where they can't see us," he growled.

We stepped hurriedly into the ante-room, deserted except for a footman asleep in a corner and there, when we were hidden from view, he turned furiously on me.

"I saw you in childbed! No doubt you buried your secret in the woods," he raged, and turned his back on me. I tried to speak as tears welled up behind my eyes, but he walked swiftly away from me, towards the gardens. I stood there alone, choking back the hurt and trying to compose myself.

I felt a tug at my dress and a tiny hand crept into mine. "He's walking away towards the courtyard. The horses have been saddled for his journey." Tienne stood almost crying by my side. "You must hurry or it will be too late, he already has his cloak on."

I answered automatically. "Yes, you are right, dear."

Burying my pride, I ran after Fernando, not caring if anyone thought my manners unladylike. My breath came quickly as I hurried to catch up with him. In the courtyard, the mules and baggage carts had been made ready for the travellers and surrounded Fernando as he sat astride his stallion. He was laughing merrily with his companions, who were slapping each other on the back, eager to be off in the pale winter light. I ran between them.

"Don Fernando! Listen!" I begged, and grasped his knee.

Panic seized me as they started to move away. I held on to his riding boot, pleading with him, but he shouted down at me, "Get away or I'll trample you down!"

I fell back, holding my head high and kept the tears in check until I heard him ride at a furious pace out of the courtyard. I dragged myself away to the shadows of an arched doorway and sank to the ground. My strength had given out. Sobs racked my body as I leaned against the cold stone, oblivious of everything but the injustice of my position. He wouldn't even let me explain. No doubt he was joking right now to his friends about me. I sobbed to myself. If they could see me now, how they would have laughed at the country bumpkin, breaking her heart over the Spanish gentleman, who'd used her for his pleasure!

Chapter 9

Time dragged wearily by.

"How lucky we have kept everything secret, Thérèse," I said to my friend one day.

"Ah yes, but I've got to get away!"

"Yes, *chérie,*" I soothed. "Just as soon as you're stronger. A few more weeks and it'll be Spring."

"Oh, I can't wait until Spring!" her dark eyes pleaded.

"Shh. Be patient, dear."

Thérèse's hands looked transparent against my blue velvet gown, her delicate veins prominent.

"You're looking much better now. There, look in the mirror," and I held it in front of her face.

"Yes, I feel much better. You've been so wonderful to me, Solange, but I'm afraid my mother will soon have me sent away and locked up behind iron bars if I don't promise to marry the Count."

"I don't think she would go as far as that."

"If I crossed her she would. She might even get a *lettre de cachet.*"

"What's that?"

"It's a document that can only be signed by the King. You

are arrested in secret and taken in a closed coach to the Bastille."

"Oh no, *chérie!* I can't believe it!"

"It is quite true, Solange. People have been taken there to be buried alive in a cell, deprived of identity, without word from any living soul outside. They are abandoned, forgotten, their fate a secret which will never be divulged. Only the King can release them. I know of people who have disappeared and have never been heard of since."

I was shocked beyond measure. "I don't think Madame de l'Eglise would do that!"

"I *know* she would. That's why I've just got to get away. We've made our plans in some detail, you know."

"Oh, Thérèse, you can't go yet! Is she still determined you shall marry the Count?"

She shuddered. "Ah, the thought of being in bed with that yellow-faced dandy with the big gray teeth! I can't bear to think of it. Almost daily she threatens me with it."

"What plans have you and Charles made, dear?"

Thérèse became agitated and she seized my hand. "I'm a little afraid." Her thin fingers pinched the lace of her sleeves.

"I feel more desolate than you, Thérèse. Your Charles is ready to run away with you, but my love has gone far away."

"He'll come back for you. I know it, dearest. You should have told him then and there that the babe was mine. He wouldn't have betrayed my secret."

I heard a bare branch scrape the window as it brushed past and I became lost in thought.

Thérèse began to pace the room. She turned to me, her white face seeming bleached against the crimson velvet dress she wore. "Will you help me to escape, Solange?"

"You know I'll do whatever you wish. Come over here by the fire and tell me of your plans. Worrying and fretting won't help." I patted the green silk chaise longue.

"I promise to send for you, Solange, when we are married."

"When do you plan to leave?"

"Tonight. I can't stand it here a moment longer. I'm well enough now."

"What? Out of the question!" I jumped to my feet and stood in front of her. "You're out of your mind—you're not strong enough to travel!"

"Don't stand over me!" she shouted, and brushed past me, her chin up. "Charles and I have been planning these past weeks and have arranged to leave tonight."

I held her small, cold hands in mine. "If you go tonight, what if you collapse? How are you going to travel?"

"I won't collapse. I've never felt better, and it's all settled."

"Very well, dear. But what do you want me to do?"

"I'll retire early with a headache, and you shall stay with me, saying you're tired as well."

"Yes! Yes! That is a good idea, but you seem overexcited, dear. I wish you would try to calm down a little."

"I don't *want* to calm down! I've waited too long for this night. As the midnight hour passes, I'll dress as a serving maid with a hood to cover my face, and then I'll slip out through the kitchens."

"I see. And Charles will be waiting for you with horses?"

"They'll be freshly fed and watered for the long ride through the night, as we go towards Calais and the boat to England, where he has a favourite aunt who is married to an Englishman. They have no children, and adore Charles as they would a son."

"Ah, that seems sound policy."

We hatched our plot and realised suddenly that it was already time to dine, but neither of us could summon up an appetite. We went to the supper room and pushed our food around our plates so that no-one would notice anything amiss. It was surprisingly easy for me to yawn convincingly as Thérèse puckered her brow and complained to her mother of a migraine.

"Oh, my poor head! How it aches, *Maman!*" She pressed the back of her hand to her forehead.

"No wonder! You're both exhausted," Madame de l'Eglise snapped. "One of you up till all hours and no nap of an afternoon, and the other one hardly leaving her room for air and mooning about all day. It's time both of you had a good night's sleep."

"Oui, maman."

"Yes, Madame de l'Eglise, you are right."

"To bed with the two of you, and don't let me set eyes on you until the mid-morning dinner in the Salle de Venus. I'll send a posset to your chamber."

We curtsied and pecked the dry cheek before walking sedately, concealing our desire to run.

When we reached our room, we couldn't believe our luck and hugged each other, rolling on the bed and stuffing our pillows against our mouths so our giggles couldn't be heard.

"What a fool we've made of *maman!* I'm not sorry. She'll just have to manage without the Count's fortune. She lives well enough at Court."

"That is true."

When the posset arrived we hastily shooed the maid away and emptied it out of the window.

Berthe, who had come to help us undress, looked very disapproving. "Why didn't you drink it? What a waste of a good posset."

Thérèse quickly explained our plan.

Berthe's hands flew to her face. She clasped her darling against her ample bosom. "Oh, I will not hear of it! It is far too soon!"

"It's all right, there's no need to worry." Thérèse's eyes were moist. "You've been more than a mother to me, Berthe dear. But it's all arranged. I'll be fine. I'm strong now and our minds are settled. I'll remember all you've taught me and I promise not to neglect myself."

"But, my pet, you'll never be able to manage without me! I'll come with you."

Both their faces were wet with tears as they argued in exasperation, neither willing to give way.

"Just look how peaky you are still," sniffed Berthe, wiping tears from her eyes.

"Oh, Berthe, I want you to stay and look after Solange.

She's the one who'll need you."

Berthe, still troubled, looked at her, considering, her eyes screwed up. "Well, you have filled out a little these past months. The rest and all those good broths do seem to have done you good."

"See—I told you!" Her face was triumphant and flushed with excitement.

I turned to Berthe to give her something to do to stop her worrying. "Come, we'll get her warmly dressed. It's a cold night."

I held the thickest gown I could find for Thérèse to step into. We heard the church bells chime as we spoke. I pulled the hood over her head.

"It'll be very frosty tonight. Take care, Thérèse."

"You can't go in those shoes, Thérèse. They're not strong enough," Berthe clucked. "You'll wear my good pair."

"But they're cracked! And they're servant's shoes!"

"I'll wrap some rags around your feet. You want to look like a serving maid anyway, so there will be less chance of your being noticed," Berthe replied. "I'm not a bit happy about this elopement, my lamb. I really should go with you."

"Oh, shush, Berthe! We've discussed all that."

"When Thérèse is settled, she'll send for you, Berthe, and you'll go to England," I added.

"Hmmm. Don't know if I'd want to go," she answered, sulking.

"Brush your hair back further to hide it," I advised Thérèse. "There's a strand showing at the side. Here, let me do it. The colour is unmistakable."

"Yes, thank you. I've a little store of money ready and I'll take my jewellery, too."

I laid a handkerchief on the bed and put her little pile of money and jewels on it and tied them tight. "Wait a minute, Thérèse. I'm going to take your mother's jewellery!"

"Oh, you can't!"

"Hush, don't argue. She won't have to pay your dowry, so she's getting off lightly."

"But it's stealing!"

"We're already in trouble. Best be hung for a sheep as a lamb."

Before she could protest further, I flew from the room and stealthily crept down the many corridors as the servants slept or leaned, dozing against the tapestried walls. Silently I sped through the dim passageways until I reached Madame de l'Eglise's room. I thought I heard footsteps approaching, and stopped with lurching heart, hiding in the shadows until they had receded.

Cautiously, I opened the door and entered the bedchamber as quietly as a cat. Deep in the curtained bed Madame de l'Eglise lay lost in sleep. I gently pushed the heavy drapes until a small aperture appeared. Her mouth gaped open and the wisps of gray hair from under her nightcap were spread on her pillow. I paused, and was relieved to hear that she was snoring rhythmically, totally unconsicious.

How was I to get the key from under her pillow? I crept on tiptoe and leaned forward, reaching out to slide my hand gently underneath, without disturbing her. Just as I was about to draw it out, Madame snorted and turned her head. I huddled down, petrified, but, praise God, she didn't wake. With a grunt she settled herself on her back, making bubbling noises with her sunken lips, and I breathed a silent prayer of gratitude as her snoring came evenly again. I had a mad impulse to drop a feather in that cavity of a mouth, but the chance of her being roused and finding me in her room forced me to push the delicious thought from my mind. It was more important to get the key and be gone.

I crouched over the ugly creature and carefully lowered my hand again, holding my first two fingers out, and touched the key. I slowly gripped it and slid it smoothly from its nesting place. I almost gasped, as there was a whole bunch of keys which jangled and clanged together, causing Madame to shift restlessly and turn onto her other side.

Holding my breath, I waited, and when she continued to sleep peacefully, I crept towards the *secretaire* against the wall. In the semi-darkness, I stumbled against a chair. She couldn't fail to be disturbed by the noise as it tumbled, and I froze for precious seconds till I was sure she hadn't wakened. I straightened the chair against the wall and rubbed my tender shin bone. Quietly, I inserted a key in the lock, but it wouldn't turn properly, so I tried another. The second key went in easily enough, but it still wouldn't turn. How could I find which one would fit? Perhaps the smallest one...

At last, the key slipped in easily and I quickly turned it. The lid sprang back and I shuffled the papers, groping until I found a velvet box and two leather pouches. Without waiting to examine them, I clasped them to my bosom, re-locked the *secretaire* and carefully returned the bunch of keys under the pillow.

I stole to the door and stuck my head out, making certain that I was unobserved. Then, lifting my skirts, I raced back to our wing as swiftly as I could, and leaned against the door as I banged it shut behind me, panting for breath.

Berthe came to me and retrieved my treasure. "Oh, God, what a time you took, Solange!"

"I was sick with worry," Thérèse added, putting her arms around me.

"Oh, it was easy," I boasted, though I still trembled.

Berthe emptied the contents of the jewel cases on to the bed. We leaned over and Thérèse gave a gasp. I don't know which of us was most surprised to see so many chains of gold and jewels, links of pearls and golden louis.

"You've taken *everything,* Solange!" Thérèse shrieked, covering her mouth with her hand. "I didn't know *maman* had such a store of valuables."

"Well, I wasn't sure what to take," I laughed, "so I took the lot for good measure!"

We clung together, laughing, till our eyes watered.

Berthe thumped me on my back, nearly doubled up with laughter herself. "Oh, I'm in pain," she choked out. "You're a terrible girl, Solange!"

"Ooh, you've a heavy hand, Berthe! Please," I gasped, between gulps of air. "Stop pounding on my back or I'll end up on the floor!"

Thérèse stood, with worried eyes. "I can't take them all."

"Yes, you can!" Berthe nodded and quickly gathered them all together and piled them with the other things in the large handkerchief. "She's probably got plenty more in other hiding places."

"Oh, Berthe, I feel awful!"

"And anyway, she always said she had hardly anything valuable, so now, for sure, she isn't lying," I added.

"Ah, Solange is right," Berthe chimed in, as she wiped her wet eyes on the corner of her apron.

I put my hand into my own little store of treasure in my special drawer and drew something out. "And here's a little portrait—a likeness of myself painted on ivory. I want you to have it."

"Oh, Solange!"

"I had it painted for Fernando. But I won't need it now," I whispered sadly.

"Oh, I'm sure things will be all right again between you, Solange."

I pressed it into her hand and we embraced tearfully.

"I do want you to have it. It would make me very happy."

Thérèse was moist-eyed as she examined the picture. "It's lovely, Solange. Thank you. I will always treasure it."

"And I have a little money Madame de Maintenon gave me. You can have it. I have no need of it."

"I can't take it. I have enough." She pushed the purse back at me.

"You can't have too much. I want to be sure all will be well with you."

She smiled and reluctantly tucked the coins into her bodice with the portrait, pressing her hot cheek to mine. "You are my dearest friend, Solange. I'll never forget you. Try to conceal my escape as long as you can."

"You know I will. No one will hear a word from me."

"And I won't give you away, my lamb," Berthe assured her. "But you know how nosey the chambermaid is."

The door opened a crack and Tienne slid into the room. "All is ready."

"Poor Tienne will get a beating, for sure," Berthe said.

"I don't care," he answered bravely.

"Oh, you are a darling." Thérèse flung her arms about the little soul and kissed the top of his head.

I opened the door an inch or two, and whispered, "Come on. There's no one about. Good luck, dear."

We embraced again and a brown ghost slipped out, Tienne leading the way, as Berthe went to stand guard in the corridor.

I now waited in terror as the minutes ticked by, until I was sure that the bright-eyed, eager bride-to-be was galloping with her beloved down the long, straight road and through the dark villages. As I dared to relax, an owl hooted. I shivered as I stared out across the sleeping roofs and quickly shut the window.

Chapter 10

All that night I tossed and turned until nearly dawn, when I fell into an uneasy sleep. It was early afternoon of the following day when Madame de l'Eglise's high-pitched voice roused me from sleep, and I blinked in the cold, sunny daylight through half shut eyes.

She screeched at me as she stood at the foot of the bed, hands on hips. "Where is my daughter, you good for nothing farmyard chit?"

Her eyes bulged from their sockets as if out on stalks. She charged over to the side of the bed and shook me frenziedly. "Answer me at once, d'you hear!"

I gathered my startled wits. "I don't know what you mean!"

"Oh, yes, you do! You know that Count Bissot was calling this afternoon especially to see Thérèse. Where is she hiding?"

I remembered with horror the planned visit. In our excitement we had overlooked this appointment made by Madame several days before.

"Oh no, no, I didn't remember that. Why do you think your daughter's hiding?" I asked innocently.

The serving maid stood, half-crouching, at the door, one red-knuckled hand between her teeth. Her eyes were popping with fear.

Madame de l'Eglise shook me again. "No one has seen her this morning." She roughly pulled the covers off me and dragged me onto the floor. "What do you mean, pretending to know nothing!"

"Don't hurt me," I whimpered. The longer I held back, the better Thérèse's chances, I reasoned. "What time is it, please, Madame?"

"I'll ask the questions!" she snapped, and shook me again until my teeth rattled and I thought my head would drop off.

Berthe looked white and scared, and pretended to look for Thérèse under the bed. "They were all right when I saw them to bed last night."

"What did you do?" Madame de l'Eglise twisted my arm. "Where is she?"

"Ow! Maybe she felt better and got up early, and went for a walk in the garden," I ventured.

None of the ladies could placate Madame. Some of them who had been standing near came over and tried to drag her away from me. "You will do yourself an injury, Madame. Come and sit down. Do not upset yourself."

"Get away from me!" She brushed them aside. "I'll get the truth if I have to thrash it out of her!" She choked and her face turned crimson with rage and, snatching off her wooden-heeled shoe, she pushed me over face downwards and whacked me again and again hard across my backside until I screamed for mercy, even as the women tried to restrain her.

"Stop! You'll kill her, Madame!" Berthe shouted, eyes frantic with fear.

At last, Madame tired. She was breathing heavily. The women fled before her out of the room and she followed, slamming the door.

I breathed a sigh of relief, but just as I thought I had weathered that storm, she burst back into the room holding a riding crop. I held my hands in front of my face and cowered.

The pain drove me to fury as she brought the lash down on my thighs and on my back, and I could not stop myself yelling at her, "Your daughter's gone beyond your reach, you old harridan!"

She checked her arm in mid-air. I picked myself up and collapsed into a chair gasping and choking.

"What do you mean?" she screamed.

"'What do you mean!'", I mimicked her nasal twang, my face alight with malice. "You greedy old witch, trying to push your daughter into bed with an old man to feather your own nest!"

I felt a surge of triumph as I saw her jaw drop open with shock, and she was at a loss for words. Her eyes narrowed. "I'll tell Madame de Maintenon what you've done and she'll have you sent back where you came from," she snarled. "I'll see her straightaway."

She turned on her heel, exhausted, and the ladies, who had been looking on aghast, crowded to the door. I heard the key turn in the lock after they had followed her out.

"There'll be no food for you today, either!" she shouted through the door. "I'll see that you suffer for this!"

I shouted back, "You won't dare raise a hue and cry about your daughter. What about the shame?"

I lay on my stomach as I heard her shouting down the corridor. "Smelling salts!" she whined, as her voice died away. "Smelling salts!"

There I lay the rest of the day. But by evening, Berthe had obtained a spare key from one of her friends and after soothing my bruises, I slept a little and felt better. I let Berthe drag my clothes over my aching limbs.

"I think I'll just lie on the bed again for a moment, Berthe, before I go to dinner." But it was not to be, for I was summoned to Madame de Maintenon.

I was in tears as I entered Madame de Maintenon's *appartement,* where beautiful flowers were displayed in abundance. I sank into a deep curtsey. My legs were shaking as if I had a fever, and my arms were without strength.

"Madame de l'Eglise has come to me with a curious tale. I

wish to know the full story, child. Leave nothing out."

"Certainly, Madame," I said miserably.

She lay on her chaise munching grapes whose skin was the color of her black-purple dress. She dismissed her maids and nodded her handsome head as I related the simple but true facts. Madame sat up straight-backed.

"You were very wrong, Solange. I am most displeased with you."

She gazed out of the window thoughtfully, her rich dark gown shimmering in the gathering twilight.

"I will have to decide what is to be done with you. His Majesty will have to be informed, I think, and he is worried as it is. Although life at Court goes on as usual, the war is very trying."

"I have heard talk of the war, Madame," I faltered. "What is it about?"

"There is the Spanish Succession, in which Austria and nearly the whole of Germany, Denmark, Holland and England are in league against France," she sighed abstractedly, and popped another grape into her mouth.

"They want to dethrone Philip V of Spain, in favour of the Archduke Charles of Austria," she continued, "and we are fighting against Spain because our King had no choice but to accept the Crown of Spain for the Dauphin's son. Charles II had no heirs, you see, and was advised to leave everything to his great nephew, the Duc d'Anjou."

"I see, Madame," I said, feeling rather confused, however.

"If we allowed the Archduke Charles to take the Throne of Spain, it would mean that our enemies would be on two French frontiers," Madame explained in a dry voice.

"I didn't realise things were so bad, Madame," I almost whispered.

"Your silly little-girl brain doesn't think beyond the Court and its pleasures," she said tartly.

I lowered my head.

Madame continued, frowning. "The news from the fighting line wasn't too bad at first, but now the King is heartsick at the defeats at Blenheim. They have cost us the whole of the country between the Danube and the Rhine, not to mention an extremely well-equipped army, and we have been driven out of Italy again, as we have been since the days of Charlemagne."

"Is it because of the war that the King hardly ever appears at *'Appartement'* now, Madame?"

"Indeed it is, child. The money in the royal coffers is very low, and trade is almost non-existent. We cannot afford to pay our soldiers and they are very short of food." Madame looked tired as she worried over the situation. "We feel sure there is someone at Court, perhaps in a high position, spying for England. I wish we knew who it was."

I gathered my strength and spoke in a voice I barely recognised as my own. "Madame, may I ask you something?"

"What is it?" she answered, touching her brow with outstretched fingers.

"You do not think Don Fernando is the spy? I know he is a loyal subject of France as well as Spain. I hope he's safe."

"Oh," Madame smirked, lifting the side of her mouth. "The gallant who was so attentive to you! Don't worry. He doesn't go anywhere near the fighting. The French half of him keeps him loyal to Louis. I do not think for a moment that he is the spy."

I was relieved that Fernando's loyalty was not in question.

"Don Fernando is to return soon from a mission for his Majesty. You may pour me a glass of wine and sit beside me." Madame indicated with a glance the carafe and glass on a silver tray resting on a table near the window.

I was stiff from standing so long, and gladly did as I was bidden.

When I had poured the wine and was seated near her, Madame, almost as an afterthought, said, "You may pour yourself a glass of wine and join me in a toast."

As I did so, she raised her glass. "To Anjou, the King's grandson, Philip V of Spain."

I drank with her, and then was foolish enough to continue speaking of Fernando. "If Madrid should fall, Madame, what would happen to Don Fernando's family near the foothills of the Pyrenees?"

"Ah, those Pyrenees!"

"Even if he lost his lands in Spain and the revenue from his vineyards, I would still love him, although his French chateaux are not as vast as his Spanish ones."

"You are still a child, Solange. Our country is at war," Madame admonished. "It is bound to affect all the big landowners."

"I know Don Fernando's peasants are loyal to him, but who can say how things will go?" I insisted.

"Indeed. Who can say?" Madame repeated quietly, lifting her goblet and sipping.

I was flattered that Madame was taking the trouble to explain the situation to me, but was still worried for Fernando.

Madame absently placed her glass on the tray. "The King directs the plan of campaign to his War Minister, Chamillart, in my bedroom," Madame sighed. "It's no good to me at my age to be undressed and assisted to bed with the Ministers there. I have to wait until they leave to ask my maid for a certain piece of china."

"Oh, Madame!" I was shocked. "I have heard it said, Madame, that Marshal Catinat has disgraced the name of France and Marshal Villeroi urged that he should redeem the nation's honour and so Marshal Catinat has been forced to serve under him."

"The King is most impressed with Marshal Villeroi. I think the lieutenants inveigh against him simply because he is the King's favourite." Madame had raised her voice.

I gulped and shifted uncomfortably in my chair.

With voice still raised, Madame went on, "The Archduke has acquired the help of the English, and Queen Anne has supplied enough money to conquer a kingdom."

After a lengthy silence, Madame seemed to come back to me with a start, and folded her arms. "So that is why I cannot go to the King with Madame de l'Eglise's problems."

My heart sank as I wondered if I was to be thrown out of

the palace. "I am sorry, Madame. I had no wish to displease you. I only wanted to help a friend clutching at happiness."

"You're too young to judge happiness, Solange. Leave me to think, and see that you say an extra prayer for forgiveness for the terrible distress you have caused Madame de l'Eglise."

I stood and glanced up under my lashes. "If I've done anything wicked, I'll pray to be forgiven, my Lady."

"Do not be impudent and remember your manners," she said sharply, but I caught a glimpse of humor in her magnificent eyes. "You will make me sorry I gave you such an opportunity to better yourself. Always remember," she wagged a finger at me. "Irreproachable behaviour is the cleverest policy. Now leave me at once before I lose my temper."

She turned her head away as I dropped a curtsey. With hot tears ready to flow, I rushed from her *appartements,* my heart heavy. I determined to say a prayer also for Fernando.

I was met at the passageway by my faithful Tienne. He held out a note to me and looked up at my face most anxiously. "What does it say?" he asked.

I glanced hurriedly at it and my heart began to thump painfully. "I'm to meet Don Fernando in the Summerhouse. Run for my cloak—bring it to me in the garden."

"Very well, Mam'selle."

My thoughts were miles away, knowing that the note was from Fernando. I wanted to be alone when I read it properly. Perhaps he was writing to tell me he was safe, or maybe he had been hurt on his mission for the King. I couldn't bear to think of that.

The air struck a chill right through me. I had not realised that it had gotten so cold. I strolled through the ornamental gardens in the palace grounds, past the elaborate fountain, Basin de Neptune, as if I were just promenading in the sunshine, but I was anxious to read the note again properly and turned quickly from the main path towards the huge jets of water from another fountain.

It seemed it was almost impossible to have any privacy

even at this hour. There were many people walking, cold as it was, on their way back indoors, no doubt, to the dancing in the Galeries des Glaces. It was too dark now to see clearly as I hurried past the large marble fountain while the spray whirled above me. The thought of Fernando was urging me on. Since the war had started, I knew he had to visit his Spanish lands in secret, and they could be confiscated at any time by the Crown.

As I reached the Summerhouse, I peered into the gloom and looked for a candle. I put my hand against the doorpost and took a step forward. "Fernando, are you there?" I faltered.

There was no answer and a premonition came over me. Something was wrong. I turned to flee, but it was too late. Darkness engulfed me and the weight of a foul-smelling blanket nearly smothered me. I felt hands fumbling at my bodice.

"Help! Help!" I tried to scream. "Tienne, I'm being murdered! I'm suffocating!"

I couldn't move my legs or arms, for a rope was tightening the stinking horsecloth around me. "God in heaven, I'm dying!" I thought. Oh, why did I rush so blindly into danger without thinking?

"Fernando—is it Fernando?" I was whimpering. "Why are you hurting me?"

Stars were dancing in front of my eyes and I felt the blood coursing faster through my veins. Then everything turned from red to black, and I felt that death had come at last.

It seemed ages later when I felt my senses returning, but still the blanket enveloped me. I blinked my eyes and saw red patterns under my eyelids. I rubbed against the rough blanket with the side of my arm and choked with the smell of horsedung. I must be in the stables. I could feel the dirt floor underneath me. I struggled to sit up. My legs felt numb and I was shaking with cold, but at least I was not dead.

Then I heard a voice quite close to me. "Look, she's moving. Have you tied her securely?"

I was astounded, for there was no mistaking the high-pitched voice of Madame de l'Eglise. What was she doing in the stables?

"I'll make her pay for all the frustration and distress she's caused me, the little bitch."

"Don't worry, your Ladyship, your honour, she's tied fast."

God in heaven—that beast Pierre! I knew too well his fawning voice and he sounded as though he was kneeling beside me.

Then came a gasp from Madame. "What's that fallen from your pocket?" she enquired sharply.

"Oh. I was about to give that to you, your honoured Ladyship." Pierre's voice changed. "I pulled it from the prisoner's bodice," he said obsequiously.

I tried to squirm. "Mmm . . . mm . .," my voice was muffled. He must have taken my diamond! I could not tell for sure, for my hands were tied, but I was certain it was gone. I tried to slacken the knots. I pulled and pushed, but the rope was too firm and the effort left me sweating and exhausted.

"A diamond—but not one of mine!" Madame de l'Eglise exclaimed with astonishment. "How did she come by it? The girl could not have had such a stone without my knowledge. Hand it to me at once!"

"I spake the Gawd's truth, Ladyship. She must've stolen it, the crafty slut!"

"Hold your tongue, rogue. You're paid to do a job, not to pass ignorant opinions."

"With respect, we ain't been paid yet, me bully boy and me," a third voice chimed in gruffly. "And I've been kicked and scratched worse than in a fight. Look at me shin bone!"

"Ugh! Take your filthy rags from my sight, cutthroat! You'll get your gold when you've done what you were hired for."

A shiver went down my spine. They must mean to kill me. But what good would that be to Madame? It would not bring Thérèse back—nor her jewels.

"'Tis dark in 'ere, mistress. I'll bring the lamp closer.

You're sweaty," Pierre remarked.

"Be you getting a fever, Ladyship?" came the gruff voice again.

"I do not feel well, to be sure. I'll leave you to finish the job."

"But the diamond?" Pierre enquired hopefully.

"I am ill, confound you! Give me your arm. Help me up."

There was a heavy thud, and I felt a body fall across my legs. I tried to scream, but only managed a small cry, "Help me, help me!"

Madame gave a choking gurgle, and I thought I heard my name called in a man's deep voice.

"Solange!"

Oh, thank God, it was my name. I tried to shout again, "Help me!"

There was a scuffling and I strained to make out what was happening. The blanket was pulled away from me and I was rolled over as I felt firm fingers loosening my bonds. I struggled to my knees on the dirty straw, and a strong arm was placed around my shoulders. It was Fernando! I felt dizzy with relief.

Behind me, struggling in the grip of a stout servant, Madame screeched, "Loose me, rogue!"

"Are you all right, Mam'selle?" Tienne put my cloak around me carefully and I rubbed my wrists to get the blood circulating again.

"I can't believe I'm safe!"

Fernando laughed with relief. "The men have fled, but we've caught this old woman. Tienne saw them overpower you, but knew he couldn't tackle them alone. He was hastening for help and ran straight into me."

"Oh, my darling Fernando! I thought you were in Spain. I haven't even read your note properly yet."

He tightened his arm around me. "I sent you no note."

"But I still have it . . ." I looked down at the trampled straw at my feet. "It should be here—I was holding it as I was seized. Ah, there it is!" I bent and picked up the crumpled paper and gave it to Fernando.

He looked down at it, and I saw his face change. Firmly,

he put me from him. I was bewildered. How could he look at me so coldly after what had happened?

But it was to Madame he spoke sternly, as she tried to twist her scrawny arm from the strong grasp of his servant. "You wrote this note, you evil woman! Berthe heard of your plot and came to me. I went straight to the King and laid all before him. As for you, Solange, go to your room!"

Suddenly, he turned his back on me and my heart sank. I just couldn't believe that he was talking to me like that.

I scrambled to my feet and held out my arms to him. "Fernando!"

He quickly turned his head. "I love you, but I know you for a slut. I must rid myself of the fever for you in my veins."

I was hurt and bewildered. He'd saved me from danger and certain death, but I knew he must still think Thérèse's babe had been mine. I could take no more. If he chose to believe ill of me, so be it. I felt too weak to care.

I grabbed the diamond in its linen bag from Madame's hand. She tried to snatch it back, but suddenly swayed on her feet. She all but fainted, but I took no notice and stumbled through the stables, trying to hold on to my senses, followed by a worried Tienne.

At last I gained the warmth and comfort of my room and collapsed on my bed, feeling that my heart was broken.

For days I kept to my room, although Fernando sent me many notes that seemed to me brittle and flattering, rather than loving. I tossed them aside. I cried out only for his understanding and scarcely heard as Berthe scolded, "Solange, you're not listening!"

"What is it, Berthe? Don't go on so."

"Madame de l'Eglise has been very dizzy and is constantly vomiting."

"Well, what of it? There are plenty of people to look after her."

Berthe stood in front of me. "You don't understand, Solange. It's rumoured that she has the smallpox."

"And what do you expect me to do about it? She's no friend of mine."

"Solange, it isn't like you to be so hard, my pet. She's lying there alone. All her servants have fled. Don't you think you should at least see if she is as ill as they say?"

"Is that true, Berthe?"

"It's true. Her ladies fear to tend her."

I didn't move, but as the day wore on, I became more and more sorry for the loveless woman.

"Oh, very well, Berthe. I'll make the effort. Madame de l'Eglise is Thérèse's mother, after all. I know she would want me to see that she is looked after."

"That's more like my pet. I knew it wasn't like you to be so selfish."

We made our way down the corridors until we reached Madame's room and I tentatively pushed open the door a crack. I peered around, but before I noticed anything else, we were hit by a most peculiar smell. It was suffocating and sickly sweet. Covering my nose with my handkerchief, I crossed the room, and as I drew near the bed, I quickly pulled back the bed hangings. I was horrified at the sight that met my eyes.

Berthe had fearfully followed me in, and we looked down at the scarecrow-like face of Madame de l'Eglise. She lay there, barely breathing, soaked in sweat, like a heap of bones wrapped in wet sheets. The foul smell was so strong I had to turn my head away.

I knew I had to get help quickly and, rushing to the door, shouted, "Won't someone help me? Madame l'Eglise is very ill!"

A little maid came hesitantly to the door, and I snapped at her, "Open the window!"

I could see the greenish froth at the corners of Madame's tightly clamped lips.

Berthe spoke tearfully at my shoulder. "What is it? Is it the pox, Solange?"

Madame was mumbling, "Mm . . , mm . . , where's Thérèse?"

I realised she was delirious.

"She's out of her wits. Get the physician!" I shouted, but already I was certain what ailed her. I lifted the sheet and was sickened by the revolting sight of a crusted eruption of pustules on her breast.

A couple of maids and several ladies clustered in a huddle around the door.

"Let no one come in! It's the pox!" They paused in terror and then fled, but I quickly grabbed the maid who would have gone also.

"Help me wash her!"

"I can't stay here!" Her horrified face drew away from me. "I'll be stricken for sure!"

"Rubbish! Bring blankets!"

The scurrying girl was already half out of the door.

There was no doubt Madame was mortally stricken by the dreaded illness. The maid brought the blankets, threw them through the open doorway, and ran. I heaped them over Madame to make her sweat, and called to the women outside, who kept their faces covered and skirts tight around their legs, lest they catch the infection.

"Bring a posset of canary and spirits of sulphur at once! Have you sent for the apothecary and the doctor? She'll have to be bled. Will none of you assist me?"

Nobody seemed willing to help, and one by one they slipped away. Only my faithful Berthe stayed by my side. She went for the doctor, but Fagin was too busy and none of the other doctors would come.

"You'd better go and get the plague nurse, then," I sighed in despair.

She nodded at me and went out. I called after her, "Get a poultice of mallow lily roots, and figs and linseed oil."

My country knowledge was of good use here. No one would enter to light a fire, so I had to kindle it myself.

There was a knock at the door and I took the salve from the apothecary's hand as he hastily thrust it at me. He tried to scurry away, but I grabbed at his cuff. "Wait! Tell me how to use the unguent."

He cowered there, rubbing his hands in a washing motion, drawing away from me with bent shoulders, as his sallow face worked with distaste.

"Should I rub it in the affected part only, or all over her?" I asked him.

"On the pustules!" he croaked as if I was stupid, and he pulled free and hurried away, his wizened body crab-like as he shrank from the disease.

I rubbed in the ointment as Madame moaned and sweated. "Oh, the heat!" she complained, as her head rolled from side to side on the damp pillow.

Then I administered doses of mithridate and Venice treacle. As time passed, she became a little easier, but her eyes seemed muddy. The room smelt like an apothecary's shop and I myself could scarcely breathe, the odor was overpowering. I looked at her with foreboding as I felt the fever burn in her.

Just as I was at my wits' end, there was yet another knock at the door.

"Entrez!" I called, and an inexpressibly revolting creature entered; a raw-boned, rough woman, thick-lipped, with a look of mingled ferocity and cunning.

"I am the nurse," she announced, as she flung off her shawl.

The plague nurse took a quick glance at the patient, her potato face impassive.

"It's the smallpox alright. You're a silly fool to stay with her. Send out for a brazier and herbs to scatter on it, and I'll bathe her in vinegar."

"Will she live?"

"If the fever breaks, she'll have a chance. But you'd better get out, because if you catch it, it'll ruin your pretty looks."

"Oh, I'm all right. I had the cowpox that milkmaids get when I was a child. They pricked me with a brooch to make sure it took."

"Hmm..."

"I'll tell the page to get the vinegar."

As soon as I had spoken with the page, I was horrified to hear the beldame demand, "I want my dinner!"

She was sitting unconcernedly on a chair by the fire, pushing her dirty knitted stockings forward and holding back the ragged petticoats.

"You think of dinner now! What about attending the patient first?"

"Oh, she'll be gone by morning anyway, probably." And she sat with her feet turned to the warmth of the fire again, as if all was well.

I had ordered some chicken, hoping that Madame would take a little to give her strength, and it was brought quickly by the maid and left outside the door. But Madame was too weak to open her mouth, and I had left the tray forgotten on the table.

I slumped down by the bed, the heat of the room was making me feel faint. Then I heard a very faint whisper from Madame. I leaned over the shrunken woman, her voice a thread of sound. "My Thérèse..., help me... Where is she? My daughter..."

The nurse caught the words. "Your daughter? And what good would she do?"

"You don't understand. Be quiet," I told the vile woman. "Attend to the patient."

"Thérèse will come," I soothed Madame. But still she tossed and turned, and I wiped her brow ceaselessly. Her hair was lank and hung limply in thin gray tufts.

"You'll do her no good," the potato-faced nurse threw at me, as she munched a chicken leg. "Oh, you should try some of this—it's delicious!"

"No!" I became violent. "The chicken is for the patient! How dare you touch it! Seeing that you have mauled it, you'd better bring some broth for her, and open that window again at once!"

She muttered something under her breath about night air being bad for sick people.

"Be careful with that jug," she said to me, sly-eyed. "There'sh good physhic in it! You'd better take a shwig of it. It may not do the patient any good, but it'll revive you shomething marvelloush!"

"What jug?"

"The jug with the... er... physic... er... gineva..." She seemed uncertain what to call it, as she drank deeply from the metal jug. Whatever it was, it seemed to have a mellowing effect upon her. She grinned through broken teeth and tottered towards me with the gineva in outstretched hands. I snatched it away from her greedy fingers.

"Give it here, you stupid girl!" she screeched at me.

"You're drunk!" I said in disgust, as I handed it to a servant by the door.

I was too upset by Madame's drawn features to ponder much about the gineva in the jug. Madame's face was sunken and blemished, and as I straightened the sheets, I felt them still damp with sweat.

"Oh, I fear she's gone. Shall I send for the priest?" I sighed.

But the plague nurse came weaving over to the bed. "No, she's not, she's shleeping," and she peered at the patient.

"Is that good?"

"The besht thing ever."

All that day and night I watched over Madame de l'Eglise as she mumbled incoherently and whimpered in delirium for her daughter. I tried to spoon a little of the broth through her sunken lips, but it just dribbled out down the side of her chin.

By the next night, Madame was skin and bone. The fever seemed to have burnt away what little flesh there was on her slender frame.

"Where's Thérèse? she whispered constantly, "I want Thérèse!"

"Rest a while," I would answer gently.

I had heard from the attendant that there was some pox elsewhere in the chateaux. Count Bissot had it in his country house, the little maid had told me, and two people had died in the north wing, where her friend attended.

Madame de l'Eglise's movements became weaker.

"Where is Thérèse?" she sighed, as a glimmer of intelligence returned to her eyes, and she slowly turned her shrunken face towards me. A feeble claw clutched at my hand. Tears glistened in the dark, shadowy eyes. "I knew you would come!"

"Yes," I whispered, realising she was mistaking me for her daughter.

Her lips moved in the grimace of a smile and I noticed that her nose had become like a little beak.

"Do you remember..." she asked weakly, as her voice trailed away, "how you used... to... run..?"

She seemed to be back in the time of Thérèse's childhood. Her voice faded and her eyes closed, as her hand slowly grew limp in mine.

I called out to the plague nurse, who ambled over.

Tears trickled down Madame's yellow skin and her head looked skull-like. She had been an evil woman. Now she was suffering and getting her just deserts, but it didn't seem to matter any more what she had been. Her jaw dropped and her eyes rolled up until I could see only the whites, bloodshot under her shrivelled eyelids. The plague nurse put a big thumb out and pushed back one eyelid. There was no flicker of response.

"Too late for the priest. She's gone. I'll call out for the cart."

"No!" Tears were in my eyes. Madame had got what she deserved, but she was still Thérèse's mother and she had tutored me. "I can't let her go on the death cart!" She must be buried in hallowed ground, even if she had died unshriven.

Not surprisingly, no one would have anything to do with victims of the contagious disease. The nurse had done as little work as possible, just stuffed herself with food and gineva, as if each day was a feast day. She shrugged her shoulders and treated the death as an everyday occurrence.

I forced her to help me lay out Madame in fine linen. But do what I would, I could get no one to help me bury her in the family tomb. For Thérèse's sake, I sent for some lilies and I had to let them take Madame on the cart in the end. There was nothing else for it.

When all was done, I desperately needed a hot bath to rid me of the smells and horror of the last few days. The sickly reek of death clung about me. I stripped myself of all the clothes I had worn day and night and gave them to the plague nurse to burn.

"Get out of here, you disgusting woman! You should be

ashamed of yourself, hindering instead of helping the sick!"

She just stuck an elbow in my ribs. "And *you're* a fool! You should enjoy yourself more, a pretty thing like you, instead of wasting your time on a dying woman." She trundled out of the door on her way to the next poor, helpless soul, no doubt.

I wrapped myself in a newly-laundered sheet and hurried to my room. There was a tub of very hot water waiting for me. I had my hair washed and after lying soaking for a long time, I dried myself and lay down on the bed, but thoughts kept rushing through my mind and sleep would not come.

The pressure of nursing had driven Fernando from my head, but now as I lay waiting for sleep, my thoughts returned to him. If only he had sent me a truly loving note! I wondered what he would have said to me. I remembered the time he had loved me and then, afterwards, his rage as he turned against me. I couldn't expect to take my place at Court while there was still contagion, but now that Madame had died, there was no reason why he couldn't come to see me. How could he ignore me after all that had happened between us?

I stared into the darkness and saw his eyes full of soft love as I remembered them, sweeping upwards over my body to rest on my face. My heart lurched at the memory of the look of naked desire that flashed for an instant as our eyes locked. I was in pain as my heart cried out for him to hold me. I yearned for the comfort of his arms, and craved to hear his voice that was so very dear to me; just to hear him say, *"Je t'aime."*

Day followed lonely day, and oblivion did not rescue me as I lay night after night in my dishevelled bed. I would close my eyes and see again that terrible scene in the hut, and remember the glance of contempt that he had given me. It made me twist and turn with anguish, but I knew that if only he would come back to me, I would lose all my pride and throw myself at his feet, begging only to let me love him.

"I need you so, my beloved," I would weep into my pillow.

"The world is dark without you. There will never be anyone but you! I live only for the moment when you return to me!"

But my tears could not wash away the pain.

Chapter 11

Life at Court continued more or less as before. Deaths were common enough here as elsewhere. It was indeed fortuitous, that the demon disease had been kept at bay and that very few had contracted the dreaded pox. I could not unburden myself to Berthe and, curiously enough, I found I missed Madame de l'Eglise.

One day Tienne came rushing to my room. "Mam'selle!" His huge eyes seemed to be popping out of his head as he stumbled over the words. "Don Fernando . . ."

"Speak slowly, dear." I remained calm, but my heart beat faster.

"I came directly to you, Mam'selle," and he handed me a crumpled wad of paper, warm from his sticky fist.

"Shall I leave you to read it, or will you tell me the contents?" he begged.

I wondered if this note was genuine, not like the last one from Madame de l'Eglise, which had resulted in my being seized by Pierre.

"Don Fernando must travel to Spain in haste, Mam'selle."

I turned quickly, alarmed. "What! Who told you this?"

"A courier brought word. All the Court knows."

"When did you hear this, *mon petit?*"

"Just now. The King has given Don Fernando official documents that will allow him to go to Burgos, although there is war with Spain."

So I read the note with mixed feelings:

"Bad news at home, my little vixen. Although I am loyal to Louis, I fear for my estates in Spain because of the war. Perhaps we'll meet again one day. How many more babes will be born to you before then? Strangely enough, that does not seem to quench my desire for you! Fernando."

That was typically Fernando! I stamped my foot and cried aloud, "How *dare* he address me in such an insolent manner!"

"But, Mam'selle, didn't you tell him the child was Thérèse's?"

"Don't be impudent!"

"If you didn't tell him, why not?"

"That has nothing to do with you, you're too young. You shouldn't discuss things like that."

"But, Mam'selle, I was there!"

I wasn't listening to him. My thoughts were with Fernando. "He jumped to conclusions, the pompous ass, but I confess I should have explained. He won't listen to me, so I had better put him out of my thoughts. Yes, that's it. He is going far away and there's an end to it. I'll live my life and enjoy it. Why shouldn't I? He's certainly not the only man in the world! I hate all Spanish grandees—they're too arrogant by far. They hang around women like dogs around a bitch on heat!"

"He isn't arrogant; I like him. He's a real man!"

"That's enough!" I gave his shoulder a little shake. "You can't make me change my mind. Send me my maids. I'll wear my finest gown and enjoy the Court to the full this Spring. I am too young to endure all this heartache!"

Swiftly I crossed to the big mirror and scrutinised my face carefully. "If I yearn over fickle love, I'll be haggard in no time. Raoul still admires me; I'll make use of him."

Tienne shot me a sidelong glance. He hadn't seen me like this before.

I was as grand and brightly decked as any lady born to a life at Court as I took my place in the antechamber, escorted by Raoul, who danced attendance on me as we waited for dinner to be announced.

"Come and sit close to me," he smiled quizzically, and he pulled out my chair.

I looked at him with my eyelids lowered. "How close?"

What difference did it make, I asked myself. He didn't mean a thing to me. I would play the Court games to suit myself.

His glance swept over me as he licked his lips sensuously, and I looked boldly back at him.

"Ah, it seems you've grown to full flower at last." His hand lingered on my bare arm. "Am I to pick a petal, my sweet rose?"

I drew away a little, then I remembered I was deliberately encouraging him. "We shall see!" I smiled.

The chamber was beginning to fill up, and several people were noticing our flirtation. Raoul was using his charm on me to the full. He took my fan and waved to the plump de Villette. She waved back, nodding beguilingly, the false red curls bobbing and the podgy, pale hand flashing with rings. It was a coquettish gesture that I was sure she had perfected many years ago. So I took my cue from Raoul, when we went into dinner, flirting with the gentleman across from me and was pleased with the effect. The Compte de Toulouse was ancient, but my charm was working nevertheless.

We had a great delicacy, I remember, sardines cooked in wine.

A steward lifted the lid from a dish.

"Oh!" I exclaimed. "Don't say we're to have peas again! I believe his Majesty sends to Italy for them. How he loves them! The Duchesse de Seasti even found some in her bed last night!"

"And what did she do with them, my little sweetpea?"

"She ate them, of course, before going to sleep!"

Everyone laughed heartily.

"You're a real country girl. I heard Madame de Maintenon wrote to the Duc de Noelle of the King's passion for peas. She is so sick of them appearing at every meal each May."

"What did she say in the letter?"

"It was terribly *drôle*—something like 'The saga of the green peas goes on; looking forward to eating them, the pleasure of having eaten them and the joyful pleasure of soon eating more!'"

"She certainly has a very dry wit. No wonder the King enjoys her company."

"You are more to my taste, my wild lily," Raoul whispered, as he kept my goblet filled with wine, which presently began to affect me.

I felt quite abandoned when later he whispered in my ear, "Come ride with me by moonlight."

My head was dizzy with drink as I leaned against him, and he took my agreement for granted. In my tipsy state, I began to think that he wasn't as bad as I had thought. At least he wasn't always sulking and storming out in a temper as Fernando did. I giggled as he nibbled my ear. It tickled when he kissed the hollow of my throat. Then he pressed me to him and we laughed conspiratorially. As we stood, I swayed and waited for a moment while the others moved off to the gaming tables. Then he drew me into the garden.

The moon was shining on my gown, making the white satin shimmer, and he clasped around my neck my white velvet cloak lined with ermine. My legs would not support me, so I used him as a prop as he guided me to the courtyard. He clasped me around the waist, and suddenly I was up in front of him on the horse. I hiccuped as the horse trotted off, and clinging to him I had only a muzzy impression of the ride. I do remember singing snatches of songs as the horse cantered along.

At last Raoul reined the horse to a standstill. I clutched the saddle as he dismounted, swayed and let myself fall into his arms as he put a hand out to steady me.

"Goodness me, where have we got to?" I saw, as in a dream, a building looming dark under the trees. My wits were so woolly I stifled the urge to giggle.

"Here we are," he said.

"Where is here?"

"A hunting lodge."

He planted kisses up my bare arm and drew me towards the door. I stumbled over the threshold, tearing my beautiful gown as I pulled it from the metal bootscraper, leaving a piece of white satin like a flag. He swung me up into his arms and carried me inside. I clung to his strong neck and closed my eyes for a moment. When I opened them again we were in a wood panelled room.

He placed his riding crop on the table as he set me down on my feet and, as I looked around, noticing a table laden with food and wine, I exclaimed with surprise, "Supper, laid for two! I hope there aren't any peas!" I giggled.

He went to the table and grasped a long-necked bottle. "We must drink a toast," he said.

"A toast? To what?"

"To us, of course."

But I couldn't focus my eyes properly. The room felt so close and stuffy after the fresh night air. I fumbled as I reached to take the goblet from his hand, spilling the wine half down his leg and onto the floor. It struck me as hilarious and I began to laugh. He was angry at first, and then joined in my laughter.

Putting his arm around me, he pulled me down onto a sofa and began to kiss my bare shoulders passionately. I had been glad to sit, as my head was reeling from the heat of the log fire and I wasn't too sure of my legs, but then I felt my bodice being unlaced and tried to wriggle away. I hated his soft, moist hands and the reek of his fine clothes, for he perfumed himself as lavishly as a whore. Suddenly I realized I'd made a terrible mistake.

I noticed a red patch on his forehead which deepened as he became impatient. "Stop struggling, darling! You're going to have the most wonderful night of your life."

"Not with you!" I tried to pull away from him, but he was too quick for me and, throwing one long leg over me, pinned me to the couch.

He panted as I struggled with him. "You agreed to come, remember. Don't be such a tease. I've waited a long time to hold you in my arms. There's no sense in behaving like a country simpleton."

His breath felt hot on my neck as I reasoned with him. I tried, as a ploy, "Just let me tidy my hair, darling. I want to look my best for you."

He leered knowingly and held back a moment. I pushed him off and stood up, but the floor wouldn't stay still and felt unstable under my feet.

"Whoops! God's breath, I'm drunk! You must take me back, Raoul."

I staggered to a wooden chair, clutching its back for support. "Where are we, anyway? I can't even remember coming here."

"You're not drunk, sweeting. What you need is more wine." He jumped to his feet and held a glass to my lips, and with his other hand clasped me in a tight grip around my waist.

I jerked my head to one side. "No!" I put up my hands and dashed the glass away. His arm was like a steel band and I grew alarmed as I felt his strength.

"Don't be a spoil-sport. You know I have a wife who's eternally pregnant, and that is a poor life for any man."

"What is that to me," I tossed at him. "And who makes her pregnant?"

His face hardened and he pinched my breast savagely, so that I screamed with pain and became still more frightened.

"I'll teach you to play with me," he snarled, as his hand tightened on my chin to make me face him.

I struggled mightily, but he just threw back his head and laughed uproariously at my feeble efforts. Desperately I twisted my head and sank my teeth into the base of his thumb. He shouted, and I felt his grip slacken. As I pulled free and darted away, he caught my skirt and I heard it rip. It came away in his hands as he lunged at me, and though I beat him about his head with my fists, he flung me over his knee.

"So it's a fight you want, little vixen. All the better!"

He reached across me and grabbed his riding crop. I heard a whistling noise and with all the strength of his arm, he brought the whip down across my backside, clad only in a thin underskirt. Again and again the cruel lash came down on me as I screamed and writhed, but hard as I tried, I couldn't escape his venomous anger and I tasted the salty tears that streamed down into my open mouth.

He pushed me off his knee onto the floor and bent over me as I locked my legs automatically. My bodice was ripped away as I felt about to swoon.

Above the thunder of the blood in my ears I heard a loud knock and then a man's voice. "What's going on here? This ain't just the gentry gettin' up to their tricks—it sounds like murder bein' done."

Raoul quickly threw a purse at someone, as he held me down with one hand.

He undid his lacings, unleashing his straining manhood, then clamped his body to mine. I was determined to hold back and not move a muscle. I lay like a plank of wood and kept my teeth clenched, but as the motion of his body increased its rhythm and his panting breath hissed in my face, I tried to close my ears to his monolog of, "I knew you'd like it once you felt how special it is. You're surprised, aren't you, darling? Isn't it wonderful? Go on, tell me," pounding away as he talked between gasps.

Then suddenly, against my will, my body began to respond. I felt myself move in rhythm with Raoul. "That's it, darling. You love it, don't you? I'm the biggest in Versailles, so I'm told!"

I couldn't help myself, I had to have more. "Go on," I heard myself scream. "More, Raoul, for God's sake!" I felt myself become moist and had to draw him in closer. My legs tried to go wider to feel the more the pounding member that caused such exquisite pleasure that I knew I shouldn't want.

My breasts throbbed at his touch, and I heard my voice,

as if from afar, moaning unintelligibly. And then we crashed together in one long climax.

I realized then that I had no control over my own sexual desires, and I was sick at the thought. Turning myself away from him, I found that I could not stand properly and oblivion claimed me.

Something was wrapped about me, and I was gathered up. My eyes flickered open, and I was relieved to see that Raoul was gone and it was a peasant with a stubbly chin who muttered, "Who was it hurried out into the night? Not that it makes any difference. They think they can do as they like, them whoreson nobles."

"Heaven thank you," I managed to murmur before I passed out again.

As I came to myself, we were entering a flagged passage and the peasant carried me into a tiny warm room. He put me on my feet and I stood shakily.

He held a lantern in front of him, and I saw he had swathed me in a brown velvet curtain to cover my nakedness.

He stared at me with piggy eyes. "I'm usually abed at this hour. Lucky for you I heard you scream and thought I'd better look into it."

I put out a hand to steady myself and clutched his ragged coat. "Thank God you came!"

I could see a question in his eyes, as he eyed my fine petticoat peeping out from under the curtain.

"I have been served a sorry trick," I told him, not quite truthfully.

When I turned to grope for a stool, in the light of the embers of the fire, I spied a frowsy woman sitting up in the box filled with straw that served as a bed, and staring at me with disbelief in her bleary eyes.

"Wot she be doin', half naked, in these parts in the dead of night? No good, I'll be bound," she grumbled, questioning and answering herself as the lodgekeeper jerked a thumb at me.

"Get 'er some wine, woman, before I shut yer trap fer good."

"I don't think the likes of 'er needs any more wine!"

"I'll have to stay till daybreak," I told her, as I dragged my aching bones over to the fire. I was tired to the point of exhaustion. "If you'll lend me a horse, I'll be gone at first light."

I slumped in the corner on the stool against the wall, shifting painfully till I found a position where my back didn't hurt too much.

"Get off that pallet, woman," the lodgekeeper dragged his wife out of the bed by her skinny shoulders. "And get that wine, I told yer."

"Yer lie down and rest, me Lady," he advised me.

"Yer lie down and rest, me Lady," the crone simpered in imitation of her toothless spouse. She found me a ragged shift in an old chest by the window.

"Turn yerself 'round, husband," she said to him and, removing the curtain, helped me unlace my stays, which she shoved under the dirty pillow. She then covered me with the smelly garment as waves of sleep descended over me. I climbed wearily into the bed and lay close to the wall, as I felt the woman push up against me, and then the bed creaked as the lodgekeeper crawled in beside his wife. In spite of the stale smell, I lay my head on the rough pillow as I felt her animal warmth, and heard her mutter to her spouse as sleep came to claim me, "Are yer sure she can pay?"

"Don't worry," I answered her. "I'll pay. Just let me rest."

"Are yer sure?"

"You can have my gold ring. I must have some sleep."

With that she was satisfied and lay down again as the man began to snore from his side of the bed.

It seemed no time at all before the woman shook me awake. I pushed myself up in the bed, aching in every bone of my body, as if my limbs had been pulled from their sockets.

"Come on, it's time yer were ready." She had grain in a basket over her arm. "I'm goin' to feed the chickens; I won't be long," she called over her shoulder as she went out.

The lodgekeeper stood in his sweat-stained hat, which half covered his grizzled face, as he leered at me.

I forced my bare legs out of bed. "Turn away from me, please," I asked him.

He turned slowly, his grin showing the few remaining yellow stumps of teeth the color of old boar's tusks. "Yer a nice little filly, now I can see yer by daylight. D'yer want any help with yer corset lacin's, dearie?"

"Mind your manners or I'll call your wife in," I snapped at him. "Keep your looks to yourself."

He shambled towards me and grabbed the lacings of my stays. I clouted him with the pillow, but he only grinned.

"Ger away, yer randy bugger!" the wife threw at him as she banged the door shut behind her.

"Ain't yer ready yet?" And she shuffled over to a cupboard, took out a pot and slapped some hard, crusty stale bread on the table.

"Come on, girl, I want yer out of here as quick as yer can."

I pulled the small gold ring that Madame de Maintenon had given me from my finger.

"How do I know yer won't say that we stole it?" she asked as she snatched it from me. She spat on it, rubbed it on her hip and then held the gold band away from her to the light to admire its shiny brightness.

"I most certainly wouldn't do that. Your husband saved me."

"Oh, well," she began to soften, "yer none but a lass. All right, I'll keep yer ring. It ain't the first time the lodge has been used, for there's many a fine gentleman has slipped us a couple of louis to keep our mouths shut."

She stuffed the ring into her pocket.

"I'll send you money when I get back," I assured her.

The husband was slurping his bread soaked in the coffee. "I'll take yer in the cart when yer've broken yer fast. I've got to take the pig to market."

"I'm very grateful, lodgekeeper." I walked with aching back to join him at the rough table.

His wife eyed my tattered finery. "Yer'll be a right show sittin' up in the cart in a satin underskirt and underbodice, an' those silk shoes won't get yer far. Here, take this cloak an' these old boots. I'll stuff them with straw so they won't slip off."

The man went out. I was surprised to see the cart was already there as I looked through the window. The lodgekeeper tied the fat pig with a piece of rope in a corner on the straw. I gathered the smelly cloak around me and bade goodbye to the woman.

As I walked through the door, I caught my foot in a tear in the cloak, and descended in a flurry into the arms of the foul-smelling lodgekeeper. I kicked him hard. He cursed and rubbed his leg, but I had pulled away too quickly and landed myself in the mud. Every movement hurt my thighs and sore back. I carefully got to my feet and wiped the mud from my face with my hands, and crawled into the cart next to the pig, who grunted and snorted in the mucky straw, his little eyes blinking.

On the journey, as the rickety cart zig-zagged along, it began to drizzle and I pushed the straw around me and scratched at the lice I had collected in the night. I was grateful to the man for helping me, but I'd have to keep an eye on him. It wouldn't be hard, I was thinking. He was too old and feeble to be much trouble, not like that bully, Raoul. I shuddered at the memory of the way he'd treated me, half in horror, half in sensual pleasure, and wondered if he'd dare face me at Court again. As for Fernando, the very thought of him made all the hopelessness of my position come flooding back. Salty tears stung my eyes as the rain beat down.

"We'll be at the market soon, Mam'selle. Here, take a swig of this wine. It'll warm yer innards."

I gratefully took a gulp of the rough liquid and was glad of the warmth it gave me. "You will be well paid if you follow the road and lanes to the back of the Palace."

"Wot! The likes of me drive up to the Palace? I wouldn't dare!"

I was sick and weary and soaked to the skin and was even tempted to hand over the diamond as a bribe, as I knew I wouldn't be able to walk. It was a miracle I'd managed to keep it on me after the beating I'd suffered. It had dropped between my breasts down to my middle.

"I am a friend of Madame de Maintenon. Believe me, she'll show her gratitude."

"Well, them were fine rags yer wore. If yer sure, yer Ladyship." His manner had become resigned as he realized I was speaking the truth.

We left the bustling villages behind as the heavens opened and it rained with a vengeance, but I was too weary to care. I didn't even bother to move as the cart lurched in a rut in the road and the pig fell against me, opened its pale eyes and grunted. Better the pig than Raoul, I thought.

At last the motion of the cart stopped and I sat up with a start. My journey was over. We were in the kitchen courtyard. It was so cold and there didn't seem to be anyone about. I heaved myself down from the cart and told the man to go inside and get warm.

"I'll get arrested, yer Ladyship!"

"Go in. I'll tell them to make you warm and give you some food. I'm too tired to argue."

The heat of the kitchens hit us like a welcome blanket of steam. He awkwardly followed me amid the scullery boys and wenches.

"Send word to Berthe quickly," I ordered a hurrying girl. She gaped at the two scarecrows slumped before her, but everyone else was too busy to notice, thank goodness.

"I'm Mam'selle Solange," I told her. "I've been set upon by robbers."

She quickly snatched her sabot off her foot and was about to clout the lodgekeeper, who was standing holding his pig in his arms like a baby.

I grabbed her arm. "No, not by him! Hurry, girl, and get Berthe. Tell her to bring some money and a gold chain."

It seemed an age before Berthe arrived, worried and anxious lines on her brow and around her mouth.

"Oh, my lamb, you're safe!" She nearly suffocated me as she crushed me to her, and then quickly began to rub me with the kitchen cloth she grabbed from a scurrying pastry chef, who didn't even miss it. The aroma of the pies and fowls was making my head reel.

"See that he is fed, Berthe, and get me to my room quickly."

I took the little bundle of louis and the chain she had given me and handed them to the lodgekeeper, who was already gulping down soup with his free hand as the pig wriggled frantically under his arm.

"I am more than grateful to you and your wife," I whispered hoarsely, and made my way with a grumbling Berthe to the sanctuary of my room.

"You look half starved, my lamb."

I collapsed onto the bed as she quickly removed my soaking rags.

"Oh, my God, you're black and blue! Tienne told me that that lecher, Monsieur Raoul, carried you off."

She dabbed my bruises with witch hazel and forced one of her concoctions down my throat before tucking me into the soft bed. Lifting my head, she spooned some soup through my parched lips.

Tienne stood at my side, tears of joy shining like dewdrops in his innocent eyes. "You should never have gone with that Monsieur Raoul, Mam'selle."

"You saw us?"

"I told Madame de Maintenon that he took you on his horse. Since then, he hasn't been seen. He told everyone his wife had been brought to bed sick, and he returned to his country estate at great speed."

I patted his head and sank into an exhausted sleep.

I awoke the following day to afternoon sunshine. There was still a dull, persistent ache in my limbs and my heart was heavy. Tienne stayed with me.

"Madame de Maintenon is thankful that you have been safely delivered back to us, Mam'selle, and hopes you will soon be well enough to resume your place here."

"I've finished with Court life, rascal!" I propped myself up on an elbow. "How I wish for peace! My very soul is weary. I think the place for me is a convent. There I could shut out the world."

"Then I'll come with you."

"You can't enter a convent, my *petit bonbon.* You will soon grow to be a man, and men do not live with the nuns."

His eyes brimmed with tears, and his little head fell.

I grasped his hands in mine. "We will be the greatest of friends all our lives, Tienne. You will always be able to visit me and we need never be far away from each other, no matter where I go. You're as dear to me as the brother I always longed for."

He stifled a sob and rubbed a clenched fist across his eyes.

"What's all this about convents?" Berthe scolded. "I won't hear of it. Now sit up and drink this honeyed milk."

"I don't want anything. Just let me rest, Berthe dear."

But she forced a couple of spoonsful of the sickly drink down me. I closed my eyes and lay there, nursing my broken heart. I was certain I would never see Fernando again. I was finished with men. The more I brooded on it, the more convinced I became. I longed for the peace and solitude of the cloisters, to end my life in meditation with the quiet nuns.

I stayed in bed for the rest of the day and feigned sleep if anyone came near. Perhaps one day my bruised heart would stop aching.

Chapter 12

When I awoke I refused all food. The very thought of eating made me ill. The maid told me that Madame de Maintenon had sent for me, but I didn't even care.

"I can't go to her. Please leave me alone."

Her jaw dropping, she said, "No one refuses to go when Madame calls!" She was shocked.

"Go away!" I shouted, and turned away from her in the bed and kept my eyes shut until I heard her leave the room.

But a little while later, I again heard the door open. "I told you to keep out!" I thought the maid had re-entered, but when I opened my eyes, it was Madame de Maintenon herself standing by the bed. A black lace coif covered most of her gray hair and her bodice was adorned with a bow, replacing the usual cross, and at each elbow above the lace was a similar knot of ribbon, enhancing the dark wine hue of the gown.

"You wouldn't come to me, so I've come to you, child. Now pull yourself together. This has gone on long enough. No man is worth making yourself ill over," Madame censured me.

I sighed, "It is very good of you to visit me, but I feel I've nothing left to live for."

"Nonsense! You must divest yourself of your passion for Don Fernando, exactly as if it were a garment that could be put on or off at will."

"My only wish is for solitude, Madame. I cannot overcome my passion."

"Zut! You must take this sleeping draught, and I will come here again when you have rested, and then we will talk."

The maid poured the potion into a cup, and Madame herself took it from her and stood over me until I had swallowed the last drop.

"I am so weary of my life. I have been thinking about it so much. The only place where I could find peace is the cloisters. I realize how much you've done for me, and I do thank you, dear Madame, but Court life is not for me."

"We will see how you feel tomorrow."

"No, forgive me, I've finished with the falsity of this life."

"Things may look different when you can think rationally."

"Nothing you can say will alter the way I feel, Madame. My mind is quite made up. I would be grateful to you if you would let me go to your convent at St. Cyr, if you and the King would allow me to leave the Court," I said in a tight voice.

"Why has this man made such an impression on you, child? There are many fine Frenchmen at Court."

Helpless tears came to my eyes. "He is adored by all who know him," I sobbed.

"Hm..." Madame smiled wryly. "Yes, he can be frivolous, but he has a fine mind. Who can tell where Cupid's arrows may fall?"

"But he always has to hurt me. He's taken my heart for a plaything, and I cannot withstand him."

"I will speak to the King about the convent and we shall see, Solange. Now try to sleep."

Already I felt my eyes grow heavy as the drug took effect, and Madame lifted my limp arms and placed them inside the coverlet. The last thing I remember was her beckoning the maid to close the curtains around the bed.

After a dreamless sleep, I was even more resolved to enter a convent and I sobbed into my pillow, praying that the King would let me go.

It was late afternoon the following day when I lifted heavy eyelids to see that Madame had graced me with yet another visit.

I looked up. "It is good of you to bother with a weak-natured thing like me, Madame. Have you talked to the King?"

Madame settled herself comfortably in the armchair by the side of the bed, fluffing out her midnight blue velvet gown about her.

"Yes, I've talked to the King. He will tell you what he wishes you to do. But I'm afraid he is unwell today and has taken to his bed."

I felt a pang of remorse. "Oh, Madame, in my selfishness I hadn't given a thought to the King's health!"

"Come along. Let us have no more of this nonsense. Up you get, Solange, and I'll expect you to present yourself to his Majesty in one hour."

"Is he very ill, Madame?" I asked anxiously.

"No, it is just an old man's complaint and he's a little better this afternoon."

"I've been so self-centered. Forgive me."

Madame left me to dress. I listlessly pushed myself out of the sanctuary of the bed and Berthe forced me to attire myself carefully. I had to make an effort for the King.

"You can't wear that to visit his Majesty," Berthe scolded and snatched the gray dress from my hands. She laid out for me my gold brocade edged with the ruffles of silver Spanish lace. There were little black flowers woven into the gold and the skirt was striped with silk.

"Should I be wearing such an elaborate gown to visit a sick person, Berthe, even if he is the King?"

"Sh!" She piled my hair high with small rosettes of black lace. "There, that's better," she clucked, standing back.

I took my diamond from the secret drawer. It meant

nothing to me now, but from force of habit I stuffed it down my bodice. It was a ritual that had become part of dressing. I remembered the many times I had been tempted to wear the diamond on a gold chain, but discretion had persuaded me it was not wise.

I wished I had never left Clagny. I would gladly have changed the Palace with all the flashing jewels, affected voices and arrogance of the courtiers for the solitude of my Grandmère's cottage with only the animals for company. To a contented mind, a hovel is as fine as the grandest palace.

I wearily made my way to the *petits appartements* through those of Madame de Maintenon by the Salles des Gardes. I was ushered in by the *valet de chambre,* Bontemps. His father had been the King's friend and confidant as well as his servant of many years, until he died at nearly eighty. It was said he had witnessed the King's so-called 'marriage' to Francoise de Maintenon over twenty years before.

I quietly entered the King's bedroom. The King's dog moved away from the door and lay down nearer the bed watching him. His Majesty lay stretched out on his back in his magnificent bed, his large stomach lifting the embroidered counterpane. His nose seemed more prominent and pinched above the nostrils, and he looked older in his nightcap. I'd always imagined him wearing one of his towering peruques in bed. He seemed much fatter than I had realized and more vunerable with part of his bald head showing. Madame was seated by the bed reading aloud from one of Racine's plays. I was amazed to see she had a pair of spectacles on the end of her nose.

"Thank you, Your Solidity," I thought I heard the King say to her, and then I remembered Madame de l'Eglise had told me that she had heard him address Madame by that name before. What a funny pet name! Dr. Fagin, who was putting some instruments back into a box, was waved away, his face heavy and disapproving.

"Is he dying?" I whispered, with terror in my heart.

Madame looked up and smiled slightly. "Of course not, Solange. It's just one of his Majesty's headaches and stomach weaknesses that come with the dizzy spells."

"I'm so relieved, Madame." And I moved to stand beside her.

She leaned down and whispered to him.

"Prop me up," he instructed his servant, who expertly took hold of his elbow and with another servant, heaved him to a sitting position, plumping out the lace-trimmed pillows.

"How are you feeling, Sire?" I asked.

"Better than Fagin, my physician, would have me believe, Mam'selle Solange. So," he addressed me quizzically, "you want to go into a convent? My dear, you're too pretty to shut yourself away."

"Oh, please, your Majesty," I bent to kiss the proferred hand and answered sadly, "I feel I have have nothing left to live for."

I glanced up and saw a rueful, pained expression appear on his countenance.

"Can you be sure?" He patted my hand and cupped my chin, staring into my face. "I have some news that will cheer you, my little flower."

"There's no news that could do that, your Majesty. My life is over."

He pursed his lips and sucked in his breath, as if in pain, and his eyes almost squinted.

"There is no need for you to enter a convent. I have arranged a superb marriage for you and I am going to give you a dowry, Solange."

"No, your Majesty!" I gasped and fell to my knees, clasping both his hands in mine. "Please don't ask me to marry!"

"Would you displease your King?"

I choked back a sob as my heart sank. I looked around at Madame de Maintenon, Dr. Fagin and the servants. "I would speak with you alone, Your Majesty."

The King was always more relaxed when we were alone. As soon as a door opened or someone appeared, his facial expression would change like that of an actor taking the stage. He was even better at play-acting than Monsieur

Moliere. No one seemed to realize he was playing a part, but I knew.

The King lifted his hand slightly and the servants silently withdrew, but Madame didn't move and Dr. Fagin began fussing around with an evil-looking draught.

The King wagged his finger. "I know you are prolonging my treatment so as to get a bigger fee. The body knows what it needs, so take this mess away. I will not be bled, either."

Dr. Fagin looked hurt and was about to protest, but seemed to think better of it and respectfully bowed low to the King and Madame de Maintenon before taking his leave.

"Forgive me, your Majesty, I cannot marry anyone," I implored. "My heart is truly broken. Please don't force me to obey you."

I looked away from him to keep my tears in check, and tried to concentrate on the clock embellished with precious stones that ticked on the mantelpiece.

He patted my head affectionately. "My poor child, you've suffered enough but, no, I cannot allow you to go into a convent. I'm afraid I must insist that you marry."

Blinded by my tears, I thought I felt Madame take me by the shoulders. I blinked and saw the King smile.

Warm hands covered my eyes and I gave a startled cry, turning around. "Fernando! Is it you? It can't be..." I clasped his hands.

He moved before me and his look told me everything I needed to know.

I loosed a hand to brush the tears quickly away, my heart in my throat. "I must look a fright."

"The word," he said, "is gorgeous!" And I could see all the love I'd longed for in his eyes. "You are even more beautiful than I remember, my Solange."

"Well?" the King questioned with a smile. "Do you still insist on entering a nunnery?"

"Oh, your Majesty, I do not!"

He laughed, leaning backwards against the carved gold headboard. "I told you I had an excellent marriage for you, and a duchy for a dowry. The rents are yours for life."

"Why have you been so good to me?"

He looked deep in thought for a moment and stroked an imaginary beard, cocking a quizzical eyebrow.

"Surely you can guess?"

Madame de Maintenon kissed my sweetheart and myself and took her leave.

Fernando whispered in my ear as we stood hand in hand at the bedside, "You will come away with me, beloved, and I will make you happy."

He brought from his pocket a huge, blazing emerald and slipped it onto my third finger, pressing my hand to his lips.

"To match your lovely eyes," he said huskily.

"It's beautiful," I stammered. "So you don't distrust me any longer? What made you change your mind?"

"I saw Thérèse in England."

"So she told you?"

"She told me all. I realized what a crass fool I'd been and you were the only woman for me."

His arms went about me and I pressed myself close to him, lost to my surroundings.

The King cleared his throat loudly, and we sprang apart, startled.

"Your Majesty," I stammered. "I'll not leave immediately. I'll stay until you are quite well again."

He drew my head down and kissed me, first on one cheek and then on the other. "Go now, before I selfishly change my mind."

Fernando drew me to him and the King put a hand on his arm. "I charge you to cherish Mam'selle Solange, for she is more precious to me than diamonds."

"She is my dear life, Sire."

As I stood there, in the arms of my beloved, I knew at last the peace of perfect love. Whatever life held in store for us, we would face it together and the sun of France, Le Roi Soleil, would always shine for us. Or so I thought.

Book Two

Chapter 13

We began the long journey for Burgos with outriders and coaches piled high with boxes and furs, but I noticed little as Fernando prepared me for the reception that awaited us at his Castle Grandé.

"Donna Isabella, my mother, will be delighted to receive you, dearest. I have sent a messenger on ahead."

He held both my hands in his, and I felt a momentary pang of guilt that I was the only person in the world to know such happiness.

"I can't believe this is really happening, Fernando! Are you sure Dona Isabella will like me?"

"I know it, for how could she help but adore you? And my sister Manoela will be your great friend. We are so alike, she and I, that we could never even tell each other a white lie, for our eyes would give us away. We know each other too well."

I laughed happily. "Is Don Miguel like you?"

"So I am told, but far more serious. However, his brother, Don José, is quite an old roué and has never married."

He put out a hand and drew the pale silk curtains across the windows. I looked at him questioningly.

Slowly he undid the front of my gown beneath my cape. "Look at me," he said quietly.

I looked up into his face and saw that he wanted me there in the coach.

"I can't, Fernando, not here! One of the men on the box might jump down." But even as I spoke, I felt the familiar warmth descending down my body and knew that my flushed face would bely my words.

"I have given instructions that we are not to be disturbed," he continued, as he loosened my underclothes.

"That's why we are alone, after all, darling Solange. We are betrothed, and this is our bridal journey."

I didn't need much persuading, and placed my hand-warmer down beside me. My hands were warm enough; in fact it might have been the middle of summer in a garden, not a rumbling coach jogging along rutted roads of a Winter morning.

I loved the feel of the fur cloak about my bare breasts and shoulders, my gown pushed up behind me, the velvet seat against my naked flesh.

I had no need to undo his lacings, he had done it for me. I encircled his hardness with my fingers, as I lowered myself onto the floor that rocked and jostled, busying my mouth over him, and was filled with joy to hear him gasp, "Solange, ah, Solange!" I couldn't contain myself and pulled him down, my legs spreadeagled in the constricting coach.

He opened my cape to reveal my breasts, and leaning over me, touched each nipple with his lips, causing me to shudder. "Fernando!" I cried. "Oh, God!" And then I felt his warmth enter me like a steel sword, but only for a moment. He looked into my eyes and I could see myself reflected in the black pupils.

Suddenly I lifted my arms and pulled his head down to my breasts, and moaned in ecstacy as he sucked my bursting nipples, causing me such exquisite agony that I moaned and writhed and pulled him, trying to guide him back where he belonged.

"Don't be in such a hurry, darling," he whispered hoarsely. "It's a long journey to Spain."

"But I can't wait, dearest." I begged. "I promise I'll hold back." But I knew I was lying, I just had to have him quickly.

"Ah!" He plunged into me and I locked my legs around his middle. I cried out, and sobbed as he plunged in and out till I screamed with pleasure.

Time stood still and we were lost together in a world that existed only for us in that moment as we reached a heaven that I would gladly have died for. I lay with my head on his shoulder and blinked away the tears.

He stroked my hair and tilted my chin up to kiss me tenderly. "I've never known a girl who loves it as much as you," he smiled contentedly.

Furious, I pulled myself away from him and crashed my metal hand-warmer onto his head. I felt the coach lurch giddily and we were both thrown to the floor again, but I grappled with him this time and slapped him about his grinning face.

"How dare you compare me with your tarts!" I shouted, as he gasped with helpless laughter. I was gratified to see a trickle of blood slowly zig-zagging down the side of his face. "How dare you compare me, your future wife, with those whores! Everyone knows they all pretend anyway."

"There's no need to be jealous, dearest. But I love you to be angry, it suits you—the colour comes to your cheeks."

"You needn't feel so smug, you're not as good as Raoul by far!" I snapped.

His eyes clouded over and I knew I had gone too far. I felt a sting on my cheek as he slapped me and couldn't control the tears pricking my eyes. "Don't look at me like that," I whispered, and touched my burning face.

He stared coldly at me and returned his clothes briskly to order.

"I didn't mean it, Fernando!" I dabbed his wound with the bottom of my petticoat. "I just wanted you to feel as jealous as I did."

But he wasn't listening and pushed me roughly from him. "Cover yourself," he ordered.

"No," I forced mystelf to stand, and stamped my foot. "I won't!"

"You can do as you like, I'm going to summon the servants. Cover yourself at once!" he snarled.

"You do so," I said defiantly.

To my horror, he banged his sword three times on the roof.

I lunged at him, pulling his hair. "You pig, why is it all right for you to compare me with those tarts?"

"It's different for a man and you know it. You told me that Raoul raped you; I should have known you lied!"

The axles creaked and the leather squeaked as the coach slowed down and the rocking almost stopped.

"I didn't lie!" I shouted, not caring if the servants heard me. "I spoke the truth, but I didn't say I didn't like it!" I knew before I'd finished speaking that I'd gone too far, but I couldn't stop the words from pouring out as I watched his lips clamp shut and his skin turn a sickly grey beneath the olive tone.

I quickly returned my clothes to order and sat beside him on the seat, but he turned his head away. I was filled with fear that he would have nothing more to do with me. I could hear the horses being reined in, snorting and coughing as the chains jingled. Then the rocking stopped as the coach ground to a bumpy halt.

I peeped out of the window to see the inn servants gathered at the door in the falling rain. I ducked my head as our footman let down the steps, being careful not to drag my gown in the mud.

I didn't look to see what Fernando was doing, but kept my back straight; I wouldn't let him know how upset I was.

I was carried by one of the servants before my soft, leather shoes could be splattered too much, into a low square room, so small there was barely space for our party, and I was forced to sit opposite Fernando at the gate-legged table.

Small windows reflected the firelight. The black shelf

above the fire, holding pewter mugs, looked dusty. I stretched my fingers to the crackling blaze and closed my eyes, feeling the warmth soothe my aching bones.

A tousled-headed female thumped hot brandy at our places, as she brazenly eyed Fernando, who seemed flattered by the filthy slut; her brown cotton dress was stained with sweat where her bosom pushed it forward.

As she returned with the meat, I daintily stretched my leg whilst staring into the fire, and was gratified to hear her shout of rage as she fell headlong with the meat on the muddy floor.

The innkeeper boxed her ears with a pan, and after a mug or two of good wine I felt much better and chanced a sidelong glance at Fernando, who was watching me whilst pulling the meat from a bone with his strong white teeth.

Fortunately, our quarrel was soon forgotten, and the rest of the uncomfortable journey continued through swirling fog as we were driven nearer to the Spanish border.

Slowly the fog cleared and Fernando looked out of the window, pointing exuberantly; "Look, Solange, come closer. What do you see?"

I peered out and felt my jaw drop. "What are they? They're frightening."

"They're beautiful!" he laughed, drawing me closer to him. "They are the Pyrenees mountains. Look how the sun lights the snowy ice at the peaks. Isn't it incredible? Have you ever seen anything so magnificent?"

"No, I suppose not. They're like blue pointed mirrors at the top, but so big and, look, that one has a halo of blue-gray cloud encircling it."

As we left the mountains behind, Fernando asked, "Can you smell the olive groves?" and breathed deeply, shutting his eyes as if in a trance.

I glanced at green fields of wild flowers on one side and miles of grey bushes on the other. "It's a musky smell," I told him. "Not very nice."

"No other place on earth has the dusty, earthy smell of Spain. It's a warm smell—you will learn to love it above all else as I do, dearest. Wait till you see the Castle, my love, I can't wait to show it to you."

I snuggled closer to him and became as excited as he was at being so near his home.

The sun climbed higher and the coldness of the morning disappeared. We entered a little Spanish town. At the sides of the roads, tired-looking dark-haired women washed clothes, the water coming from pipes into the troughs; it looked like very hard work. Old men were sitting beneath the trellis of vines on wooden benches, their weary faces unshaven and their clothes drab and ill-fitting, drinking from thick mugs.

"Look at that poor old dusty woman with bare feet—her basket of vegetables is too heavy for her." She squinted up at me through beady, dark eyes as if she'd heard.

"She's lucky she has land enough to grow things. They are used to their way of life."

"There's another one with reeds on her back. Why do the women do all the work?"

"It is the way of the peasants; that is the way they have done things for generations."

Some of the peasants stopped and doffed their hats at our travelworn but grand procession.

"Oh, Fernando, I'm suddenly afriad! Supposing Madame, your Mother, doesn't like me, or Don Miguel would have preferred a Spanish bride?"

"You forget, Solange, my mother is French. Donna Isabella is sure to love you just because you are you, dearest."

I was still apprehensive, however, as I could see in the distance the high stone walls of sand-colored bricks that wound around and around the hillsides in front of us, covered with green foliage that climbed up the menacing side of the Castle. There seemed to be many turrets and one much larger at the very top. It looked sombre and more like a prison than a castle to my French eyes.

The outrider had made good time, I could see scurrying servants running in all directions as our coach just managed to scrape under an old archway with little room to spare. The family were waiting on the steps and I peered out and looked at the people to see who was who. They certainly looked drab. The peasant faces of the servants were blank, but I could tell what they were thinking, "Let's see what's so special about Don Fernando's French bride."

"Look, there's my father in the red coat!"

I saw him at once, doubt apparent in every tense muscle of his body. I scanned the many faces for a glimpse of my future mother-in-law. My heart was fluttering as Fernando motioned to wait for him to get down, then gave me his hand to escort me to his family. A warm breeze caught my face and I took a deep breath of the welcome air after the stuffiness of the coach.

I waited while Fernando kissed his father's veined hand, bowing low. "May I present your new daughter, Mam'selle Solange, Don Miguel."

I was kissed on the cheek by the man who could be no other than the father of Fernando. A little shorter, thinner hair and a face creased with the joys and sorrows of fifty or so more summers. I sighed with relief when I saw the doubt leave his eyes.

"Welcome to your new home, my dear daughter. Manoela, come, meet your sister."

A black haired beauty with skin like ivory peered over her fan and offered her cheek with downcast eyes. Her glossy mane was parted down the middle and drawn to a fine bun at the nape of her slender neck. I touched her cheek with mine and took her hand, which felt cold and was weighed down with old-fashioned rings. She drew back a little and gave me a shy smile. Her duenna was not far behind.

The servants bustled with the baggage and the dogs barked and ran about getting in the way of everyone, but as happy to receive us as the others, it seemed.

I looked for Donna Isabella, and Fernando intercepted my look. "It is really the time of siesta. My mother, Donna Isabella, will appear shortly."

He was fending off the joyous leaps and licks of his dog, a huge brown animal who obviously adored his master. It made me smile to witness such a happy reunion.

We walked arm in arm, my sweet sister-in-law, Manoela, Don Miguel and I, up the stairs and under an old archway into a garden of cold shadows. Water trickled from the fountain jaws of a lichen-encrusted lion's head in the centre. On either side spindly fig trees reached towards the sunlight. We entered through a huge heavy doorway studded with black iron nailheads and came to the hall, where our footsteps echoed. Wood was stacked in the stone fireplace but not lit. I wished it had been, as the chilly air made me shiver. High backed tapestry-covered chairs of heavy dark wood were assembled around a refectory table laden with wine and tasty things to eat. The stone walls were decorated with ancient banners and flags dating back to the crusades, swords and jousting sticks ensconced on either side of the cheerless fireplace.

I was about to ask who the woman in the portrait was (she looked tiny, a delicate and proud Titian-haired lady) when I heard dainty footsteps and the rattle of rings as the tapestries were pushed aside.

I turned, and knew that the fairy-like creature was Donna Isabella. She had a servant with her, holding her embroidery. A waft of heavy perfume caught my nostrils as I curtsied deeply to the exquisite creature who smiled, and held out a dainty hand to be kissed, but before I could do so, her slender arms embraced me, the scent of the gray silk gown as delicious as a spring morning in France.

"You are truly welcome, dear daughter, and much prettier than I anticipated. Thank God for delivering you both safely to us!" Her French was perfect.

"Thank you, Donna Isabella," I whispered with relief.

It didn't seem possible that she could be the mother of so large a son. Fernando bent nearly double and picked her up in his arms and twirled her around and around like a doll, as he roared with laughter.

"Put me down at once!" Donna Isabella spoke sternly, her tinkling voice outraged, and held her hands on either side of his face, but I could see by the dancing lights in her pale gray eyes that she adored her handsome son and his playful ways.

When we had eaten, Manoela accompanied me to my room where my maid had already arranged my robe and slippers, a ewer of hot water at the ready. After she had loosened my clothes, I got out of my dress, then dismissed her.

I looked out of the window to the courtyard below. How dull and barren it seemed compared to the thousands of neat flowerbeds at Versailles! The room was stark, apart from the beautiful arrangement of wild flowers on my dressing table.

"I do hope you like the flowers, Solange. I picked them for you this morning." Manoela smiled shyly, a gentle sweet shadow, hands clasped in front of her, but her brow was puckered.

"Oh, you startled me! I'd forgotten you were there; you're the quietest person I've ever known. The flowers are a beautiful yellow, my favourite colour. I always think yellow echoes the gold of the sun, don't you?"

Her brow cleared at once. "Thank you, dear sister." We touched cheeks lightly and then she was gone, leaving me to my siesta.

I collapsed on the bed gratefully, my very bones aching from the arduous journey. As sleep overcame me, my thoughts turned to Fernando, as usual. With him everything would be good; I could send to France for flowers and make a little arbour of my own, perhaps. Manoela would be a dear sister to me, and Don Miguel liked me, I felt sure. Donna Isabella puzzled me. She seemed so much younger than her husband, perhaps only fourteen years older than her son. But I was certain we would learn to love each other as we lived in the Castle together. I wondered why only her mouth had smiled to me and not her startling gray eyes.

A maid awakened me with a refreshing drink.

"Oh, I'm so excited," I admitted as I hurried her with my toilette. "Quickly, the red brocade and slippers to match!"

But I was met with a blank stare. "Señorita?"

I hadn't realised she wouldn't know French. I ran to the pile of gowns still spread on the chaise longe, and snatched the heavy silk. "This one."

"Ah, esta!" the old maid sighed. "Hurry, hurry! I want to go downstairs and explore the Castle."

She grinned imbecilely nodding her head.

Presently I was ready and checked my appearance. Yes, it was a fine gown, billowing and lustrous where the light caught the folds, and the decolletage revealing half my breasts very flatteringly.

There was a gentle tapping on the door and Donna Isabella entered; a butterfly in steel blue lace, sapphires blazing from her ears and throat. She carried a small black leather box tooled in gold.

I curtsied. "You honour me, Donna Isabella."

"A gift to bid you doubly welcome, my dear." She swayed towards the dressing table.

I dropped on the dressing stool in front of the mirror and fumbled with the catch. The necklace that greeted my eyes reminded me of flames dancing on the white satin cloth.

"Oh, Madame, how beautiful!" I gasped.

"The rubies will compliment your youthful colour." Donna Isabella sighed, "How I do miss the French fashions! We have them copied here, but our modistes have too heavy a hand."

"You are so tiny, Donna Isabella, please choose whichever gowns you wish." I indicated the dozens of silks and satins still being arranged by the maids.

Donna Isabella's eyes lit up and, with a step like that of a child, skipped straight to the silver ball gown.

"Oh, it is a whisper of moonlight!" She plucked it from the chair, holding it against her tiny body. "I will take only this one, for the wedding." Her fingers stroked and patted the delicate silk and held herself this way and that in front of the long mirror by the window.

"Only the French know the art of delicate sewing, to be sure. In Spain the gown enters the room before the woman." We gossiped quite naturally. Donna Isabella confided as we made our way downstairs. "Fernando has a very stubborn streak. You must be firm with him, he takes after his father, of course," she slyly admitted. I fingered my ruby necklace as we walked down the many corridors. As we entered the dining room I was met by the flashing black eyes of a guest who eyed my bosom brazenly and ran his tongue over full carmen lips.

"May I introduce my betrothed—my uncle, Don José—." I felt myself flush as his eyes raked my body. The tall grey-haired rogue bowed low and lifted my limp hand. Still holding it he stared into my eyes, causing me to prickle with heat. A look of open desire flashed clearly from his eyes. I was too stunned to speak. He turned my hand over and lingeringly kissed my palm. An electric current shot through me and I snatched my hand away, but I could see that he was amused. I was flustered as we took our places at the dinner table, alight with dozens of candles in the ornate candelabra, casting shadows on the company. The walls were hung with sombre tapestries and portraits of men in stiff white pleated collars, below small pointed beards. Their eyes stared as if all-seeing, and I knew a moment of apprehension. I caught Donna Isabella eyeing me curiously and remembered my manners. Fernando seemed different here, more relaxed and jocular. I was embarrassed as his eyes openly admired my décolletage. Donna Isabella flushed and pretended not to notice, but he was not to be discouraged.

"I see you wear my Grandmother's rubies, dearest," and he touched the necklace lightly, his fingers warm against my throat. I prayed that no one would notice the color rise to my face. I glanced out of the corner of my eye at his mother and although she was sipping daintily from her glass goblet, something told me that she missed nothing. I caught a flash of dislike, but it was gone so quickly that I couldn't be sure if it was my imagination. I realized that Don Miguel had been speaking to me.

"I'm so sorry, Don Miguel, what did you say?"

"Ah, love! You are lost in love, dear child, and that is as it should be," Don José smiled sarcastically, looking sideways down his aristocratic nose. Manoela looked down at her plate.

"Don't be ridiculous," Donna Isabella interrupted. "Puppy love," she sneered. "She'll learn in time what love is, but by then who knows?" she shrugged.

Don Miguel looked at her sternly, "I think perhaps you've had enough wine, my dear."

Donna Isabella's eyes flashed cold hatred. I gasped, realising she loathed her husband. Don José, sitting back in his chair, threw me an amused glance.

Donna Isabella indicated to the servant who was standing obediently behind her chair to fill the goblet, and just like a child who has been advised not to do something, she deliberately took pleasure in disobeying and proceeded to drink in one continuous swallow, her slender neck showing the muscles as the wine slid down. The meal continued as we all made polite conversation. Fernando and Manoela joked about the many things they had enjoyed as children. I realised Manoela must have been a happy child, but now the life seemed to have been crushed out of her. I wondered if it was an unhappy love affair or the rigid rules of the Spanish household. Donna Isabella picked at her food, jabbing the meat and pushing the pastry round her plate. At last the charade came to an end and we made our way to the withdrawing room. Donna Isabella staggered a little, although her husband had tight hold of her arm above the elbow.

"I think an early night would do you good, my dear," I heard him mutter under his breath. She wrenched herself away from him.

"Don't you tell me what to do, you uncouth Spanish peasant," she spat through her teeth.

I wondered what kind of a household I had got myself into. We all stopped where we stood, just in the doorway to the room. I couldn't help thinking it was just like a game we played at Versailles where nobody moved when the music stopped. Fernando went to kiss his Mother and led her gently but firmly away, throwing me apologetic glances.

"Come, my dear Solange!" Don Miguel guided me to a chair by the window which overlooked the lawns. I was conscious of Don José's eyes on me. Without looking I knew he was mentally undressing me from his position by the fireplace as he drank deeply from his goblet.

"It has all been too exciting for my wife, I'm afraid. I think perhaps she has been away from her beloved France too long."

"Of course," I spoke rapidly, trying to show him that I felt pity for what I could see was a difficult marriage, thinking in my innocence that my marriage would never be less than perfect.

As I lay in bed that night I tried to picture my darling Fernando, but Don José's eyes were as clear in my memory as if they were in the very room. Why did he make me feel that we were irresistably drawn together? He must have been nearly as old as Don Miguel, his brother. I prayed that no danger would come of what I could not quite understand. If only Thérèse were here. There was no one I could confide in, certainly not Donna Isabella. I had the unmistakable feeling that she was just waiting for an opportunity to cause trouble for me. I shuddered and closed my eyes, trying to imagine Fernando's lips on mine, but I writhed as I realised it was Don José's mouth I could feel and the hands of Don José that were caressing me as the flashing black eyes mocked. It was as if I were under a spell, I told myself, but as I fell into a sweat-soaked sleep I had the most terrifying dream.

I was immersed up to my neck in a slimy green pond crying for Fernando to help me out. All his family was standing round laughing and pointing at me. Donna Isabella had tears of laughter trickling down her face as she rocked in glee. Even Don Miguel threw his head back as he roared with the others. I held out my arms to them. "Won't you help me, please?" I screamed, feeling the water reaching my mouth. This only caused more laughter and Manoela held on to Fernando for support as they clung together weak with pleasure. I felt as if I were choking as the filthy tepid water lapped into my mouth, tasting of one of Berthe's vile concoctions and other unspeakable flavours. I turned as I felt someone's arms pull me by the waist and fell into the arms of Don José. He kissed me passionately and I returned his rough embrace as together we fell beneath the putrid surface of the pond.

I awoke shaking with the clarity of the nightmare. I touched the wood of the table by my bedside and the cold wall behind it to make sure it was only a terrible dream. I lay there, frightened, for the rest of the night, and only fell into fitful slumber as the dawn light came peeping through a chink in the heavy drapes.

The following day Donna Isabella was quite gay, and it was hard to believe her embarrassing behaviour of the night before. Fernando had ridden off with Don Miguel to inspect the vineyards and so Donna Isabella, Manoela and I sat in the chilly morning room busily making lists for the wedding. The room seemed quite bare with its dark high-backed chairs and small windows. The bright morning light fell coldly on Donna Isabella's face. Faint lines ran from nostril to mouth which I knew would be harder etched as each year went by. The downward droop of her mouth when she thought herself unobserved gave her many more years.

"Oh, isn't it exciting!" Manoela clapped her hands, "I am to be a bridesmaid," and she jumped up spontaneously, flinging her arms about me. Her face fell as her Mother sighed softly.

"Sit down, Manoela, remember you are of marriageable age yourself, and do fluff out your gown. I never did like you in yellow, it doesn't go with your complexion."

"Yes, Mammalita."

Manoela, with head bowed, sat on the corner of the dark red chair, hands folded tightly in her lap. I straightened the pages on the table in front of us neatly.

"I was just thinking how well the color became you, Manoela," I ventured before I could stop myself. "Yellow is so refreshing against youthful skin, I always think." My sister shot me a grateful look, but Madame screwed her eyes up and quickly rang the little bell resting on the table at her side, and began to tap her foot, a gesture I was to come to know quite well. The black-clad maid entered, keys jangling at her thick middle.

"I will take a walk in the garden, fetch my cloak." The foot tapped on as the silent woman went to do her mistress's bidding.

"I shall do the lists myself. What use is a stupid girl, no wiser than a child and an ill-mannered bride-to-be who had better watch her manners if she is to be allowed to join a noble Spanish household." Tap! tap! tap! the foot continued. I felt the blood rush to my face and stood quickly in front of her, raising my voice.

"I beg to contradict you, Madame."

"What, you dare to doubt my word?"

Madame turned, glaring up into my face, two spots of color appearing below her eyes. I don't know what made me lie to her then, I knew Fernando would not let me down.

"Are you awarc, Madame, that you are addressing the daughter of the King of France?" I held my chin high and looked disdainfully down my nose, then walked slowly around Madame, eyeing her up and down disinterestedly, although my heart was beating fast. I was gratified to see she was speechless with shock. Out of the corner of my eye I could see Manoela crouched in the corner of her chair like a little mouse, her thin fingers covering her mouth.

"The question I think is not if I, the Princess Solange, is allowed to join a noble Spanish household, but rather," my voice slowing its pace as I faced her again one hand on hip, "If the household is worthy of the honour bestowed upon it of the Royal blood of France. Now," I said haughtily, lifting my other hand slowly, causing my jewels to flash, "I'm sure you and your charming daughter will excuse me—I've a most important letter to write to my Father, the King." I gave a bored yawn behind my hand. "He insists I keep him well informed. I think I have made my position clear."

Allowing a brief smile to touch my lips for an instant, I walked regally as befitted my position, sailing past an open-jawed Donna Isabella, and the gaping maid who must have heard most of the conversation. The news would be all round the castle in no time for sure.

Chapter 14

I stood at my window looking for Fernando's return. Although I felt quite weak after my dealings with his Mother, I hoped he would understand that it wasn't seemly for her to speak to me as if I were a common peasant. I scanned the paths and hillsides, screening my eyes from the midday sun. A cart and an old man were trundling along down to the village. All looked bleak and grey apart from the pale blue sky. The dust on the castle walls seemed to cover everything. I must respect Fernando's mother, I told myself, but she must be put in her place, none of the ladies at Court would allow one word of impudence from a noble, relative or no. Their horses were carrying them over the hills now, I could just see them bobbing then disappearing round a bend in the hillside. I quickly rearranged my hair, the gloomy-faced maid obsequiously bowing more than usual.

"Don't be so busy scraping near the floor, you stupid woman. Hurry and bring me the brown taffeta." She continued her bowing, grinning now as well. "Oh God's breath, you can't understand a word, can you, you simpleton?" She obviously thought I was flattering her for she smiled the more.

"Bueno, bueno!" she simpered.

I pointed at the dresses in the cupboard and dropped the fine silk I had chosen over her arms, and between us I was gowned in no time. One last look at the effect in the mirror—

"Bueno, bueno!" she grinned. "La linda senorita!"

"Princesa, if you please," I answered, pointing to myself. I felt like an actress playing a princess. I had forgotten her name.

"Amelia?" She shook her head, and pointing to herself proudly she said, "Lucia".

"To be sure, the beading is most prettily arranged down the skirt, Luthia. The topaz brooch, I think." She stared blank-faced. I indicated my jewel box on the dressing table and she rushed to do my bidding.

"Princesa," she said, and held it open for me. I pointed to the cushion-shaped jewel set in gold filigree. She obediently snatched it and the matching earrings, lifting her black eyebrows, quizzically.

"Bueno, bueno, Lucia."

A smile like a summer's day appeared like magic at the compliment. My skirts swished as I made my way down the staircase, not quite knowing what kind of a reception would await me, but there was no need to worry. Fernando held out his hands to me from the hall. He looked more handsome than ever. His eyes were full of love for me. He kissed my wrists slowly, causing the familiar shivers to run through me.

"I think a short stroll before luncheon, Princess," he spoke mocking me lightly, holding out his arm. I placed my hand on top of his.

"I should be charmed, Don Fernando," I answered in my best Court voice. Under his breath as we walked slowly to the gardens so that no-one could hear, he spoke quite differently whilst keeping his face quite placid.

"So, I hear the Iron Butterfly has had her wings clipped. I wonder when I shall be put to bed outside the door by my royal bastard."

"We shall have to wait and see, shan't we?" I replied sweetly. We stopped by the fountain, and Fernando turned to me, a stern expression on his handsome face.

"Don José is still here I believe, and I would appreciate it if you would try to behave as my betrothed, not some cheap whore from a bawdy house."

I flared up in rage. "Don't you dare tell me how to behave! I've had enough from your Mother. A fine example of behaviour, she is."

"There is no need to bring my Mother into this. I'm speaking of you, my dear."

I flushed, knowing he had a right to reprimand me, but I couldn't deny the effect his uncle had on me. A servant hurried towards us bowing obsequiously. I took Fernando's arm as he smiled stiffly, and we made our way to the meal that I dreaded, knowing that Don José would be there.

His back was to us as we entered, broad and strong in a black velvet coat. I quickly looked away, not wanting to meet his all-knowing eyes. I managed to avoid him throughout the meal, and when the others retired for their siesta, I decided to take a walk alone. It was warm on the terrace and I could smell the wild flowers of Spain, heady and sweet. I entered the parkland surrounding the Castle and strolled beneath the trees. I stooped to pick an unusual pink flower and held it to my nose. Suddenly I felt my breasts grasped from behind, and warm lips gently touching the side of my neck. I gasped, whirling round into the arms of Don José. Before I could protest, he held me in a vice-like grip and I could feel his muscular thighs pressed against me.

"Let me make love to you, querida. Only an older man knows how to cherish beauty. It isn't too late for you to belong to me."

"Let me go!" I choked, kicking his legs. He cradled my neck in the hollow of his hands as I twisted violently, trying to free myself. "Let go of me at once!"

"You know you don't mean that, vida mia." I felt weak, realizing that as I pushed and pummelled his broad chest, even the feel of his body caused my pulse to beat faster. I could not mistake his look of deep passion. It enveloped me like a quivering screen of heat. He sensed my hesitation and covered my mouth with his own. I had never kissed a man with a beard before. It was sharp and prickled my face lightly, a sensual caress. My knees buckled weakly and we collapsed together, sprawled on the grass.

"Vida mia" he said huskily, and I couldn't break away from him. I lifted my hand to strike him, but he just laughed softly and grasped it between his lips, covering my fingers with tender kisses, one strong leg pinning me to the ground.

"How dare you?" I choked as his heavy body covered mine. "They'll see us from the Castle, please let me go. I am affianced to your nephew!"

"You can't marry that young pup. You need a real man." The throbbing between my legs wouldn't stop.

"Oh, God help me," I whimpered. "I am lost!"

He pressed his lips between my breasts and down my body where he pulled my gown away.

"I want you for myself, vida mia. I will make you happy, we were meant to be together always."

The bird songs were muted and the sun seemed to pound down on me as through a smoke screen.

"You're raping me," I moaned, knowing that I wouldn't let him go now even if he wanted to. He made love to me slowly, savouring every secret crevice of my body. I could feel the warmth of the sun caressing my thighs and closed my eyes to feel it on my eyelids. I was floating as if in an exquisite dream while his experienced hands and tongue showed me pleasures that must have been the Devil's own creation. I lay there, waiting for him to take me—to release me from the delicious spasms of agony.

"José! José!" I pulled him down and heard myself moan like an animal.

"You belong to me, querida. Your beautiful body belongs to me!"

I held him long after we had exploded together, not wanting to lose his vibrant maleness. We lay, partly clothed, under the sun.

We must have slept joined together. I felt him being pulled away from me and covered my breasts automatically with my hands.

"Defend yourself, you old roué!" Fernando stood there, his face bloodless, eyes black as thunder.

"I stand by my honour," José answered him politely, quickly putting his clothes back to order.

"You'll pay for this with your miserable life!"

"Solange is not for you, Fernando, she will tell you herself." He turned to me and I opened my mouth to speak but I was interrupted.

"Go back to the Castle at once!" Fernando ordered, his voice as cold as a beggar's grave. I turned to José who nodded, helping me to my feet.

"I won't go." I was frightened by the murder in Fernando's eyes. He drew his sword. "No!" I screamed, "No, don't be a fool," but it was as if he couldn't hear me as José defended himself skillfully, perspiration dripping from his brow.

He was superb, but Fernando was quicker—I clutched the trunk of a tree for support as I prayed there would be no bloodshed.

"Stop this at once, I beg of you, Fernando," but my voice trailed away as I saw a scarlet stain appear on José's upper arm. I knew I was crying while I begged them to stop. José's injured arm hung limply as he continued fighting under the gruelling sun, his steps becoming slower as each moment passed. And then it was over. He clutched himself beneath his heart and almost twisted round, the sword sticking out grotesquely, and then he fell. I rushed to his side and wiped his brow with my gown. He smiled at me weakly, his lips hardly moving.

"For you," he gasped, "for you I give my life gladly, vida mia."

I was about to protest, but I knew it was useless. The eyes that had been filled with passion such a short time ago were now blank in death. I felt myself being lifted and carried back to the Castle, not caring what became of me.

Chapter 15

"We have managed to keep the scandal within the family," Donna Isabella assured me from her seat by my bedside. "I knew something like this would happen one day." She said it as if everything occurred as she anticipated. I was surrounded by the entire family, Fernando's hands covering mine.

"But you don't understand," I stammered as I felt the tears slowly slide down my face.

"Quiet, dearest, you must have rest after such a terrible shock." I twisted my head from side to side.

"It wasn't what it seemed," I moaned.

"Hush dearest, we know, we know."

"You don't know," I insisted. They all tiptoed out of the room, Don Miguel practically pushing his wife before him, and I was left alone with my betrothed.

"Of course, there is no question of a wedding now, Fernando."

"You mustn't think of this day again, dearest. Try to blot it from your mind."

"You must listen, Fernando," I pushed myself up on my

elbows and he fluffed the pillows for me, his hand lingering on my hair.

"I know what happened, Solange, it was obvious, unspeakable. I can't forgive myself for allowing him here. My mother never trusted him."

I was too drained of emotion to argue, but I felt I had to tell him the truth. I took a sip from the glass beside me, the strong cordial giving me a little strength. I felt as though my arms were shaking, but when I looked at them they seemed perfectly still.

"Try to get some sleep, my dear love, the wedding is in three days' time. That old fossil must have been deranged to do such a thing! Only a madman would rape a lady from his own family—but I have upheld the family honour, may his evil soul rot in Hell." He stood and paced the room, thumping his fist against his palm. I wept into my hands, hard and long sobs racking my body as I remembered his beautiful lovemaking and then his last words to me. Fernando put a protecting arm around my shoulders and tried to wipe my tears away with his white silk handkerchief.

"Please stop crying, my love. It's all over now—that beast will never bother you again."

"Will you try to understand that he *loved* me, he didn't really rape me, Fernando, you must know that!"

"Ah, Solange, you are too trusting. Of course, he told you that he loved you; he told my mother he loved her too. What did you expect him to say—'Lie down and let me rip your clothes off'?"

"Stop it! Stop it! I won't let you talk to me like that, I don't care what your mother said, it wasn't like that at all. You don't understand. I can't marry you now, it wouldn't be right."

"It makes no difference to me, Solange. It wasn't your fault. Now promise me you'll rest."

I sighed, knowing he wouldn't listen. He kissed me tenderly on the forehead and drew the bedcurtains. I lay back and prayed for the soul of Don José. Don Miguel was sure to be pleased to inherit the estates of his unmarried brother and grieve in private. But I knew in my heart the fault was mine and I should have had more control over my emotions, for although Don José had made the first move, I could have tried harder to resist. It was hard to understand that much as I loved Fernando I was capable of a consuming passion for other men. Was it fair to marry him knowing how my emotions ruled me? As I drifted into an exhausted slumber I whispered, "Buenos noches, vida mia."

Chapter 16

We were married by the Archbishop of Toledo, and the wedding was attended by the grandees of Castille and the Aragon nobility. All over the village there were tourneys and fêtes. Banners hung gaily across the narrow streets. The hall had been richly decorated for the occasion and a lute played the notes of a pavanne. Over my gown of cloth of gold sprinkled with purple lace buds, I wore a castillian cape of purple velvet worked with flowers in gold thread. Fernando's white breeches and matching coat were decorated with gold chains, and I saw many a lovely señorita eyeing me covetously. On our wedding night Fernando gave me an emerald bracelet which the King had instructed him to keep for the occasion.

The very next day my husband was called away on a mysterious journey. All he would tell me was that it had to do with the war between France and Spain which was still being waged, and I was left in a strange country with a family I hardly knew, a bride of one day without a husband.

I lay in the big bed and rolled to the warm spot where my husband's body had left its indentation and smelt the familiar scent his body had left. I buried my face in the empty space and sobbed. What was I doing in this miserable castle with a meek-eyed virgin as my only friend? I was haunted with the fear that Fernando would be killed, and at other times I remembered the death of Don José, reliving the agony of that whole unfortunate business.

There was no word from my husband as the endless days turned into weeks and the household was filled with gloom. As the heat of summer continued I realised I was to have a baby. At first I was thrilled. At last I would have someone of my very own. But then I worried day and night, wondering if Fernando was safe—if only I could tell him that he was to be a father! I waited until I could hide my secret no longer, and confided my news to Manoela. Her sweet face took on a beatific glow. She held her cheek tenderly to mine and comforted me as I sobbed my fear for Fernando.

Living in the Castle with my mother-in-law was not pleasant, and as we sat at table one Autumn evening, the wine made me fuddled. I cradled my belly in my arms unthinkingly as the servants waited on us in that gloomy room. Catching the sweet smile of my sister-in-law as I raised my glass to drink, I was unaware that she would take this gesture as a signal to break the silence of the meal.

"Solange has something marvellous to tell you both," Manoela almost sang in her breathless voice.

My father-in-law lowered his fork slowly, and facing me he lifted his own glass, his dark old eyes uncertain.

"Is it a toast, my dear daughter?"

I blushed, and looked into his happy face that was creased with pleasure.

"You knew, Father?"

"I guessed. But this is the best possible news, my dear. Isn't that so, Isabella?"

But Isabella shot me a glance of pure hatred, and one of utter contempt to Don Miguel. Her high-pitched voice tinkled across the table, "To what do we raise our glasses, may I ask?" I could hear her foot tapping against the table leg. How I wished Manoela hadn't spoken. She was so impetuous, little more than a child at times. Didn't she realise that my mother-in-law despised me?

"I think our daughter will tell us the glad tidings," said Don Miguel standing and placing his napkin on the table before him and coming over to me, arms outstretched. Cupping my chin gently, he kissed my burning cheek. Manoela clapped her hands,

"Go on, Solange, go on!" she prompted.

"I am with child," I said quickly, and heard Donna Isabella suck her breath in. "I had hoped that Fernando would be here when I told you."

"I'm sure he will return to us quite soon. We couldn't be more delighted." Don Miguel kissed my other cheek. "Isn't that so, my dear? We look forward to Fernando's son with pride."

"Ha! his son! Who says it's Fernando's son? I won't drink to your brother's bastard!" Donna Isabella spat.

Manoela gasped, and covered her mouth with her hands. The fear I had pushed to the back of my mind had been spoken. I was forced to face the agony of uncertainty. Was Fernando the father of my child, or would his dead Uncle José live on through his child to remind us all of the tragedy I had brought to this miserable place? The blood pounded in my head as I stared at the scene before me. Flickering candles in elaborate candelabra threw a ghostly glow over the room, causing the people to seem unreal. Don Miguel patted my arm gently, then returned to his chair at the head of the table. A gleam of candlelight touched the delicate features of Donna Isabella. Crimson spots appeared on either cheek as she continued eating. Don Miguel finally addressed his wife.

"It would seem you are not altogether pleased that we are to have a grandchild, my dear. I wonder if I can guess the reason?"

Isabella's fine grey eyes narrowed, and before her husband could speak again, she raised her glass and tossed the contents towards him. Instead of reaching its target at the end of the table, the rich red wine rained onto the center candelabra, causing the flames to splutter, then drip slowly onto the fine lace cloth. A stony-faced manservant was about to remove the cloth, but Don Miguel, with a tired movement, waved him away.

Enraged at missing her target, Donna Isabella stood, and with eyes blazing, walked up to her husband and slapped him hard across the face. The hand left a pink mark which darkened as each second passed. Manoela began to snivel, but Don Miguel only shook his head.

"Perhaps you would leave us, my dear daughter," he sighed.

I gratefully rose and held my trembling hand out for Manoela to join me. With bowed head she followed me to the door. Before we could make our exit, words reached us which slowed our hurrying steps.

"Is it the idea of becoming a grandmother which displeases you, my love? Would you rather our daughter's child was to be yours, and that of our son?"

I turned, my hand on the iron door handle, not daring to breathe. Don Miguel had gripped his wife's arm above the elbow and I could see she was trying to wrench herself free, her teeth clenched in anger.

"Let go of me, you peasant!" she screamed.

"Is it not an unnatural love you bear your son?"

I saw her color rise and she spat straight at him, still wriggling to break away from his grasp. The spittle etched an ugly trail as it slowly moved down the side of his nose. Manoela crouched against the door, hands over her ears, as her father's hollow voice reached us again.

"So, it seems I was right, wasn't I, Bella?"

"You fool, you stupid old fool!" she choked in fury. "Fernando is *not* your son."

There was no sound but our breathing and the thudding of my heartbeats. Isabella's voice, when she continued at last held a note of triumph.

"That surprised you, didn't it?"

With a painful groan Don Miguel fell into a heap at the

feet of his wife. Her voice changed into the laughing screech of a mad woman. Her dainty head was thrown back as she rubbed her freed arm against her side.

"Father! Father!" Manoela ran and flung herself at the still form of Don Miguel.

The servants hurried forward, as, half-fainting from shock, I fled to the sanctuary of my room without a backward glance. Leaning against the heavy door, I pressed my face against the hard wood, praying for the health of Don Miguel and my unborn child. Tears of anguish filled my eyes as I longed for my husband to comfort me in this crumbling old castle, so full of hatred and dark secrets. I beat my fists against the door, while the wind howled round the buttresses, causing me to shudder and reminding me that I was a stranger here in this foreign land. I prayed aloud for Fernando to return, and to assure me that he at least believed it was indeed his child that I carried. I tried not to think about the terrible scene I'd witnessed downstairs, and wouldn't allow my mind to work out the relationships in this strange household. I was relieved when Manoela's gentle tap came, and on opening the door, I could see by her calm features that the crisis had passed. The stern-faced Duenna allowed her to spend the night with me, and Manoela assured me that Don Miguel had been attended by a physician from the village, and seemed only to have been overwrought. Fortunately she had not heard the dreadful words that had passed between her parents. As we lay in the shadow-filled room listening to the wind beat against the Castle walls, I held my swollen belly and thought of the child who would soon be born to me. As my eyes grew heavy with sleep, I thought I felt him kick with life, and a glow of happiness enveloped me unlike any I had ever known.

Chapter 17

Although we sent messages far and wide, we received no news of my husband. My son arrived early with the December snow, and he was christened Louis Fernando. He was a beautiful baby with his father's eyes, and a tuft of tight black curls. He brought a glow of happiness to the Castillo, pushing our fears aside. When I looked down at my son, my heart would melt with love. His chubby arms lifted above his head and the tiny fists clenched shut in sleep. He was round as a peach and his merry dark eyes never left mine from the day he began to sit up. If only his Father could have seen him!

Louis was six months old in May, and as Manoela played on the rich flowered rug throwing a brightly colored cloth ball for him, I told her, "I have decided to take Louis back to France."

She held the ball in mid-air. "Oh, Solange, you can't!" she dropped the ball and clasped the baby so tightly that he squealed and tried to wriggle from her embrace, kicking his legs. "What if Fernando returns home? You belong here, this is your home, and Louis' home."

"I'm sorry, Manoela. Why don't you come with us? I know you would love the gaiety at Versailles."

Her grip loosened, and Louis swiftly wormed his way across the room, chortling to be free once more to play with the ball. Manoela clapped her hands, causing her many rings and bracelets to tinkle.

"Even if Don Miguel would give his permission, I know Donna Isabella would not."

"Would you like to come to France?"

She sat back on her heels, smiling shyly.

"I'm not sure, Solange. My Father needs me here."

"He would be happy for you if you returned with a fine husband."

She lowered her eyes and a faint flush crept up the ivory skin of her neck. I felt a hundred years older than she at that moment. She was so innocent, but a short time at Court would soon alter that.

"I will speak to Don Miguel at the first opportunity, and we shall see if he is agreeable. Louis! Louis!" I ran to retrieve Fernando's brown dog, who had been rudely awakened from his position by the door. Louis was pulling his tail with sticky pink fingers, and as the poor animal tried to escape, Louis pulled the harder. Lucia, silent as the grave, came into the room, her capable face disapproving. She removed the yelping dog's tail from its trap, and lifted my son up, tutting all the while in her gutteral at 'foreign ways, allowing babies to run wild'.

"Tante Mella! Tante Mella!" Louis yelled, turning from red to purple. "Maman!" Two little arms stretched toward us, but he was already being taken for his *petit dejeuner*.

"Be a good boy, Louis. Tante Mella and I will be up to play with you later." I blew him a kiss and sighed, "How he loves his Tante Mella!"

"He is a darling child, your son."

I stole a glance at myself in the huge mirror over the mantel and patted my hair into place and gave my waist a critical look.

"My figure is back to normal at last, Manoela, is it not?"

Manoela nodded absently and joined me.

"If I do go with you, dear sister, it would be only to look

after Louis. I've no desire to take part in the merrymaking you've told me of."

"Nonsense! With your dark beauty you'd be a great success." She stood behind me and in the mirror her frightened black eyes looked uncertainly into mine. I swung round and kissed her lightly. "Silly, there's nothing to fear. I have many good friends at Court. We'll look after you. Come, it must be time for luncheon. I will speak to Don Miguel before siesta."

Arm in arm we made our way to the dining hall which never failed to chill me, in spite of the heavy hot food that was always served. There were too many unpleasant memories. I let a sigh of relief escape as I realised that Donna Isabella had excused herself to have a tray in her room.

"A slight migraine," Don Miguel muttered as he finished his wine. I realised with a start how old he was looking. His olive skin had a yellow tinge, and the once proud back was stooped, as if the weight of his problems was too heavy for one man to carry. He greeted us warmly, then sat down heavily as the soup was brought in. I shot Manoela a worried glance, but she took her place with head bowed, and slowly began to sip her soup. As the meat was served I decided to broach the subject of our departure, but found it more difficult than I had imagined. There was no sound but that of the cutlery touching the plates, or the slight tinkle of glass. It was a sad meal which the three of us ate. I wondered for the hundredth time if Fernando was eating, and if he were safe. For we still knew no more than on the day he had gone from us. Don Miguel stared into space from his slumped position. I finally found the courage to speak,

"You look tired, Don Miguel. I would like the physician to visit you, don't you agree, Manoela?"

"Are you ill, Father?" her startled gaze met his.

"What did you say, Manoela?"

"You are ill, Father. You don't look well." Her hand reached out to touch his. He clasped dry fingers over her slender ones.

"I'm very tired, Manoela, forgive me my dear. You must

excuse me, Solange, I am very poor company tonight."

"You seem very weary, dear Don Miguel."

"My thoughts were with Fernando. Without little Louis I couldn't face another day."

I noticed his shirt gaped at the throat of his scraggy neck. He, who had been so fastidious about his appearance. How could I leave him at the mercy of the Iron Butterfly? She'd surely try to smash him with those evil words she used; crush him till there was nothing left but an empty shell.

After the meal we made our way to the courtyard and the fountain. How barren it looked in the pale sunlight. We sat in the shade of a tree which sheltered us from the faint breeze that came whispering from the mountains. Taking a deep breath I spoke carefully, choosing my words with great consideration.

"Don Miguel, you've been very kind to me; you've made me truly welcome here."

He looked puzzled.

"But of course, my dear, why should it be otherwise? You belong here at the Castillo Grande."

I felt rather than saw Manoela slip away through the trees.

"Please don't think I'm ungrateful for your love and understanding, but I'd like to go back to France now."

"Ah! So you wish to leave us, Solange."

"I would like his Majesty to see my little Louis. The King's an old man now. We wouldn't be away too long, perhaps only till next Spring."

He looked at me thoughtfully, slowly nodding his head.

"I feared you would pine for France, daughter. But what of my grandson? He dotes on his Tante Mella."

Renewed strength seemed to enter his body as he talked of my little Louis, and some of the old *bonhomie* returned a sparkle to his eyes.

"I think it would be better for Louis to have his Tante Mella with him," I suggested. He looked at me solemnly, then shook his head sadly and said, "I have a shrew for a wife and now my two daughters are abandoning me with my adored only grandchild."

He wiped his red eyes slowly with a large lace handkerchief and I rose to kiss his bony cheeks.

"You do understand?"

"I understand too much, and perhaps not enough. But go, my daughter, with my blessing. When Fernando returns we'll all be together again and then there will be many grandchildren."

"I knew you'd agree. Thank you, Don Miguel. But what of Donna Isabella?"

He waved his hand with a gesture of despair.

"Will she allow Manoela to leave?"

"I will speak to the Señora, my dear." He stood and took both my hands in his. "It will be good for my Manoela to be away from her Mother, and perhaps better for you."

I could guess what it cost him to make such a statement after his wife's outburst as to the paternity of my child. As if he'd read my thoughts, Don Miguel continued,

"Fernando has been my son for too many years. I am too old to change my affection. I feel sure your mother-in-law was only trying to wound me. I tell myself not to think about it. Marriage can be a venomous relationship sometimes. I don't know why I still love her."

We walked slowly across the courtyard back to the Castle. It was the last time we would do so before my journey.

Chapter 18

Lucia settled my son on her lap in the coach and a manservant tucked a rug around Manoela's knees. I took one last hurried look at the Castle Grandé and shivered in the cold morning air. We had said our goodbyes the night before, and surprisingly the Iron Butterfly had seemed quite relieved to be rid of us. She had kept her mouth clenched shut most of the evening, showing boredom in the tapping of her foot in its dainty grey satin slipper. She gave a glance in my direction throughout the evening, as her daughter entertained us with her pretty singing.

Glancing up to the apartments of Don Miguel I was surprised to find he was not at one of the windows. Suddenly he appeared at the door of the coach.

"You'll take a chill," I chided him, secretly pleased he'd risen at such an early hour to bid us *au revoir*. Before I could hurry him indoors, he stooped inside the coach to have one last look at his grandchild. Louis reached out a chubby fist and pulled at Don Miguel's nose.

"Oh, Louis," I laughed, "what a way for dear Grandpapa to remember you!"

Any tears which might have been shed were brushed aside

as Lucia tut tutted her disapproval, and Manoela giggled into her handkerchief. Don Miguel stood on the steps with the servants, waving, a brave smile on his tired face. I watched till we turned a corner of the road and they disappeared from view. Louis fell asleep almost at once as the coach swayed along. I looked back at the same scene I'd craned my neck to glimpse as Fernando's betrothed. That seemed so long ago. I held my cape more tightly round my shoulders.

"You're shivering, Solange," Manoela whispered. I came back to the present with a start.

"The sun will soon be up and I'll feel warmer."

I opened the valise and drew a bottle of cognac from its resting place and held it to Manoela's lips. She coughed as she swallowed, and caused little Louis to open his eyes, but seeing us and Lucia near him, he was content and dozed off again at oncc. His cheeks were like freshly plucked peaches under lashes like black fur. I felt elated to be leaving that miserable Castle Grandé.

"What's the matter, Manoela? You're not frightened, are you?"

She shot me a troubled look.

"I've never been out of Spain before. I know I will make a fool of myself at Versailles."

"Don't be a goose, of course you won't! Anyway, I'll be with you and Louis will need you more than ever, so there won't be much time for being a fool. You'll be far too busy."

Her pale face broke into a smile at this, and she leaned over to place a gentle kiss on Louis' tiny nose.

"Promise me you'll always stay near mc, Solange."

"You know I will, silly. But wait till you have a lover. You'll be asking me to stay away then," I teased.

"What talk!" Lucia admonished, and her flat face held a look of shock. "I knew Donna Isabella should've accompanied us. Most improper! Most improper!"

"Look!" I pointed to distract her, "The Pyrenees." The coach began to climb as we saw in the distance the white and icy mountains with here and there tufts of greenery. The sun shone on the peaks of snowy brilliance as we gazed at the heavenly view. Time passed quickly. Louis awakened and began to complain, and I was about to ask Lucia to unpack the food, when suddenly the coach lurched to a stop, flinging us against each other. Fortunately, Lucia had tight hold of Louis, who began to cry lustily.

"We must have lost a wheel," I assured Manoela, putting my hat to rights. "Lucia will soon give you a drink of milk, Louis, to fill your empty little belly," I soothed.

It was then that we heard shouts of surprised dismay from our coachman.

"There's ladies inside, mercy for the love of Heaven!"

There were unmistakable sounds of steel meeting steel. I leaned my head out of the window, clutching the baby to me. I heard shouts of "Hurrah!"

"The bloody aristocrats and their fancy coaches!"

Lucia crossed herself and mumbled a prayer, her sallow face drained of color. The baby continued to scream, and I quickly covered Louis under my cloak. In that instance I cursed myself for taking this ill-fated journey.

There was a battle in full swing as I peered past Manoela, her eyes bulging in horror at the sight of the blood pouring from our coachman's throat, as he disappeared from view beneath the wondow. I felt my body go slack with fear, cowering back as the door was pulled open and Lucia was dragged, screaming, into the road by the dirty hands of my old enemy Pierre.

Chapter 19

Before our eyes a long, rusty blade was thrust through Lucia's chest, and the life gurgled out of her. There were three highwaymen, including Pierre, the murderers of innocent travellers.

"Out!" Pierre ordered, blowing his nose into his hand then wiping it at the side of his too-small greatcoat, "and be quick about it." He eyed Manoela and his face broke into a toothless grin. "I like 'em dark, don't I, Enery? That's if I can't get 'em fair."

This was met with snickering from a bloated little pudding of a man. He answered from a grey-green beard, matted with filth, "Aye", and dug the end of a long evil-looking knife hilt into the ribs of his dough-faced companion. "Cockermouth can vouch for that, eh lad?"

"Well, I'll be the Pope's mistress!" Pierre leaned forward and jeered at me through narrow eyes. "If it ain't the high and mighty Lady Muck herself!" He stood there hand outstretched while the baby continued to scream. I forced myself to answer him, trying to bargain for our lives.

"I hope that you'll explain the meaning of this outrage."

Before I could continue, the baby's cries were drowned by

their laughter. Pierre held out a calloused fist and bowed mockingly.

"If modom would care to step this way..."

Hoping to humour him I managed to raise myself from my seat, holding a trembling hand forward out of habit. I then drew it back quickly as I descended from the coach step and lost my footing. He moved aside and they roared their pleasure as I landed full length amongst the bloody bodies of our servants. Before I could regain my balance, I felt myself being heaved up by my petticoats from behind.

"Always help a lady when she's down, I always says."

Enery rocked on his short rag-covered legs.

"Shut the brat's mouth, will yer or I'll shut it for good!" Pierre was growing impatient.

"The baby needs his milk," I begged.

"Get the dark-eyed virgin out", Pierre ordered. Enery made to obey without changing the expressionless eyes.

"Leave her alone! We'll give you whatever you want," I cried.

"We'll take what we wants," Pierre grinned, "but thanks for the offer. And for starters we'll take Gypsy Eye's brat and stuff it's gob shut."

I planted myself in front of the door, but was pushed aside by the silent Cockermouth. Manoela got to her feet, and turning, lifted Louis and placed him firmly in her arms before descending gingerly from the coach. She stood like a madonna, her eyes luminous and terror-filled, clutching the screaming child who kicked and pushed at her.

"He won't give you any trouble, I promise you, only let me feed him, please," came her breathless voice. They looked too stunned to answer, and I held my breath as they looked to Pierre.

Enery interrupted, "For God's sake, let her feed it. I got enough of that at home with me own brats."

Pierre jerked his head towards the coach, and as if she were back in the Castle, Manoela turned slowly, and lowering her head, stepped back into the coach and shut the door.

"There! There!" she cooed, and soon there was no sound from within, and I faced Pierre, renewed hope of his mercy spurring me on.

"I can see you are a reasonable man, Pierre, and so," I reached my trembling hands to my neck and removed the diamond I remembered he coveted and handed it to him. Enery and Cockermouth eyed it disdainfully. Only Pierre smirked, "The star, by all that's holy!" and he snatched it in one motion and stuffed it in his pocket. "We'll leave the road before dark," he ordered. "Get on the horses lads, and tie the others together; we'll leave the coach here. Get in," Pierre ordered me. I left them gladly, and entered the coach again. Plucking my baby from Manoela's arms, I marvelled how peaceful he was. His eyelids drooped contentedly over rose pink cheeks.

"Stay calm, we daren't talk now," I hissed.

"I heard," she whispered, pulling her shawl tightly round her slim shoulders.

Later we left the coach and joined the others who had stopped work and were passing a bottle from one to the other. I settled Manoela on a trunk by a tree and placed Louis in her arms. I wrapped a fur tightly round them for a breeze had sprung up. I felt my throat constricting as I watched the ruffians plod through the dead bodies, kicking at them in their haste. I mouthed a silent prayer that Pierre wouldn't harm the child, knowing he believed that Louis was Manoela's. Thank God Louis had the same dark hair and eyes as Fernando and his sister!

"I'll gather our belongings. Where are you taking us?" I asked.

"We'll ask the questions," Pierre retorted. "Help get the trunks loaded on the horses. Fancy pickings they are, I'll be bound."

There wasn't a sign of another coach on the lonely road as it began to darken. I helped them as best I could, stalling for time, keeping my eyes averted from the mangled corpses and shuddered, realising that it would be dark very soon. The horses were frisky after their rest and tossed their heads.

"He's a bonny babe for a bonny lass, dark as midnight, like his Ma," Pierre flattered, wiping the neck of a wine bottle on his sleeve before he held it out for Manoela.

"N . . . no, n . . . no, thank you." She pulled herself away from him.

"Drink it or he'll push it down yer," Enery advised. She threw him a terrified stare from under raised brows.

"Shut up, Enery! It'll do you good, me lady."

Manoela began to shake visibly.

"My lady is cold," I advised, and gathered more furs from our trunks. "The drink will warm you, My Lady. Pierre is right." She stared up at me while I made myself busy tucking the rugs round her almost limp body. Then she lifted a pale hand for the bottle. Pierre's eyes glistened at the sight of her shining rings as she sipped from the bottle.

"If you'd be happy with the rings, I'm sure My Lady would be glad to make you a present of them," I tried hopefully. Cockermouth leered drunkenly,

"D'you hear that, lads. Present, ha! We don't want your presents; we take what we wants, right, lads?" and with that he lunged over and pressed his stinking mouth on mine. His grizzly beard scratched my tender cheek. His calloused fist fumbled at my gown, but Pierre pulled him off.

"I'm saving her for you, Cockermouth, but first to business. Come on! Pull the coach off the road and leave it with the bodies." I sat next to Manoela, and placed a comforting arm around her shoulders. She'd stopped shaking and handed me the bottle. I drank gratefully, and felt a little warmer. As they began to move the coach, I stood quickly.

"I'll take Louis now." Mercifully he stayed asleep as the wind whipped up and darkness fell. Shadows lingered behind the trees which rustled, whispering secrets of countless unknown robbers who had passed through the Pyrenees, and of their unfortunate victims.

The three of us huddled together beneath the friendly branches of one of the great trees.

"Be brave, Manoela," I whispered. "I feel we'll be all right.

Just do as I say. Pierre only wants our jewels. He'll let us go, I'm sure."

"How does he know you?"

"I'll tell you when all this is over; we must concentrate on staying alive for the present."

It was dark by the time the coach was off the road. The horses were led, and we were urged to walk in front over the gravelled, grassy roots and stones. Our delicate leather boots were poor protection as we stumbled and held the sleeping child in turn. Our only light was a lamp carried by Enery, its beam causing their faces to look eerie and more frightening than in daylight. It was no use trying to escape at this point, I was certain, for I didn't even know how far we were from a village. I had been much too busy with Fernando on the journey down from France to take much account of the distance. I sighed as I remembered his dear face and my throat filled with longing. Perhaps he was a prisoner somewhere, suffering a worse fate than we. I cuddled little Louis closer and felt the tears sting my eyes.

We were a few steps behind so we hurried to keep up with our rowdy captors. Fernando didn't even know he had a son. I refused to think that perhaps poor José was Louis' father. Manoela stumbled, bringing me back to reality with a start. Pierre heard her cry, and ran back to help her to her feet, but she cowered away from him, her face a ghostly shadow, her skirts blowing like clouds in the gusty wind. Thank God, I was carrying little Louis. Manoela limped beside me, her ankle twisted by the fall.

"How much further?" I asked, as large drops of rain began to fall from the black sky. But even as I spoke, we entered a small wood where branches crackled underfoot and foul smells filled our nostrils. The rain became heavier and pelted us mercilessly while the horses were tethered to a tree stump. Then we followed a few steps more to a ramshackle dwelling.

Chapter 20

The moon shone from behind the trees, showing the hut more clearly; a small, make-shift abode it was, but at least it had a roof. We were soaked to the skin by the time we were half pushed through the door. It creaked its welcome, and I could see a rough table and broken chairs, the rooftop black in the moonlight. A fallen bottle lay on its side and three mugs stood alongside. At least there were not more than three. We knew how many jailors we had.

"Get a fire going, and be quick about it," Pierre barked at me.

I was too tired to argue, and meekly handed the baby to Manoela and gently guided her to a chair. Looking towards the make-shift fireplace and the pile of logs in the corner, I removed my soaking shawl and set to work as Enery lit candles and shoved Manoela towards the other room. I followed them after kindling the fire. Soon tongues of flame caught the logs and twigs. Enery was hauling one of our boxes across the room, lifting our clothes out and flinging them into a pile.

"Pierre," I called, "Would you be kind enough to let My Lady and the baby share this room?"

Manoela just stared, the baby on her lap, from the corner of the dismal room.

"Shut up, you!" Pierre growled. "Make us some grub, and if it's good, I'll think about it."

The mention of food reminded me that we hadn't eaten since daybreak. I felt weak and my mouth moistened at the thought of it.

"Let me bring them to the fire, and I'll set to work right away."

I noticed they'd brought all our boxes of belongings by now.

"I'll need some dry clothes," I said and retrieved two boxes that I knew contained some of the baby's and our clothes.

"Only take the clothes, mind. The rest is ours now!"

I pricked my ears up to every word they spoke to each other, whilst appearing to only take notice of the cooking pots over the fire. I felt warmer after we had quickly changed our garments in the other little room. Manoela sat by the flickering flames, Louis curled up comfortably at her feet. Then, at my insistence, she wiped the table and rinsed the mugs in a bowl of water brought by Enery from I knew not where. It must have been her first attempt at domesticity. I knew she was better busy; it would stop her fretting. I pushed the thought of the sleeping arangements to the back of my mind, a habit I was becoming quite adept at. Meanwhile, I threw everything they brought me into the steaming pot of water, scraps of meat and vegetables.

"As long as we don't see no soldiers we're alright," Pierre said while biting into a hunk of bread.

They sat drinking round the table, wiping their mouths with the backs of their hands.

"No soldiers come up here, they're too busy fighting for their bloody lives at the border," Cockermouth interrupted.

"Are you sure they were all dead back at the coach?"

"I be a thorough worker. Dead as mutton chops, no trouble at all from them. With this little lot we'll be made for life."

Enery grinned, and laughed into his beard, "My missus'll be right pleased with me for once. She'll keep her bloody gob shut when I get back. Always saying we got no gold. Thinks I'm still in the army, she do. Might decide not to go back to her nagging, mind 'ee, this little filly'd suit me better, I reckon." He loped from the table, and before I realised what was happening, slapped me heartily on the backside. I gritted my teeth.

"Supper's ready. Help me to dish up, My Lady, please."

Manoela crept from the corner and passed the crude plates from the stew pot to the table. They slopped the food down greedily as did I; I couldn't get my fill. Only Manoela pushed the crude fare round her plate, her head held low, staring down. Pierre stabbed her in the ribs with his elbow.

"Eat up, me beauty, I likes me women with a bit of meat on their backsides."

Manoela leaned away from him, her terrified eyes about to pop. This was met with bawdy winks and guffaws.

"She isn't well, leave her alone! My Lady isn't over her confinement yet, she had a bad time."

Pierre guiltily shifted in his place.

"If she don't want good food, I'll have it then."

He let the stew drip onto his plate and mopped it up with a hunk of the rough bread. Then he leaned back and belched loudly with pleasure, rubbing his protruding stomach which overlapped the string holding up his breeches.

"That'll do for starters." Cockermouth complimented me. "Ye're not a bad little cook."

He stood, pushing back his chair and scratched his crotch absently. The fire flickered and threw red shadows over the men's faces. I was weary to the very bone, but knew I must not sleep yet. I had to try and bargain for our lives—and Manoela's virtue.

"Pierre, I think we should have a talk."

This was met with laughter.

"She don't waste much time, do she?" Enery shot at Pierre.

"Shut up, you! Talk away, me beauty. We've got the lot;

you, Me Lady here and the brat."

"Aye, we have that," the others agreed, "And wot's more, the valuables."

He let his grubby hand slide over my hip. I pushed his hand away.

"Get away from me! Do you realise who you are addressing?"

"It's *undressing* we'll be doing, eh lads?" Cockermouth lumbered over to the largest box that had been left in the room, and began to unbuckle it, removing clothes and flinging them at random round the room. Enery joined him, and donned a fur bonnet and muff. He made a moué and held his hands in front of him imitating a lady. This was much appreciated as he minced round the room.

"You've got all our belongings, let us have the horses at least, and by first light we can ride to the nearest village. We promise not to give you away."

Pierre clambered over and his blubbery lips parted, revealing the gap where his teeth had been. He grabbed my neck and pulled my head back, forcing me under his own ugly visage. Cheering went up from the others, but I kicked his shin with all my strength as the sweat trickled down the back of my neck. He let go of me and held his leg, cursing,

"You little bugger. You'll pay for that. Ye're not going nowhere. I ain't forgot the last time I had trouble with yer. Grab her, fellas."

My clothes were ripped off from the waist down, as my hands were held behind me. Quickly they pulled the top half of my clothing from my breasts.

"Swine! Swine! Vermin!" I shouted, "You'll be guillotined for this! My Lady's husband is a Spanish Don."

For an answer I received a hard slap across the mouth from Enery.

"That'll do her a lot of good here, eh lads?"

"A fat lot o' good," the others agreed as I was lifted and thumped onto the table, causing the contents to fall on the floor, scattering the dirty dishes. I caught a glimpse of poor Manoela, shaking with horror, her back flat against the wall, cowering like a captive animal as she stared through eyes wild with terror. Her mouth was open, but no sound emerged.

I felt hot stinking breath on my bare flesh, and as I tried to move I realized with utter despair that my hands were securely tied behind me, and then I felt the weight of a heavy body, legs astride me and I closed my eyes tight and bit the first thing that came into contact with my mouth. I tasted the bitter stale hair that must have been Enery's beard. I was slapped hard across the face. The blow jarred my teeth and made me dizzy, as I was entered by a bar of male flesh that tore in and out of me.

I was soaked with the sweat from his heaving body, my tongue trying to spit out the hair from his stinking beard. It was the first man I'd been with since Fernando had left. I tried to imagine it was Fernando on top of me, and before long I felt my body lift to meet the rhythmic movements.

"Ah, that's it, my girl!"

I tried to close my ears and just forget where I was. One last heave and he was through with me and rolled off the table, lifting his breeches sheepishly. I was about to sit up to wipe away the sticky mess from between my thighs when I realized my hands were still bound.

"Not so fast, me beauty. Fair's fair. I ain't 'ad my turn yet."

My heart sank. I had imagined my punishment was over. In spite of myself, I sobbed. The hot tears rolled into my mouth and I gulped, hoping Manoela had left the room with the baby. But before I could summon up enough strength to look, a hard calloused hand had cupped my bare breast, and wet lips sucked and kneaded the nipple.

"Not again, please not again. I'm in pain, please . . ." but I needn't have wasted my breath. Enery's beard brushed my wet cheek and he clapped his hand hard over my mouth. With one hand he turned me over.

"Pigs, let go of me!" but I was pinned down on my stomach.

"If you wouldn't fight so hard you could have it in comfort," Enery promised. "You'd enjoy it."

I looked up and spat at him. For answer he pushed my face down in an empty tin plate so that I couldn't speak or move. I didn't know who entered me from behind. It hurt terribly. My limbs trembled and I clenched my teeth with loathing. At first he plunged slowly, then harder and harder as I heard him panting. My eyes stung with tears and the pain was tearing me apart. I must have passed out for part of the time. The next thing I remember was Enery slapping my face with cold water from a jug.

"Come along, beauty, you're not going to let Cockermouth down, are yer?"

I realised that it must have been that swine Pierre that had nearly killed me. I tried to focus my eyes in the flickering room. I was aware that I was unclothed apart from my silk stockings, ragged and torn round my ankles, and a soft brown boot on one foot like a rag doll. Since my hands were no longer tied, I wiped my eyes. Manoela had gone, but the baby was sleeping peacefully by the fire. It was a miracle, I remember thinking, and was thankful for that at least. My heart sank with foreboding as I imagined what had been Manoela's fate. Greedy little hands were fondling my breasts. I slapped them away.

"You'll be tied up again for that."

"Where's My Lady?" I managed through swollen lips which felt huge. I could taste blood in my mouth.

"Never mind her, she's taken care of. She'll get her share, don't you worry."

I pushed him off me.

"Here, watch it, you. I'll call the others back if you don't behave, you little wild cat!"

I staggered on to the floor and realised that what was slowly seeping out of me was tinted with blood. The sound of moaning came from the other room, but as I tried to stand up, pain stopped me. I picked up my torn dress and slowly tried to wipe myself dry. I was raw and throbbed with pain.

"Is she in there?"

"Aye, she be asleep. A lot of good she be!"

At least I knew Manoela had been left in peace for the moment. Cockermouth lunged towards me as stealthily as a cat after a mouse. To scream was useless. I knew I might as well get it over with.

"Go on then, you pathetic excuse for a man. Are you sure you can manage?"

A shadow moved across his face and I was sorry I had tried to goad him. He pushed me against the door and banged my head against it, holding me by the hair.

"You'll see how I can manage, me fine lady." His words froze me, reminding me to watch my tongue if I wanted to survive.

"Some wine, I beg of you, or I'll be sick."

He released me suspiciously, examining my face for signs of trickery.

"The door's bolted. You can't escape me. Go and get some wine then, and be quick about it. Perhaps it'll make you more friendly. I want to get started. I saved you for last so I could have longer. Yer glad, aren't yer?"

I shuddered and forced the sour tasting wine down my aching throat, then filled the mug a second time. I felt him bite my behind, and whipped round as the mug fell from my grasp on to the mud floor.

"I likes a girl with passion an' a bit o' fire in her."

He pulled me towards his gnome-like form by the breasts. The feel of his bony fingers made me want to throw up. He pushed a leg between my thighs, and his organ felt hard as it pulsated against me. I fell to the floor and we rolled together. The stained coat of one of the dead coachmen lay on the floor, and it became our bed.

"No need to worry, we got all night," he grinned, panting as his raisin eyes caressed my body. "You're a bit too skinny for my taste, but you'll do nicely."

Rage welled up in me and I forgot to hold my tongue.

"You loathsome, filthy pig," I spat, "Get your smelly body away from me. You sicken me beyond words!"

He grunted, flattening me underneath him. Pierre's voice came from the doorway, "Want any help, Cockermouth?"

I cursed under my breath as Pierre came lumbering over and stood with his back to the fire enjoying the fact, no doubt, that I was pinned like a butterfly.

"Give 'er a clout, Cockermouth. It works wonders, she'll enjoy it more, they allas do."

"I'm not interested in her enjoying herself," he panted, "I knows she'll do that, don't I, lady?"

I was about to spit in his face, but he slid his heaving body up mine till he rammed his throbbing member against my mouth. With my legs free now I tried to roll over, but Pierre obliged and crushed my legs with his weight. My teeth were forced open and Cockermouth's revolting member pumped in and out of my mouth. I retched and gagged, certain I was about to choke as each second passed. I couldn't see and had no control; a helpless prisoner being doubly tortured. The pumping got faster and faster, and the pain became an agony. Then my mouth was filled with his warm, sticky juice and I vomited again and again until I was left in peace, exhausted and faint, unable to cover myself as the cold sweat began to dry on my ravaged limbs. I lay there a long time, and at last struggled onto my trembling hands and knees. I was shivering with cold and remembering with horror the ordeal I had experienced. I felt myself sway as I scrambled to my feet.

The fire was almost out and the only light was the grey dawn peeping through the cracked window. The smell was terrible. Vomit was all around me, but my first concern was for little Louis who stirred restlessly in his makeshift cradle. My legs sagged at the knees as I groped my way along the wall with one hand. I had to get warm, my teeth were chattering. I lit a candle from the last dying embers of the fire, and began slowly to clean myself as best I could. I must think clearly and unemotionally, I told myself. Manoela was relying on me. I was really the only one who could plan for our survival. I dragged my body to the cradle and heated the remaining milk for little Louis' breakfast. A wave of love descended over me as he drank lustily.

Chapter 21

I wasn't sure how long we were prisoners as one toil-ridden hour followed another. I tried to count the nights, but had to give up eventually, as days mingled into weeks and I became more terrified of never becoming free. I knew Manoela was being used as I had been, but my main concern was for the baby's safety.

I was awakened one morning by the sound of rain beating against the roof. Instinctively I knew that something was terribly wrong. The stillness was too intense. I blinked in the grey dawn light and squinted through half-closed eyes to where Louis was sleeping in his box by the fire. My heart lurched with relief to know that he was unharmed. He lay like an angel as unconcerned as if he were in the Castle, a pink thumb between his pouting lips. Turning, I touched Manoela's arm. My hand felt sticky, and I wiped it on my nightshift, and creeping out of bed I lit the night candle on the upturned box which served as a bedside table. I sucked in my breath at the brown stain which streaked down my nightshift, and saw that my nails were rimmed with the same congealed mess. My body began to shake as I stared at my hand and realized that Manoela was dead. I fell to my knees at the side of the bed, and touched her clear cold brow. Crushed with sorrow, I buried my face next to hers and bit the covers to stifle my screams of horror. I blamed myself for her death. It was because of me, I had done this! Impatient, refusing to wait for Fernando to return to me; bored in the Castle, selfish, only thinking of myself, that was why my lovely sister lay dead beside me.

Forcing myself to look at her, I held the candle up and peered down at her staring eyes, the blood-soaked garments and the filthy kitchen knife with only half a handle which was clutched tightly in her small pale fist. Strangled cries choked me, and I remembered that Manoela had never seen a man before. She must have suffered a hundredfold more than I had at those brutes' hands. And so she had taken her own life.

I'd never be forgiven for this. Fernando would hate me for the rest of his life. His Mother would convince him it was my fault, just as Don José's death had been because of me. Through the blur of my tears I whispered, "Forgive me, Manoela." I was naïve to have fallen into an exhausted sleep each night after one or all the men had used me. I thought even they would have been satisfied with me at their mercy without forcing their loathesome torture on Manoela who hardly spoke a work and never looked at them. We should have taken turns sleeping. In fact, no food had passed her lips since we were captured; dark shadows had appeared beneath her eyes and each day her nose became more prominent as the flesh fell away from her bones. She lay there in peace at last. I covered her gently with a rug. I closed my eyes and tried to pray for help for my child. I knew it wouldn't be long before one of the men came to use me and demand breakfast, and I trembled anew at the thought of how they would view this tragedy. If there had ever been any hope of their letting us go, now it was out of the question. They would be afraid of being implicated in Manoela's death. Panic overcame me, knowing I might be kept here with little Louis for ever, slaves to those animals. I began to tremble with fear again and in spite of being cold, sweat prickled my forehead.

There was nothing to lose now. I had to try and escape with Louis. Although we'd never been allowed outside, I knew the horses were still kept at the back of the place, because Enery always stank of horses. In fact, I could smell him from across the room. He would disappear for whole days, and return weighed down with meat and bread. But I'd never been able to see from which direction he'd come. Obviously there must have been a village half a day's ride away, I reasoned with myself. I looked at the narrow cracked window, wondering if I smashed the glass, if I could squeeze through.

They had been too careful for me to try to make a bolt for it till now. The only time I felt they were not watching us was when they had finished with me for the night and by then I'd been only half conscious with fatigue. I made up my mind to try when Enery made his next expedition. There would be one less to watch us, and I knew he would be off as soon as rations were getting low. Drying my eyes with the hem of my nightshift, I crawled out of the bed and dragged myself over to the window, but the only view was the trees dripping with rain; it wasn't possible to see further, we were completely hidden from view.

I sighed, and forced myself to think rationally. I kindled the fire and put the pot of water on to boil. It took me a long time. My fingers were clumsy and shaking with shock. Presently, Pierre appeared, scratching his chest through the shirt which he never changed, and yawning loudly, his bleary eyes heavy from sleep.

"What happened to My Lady last night?" I hissed, hardly recognising my desperate voice. He leered knowingly.

"A frigid little bird my Lady be, but she'll come round in time, they allays do."

He yawned again and scratched his stomach leisurely, like a cat.

"My Lady is dead," I told him tonelessly.

"Dead! Don't talk rubbish."

"Look! I pointed to the body on the makeshift bed. He lumbered over, "No, don't touch her."

"It's a trick, you nearly fooled me there."

"It's no trick."

Something in my voice must have warned him that I spoke the truth.

"What did she die of, shock?" he laughed cruelly, not caring a fig that the life of a lovely young girl had been wasted.

"She killed herself because of what you did to her. She was reared gently, not like me. She couldn't face any more degredation."

"That's too bad for her, then. Where's my breakfast, I'm hungry."

I couldn't believe that even he could talk of breakfast with a dead body only a foot away. He caught the look of shock I gave him.

"Enery! Cockermouth! There's work to do."

"I'll do it," I told him.

"Oh, no yer don't, you're not going out of here."

When the others appeared, dishevelled and bleary eyed, he told them, "My Lady done herself in, rather than submit to our charms. Ain't it a laff boys, eh?"

They both took an interested look at the body on the bed.

"Well, stone me!" Enery remarked, "Thought she was a nutter from the start, never speaking like that. I had to cover her face with a sack before I could touch her, couldn't stand her nun-like face."

"You swine!"

Rage welled up in me and I rushed at him with the skillet in my hand, smashing it in his face. Cockermouth dragged me away and flung me to the other side of the room where I crashed into the wall, dizzy and shaken.

"Get rid of her," Pierre ordered, "But first make sure it isn't some trick."

"Aye, don't worry. Come on, Enery."

Enery rubbed his face where the skillet had cut the flesh on his cheek.

"Little wild cat, you'll pay for this."

I watched while they bundled Manoela's body over their

shoulders between them, while Pierre sat ready to spring if I made a false move. The knife fell to the floor, and drops of blood dripped down. My stomach retched to see them manhandle her body as if she were no more than a bundle of rags. The noise had wakened Louis, but mercifully he was too young to know that his darling Tante Mella had gone from us forever. He just played with the coloured ball she'd brought for him from the Castle.

Chapter 22

The door banged shut after Enery and Cockermouth who were cursing under their breath. I stared at the dampened ground where Manoela's blood stained the earth and I swayed with grief, and the pain of having to watch her lifeless body taken to a pauper's grave.

"Can I look for a few wild flowers for her grave if I'm quick?"

Pierre continued to pick his nails with a knife and sucked at something in his mouth.

"Oh no, you don't. I warned you before. Now, get the breakfast going. It's too much fuss you're making, be thankful it isn't you they're burying with the brat."

With more strength than I knew I possessed, I held back the anger that boiled in me.

"If M'Lady weren't satisfied here, that's her look out, now get crackin'!"

Biting my tongue I listlessly walked over to the makeshift chair by the bed, and lifted my heavy brown dress off the back and stepped into it, covering my blood-stained nightshift. Pulling the pot over the fire to boil the water, I fed dollops of bread dipped in milk to Louis as the tears started to flow unchecked. The baby didn't seem to notice that they splattered on him. He just continued to break his fast as if the rotten hovel were a palace.

As usual after his tummy was full, Louis' eyes closed, and soon he was lost in slumber. As I gently lowered him into his box of straw, I realised that Pierre was snoring by the fire. Without wasting a second's thought, I snatched my baby and crept over to the door, undid the latch, and held my breath as I carefully shut it behind me. The others were nowhere to be seen. I came round to the back of the building, undid one of our dapple greys from the tree that glistened with rain. I crawled onto the mare's back, my son wedged in front of me, and instantly kicked her sides. The unexercised mare snorted, her head thrown back, and broke into a canter down the narrow path. I'd no idea which direction to take, just kicked her harder and whispered down into her ear, "Please, my beauty, this is a race for our very lives!" In answer she almost flew. As we reached the open plain, the sun glistened on the grass that was drying. Huge mountains rose to left and right, not a sign of smoke or a dwelling place as far as the eye could see. The fresh air caressed my face as I prayed with every hoofbeat that the men wouldn't come after us before we had reached safety. It became warmer as the day wore on and I was thankful that the child continued to sleep in front of me.

Not daring to look back, I kept alert for any sound of hoofbeats other than those of our mare, who raced as if she had wings. The journey seemed endless and I became dizzy with fatigue. Sometimes I wasn't sure if we were going backwards or forwards, and dreaded that the horse might collapse from lack of water. I promised myself I would stop when it grew dark, and try to work out where we'd reached. My hair was soaked with perspiration and my dress stuck to me like a second skin, tight and permanent. The mare began to slow her pace, and my stomach lurched with the dread that I'd pushed her too cruelly. We were passing more trees now, and dotted beside them were clumps of blue and yellow flowers. Louis was awake; I could feel him wriggling in front of me. I forced my voice to be light,

"Isn't this a lovely race, *mon cher*? Can you feel the mountain wind on your face?"

"Faster! Faster!" he shrieked; it was just a game to him. My throat ached from dust that seemed to fill my nose and mouth, and I whispered again in the horse's ear, leaning over and trying to control Louis' waving arms, "Just keep going, my beauty, and I'll water you soon!" As I straightened my back in the saddle, I wondered if I was in a trance. Blinking my burning eyes I imagined I saw, in the distance, a cluster of people, an army camp of sorts with soldiers and tents. As we drew closer their voices reached me and I knew by the colors of their great-coats that this was a French army camp. Feeling too dazed to shout, I pulled the reins in while Louis shouted,

"Battles and armies! Battles and armies!" and would have fallen as he stretched towards them if an open-mouthed officer had not caught him.

"*Sacrè Dieu*! A gypsy child, who'd believe he fell straight into my arms!"

Almost collapsing with relief, I was helped down amongst the laughing soldiers, some squatting at their fire, whilst others stood drinking.

"Water!" I begged, "Water for the love of God!"

"Your brat's got water, here, Gypsy."

A blond officer held a tin mug to my lips. I snatched it from him and drank deeply, holding it till I'd swallowed every lifesaving drop. Gasping I let my legs give way and lay in a heap on the cool grass and watched as my heaving mare was led away.

Most of the men didn't even toss me a glance, just continued playing cards or laughing with their comrades. A bowl of cognac was held to my parched lips as I saw little Louis high on a shoulder while he waved to me and called, "I'm a soldier, Mama, look at me!"

One of the men looked surprised at this.

"The brat speaks well for a gypsy."

"A woman at last!" another voice sighed.

"Only just," came the disgusted rejoinder.

"A woman is a woman, my friend. It will soon be dark."

I could have spat with disgust to hear their discussion as if I were to be sold. Could I look as bad as they agreed? Obviously I must. Considering how I felt, this was not surprising. My face was burning from the unaccustomed sun and wind, and I just wanted to sink onto the ground and sleep.

"Better take her out of the sun, Raoul, she's like a boiled lobster!"

I felt myself being carried inside a tent and laid on the floor that smelled of tobacco. Raoul, I wondered? No, it couldn't be the same Raoul. I blinked my eyes open,

"Raoul?" I croaked, eyeing him.

"My name is Raoul, Gypsy."

I was sure it was he; I couldn't mistake those slanty eyes and the thick voice.

"Raoul, it is you!"

"I'm afraid there must be some mistake."

"Don't you know me?"

He laughed, kneeling beside me. The relief of finding someone I knew, even one who wasn't a friend, was too much for me. I choked my sobs back at the thought of Raoul so long ago. He had treated me royally compared to those other swine.

"You don't recognise me?"

"I'm sure I would if I'd known you before. It's unusual for a gypsy to be fair-skinned."

He peered into my eyes.

"No, it can't be! *Mon Dieu!* Not Solange?"

"Yes," I spluttered, "It's me, Solange."

Raoul dabbed my brow with something cool.

"What happened to you, what are you doing here in rags?"

"Raoul, I've been a prisoner, miles from here with my baby. Where is he?"

I sat up, panic-stricken. He carried me to the sumptuous couch that smelt of leather.

"He's being bathed and dined in style." I breathed a sigh of relief and let my blistered hands be smoothed with ointment.

When I told him what had befallen us, he pronounced dryly that Don Miguel was unwise to allow three women and a baby to travel through the border with all the trouble there was at the moment.

"I insisted, Raoul. Please, just let me rest now."

"Of course you must rest. How stupid of me. Don't worry, Solange, I will order my men to find your jailers and your jewels will be returned to you."

He placed a tender kiss on my burning brow, and before I heard his footsteps disappear, I fell into an exhausted slumber. I slept for almost two days, as I later learned.

I awoke to cheers and the delightful sight of my son held high on an officer's shoulder, a hat half covering his face, a wooden sword tightly held in his hand. For one awful moment I remembered the knife Manoela had clutched such a short time ago. But I was pulled back to the present as little Louis smacked his officer on the head with his weapon and screeched with laughter.

"Soldier dead! Soldier dead! Fall down!"

He was thrilled at finding himself the center of attraction amongst all these burly soldiers in their bright uniforms. Raoul herded the men out with the child. His valet brought me a bowl of water and some food. Smiling down at me he said, "I'll leave you these breeches and things; they're the only clothes we have here."

I thanked him and as he turned on his heel I attacked the fresh bread and meat like a starving animal, then lay back and stretched lazily. I felt filthy, but rested, and bursting from the good solid food. The nightmare seemed far behind me as I swung out of the bed and realised that I did not have a stitch of clothing on. I laughed cynically. How could it matter, after all I'd been through, if Raoul had seen me completely naked?

As I vigorously scrubbed the grime from my body and washed my hair, I wondered if Raoul had news of Fernando.

It seemed a hundred years since I'd held my husband in my arms. With the knife from my dinner, I altered the breeches to fit me snugly, and the starched white linen shirt to hug my figure. The boots were hopelessly big, and so I continued to wear the red silk slippers I'd worn since my escape.

The tent smelled of tobacco, and neatly arranged on a small table were books and papers, men's brushes and clothes. Raoul returned as I tucked the shirt into my breeches. I recognised the admiring light in his eyes, sending a shiver of pleasure through me. He bent and kissed my breasts where I hadn't fastened the shirt.

"Raoul, you've been very good to me," I said.

He lifted my hand and kissed the palm. Not letting go, he told me, "We've caught your rogues, and they'll be properly dealt with. Apparently they have a price on their heads—wanted for murder for some time. I'm thankful you were not harmed more, my darling Solange."

I removed my hand. "Are you sure it's those men, Raoul?"

"Oh yes. They even found the body you mentioned, and a few other skeletons nearby."

I fell into the nearest chair, feeling shaky again.

"I'm sorry. Forgive me, sweeting. I know how you must be feeling. I'm a thoughtless swine!"

"No, you're not, Raoul. I'm grateful to you beyond words."

He strode over to the decanters on the table nearby and poured two glasses of cognac.

"You know I married Don Fernando, Raoul?" He drained his glass and showed his brilliant teeth, smiling broadly,

"Yes, I know that, sweeting, but I won't let that stand in our way, never fear."

I smiled back at him. It was such a relief to be in sophisticated company again, and he was most attractive, there was no denying it.

"We married in Toledo, but Fernando was called away the following day and no word has been heard of him since.

Do you think you could make some enquiries for me, Raoul?"

He pulled at his moustache, smoothing it, first one side, slowly, and then the other, "I'll see what I can do, certainly." He looked at me letting his eyes wander slowly over my face and shoulders, "Would you mind very much if he'd been killed?"

"Yes, Raoul, I'd mind very much indeed."

He sighed theatrically, "Very well, darling, I'll see what I can find out. However, I'm glad there is a favour I can do for you. I'd always hoped there might be," he said grinning.

He folded me in his arms then and held me, placing warm kisses at the side of my neck, causing my heart to pound. The blood throbbed in my ears while I felt his experienced hands caress my breasts through the shirt till they felt tight and the nipples rose and hardened. He drew away from me and stood, his eyes never leaving mine while he quickly removed his clothes and let them fall to the floor. He came towards me and I held my breath while he expertly rid me of my breeches, sliding them down my legs. How good and clean his body felt after the filth and torture I'd endured!

Raoul was a wonderful lover, considerate and sensual. He held his finger between my lips, then traced it down slowly till he'd reached his goal. I gasped and clung to him, feeling the hardness against me. I lied to myself that I was with him only to get news of my husband, but I knew as our bodies joined that I couldn't live alone in the hope that Fernando would come back to me one day. I needed to be loved now... now... We thrashed together on the crumpled bed, only the two of us living to give pleasure to each other.

"Darling Solange!"

"Yes, Raoul?"

"You do care for me, don't you?"

"You are an old, dear friend now, Raoul."

"Is that all?"

"No, that's not all. You're going to try and get news of my husband, aren't you?"

He slapped my derrière in mock regret.

"Will it be possible for my son and I to be escorted to Versailles today?"

"You can't wait to leave me when I've only just found you again!"

"If you get news for me I could stay till tomorrow."

I leapt away as he lunged for me and chased me playfully round the tent,

"Minx! Come here till I teach you a lesson!" I didn't really mind being caught in his passionate embraces again. I loved being petted and flattered by Raoul, he knew exactly what I wanted to hear.

The men took charge of my son. I think he reminded them of home. I hardly saw him while we were at the army camp. It was some hours later that Raoul brought me the news I was waiting to hear. We sat by the light of a lamp.

"Your husband is alive, as far as we know, but that's all we know."

"Thanks be to God. Where is he?"

"I'm afraid no one seems to know."

"Oh, that's ridiculous; they must know."

"No, he is doing important work for His Majesty, I gather. My friend would know if there were more news."

"I'll speak to your friend myself."

"He isn't here now, I'm afriad. You're lucky he hadn't left this morning. He had a bulletin for Paris."

"I don't believe you." I saw anger flare in his face. "Oh, I'm sorry, Raoul, of course I believe you. Will you arrange for us to leave in the morning?"

"In the morning," he promised as the lamp went out. I pushed him away from me in the dark.

"Now that I know Fernando is alive for sure, I don't feel I should let you make love to me."

He pulled me roughly to him, "I don't think you mean that, Solange. Shall I light the lamp?"

"No! No! Don't light it," I clung to him.

"I did get you the news. I didn't need to tell you", he breathed into my ear.

"I know, I know, that's true." His mouth closed on mine and we spent that night together, locked in an ecstacy of touching and tasting each other. Each hour seemed only a second as the warmth of his powerful body teased and thrilled me. We lay, our legs entwined, his hands caressing my buttocks, and suddenly he pulled me on top of him and sat me astride his slim hips. The moon must have been up, for a faint light revealed his eyes which burned with desire clearly written in them. I moaned as I felt him enter me and jogged up and down as on a horse, gasping with the joy he gave me. I held my hands behind my head because I knew he was admiring my breasts, closing my eyes as I began to ride him faster. That moment there was nothing but the two of us climaxing together again and again, till we lay back panting. Later he placed tiny kisses from my mouth down to my toes and I let my hand cover his limp manhood that had given me such endless pleasure.

Chapter 23

The following morning I couldn't help blushing as Raoul kissed his index finger and touched Louis' head while his men threw us knowing looks and smiles. We stepped outside where our horses waited, their coats glistening in the morning sunlight. The air was cool and smelt clean and fresh. Louis was snugly placed in front of an officer on a frisky black stallion. The officer's dark moustaches curled upwards proudly and he surveyed the scene around him as he gripped the child with one firm arm. In a flash Louis turned and gripped the moustaches with both hands, much to the delight of those of us who'd noticed.

"Gee up, soldier! Louis' in a hurry to race the horse."

But the officer didn't seem to be amused. He grabbed Louis' wrists, causing him to squeal. The officer's face had turned scarlet with embarrassment as his men chortled. "Perhaps Madame would care to play nursemaid to her offspring? I think it would be more fitting than for an officer of His Majesty."

I strode towards him, unencumbered by skirts for the first time.

"Stay with soldier boy. Go away!" Louis pulled sideways

but the officer had had enough, and held the child down to me smartly, as Louis kicked and shouted his disapproval. I slapped his legs.

"Soldiers don't kick, Louis, remember you must behave bravely." He eyed me, unsure of his position.

"Soldiers don't ride with their Mamas," came his quick retort.

"That is true," Raoul intervened, "Neither do they pull their fellow officers' moustaches. Perhaps if you were to apologize to the officer, he may decide to have you as his companion after all." Raoul exchanged looks with Officer Girard who seemed quite composed now that his precious moustaches were found to be undamaged. Louis looked up to the straight-backed officer and squinted in the sunlight. It was a long way up from the ground for one so little.

"I didn't mean to hurt you, Ossifer, but I've heard it said an army has to be on the move and we weren't moving."

This was met with raucous amusement from the men. They slapped each others' backs, eyes crinkling.

"He's as bright as his Mama," someone remarked.

Even André Girard showed smallish good teeth and held his hands down for Louis to be lifted up front again. "Very well, Soldier Louis. Move we shall, but," he grimaced firmly, "No more pulling of hair."

Louis' smile faded, "No . . . no more pulling, Monsieur."

Raoul lifted me up on my horse by the waist, "I'll miss you, Solange," he whispered.

"Thank you," was all I could manage, with so many eyes to watch our departure.

A small escort accompanied us, as we made our way home. The noises of the camp became fainter behind us as shouts of "Au revoir, Soldier Louis," were repeated. My son sat proudly, his little back straight, and with eyes sparkling he repeated again and again, "Faster! Faster!"

It was an almost cloudless morning as I remember, only a ribbon of grey a long way in the distance. I breathed the fine Pyrenean air that we would soon leave behind us. I loved the smell of the huge brown trees and the wild flowers, musky and scented, and I longed to sing. I remembered singing with Fernando long ago, and hoped I would soon know for sure where he was. I felt hot remembering my night of love with Raoul, and wondered if Fernando would understand and forgive me. I decided it was safer not to mention it. There would be quite enough explaining to do as it was. It felt unfamiliar riding astride the horse like a man in breeches, and I laughed to myself as I pictured Madame deMaintenon's face if she were to hear of it.

"Manners and etiquette, if you please!" I must have laughed out loud, for I felt the gaze of the dark-moustached soldier looking my way, eyebrows raised.

"We've a fine day for our journey, Madame," and his eyes lingeringly wandered over my tightly clad thighs; eyes that I felt could pierce through my very clothing.

I turned my nose up at him, causing his face to darken. He whipped his horse and little Louis shouted, "Hurrah!" and we all rode faster while the dust rose in clouds around us.

Hours later, after a mercifully uneventful journey, we entered a village of cottages, a few peasants pushing carts in the lazy afternoon. Little white cottages were clustered around a green. Our horses slowed their pace, and I wiped my hot brow and pushed the strand of damp hair that had fallen across it. A one-legged tinker blinked up at us and doffed his tattered black hat as his mangy brown dog barked, much to the delight of little Louis. André raised his hand as we approached the village Inn. The distant sound of the smithy, low and drowsy, seemed fitting on such a golden, sleepy afternoon. As the horses clop clopped to a standstill, the stable lad ran forward, and when we dismounted, led them away to be watered.

"Bonjour, Monsieur," the groom said sullenly. I looked round for André, but he was already carrying Louis towards the door and turned, waiting for me to follow. I realised with a laugh that the boy had taken me for a man. I'd forgotten I no longer wore the accustomed petticoats. My legs were stiff as I made my way and entered under the swinging sign "The Black Bull" into the dark, flagged parlor. There were hats and tankards and riding crops on the scrubbed table. Before the open hearth stood two gentlemen straddle-legged, surveying the room with total indifference. Although I longed to continue the journey after a short rest, I realised it would be better for Louis to have a proper night of sleep. After I'd settled him in our room, and watched him eat ravenously, I decided to eat my meal in the parlor. André rose and offered me a seat.

"Thank you, Monsieur." We touched tankards and I let the weariness slide from my muscles, stretching my legs out to ease them.

"Will you do me the honor of eating with me, Madame?" I saw the two gentlemen exchange knowing looks, thinking we were sodomites, no doubt. But André hadn't seen them. "The venison looks edible."

"Thank you, Monsieur, Master Louis enjoyed his dinner, it was most kind of you to wait for me."

He flushed his pleasure. The scruffy-looking serving wench refilled our tankards and I was conscious of sloe eyes looking sideways into mine. I didn't give the matter much thought, till I felt a soft breast brush my shoulder. Putting my tankard down abruptly, I turned to face her. She smiled, revealing long buck teeth. She looked back over her shoulder as she wriggled her fat behind on the way back to the kitchen. I couldn't understand why the untidy wench was casting languishing glances at me, till André laughed seeing my puzzled expression. He stretched his small feet near the fire, causing the highly polished leather to glow in spite of its thin layer of dust.

"Don't you realise, Madame, the poor wench takes you for a brave young soldier?"

"Oh! Of course, how stupid of me! The sooner I return to my gowns the better." I lifted my tankard of spiced wine and felt relaxed from the fire and the filling meal. "I'll bid you a good night, Monsieur." I rose and imagined I saw a disappointed frown. "Where are the men, by the way?"

"Oh, they're gone to the village bawdy house," he said rising, and slowly pulled his moustaches. "I had thought perhaps you would honour me with an hour of your company this evening?"

"I'm sorry, Monsieur, you must excuse me, I'm very tired."

He bowed a little stiffly, I thought, "Then I bid you a good night." I almost felt guilty as his disappointment showed clearly in the sag of his shoulders as I turned and knew he watched me leave the parlor.

The door to my room creaked as I slowly opened it, not wanting to disturb my son. There was no need for this precaution, I was pleased to see. He was breathing evenly, and smelt of damp warm washing drying in the sun at Clagny. How I wished that Grandmère had lived to see what a fine boy I had! Smiling to myself I imagined how proud Fernando would be to know he had a son. I removed the pink thumb from Louis' mouth, and gently tucked the coverlet under his chin. The strength of my love overwhelmed me as I stared down at the tousled curls and plump cheeks against the pillow. There was a subdued rattle, and I had the uneasy feeling that we were not alone. Spinning round I faced the buck-toothed wench half concealed in the shadows of the four-poster bed. She curtsied, smiling slyly.

"Get out of here," I hissed.

"I brought a jug of wine, Monsieur."

"I don't want your wine, you'll wake the child. Now, get out!" She placed the flagon firmly on the table by the bedside.

"What's the matter, ain't I good enough for you?"

"I should explain, perhaps. It's my fault. I'm the mother of this child. Wearing breeches, I grant you, because of an unfortunate accident, so perhaps it's an excusable mistake on your part." I waited for her to go, but she stood there grinning, the teeth seeming to glow in the half light and protrude further from her mouth.

"It don't make no difference to me." She smoothed the bed quilt with a sensuous gesture. I took a step forward to seize her arm and thrust her out of the room, but with a lithe unexpected movement, she slid close to me and clamped her arm round my waist. Jerking my head back in dismay, I felt her other hand fumbling with the buttons on my jacket which hung loosely on my shoulders. Her hot wine-moist mouth pressed against my flushed face.

"Get away from me." I used all my strength to push her away, but she was no court lady. Her body was coarse and muscular, and her rough hand slid up from my breast and clamped itself round my chin, striving to pull my mouth to hers. I pushed her chest hard. "Slut, you disgust me!"

She slipped back suddenly. "Oh, you're choosy, mistress, think yourself too high and mighty to have a bit of sport with a peasant girl. Come on now, you'll enjoy a little kiss and cuddle."

I wanted to yell, but feared to wake the child. "Out! before I take a whip to you."

Her shallow skin flushed with fury as she snatched a pillow and stood with it poised over little Louis' face.

Chapter 24

"If you can't bring yourself to lie with a peasant girl, I'll suffocate the brat." By the look of mingled desire and venom in her narrowed eyes, I knew she wasn't bluffing. Without thinking I flung myself at her throat, but she was too quick for me and stuck out a clumsy foot and I fell headlong onto the floor.

"Well?" she questioned. I felt giddy as I groped along the mucky floor and pulled myself up by the carved bedpost. She lifted a finger on which hung a large iron key, and swung it slowly, tantalisingly. "You're going to have to pay for this key in my coin." Seeing the disappointment I must have showed, she assured me, "We won't be disturbed, I'm the innkeeper's wife, you see."

Deciding the only thing to do was to humour her, I said, "Please go away, I'll give you money."

"But it isn't money I want." She came towards me and pushed me on to the bed, causing it to creak. She forced her too-fleshy tongue into my mouth and I began to shake. "You're shivering," she said, "Take your clothes off, and I'll warm you."

"No, I'm warm, really I am." I let her remove my coat and

rather than have her rip my shirt I removed it slowly, stalling for time, praying for someone who would interrupt this unwelcome tête à tête. But the only sound was the distant hoot of an owl, lonely and eerie. I folded the shirt and was about to place it on the bedside table when she grabbed my arm and the shirt fell to the floor. She pulled me on top of her and placed my hand in the furrow of her flat breasts. Then I felt stumpy fingers grind my buttocks.

"I always get on better with women than with men, don't you, dearie?"

"Oh, God, no, no I don't." I pulled myself to a sitting position. "I've never thought of women in the way I think of men."

"Well," she coaxed, "Never too late to learn." She let her sausage-like fingers fumble down to stop between my legs causing me to dread what was coming next. The baby sighed and turned, oblivious of his bed-partners. In a panic I jumped from the bed fearing to let those fingers explore me further. She lunged at me, but in my panic I sidestepped her, and grasped the flagon by the neck and brought it down with all the strength of my terror on that shaggy head. The thick glass splintered and wine ran in rivulets as red as blood as she cried out and recoiled, clapping her hands to her wet face. The movement dislodged the key and it clattered to the floor. Snatching it up I lifted the shattered flagon, and thrust its jagged edges towards her face. She turned her head with a snarl.

"Get over there, away from the bed," I ordered. As she backed away I edged towards the door, and groped with my other hand towards the lock. After several ineffectual probings, I managed to turn it and flung the door wide. Waving the flagon menacingly, I motioned to the woman to get out. She slunk away, casting malevolent glances at me, and as soon as she was clear of the door, I slammed it and not only turned the key in the lock, but slid the bolt. Then my strength drained away and I leaned against the door, my heart thudding until I could cross the room and fall on my knees beside the bed. The angel child had not stirred during the whole commotion. Too exhausted to undress further, I edged myself on to the bed and lay down. I didn't stir from the room until I heard André's voice, and knew it was safe to venture forth.

My jaw hurt, but otherwise I felt all right as we joined the men to eat before we left. André and his bleary-eyed men stared at my bruised face,

"My son hit me by accident," I told them. The men gave a knowing look to André, and laughed. I held Louis close, thankful that he was unharmed. André clamped his mouth shut, then stood abruptly,

"It's time we were off," he ordered. "We've more important matters waiting than to escort Madame to Versailles."

The men obeyed, sensing that this was a time to humour him, and drank their wine. At that moment the inn wife made an appearance and glowered from an unwashed face, and I was pleased to see that she had come off worse than I had. I kept Louis close to me while he banged a crust of bread on a pewter mug.

"André, please be seated for just a moment."

He frowned and I put his ill-humour down to the wine he'd drunk the night before, and decided to overlook it. All I wanted now was to get away from that foul inn.

"I would like a word with you, please."

The men ambled from the room and André sat, lifting Louis from my arms, and proceeded to ply him with milk, dipping the bread for him to suck and then chew with gusto. The innkeeper's wife retreated to the back of the room and began clattering mugs and plates.

"It's incredible what such a tiny fist can achieve," André observed eyeing my swollen jaw in disbelief.

"I'm sorry, André, I've had a terrible night," I hissed. "That woman made me her prisoner."

"What, not again, please Madame!" He laughed sarcastically. "You surely don't expect me to arrest her."

I stamped my foot, "Believe what you will. It happens to be the truth. I would that I'd spent the night with you."

He flushed unbecomingly. "If that's meant to be a compliment it's a very poor one, Madame. If what you say of the inn wife is true, I've no doubt you got what you deserved. And now it's time we were on our way."

He rose, placing little Louis on his shoulder and was rewarded with a clunk from the mug on his head. "Sacre coeur! What a family!" he expostulated, "We'll all be wounded before we meet the enemy!"

I shot him an angry glance and taking my arm, and little Louis under his other, we walked haltingly towards the door where the inn wife stood, arms akimbo, teeth to the fore.

"Pity you're going so soon," she sneered. "We could've found something to amuse you, I'm sure." The next instant she lay sprawled at our feet. "Oh dear me, how clumsy I am, André. I seem to have missed my footing. Would you mind moving over a little because we can't pass you," I asked sweetly of the inn wife standing over her. But André was already stamping over her to open the door.

"Get off me," she howled, grovelling, and grabbed his booted foot, but he was too quick for her and pulled it away. I tried the door but she was too close for me to squeeze through. She threw curses at us as she pushed herself up,

"Think they're gentry, the stinking army!"

"I've improved your appearance," I shot at her as we made our way out, "You look almost presentable without those teeth."

We ducked and ran as pewter plates and mugs came hurtling after us. We gasped in the cold morning air from the exertion as we mounted our horses in double quick time and galloped off, a screaming inn wife in hot pursuit, waving her fist, causing the men much amusement. Little Louis mimicked her brilliantly, waving his tiny fist,

"Cochon! Cochon!" he shrieked, wriggling on the saddle before me.

It was a long tiring day, our only stops behind bushes when nature forced us. André's temper had improved as the day wore on, and now he seemed anxious to please. I could hardly contain myself when at last I recognized the country lanes on the outskirts of the Palace as the night sky drew in around us. After Louis had sat with André for a few hours, he strapped him on my back and Louis slept the rest of the way. When we trotted into the environs of the Palace, it was hard to believe that at last we had arrived. We reined in, and André lifted down the drowsy little boy. I was too stiff to move, and had to be helped down. My feet felt as though they didn't belong to me and every bone in my body was making its presence felt. All I longed for was to get out of the soiled clothes I had lived in for so long, and resume my petticoats.

Thankfully when I reached my chambers and enjoyed the luxury of going clean to bed, I swore I'd never take another journey.

My tiredness swept away and I became exhilarated as I realized that very soon now the King would see my son and at last he might tell me of Fernando's whereabouts. My last thoughts were of my husband as sleep came to claim me.

Chapter 25

Far too soon I was awakened by a familiar voice. As I blinked in the candle-light, it took me a few confused moments to remember where I was. Propping myself on an elbow I cried out, unable to believe what my eyes confirmed. Reaching up I held my arms wide,

"Fernando, I can't believe it, you're safe. Oh! Fernando dear heart!"

He scowled and drew away and I let my arms drop as my heart sank.

"Don't be angry, we've been apart so long!"

He stood beside the bed, hand on hip. I took in the lavender satin breeches and purple velvet coat. "I've reason to be angry. Why did you leave my Father and sister? I imagined you all safe in Spain," he stormed, pacing up and down the room, flinging his arms about. I felt ill at the mention of Manoela.

"I've ridden a long and hazardous journey just to be with you!"

"How dare you traipse halfway across Europe when we are at war, you thoughtless woman!" He continued to pace the room, thumping a fist into his palm all the while. "Well, how could you? What of my father and Manoela?"

The thought of telling him what had befallen his sister made me feel faint, and I lay back on the pillows. Suddenly he stopped shouting and strode towards me.

"Why don't you answer me? Are you sick, Solange? You've gone quite pale suddenly."

I forced myself to speak in spite of the fear that gnawed inside me, "I'm more than sick," I faltered. The beautiful dark eyes softened as I felt mine fill with tears. I held my hands over my face and cried silently and uncontrollably. Feeling his strong arms around me, familiar after all this time, I longed to bury my face in his chest and let him comfort me, but it was much too soon for that. I choked a sob back. He kissed the top of my head, then, taking my hands in his, he pressed my wet fingers to his lips. I could see by the light of the flickering candles as his eyes held mine that he did still care for me. Perhaps it would have been simpler if he didn't, then my task might have been easier.

He would have made love to me then, and although I ached for him, I pulled away. He seemed surprised.

"My robe, please." He gathered it up for me, and I tied the blue silk about me and swung my legs over the edge of the bed.

"You must realize I've been out of my mind with worry about you all, and not one word have I heard from you in all this time, Solange."

"Don't you talk to me of worry," I screamed. "How *dare* you expect word when we never knew where you were, or even if you were alive or dead," and I glared up at him. His face fell,

"But my letters?" He rose, frowning, and pouring some wine, brought it to me.

"Somebody may have received letters from you, but not your father, and certainly not I."

He sank down into a chair and pushed a hand through his heavy black hair. "I think I know who has the letters." He sounded tired suddenly.

"Who?" I asked, "Who could have them?"

"My stone-hard Mother."

"The Iron Butterfly? Of course," I whispered. I should have guessed, she was the only one who never seemed worried." Rage boiled in me. "How could she do this to your Father, apart from me? It's made him ill."

He lifted his head, his eyes clouded over with concern, "How ill is he?"

"Don Miguel is very weary, but I'm sure if he knew you were safe he'd feel in better health."

Fernando shook his head. "I should have sent my letters to be delivered personally, not to the household, but it's a treacherous time, and everything I wrote had to be in code anyway. There are so many spies in the army. Forgive me, Solange," he croaked and held his arms out to me, but I eyed him suspiciously.

"What have you been doing at Court while I've been nearly killed trying to find you? Having a fine time I see," noting the exquisite lace ruffles at his throat, caught with an amethyst pin. "You don't look half a soldier."

"Ha! Rubbish and poppycock; you're jumping to conclusions as always." He stood leaning against the mantel, raising a goblet to his lips.

"Well, what have you been doing that made you forget you had a wife?"

"I've only been at Court two days on His Majesty's orders. Don't let's spend our time quarrelling." He came towards me, "Although I always loved you best when those green eyes flashed in anger." He smiled at me for the first time, causing my heart to lurch, and I noticed how thin and drawn his face had become. I longed to caress the tired lines and comfort him. I moved to the green chaise longue and beckoned for him to sit next to me, and searched my mind how to break the terrible news gently. But there was no way. As he sat down his nearness made me tremble. I reasoned that Fernando was a soldier and could take the truth straight and blunt.

"Manoela is dead!"

I saw the shock in his face, and the color drain away. His lips moved, but no word would come. I put my hand on his arm, "Hush! I'll tell you," then haltingly I told him the story of Manoela's death.

He turned his head away and spoke quietly in a dull monotone,

"You've always brought trouble to me. By what right did you take my sister from her home? I haven't forgotten Don José."

I felt myself turn cold, and bit my lip. I tried to reason with him, but suddenly there was a noise at the door. Who could be interrupting us at this worst possible moment? It was little Louis, scampering ahead of his nurse.

"Maman! Maman!" he shrieked, flinging himself into my arms. I felt his warm cheek against my wet one.

"Leave us, please," I told the startled nurse. Little Louis pushed a jester on a stick into Fernando's still fingers, causing the bells to tinkel around the colored hat of many hues.

"Who is this child? He calls you Maman."

"Don't you recognize him, Fernando? He is your son."

He forced himself up and stood in front of me, "He may be your son, but he certainly isn't mine."

"He is your son, I swear it, Fernando! He's beautiful! I thought you'd be proud to have so fine a son."

"A son who limps?"

I stared at Fernando. I had noticed no irregularity in Louis' gait.

"It's not a limp, he's not deformed, he must have hurt his leg at play. He *is* your son, your father will bear me out!"

"That's safe to say when he's in Spain and you're in France, but he is an appealing child and if he *were* my son I'd be worried about that leg."

Louis poked fat fingers into the sides of Fernando's mouth, hoping to coax him into a smile. In spite of himself, his lips curled up. Little Louis' happiness was so infectious. "Man won't play," he said, flourishing his jester again, but Fernando held him at arms length. Louis pulled himself away and hurled the jester along the floor dejectedly.

"Why does his foot turn out when he pushed himself up to

walk?" Fernando enquired. "Perhaps his father had a limp."

"Whatever it is, he'll grow out of it. He's seemed all right up to now."

"I suppose you've left him to his nurses all the time while you've been off enjoying yourself?"

I leaned back drained of emotion, knowing he had made his mind up not to believe me.

"If this is your idea of a joke, it's a very cruel one even for you. Your son is perfect!"

"Ha! My son! I've got to admire you, brazen as hell. But you won't catch me with that one. My son! Ha! It's a good one, I'll grant you. Quick too, but it's the last lie you'll tell me." He walked away from me and kept his back to me, and I could see he was shaking with emotion. Suddenly he turned, eyes narrowed. "When was he born?"

"December," I whispered proudly.

"Ha!" he sneered, "Worked it out well, haven't you? Was he born with a malformed leg?"

"What are you saying?" I jumped from the chaise and clawed at his shoulder, crying, my face distorted. He grabbed my wrists.

"I see you hadn't noticed. Calm yourself, Solange. Have you had the physician examine him?"

"Well, I only got back late last night. We've been journeying so long."

"You must have the physician examine him at once. I'll see if I can get Fagin for you."

The more I dwelled on it the more anxious I became. "I never noticed the child limping before. Perhaps he was just acting with the jester. Yes, that's it, he was pretending. He loves playing pretend." Perhaps he really had been play acting, but the physician would set my mind at rest. The more I thought about it, the more I realized Fernando was right. His leg did give way under him at times, but I'd thought that was normal for a child learning to walk. Had I chosen to ignore a truth I couldn't bear to face?

Fernando left the room and soon returned with Louis. I was about to go to my room, but Fernando stopped me,

"No! You stay there," he commanded. "Be a big soldier and march to your dear Mama." Louis drew himself up proudly, cheeks puffed out with importance and marched as I watched horrified. One leg dragged slowly after the other beneath his petticoats. As he reached me I shook him.

"Why are you pretending to have a bad leg? Tell me at once! Perhaps the new Court jester I heard of has a funny leg. Has Pampillon got a funny leg?"

"Stop it, Mama," he wriggled away, and I sat him on the floor. I looked over at Fernando, sick at heart.

"Wait here. I'll see if I can get Fagin."

"No, don't go yet. I want to talk to the King first."

"The King would wish it."

"Perhaps you're right. Send for Fagin."

He left us and Louis began to play, swinging on the heavy silk drapes like any normal, healthy child. I grasped at any straw.

"Louis, come here a moment, mon cher."

"No," he continued swinging on the curtains, so I went to him. Lifting the dress I probed his chubby legs from thigh to knee, then down to his ankles. They felt perfectly firm and sturdy.

"Let Maman take your shoe off."

"No! Maman, swing on curtain like Louis!"

"Do as you're told, Louis." I pulled at the blue silk shoe till it came away, and he kicked at me.

"Go away, Louis playing." His round cherub face filled with mischief as he continued swinging, happy and contented. Hope returned that there was little amiss. I shouted for the maid and hurried into my clothes, hampered by my mischievous child. A page brought hot chocolate, but I had no appetite.

How glad I was that I'd been given my old apartments, my gowns still in the *garde robe*. My fine chocolate-colored silk gown felt like the caress of a summers' day, soft and delicate, and warm to my skin. When Fernando reappeared, he'd changed into a smooth-clothed brown coat, the color I liked him in best.

"Fagin was with the King, who is delighted to hear of your return."

"Fagin is coming then?"

"The King insisted that his personal physician should see the child, as I knew he would."

"Thank you, Fernando. You are still in favor with his Majesty it seems?"

"I did manage to track down a spy from Spain, who had infiltrated the very Palace and done untold damage. His Majesty and his Ministers have known of the existence of a spy for a long time; it took me more than a year to find him. Anyway, he won't worry us any more. The King is most relieved."

"He must be. It can't have been an easy time for you, then, either." I tried not to let the pride I felt for him creep into my voice, but it came out a little breathless. Fernando seemed glad that I was so obviously impressed.

"There were moments when I only dreamed of food or of lying on a clean bed. However, I was lucky. I was only wounded once, but it held me up for weeks, freezing in the mountains with only an old goat for company."

I lifted a hand to his face, and stroked the tanned cheek where the bone stretched the skin. "Where were you wounded, Fernando?" but before he could answer, Louis crashed into him squealing. Fernando removed him from the curtain and we went next door to my sitting room.

Presently Fagin appeared.

"My dear Mam'selle Solange! . . . er Donna Solange I should say," he smiled through thick lips and bowing slightly from a heavy waist. I rose and was about to explain about Louis' leg, but he held up a hand to stop me.

"I see we have a soldier in our midst. Perhaps you would march over to the door," he asked Louis. As the child eagerly obeyed, Fagin pursed his full lips and stroked the hooked nose. "I think I should enjoy playing battles and armies, if you would be good enough to leave me with the soldier for a while. I know a very good game." Louis came running back. I hadn't dared to look till now.

"Yes, battles and armies," Louis mimicked, and stroked his own tiny nose, just as Fagin had done, causing us all to laugh. Fernando and I exchanged glances.

"I see I shall have to watch myself with this young man," Fagin laughed.

Fernando and I sat across from each other in a window embrasure overlooking the park, brilliant in the morning sun. The flowers were abundant, just as I remembered them. For a while we had no words for each other, our thoughts were with the physician and child in the other room. Then I grew restless and pleated my handkerchief, waiting for news.

"I wish he'd hurry, what can he be doing all this time?"

"Perhaps playing battles and armies," Fernando suggested, and stroked his nose. I smiled, in spite of my fears. "Does anyone else know about Manoela?" Fernando suddenly asked. I sucked my breath in sharply, but I could see he didn't really blame me in spite of his anger and grief.

"How could anyone know? Who was there to tell? After we escaped my only thought was to find you."

"But your jewels: it seems to me rather strange that these savage murders never bothered with any of your gems?" I felt his eyes fasten on my emerald ring that he'd given me for our betrothal.

"It would seem strange, you are right. I was fortunate to have them returned to me." I saw his eyebrow lift quizzically, ready to disbelieve whatever explanation I gave him. "You remember I told you after we'd escaped I..."

"Pardon, Madame." We both looked up. A page bowed, "Dr. Fagin would see you now."

We both rose and hurried back without another word. I waited with bated breath, till Louis' nurse took him away for his *petit dejeuner*. "Be a good boy, *mon cher*," I called after him, trying to keep my voice bright, but all I could see was the dear little leg tiredly dragging along. I vainly tried to read the diagnosis on Fagin's jowled countenance, but there was no sign of a good or bad decision.

"I've given the child a thorough examination and I find an interesting condition, yes, most interesting, not dissimilar to that of the Duc du Maine when he was a child. I believe Master Louis has not reached his first year. I find this hard to understand; are you sure you have your dates correct?"

"Quite sure," I answered.

"Well, he is most lucid. If you were to say he were two I should not be surprised."

"He did speak and walk early," I replied proudly. "I know the Duc du Maine limps, but his health is good now. Does that mean that Louis will limp all his life?"

"We can't tell."

"What is wrong with the leg?" I begged, "What's caused it to be slow?"

"In my opinion I'd say it's a birth injury, they're very common."

"But he never limped before," I said, puzzled.

"Was it a difficult birth?"

"Everything seemed normal at the time," I assured him.

"As I wasn't at the confinement I'd have to discuss it with those who were," the doctor informed me.

"I gave birth in Spain."

"Hmph! I will bring my associate to examine the child further if you wish, he will need to be watched and treated at once."

Fernando thoughtfully said, "What treatment would you recommend?"

"We could put the leg in irons."

"No!" I screamed, and felt Fernando take my hand. "Forgive me, I didn't mean to shout."

"I will personally see to it that the leg is stretched regularly, otherwise it won't grow properly." I listened with terror as Fernando guided me to a chair.

I remembered the snide remarks of the village children about anyone who was different, and imagined how much worse it would be here at Court where beauty was worshipped. Fernando interrupted my thoughts.

"The Duc du Maine is still the King's favorite son, even if he does limp, and there doesn't seem to be much wrong with him or little Louis, does there?"

"Not much wrong?" I shouted, "He'll limp all his life!"

Dr. Fagin bowed. "Please don't worry unduly, Donna Solange, he's a sturdy little fellow and sharp too."

"Thank you," I sighed, "It was good of you to see us so promptly."

"Not at all, don't hesitate to send for me when you have decided to take my advice."

"That's out of the question!" I told him.

Fernando tried to comfort me. "He doesn't seem to think the leg is very bad."

"He didn't even say *why* he's limping."

"Because he doesn't know. Doctors can offer only an educated opinion remember, they are not Gods."

"We'll probably never know what caused it, not for sure."

"The main thing is that he is healthy and with care he'll improve."

"What of the smirks behind his back when I'm not there to protect him?"

"Don't worry, Solange," he pressed my hand, "We'll look after him."

Did this mean he accepted Louis as his son, I wondered? He guided me to the chaise.

"You don't want to take your place at dinner?"

"I haven't the strength."

"I think you'd be wise to rest." As I lay down he held my hand in his again. "I'm going to send a letter to my father. I'll have to tell him about Manoela's death."

"I hope the shock won't be too much for him."

"I pray not. I'd go myself, but the King still has need of me. I'll assure my Father that you and Louis are safe."

"He loves the child, Fernando. Tell him Manoela wouldn't want him to grieve."

"I know. I give thanks that he arrived here safely with you after such a terrible ordeal. I could have lost you all."

He rose after placing a kiss on my hand, then left me to my thoughts. Did I sense a coldness in him? I wasn't sure. It must have been a shock, seeing his son when he didn't even know of his existence. It must upset him that the child's leg wasn't normal, equally as much as I. I lay there, my mind going over all that had happened these past months, and didn't dare to close my eyes. I wanted to memorize my surroundings and feel quite sure that we were safe. There was a faint knock on the door, then a maid ushered Madame de Maintenon into my bedchamber.

The old woman was stouter and greyer than I remembered, but seemed pleased to see me. She clasped my hands in hers.

"And how are you feeling after your adventure, child? No, don't get up, I will sit." A waft of the perfume she always wore filled my nostrils, bringing back memories. She flounced her black taffeta dress and made herself comfortable.

"You honour me with this visit, Madame. I feel quite well, thank you."

"Don Fernando has presented your son to me, a most beautiful child. He bowed delightfully."

A glow of pleasure swept over me. "Thank you, Madame, but..."

"But what?" Madame enquired.

"Did you notice his leg?"

"Yes, I did notice that one of his legs seemed a little tired. The Duc du Maine had a similar condition as a child, and that is what I am here to talk to you about. You must not allow the physicians to pull the leg on that rack contraption they have. They pulled the poor Duc du Maine's until the bad leg was longer than the good one, and made it very weak.

"Oh, so that's why he limps now?"

"Well, I'm not sure, of course, but I put a stop to all that agonizing stretching."

"Is it true that the Duc's leg is half paralyzed?"

Madame pursed her lips tightly and didn't answer me.

"I didn't mean to speak out of turn, Madame, but I'm so worried!"

She patted my hand, "Of course, you are, child, but there

is really no need. I will take him for the healing waters as I used to take darling Mignon. There will be no stretching on that rack contraption."

"You are very kind, Madame."

She rose heavily. "The waters of Bourbon have excellent healing properties. When you are feeling stronger I wish to hear all that you have been through." I felt myself redden. Madame smiled, "Well, perhaps not all. A few prayers would not go amiss, I think."

"Yes, Madame."

"I always knew you were a bright child. We are thankful that you and your child have returned safely to us." I thought I detected a twinkle in the old eyes.

"Thank you, dear Madame."

"The King is very glad, and looks forward to speaking with you this evening, so try to sleep now." She smiled and looked down on me fondly, her large dark eyes examining me closely. She patted my hand again. "You have been through a great deal, child, I can see. Perhaps you are one of those people who invite trouble, but I am sure that is not so. I think you cause a great amount of jealousy for some strange reason." My eyes widened in surprise. "Always remember to say your prayers, Solange."

"Yes, Madame, I will."

She left me then. I felt strangely soothed by her visit, and drifted off to sleep.

When I opened my eyes I felt there was something not quite right and then I remembered, and my heart sank. Little Louis' leg. But it wasn't so very bad. Hadn't Madame de Maintenon assured me of that? And she'd promised to look after him as she had the Duc du Maine. I wondered if she was fit to travel all the way to Bourbon for the waters at her age. I would ask her if I should go instead, and my spirits lifted now that the problem was faced properly and a decision made.

Chapter 26

When I took my place amongst the crowds in *appartement* that evening, it was hard to believe I had been away. But then, as I faced his Majesty, I could see that his nose looked larger and his eyes smaller. Time had taken its toll. I half expected to see Madame de L'Eglise and dear Thérèse, and just as I wondered what had happened to Berthe, a handsome young footman appeared. I held my breath,

"Tienne! I can't be!"

He smiled, bowing graciously, "Welcome home Madame, Donna Solange."

"How you've grown, Tienne, so handsome and broad!" He beamed at me. Soon we were lost in reminiscences, till there was a hush as his Majesty lifted his hand for silence.

"We have a special guest returned to us this evening." All eyes were upon me, but I was not afraid as I had been that first time so long ago. I curtsied to the King and made my way towards him. There were whispers behind fans. I heard a few comments as I held my head high, conscious of the approval of Fernando as he eyed my elegant dark pink gown of peau de soie.

"I wonder whose crippled babe she's brought with her," a

voice, not unfamiliar, reached me. "The poor child, not knowing who his father is!" I felt my forehead prickle with heat. "That color doesn't suit her sun-scorched skin," the voice continued. "No lady gets weatherbeaten like that."

I curtsied low to his Majesty and as I stood again I saw de Villette, her head to one side while she eyed me up and down, her face a study in malicious hate. I was not displeased to note that she had not improved with keeping. Music drowned the rest of the remarks, and as I sat with the King I was soon lost in conversation. I shouldn't have been surprised that he already knew almost everything that had happened to me. I was amazed that his soldiers had kept him so well informed of such an unimportant person as myself.

"I look forward to making the acquaintence of Louis Fernando. Madame de Maintenon tells me he is a lovely child."

"Thank you, your Majesty. I am so happy to see you are in good health."

"I grow tired, my dear, and have many more problems." He lifted an elegant hand, "But we carry on."

I could no longer hear what the King was saying. It seemed that the years had slipped away. There were Fernando and de Villette dancing like lovers, the whorish cow grinning like an imbecile into his eyes, while he joked and flirted for all to see. I loathed the childishness in him. He became like a plaything the moment any woman flattered him, and I wished in that moment that I hadn't married him. He was weak and too easily swayed. What a fool I was to think that marriage would alter his weaknesses! He was exactly the same, falling in with the majority.

"Enjoy yourself, my child." The King brushed my cheek with his hand. While he was surrounded by his fawning courtiers, each vying for a moment of his attention, I looked about me for a partner, but there was no need, Tienne was at my side, tall and splendid. His cap of ash-blond hair had grown a little darker.

"That scoundrel who disappeared is back, Madame. When the King hears, he'll have him in irons."

"What scoundrel, Tienne? Don't talk in riddles."

"You know, Madame, the one that held you at the hunting lodge, Monsieur Raoul."

"Raoul, where?"

Tienne's jaw dropped, as striding toward us, resplendent in blue velvet, Raoul made an entrance. He twirled me in his arms as the old faces stared, lost for words, remembering how things had been.

"No breeches tonight, I see?"

"I hope never to wear men's clothes again. These silks feel marvellous."

"Yes, they do." His hand stroked the silk sleeve. I laughed, appreciating his light-heartedness. I was pleased to see that Fernando was eyeing me suspiciously, so I decided to really antagonise him, and whispered in Raoul's ear.

"Laugh as loud as you can after looking at Fernando, then whisper in my ear."

Raoul didn't need much prompting. In fact he pointed towards de Vilette and Fernando, then stopped dancing in the middle of the floor and half choking (so that I could hardly believe he was acting) he told me, "De Villette's coquette beauty spot has slipped." He couldn't continue for laughing and he clutched his sides.

"You don't have to overdo it, Raoul."

He spluttered, "Look!" I looked, it was true, the black spot was stuck to her front teeth, causing her to look toothless as she smiled grotesquely up to Fernando. Fernando was looking at us, however, and didn't seem at all amused. Raoul and I had to leave the floor and collapsed on to chairs. Other courtiers were smiling too by now, although I'm sure it was just because we were so obviously enjoying ourselves. Tears trickled out of the corners of Raoul's eyes,

"And I thought you were such a good actor!" I screeched.

"I didn't need to be, did I?"

"Solange!" I looked up suddenly at the sound of my husband's voice. "I think it's time for us to leave," and he grasped hold of my arm.

"I am not tired. You go, by all means."

He stood in front of us scowling. "I wish for us to leave now."

"Oh, you and your er..." I turned my hand around slowly, "Your er...." I looked at him quizzically, but he just continued scowling.

"Paramour? Is paramour the word you're looking for?" Raoul suggested politely. "The one with the black patch on her teeth?"

That started me laughing again.

"Either you come with me now, or I leave on my own!" Fernando had lost his color by then; his temper was raging. His hand tightened on my arm.

"Would you mind removing your hand, you're hurting me." I tried to smile, knowing all eyes were upon us.

His grip tightened a little. "I won't ask you again," he hissed. "I'll take the child and go."

"*Don't you dare touch that child,*" I rasped and saw the look of victory pass over his face. "I'd better go, Raoul, I can see this demented fool doesn't know how to control himself in company."

Raoul bowed, smiling all the while, then kissed my hand, "I'll say what I said in the army camp, Solange. I'm always available if you need me."

"Army camp? What army camp?" said Fernando sharply.

If only Raoul had kept quiet. "I'll tell you all about it," I promised. "I must see how little Louis is now."

"Don't you fob me off with excuses, you'll tell me now!"

I could see several ladies and gentlemen listening intently while pretending to flirt and talk.

"I think you've had a little too much wine. Let's talk in the ante room. Come!" I tried to lead him by the arm, but he was obviously drunk, and grabbed hold of my gown by the shoulder, and as I turned away from him, a piece of pink silk tore away in his hand. There were gasps from all sides, and Fernando's pale color changed to crimson with rage.

"Tell me about the army camp, you slut!" He lifted a hand to strike me, and Raoul grabbed the raised arm which caused Fernando to sway and slip to the floor, striking his head on the corner of a small table. Several courtiers scattered away, but most, I'm sorry to say, drew closer for the kill. I was ashamed for him and sorry for myself. Fortunately, the King had returned to the Gaming Room. De Villette made herself conspicuous by bending over and dabbing an ineffectual scrap of lace on Fernando's bruised temple. But instead of thanks he snarled, "Get away from me!"

"But Fernando!" she simpered. He pushed her and she flopped down next to him, much to everyone's delight.

"Come along, Solange." Raoul offered me his arm.

"No, I'm sorry, Raoul. Please leave us."

Fernando scrambled to his feet and made his way from the room. I hurried after him. Then the wine fumes seemed to overcome him and he sagged, insensible, to the ground.

"Oh, gracious heavens, you must carry him to our apartments."

Two footmen were already picking him up between them. They were used to this and showed not a trace of surprise. I walked ahead, indicating that they should follow. I watched as they removed his coat and shoes and loosened his linen and wondered if I could help him overcome this weakness.

Chapter 27

When I thought about it, I realised that he'd always had a miserable disposition; black moods that seemed to take over when least expected; too much wine didn't agree with him, and he was drinking more now than ever before.

The following morning he behaved as if all were well between us, apparently remembering nothing from the night before.

"Are you feeling rested, dearest?" He put his arms around me in the bed.

"Are you going to pretend that nothing happened last night after the performance you put on?"

"Why must you always find fault with me?" He looked so taken aback that for a moment I wondered if perhaps I'd exaggerated the brawl of the night before in my own mind. Now he was sulking again, staring into space for all the world as if he had the King's own problems of the war and finances to cope with.

"So, you're sulking again? I'm quite resigned to it."

"You started nagging the moment you opened your eyes. To think I've been looking forward to seeing you again, and as soon as I set eyes on you, the complaints start."

I threw the covers back and slipped out of the bed. "Did you expect me to say nothing when all eyes were on you? There was that overblown cow mooing over you just as she used to in the old days."

"I don't know what you're talking about. I've never heard such hysterical rubbish."

"If it's hysterical rubbish about last night, take a look at the bruise on your temple." I turned on my heel and left him sitting upon the bed, fingering his forehead. When I returned the maid was setting the breakfast out. The bed curtains were still closed, but I noticed a hand mirror on the table by the bed. He must have been examining his battle scars. I hid a smile behind my hand.

"Is that you, Solange?"

"Where are you?" I forced myself not to laugh.

"I'm in bed! Where the devil do you think I am?"

"I couldn't see you."

"Get rid of the maid, I don't want any food."

"But I do", I said chirpily. "That will be all," I told the maid who winked and bobbed, then made for the door. "You can come out now."

"What d'you mean, I can come out now? If I choose to lie a-bed I shall do so. That fall I had last night has left me a little shaken."

"Oh!" I said sweetly, "You remember the 'fall', as you call it?"

"Of course, why shouldn't I? I'm not in the habit of forgetting things, and I'll thank you not to imply otherwise." I sipped my tea and sighed theatrically. "And don't sound so badly used; it was all your fault. Now, how am I going to show my face? I'll have to stay here till the bruise fades." He picked up the hand mirror from the table and examined his face carefully.

"I'll send for the physician to attend you."

"I don't need the physician!"

"Then put a piece of raw meat on it. Don't you want anything to eat?" I smoothed my pale green peignoir about my hips. In spite of Fernando's irritability, I was glad to be wearing silks again. For a moment I wished that time hadn't passed, and I was still a young innocent girl. But then I wouldn't have little Louis. I smiled as I remembered how his chubby arms hugged me as they encircled my neck for his goodnight kiss.

"What have you got to smile about?" He snatched his nightcap off in a temper, and stomped from the bed, pulling a dressing gown of red around his shoulders like a cape.

"I was thinking of our child."

"Hah! A likely story! How did you come to be in that army camp, and what were you doing? Anyway, how do I know he's "our" child?" Of course you choose to tell me he is, that's only natural. Any mother would do the same." He paced the room like a tiger. "Even an animal protects its own, but you've got a lot to answer for, Madame."

I deliberately placed my cup down and faced him squarely. "You must believe whatever you choose, Fernando. Little Louis and I managed without you till now, I'm sure we will continue to do so." In spite of my brave words I felt a lump in my throat and hoped that the tears which were not far away, would wait till I was alone.

"I didn't say anything about you being on your own again; You always put words into my mouth." He continued pacing the room, looking like a bandit from a play with that bruise on his face, and his hair still tousled from sleep.

Sniffing, I bent my head and took a gulp of the tea I no longer wanted. Ugh! It was tepid! It didn't seem possible that we were the same two people who had once loved so deeply.

"If you promise not to interrupt, I'll tell you everything, but I'm very tired. You exhaust me with your childishness."

I left nothing out but the nights I'd spent with Raoul.

He didn't speak for a long time, then began to shift about, not altogether knowing what to say, it seemed. "Well," he came and sat beside me, "Why didn't you tell me all this in the first place?"

"You didn't give me a chance," I whispered.

"Come here!" he ordered hoarsely, but I didn't move, just sat there, drained, as if I'd lived through the two journeys and the imprisonment all over again in the telling. I felt his arms around me and saw his red dressing robe slip from his shoulders, but I felt nothing; no surge of love, just disappointment that he could be so immature when it came to women and his own weaknesses.

His voice was contrite as he said, "We all have faults and you can't blame me for thinking the worst of you and Raoul after what happened the last time."

I shrugged away from his arms, although I nearly weakened when I saw the look of surrender in his eyes. "You were right to think the worst." I crossed to the bed and crawled on to it, my back towards him, and closed my eyes. I didn't want to look at him again. "It was inevitable under the circumstances. Raoul probably saved my life, and little Louis'. You could hardly have expected me to refuse him a few hours of my company," thinking to myself he hadn't bothered to mention who comforted *him* when he was far from home.

My arm fell limply over the side of the bed and I felt my body would sink through it. I heard the door shut, and with an effort raised my eyes. My husband had gone. I breathed a sigh of relief. After all the weary months of longing and waiting for him, our reunion had been a bitter disappointment. I couldn't spend the rest of my life with a man never knowing from one day to the next if, when he opened his eyes in the morning, he was going to praise me or revile me.

Someone slipped into the room.

"Berthe! Oh Berthe! I wondered where you'd got to!" I jerked upright in the bed, and flung my arms about her homely body and pulled her down on the bed. My tiredness seemed to have gone with Fernando. Tears of joy trickled from the familiar old eyes, not shining now, more sunken and dull.

"I've been sick these last few weeks, Solange." She wiped the tears away with the back of her hand, "Otherwise I'd have been to see you sooner."

"Oh, Berthe, I am sorry! Are you well now?"

"Of course I'm well now! Enough about me. Tell me all

about yourself and the baby, and Don Fernando."

"I think he's left me," I said defiantly.

"God help us! Sit back, I'll fetch you a soothing draft." Berthe's plump hands flew to her face.

"There's no need to be upset, Berthe dear. I'm glad."

"What! Don't say such things. You'll feel better after one of my tisanes." She made to rise, and I grasped a fold of her skirt to hold her back.

"I *do* mean it. He's such a bad-tempered idiot, that I'm glad, really relieved."

"You'll feel better in time, *ducette*."

"You don't understand, Berthe, I'm delighted he's gone. I couldn't be more pleased. Now, help me dress if you are sure you feel well enough."

"Of course I feel well enough. I eat too much pudding, that's all. I used to be able to eat two helpings with no ill effects, but not any more."

Berthe and I chatted away as I dressed in a beige silk dress with brown ribbons trailing down the skirt.

"You are a fine woman now, Solange. When can I see Master Louis Fernando?"

"You shall come at once, Berthe dear. I think he will be back from his walk by now." I placed a kiss on her cheek. "It's so lovely to see you again. Have you news of Thérèse?"

As we walked to little Louis' rooms Berthe rambled on, "Thérèse has two bonny daughters and has promised to bring them one day from England. She asked after you."

"Oh, Berthe I'm so happy for her! What are the children called?"

Berthe slowed her pace and drew her head up proudly. "Chantelle Elizabeth and Hélène Solange."

"I will write to Thérèse, she must be very happy."

I felt a twinge of jealousy to think of the mess my marriage was in. The nurse wasn't back with little Louis, one of the maids in the nursery wing informed us, and it was now past time for his *petit dejeuner*. Berthe showed her disapproval to the nursery maid.

"This would never have happened in my day! Punctuality

was my byword. I'll have a word or two for that woman when she finally decides to bring a starving child back for his food." She sat down and folded her arms in disgust, muttering under her breath, "A fine way to bring up a child, no meals on time!"

"Never mind, Berthe dear, they'll be back any minute, for sure," and we sat reminiscing. Berthe told me, "Ma'mselle Thérèse always had her meals when the hour struck. Madame L'Eglise never had a moments' worry when *I* was nanny."

"Excuse me, Donna Solange."

"Yes," I looked up to the little maid who had addressed me.

"Can I be of service, Madame?"

"No, thank you, there's nothing we require, is there Berthe, dear?"

Berthe shook her head, annoyed at being interrupted in full flow.

"We'll just wait for Master Louis, so Berthe can become acquainted with him."

The little maid seemed to hesitate. "What is it, girl, you seem worried."

"Well..."

"Tell me at once! Is there something wrong?" Berthe grabbed hold of the girl's arm and gave her a shake. The girl looked terrified.

"Please, Berthe, it ain't my fault. I ain't done nothin'. You're hurtin' me."

"Well, what's wrong," I cried, "Is the child ill? Where's the nanny?"

Berthe tightened her grip the more and shook the poor girl again. By now we were surrounded by servants. One of the footmen stepped forward.

"Don Fernando left with Master Louis some two hours since, Madame. Nanny said the master didn't want you disturbed as you were tired after your journey."

Cold fear prickled my body. I couldn't speak with shock, and I became drenched with the sweat of panic. I felt, rather than saw, the frightened eyes of the servants, as realization dawned on them that my husband had taken the child away without my knowledge, and perhaps would not return.

"Where's that nurse?" Berthe was the first to speak.

"Oh, nanny went too," the footman replied.

"I'll bet she did," came Berthe's quick retort.

I forced myself to my feet and leaned on Berthe. My legs felt weak and I couldn't think straight. Berthe held me in her arms and tried to console me. "There, there! They'll soon be back I'm sure."

At last I found my voice, but when I spoke it was like the voice of someone else, and sounded far away, "What shall I do? My baby, I must find my baby!" The voice was sobbing hysterically. I grabbed the jester doll from the floor under a table where little Louis must have dropped it, and the bells sounded as loud as church bells, mocking me with their cheerful tinkle. I held the doll close to me, feeling the cloth, and it seemed as if my baby's body was wrapped inside it, warm and solid. I knew that I was crying, but no tears came.

"Leave everything to me, Madame," I heard the footman say. "I will make enquiries as to which direction they took. Perhaps they are already on their way back."

"No," I answered between sobs. "They won't be back, he's taken the child to spite me, and the child is ill, he needs care, his leg! His leg! His poor leg!"

"Now, how," Berthe chided, "What mades you so sure they won't be back? Where would they go?"

"I don't know, I must try to think!" Berthe took a glass from the footman and passed it down to me. "Oh, Berthe, you and your drinks! I wish you wouldn't always fuss when I'm trying to think! I know! I'll go to Madame de Maintenon!" Once my mind was made up, I took no notice of anyone.

"You don't need to, Solange." Berthe was afronted. "We can deal with this alone."

But I didn't bother to answer her, just lifted my skirts and as quickly as my numb legs would carry me, I made my way, tripping and half running to Madame's apartements. When at last I arrived, instead of pausing for breath, I told the astounded footman, "I must see Madame de Maintenon at once!"

"I will see if Madame is resting."

"If she is, please wake her, it's most urgent."

One look at my tear-stained face convinced him and he bade me take a seat. He seemed to be gone for hours, while I sat and stood, walked and had a hundred different thoughts of where Fernando could have taken Louis, till I could stand it no more. I dropped the jester doll onto my chair and walked as quickly as I could and knocked on Madame de Maintenon's door. The footman opened it.

"I was just coming to announce you, Madame," he informed me in his most arrogant manner. I swept past him and flung myself at Madame's feet.

"Forgive me, Madame, I'm beside myself! Don Fernando has taken little Louis away. I may never see him again. I've got to go after them. Help me!"

"Now, calm down, Solange, calm down, what are you talking about?" She dismissed her maid. "Try to speak more slowly." Then she went to her chaise and arranged her dark silk gown around her. How could she be so calm after what I'd told her! "Now what are you trying to tell me, child?"

"My baby's gone, you don't understand, Madame! Don Fernando's taken little Louis!"

"Don't scream, child, you're giving me a migraine." Madame touched the lace cap which covered her grey hair. "What is wrong, may I ask, with a father taking his son for a ride? I really don't understand you, Solange. Sometimes I think you are not as intelligent as I gave you credit for."

"But you don't understand, Madame!"

"Cover my legs with that rug, would you?"

"Oh! You stupid old woman, all you think of is your comfort!" I gasped, realising what I'd said. But I think it brought Madame to her senses. "Forgive me, Madame, I'm out of my mind with worry!"

"Are you trying to tell me that you think Don Fernando has taken the child away for good?" Madame's mouth turned up at the sides.

"Yes, Madame, I do, and I've no idea where."

"Now, do stop snivelling, child, and please lower your voice. I'll try to think."

"Yes, Madame. Thank you."

"Here, use this." Madame handed me one of her lace handkerchiefs. "Why are you so sure he does not intend to come back?"

"Because he's furious with me, just because I told him the truth. He asked me a question and when I answered him he didn't like it."

"What truth is that, child?"

"I would rather not say, Madame, if you don't mind." I looked down at the carpet. "You may not wish to help me if I tell you."

"What can be so terrible to make your husband abscond with your child, I wonder? If you come to me for help I can only give it when I know what led up to this. Come, come, child. We can always ask to be forgiven for our sins in prayer."

"I'll do anything to get my baby back, Madame. Anything!" I looked with horror at Madame's lace handkerchief and saw that I'd shredded it into tatters. "Oh, dear!"

"Never mind about that. I saw Master Louis a few hours ago, so I shouldn't start worrying yet."

Then I told her what the servants had said.

"I see. Even so, I think we should wait till this evening. Nanny will look after him, she's most reliable, there's no one better."

But when evening came and there was still no news of them, Madame agreed we had to do something.

"Now try to relax, child, I'll see what I can do. Perhaps they took a coach, we shall soon know where they are." Madame called Tienne to tell the Major Domo to send riders out. "They must ride *ventre à terre*, belly to earth, in all directions to find Don Fernando." She turned to me. "When Don Fernando's Spanish blood has cooled and Master Louis is asking for his dear Mama, I feel sure they will return."

"Perhaps you're right, Madame. I pray you are." I was relieved that something was being done at last.

After Tienne had left, Madame invited me to join her as she took some refreshment, and I felt her soothing influence calming me as usual. The cool drink and little cakes made me realize I had missed the main meal of the day. Madame wiped her mouth daintily with a napkin.

"Why you insisted on marrying a foreigner I'll never know, Solange. There were so many fine Frenchmen at Court. I've always been of the opinion that the Spanish are a little too hot-blooded and given to passionate words."

"I'm beginning to think you were right, Madame," I sighed, trying to please her.

"Even if I am right, you must remember Don Fernando is of a most noble Spanish line and your husband to boot, and you will show proper respect."

"Yes, Madame de Maintenon." I nearly choked on the cherry cake.

"It's high time you calmed down as a dutiful wife should." Madame tapped two fingers on my hand as she spoke. "No wonder your husband is displeased with you. A wife's place is with her husband's family. You had no right to go wandering off, it wasn't seemly."

"Yes, Madame, but. . . ."

"No buts," Madame held up a plump hand. "I think of you as my own daughter. A reprimand from me is as a kiss from a so-called friend." Madame had that glint in her dark eyes as of old. "Do you understand me, child?"

"I do, dear Madame, you always help me to see things more clearly."

She patted my hand. "Good, now you may read me one of Monsieur Molière's plays, it will help to keep your mind occupied while enquiries are being made. I read a great deal to his Majesty. I will enjoy being read to for a change."

Madame indicated a book on the table by the window. "I remember you read well."

"Oh, yes, Madame," I answered proudly and made my way to the window. Everything looked as usual in the park on this sunny day; the courtiers were promenading, twittering and laughing; the sun shone on the beds of tulips and jasmine, pink and yellow amongst the smooth green lawns. I wondered where my little Louis was. At least I could be assured of his safety. Fernando wouldn't harm him. It was he who had noticed little Louis' bad leg and insisted on sending for the best Court physician.

"What are you doing, child, mooning by the window? Perhaps you would rather be out in the sunshine."

"Oh no, Madame, forgive me." I straightened my gown and crossed the room to her and sat opposite her. I opened the book on my lap. "Which one shall I read, Madame?" I looked up and saw that she had her eyes closed. How wrinkled she had become, her face had gone much fatter.

"From the beginning, I think, and then we shall see."

I was about to read, riffling the pages with my fingers, when I looked up. "May I ask you something, Madame?"

She opened her eyes and sighed, "What is it now, child?"

"Well, I don't really know if I should."

Madame pressed her forehead again, "I think I am becoming rather weary. Ask me the question for goodness sake, and let's get on."

"Well . . . you were married to Monsieur Scarron, weren't you Madame?"

"I beg your pardon?"

I spoke louder, "You were married . . ."

"I'm perfectly aware of what you asked me, and I think you are overwrought and forget yourself, Solange!" Madame's eyes flashed her disapproval and she tightened the rug around her lap.

"I apologise, Madame, I think I *am* overwrought." I felt sick to have forgotten myself enough to become familiar with Madame.

"I suggest a posset and a rest before dinner, and I will have you informed of any news."

I rested the book on my chair as I curtsied and kissed the plump hand. "Thank you for all your help, Madame." She nodded, "And forgive me for speaking out of turn."

"Under the circumstances it is forgotten."

I mumbled my thanks and made my way back to my own apartments, not noticing anyone or anything, but only seeing my little one's face in my mind's eye.

I suddenly realized that I had picked up the jester doll while on my way out without thinking. It jingled, and I was clutching it to my bosom as I flung myself on the bed and cried into its shabby costume.

Chapter 28

I forced myself to put on a brave face as I joined the others for the evening entertainment. I couldn't rely on news reaching me immediately if I stayed in my rooms, and I didn't dare to bother Madame again. I could tell by their faces that everyone knew what had happened. All I needed was for de Villette to make one of her caustic remarks. I looked for her so that she wouldn't catch me unawares. Raoul joined me, a crease of concern on his forehead.

"I was sorry to hear the bad news, Solange. If there's anything I can do to help, you've only to ask." His slanting eyes assured me of his allegiance.

"I know, Raoul, I appreciate your concern. I'll let you know as soon as I hear anything."

Tienne joined us then. "The King asks you to speak to him, Madame."

Raoul and I exchanged glances. He bowed and I followed Tienne through the throngs of people, pushing our way to the Grande Appartements. I knew why he had sent for me. He must have learnt what had happened. It was impossible to hurry, but we forced a path through the chattering courtiers, and at last, panting for breath, I was ushered into the presence of the King.

He was surrounded by admirers, fawning and preening. They fell back as His Majesty acknowledged me with a smile and held his hand out for me to kiss, and guided me next to him on the green chaise longue.

"Take that worried look off your pretty face. Your son is on his way to Bourbon for the waters with his father."

I felt elated with relief. "He told you, your Majesty?"

"He left word for me. I didn't realise till Madame de Maintenon told me that you had not been informed."

"Thank God I know where he is!"

"I take it you two are having another of your usual lovers' tiffs?" His Majesty smiled.

"It's no lovers' tiff this time, I'm afraid. He's gone too far!" I clenched my hands together.

The King strctched out an elegant silk-clad leg and stroked his chin slowly. He pursed his lips and looked at me, "Are you quite sure it isn't *you* that has 'gone too far', as you say?"

"What, me, your Majesty?" People turned to stare and I realized that I had raised my voice. "I don't know what you mean!" I held my back straight with indignation.

"I think you do!" his Majesty laughed, and bent his head to look into my eyes till I couldn't help smiling.

I sighed, "I dare say you could be right, your Majesty, but he had no right to take the child. I'll never forgive him for that. I must have little Louis back immediately, and I want you to have Don Fernando locked up, the man's demented!"

The King, to my horror, threw back his head and laughed. "Solange, you are incorrigible! I can't have a man locked up because he's had a quarrel with his wife!"

"You can do anything, Sire."

"Now, you don't really mean that you want him locked up." The King smiled, highly amused, it seemed.

"Oh, yes I do, your Majesty. He has kidnapped little Louis, who at this very moment is probably crying for his

Mama." Tears filled my eyes and I had to swallow and discipline myself to hold them in check.

"You could hardly call it kidnapping when a father takes his own child for the waters to improve his health!"

"But, your Majesty, all little Louis' toys and most of his clothes have gone. He obviously intended to keep him away without my knowledge."

"I think Don Fernando was in one of his hot tempers. He will have cooled down by now, and thinking of sending word to you, I shouldn't wonder."

I felt light headed. "I must leave at once. Will you excuse me, your Majesty? I know Monsieur Raoul will accompany me."

"Do you think that would be wise, Solange?" The King raised a quizzical eyebrow.

"I must go at once! Don Fernando may keep him there for weeks."

"That isn't quite what I meant. I will send a suitable escort with you, and ladies to accompany you, of course. But if Monsieur Raoul were to accompany you, it would be most unwise considering Don Fernando's passionate nature. He would certainly jump to conclusions, perhaps not entirely unfounded." His Majesty lowered his head slightly and waited for an answer.

I flushed. "I don't care about his conclusions, and if you'll forgive my plain speaking, I'm tired of his childish tantrums."

"Perhaps it was a little thoughtless of Don Fernando to take the Countess de Villette along—not the most suitable lady in the circumstances."

Rage held me in a grip of iron. My heart lurched with temper and jealousy.

"That bloody swine!" I gasped, forgetting I was addressing the King. "Forgive me, your Majesty, but I'm sick with anger."

"It seems you are," he agreed.

"May I leave now, your Majesty?" I made an attempt to stand.

"It would be most unwise to leave at this hour, don't you think? Be ready at first light, and all will be arranged for you. And if I were you, Madame de Maintenon should be consulted about the waters, and the child will benefit from a stay in Bourbon for the good of his health. They worked wonders for my Mignon."

The King held his hand for me to kiss, then drew mine to his lips.

"Thank you, Sire. I will do as you say, but Monsieur Raoul must accompany me. I need his assistance."

"So I hear," the King looked at me sideways.

"Oh, your Majesty, you make me blush!"

"I think not. You no longer have need for blushing."

As I left the King I was seething at the nerve of that Spanish swine making a laughing stock of me by taking that cow de Villette as companion to my son.

I had Raoul brought to me, and together we planned our departure for the following morning. We talked on the terrace in the cool summer air, sipping our wine.

"And now let us enjoy our evening, darling." He traced his long fingers across my shoulder, sending a shiver down my spine.

"Oh no, Raoul, all that is over now, there can be no love between us, only true and lasting friendship."

"After what you've told me that does sound a little naïve."

"What do you mean, 'after what I've told you'? That has nothing to do with it. I want to have a good rest for the journey. You can't imagine how I'm longing to see my dearest child again and hold him in my arms!"

"Then I wish that I were that child." Raoul leaned towards me, the green of his coat making his eyes seem amber in the fading light. As he took my hand in his across the table, I felt curious eyes observing us.

"Please try to understand, Raoul. I'm very fond of you, but things are muddled enough already. I don't want to make them worse."

"Why should one night of love make things worse?" His words were spoken like a caress, lingering and soft.

I caught my breath. "Stop it, Raoul, please."

"What do you think your dear husband is doing right now? Thinking only of you and begging de Villette to leave him alone?"

Jealousy gnawed at me, causing me to snap at him, "You are just trying to make me fling myself into your arms to be comforted, Raoul. That isn't fair."

"I'm not trying to be fair, darling." His voice was low and seductive. "And what if I am trying to hold you in my arms? It is a most heavenly sensation from what I remember."

I felt the effect of his words in the pit of my stomach and continue down between my legs.

"Look at me!" he ordered gently.

"No!"

"You're afraid, darling!"

I never could resist a challenge, and as our eyes locked, my legs felt weak. The look in his eyes reminded me of a smouldering fire that would burst into flame if pushed with a poker. I shivered and knew I didn't care who saw us. I rose and he held me close to him as we made our way indoors through the lawns and terraces of sweet-scented flowers and exquisitely dressed courtiers.

As we reached my rooms Raoul pinned me against the wall and covered my mouth with his own.

"Oh Raoul, Raoul," I moaned, feeling his straining body through all my petticoats.

He stood away from me. "Let me see you undress." I began to snatch and pull at my dress. "No, not like that! Slowly, and look at me while you do it."

"I can't." I ran towards him. He kissed me leisurely, then pulled away. I did as I was told and slowly stepped out of my gown, then turned for him to undo my stays which he threw into a corner. I pushed my garter slowly down my leg. "You're not looking at me," he reminded me.

I met his eyes and slowly walked to the chaise longue, my legs quavering, and lay down and lifted my eyes to his again. He undressed, smiling at me all the while. He stood there, his dark member protruding. I rushed to him and knelt down, burying it in my mouth, my hands clutching his slim buttocks. He moaned his pleasure and began to pound in and out of my mouth. I drew him in further till I could feel it touch my throat. Then the warm liquid filled my mouth, and he bent and kissed my face, holding my head in his hands. I let the sticky liquid trickle down my face, then he lifted me in his arms onto the bed.

"My darling girl." He cradled me in his arms, and poured us some wine from the table by the bed. By now I wanted him so badly that I was weak with longing. His manhood lay limp and tired, but I crept down the bed and let a breast flick it as I swung over it, first one way and then the other, till it raised once more. I was about to sit astride it when he pushed me onto my back, clamped his mouth in my mound, and a delicious agonizing warmth filled me. I caught my breath as he held me gently between his sharp teeth, and I felt his tongue dart around me till I felt myself gape open and my body lift, urging his tongue to enter and possess me. I pushed his head with my hands and entwined his hair around my fingers. His lips felt warm and his tongue hot. Suddenly I held his head tightly to me while spasms rocked my body and he plunged his thumb and fingers inside me, and my body burst with pleasure.

"Oh, Raoul, I wish you had come inside me."

"Didn't you like it, darling?"

"You know I did, but I like you inside me better."

"The night is still young." He held me to him and we dozed, arms entwined.

At last I felt his hairy legs cover mine, and then his knee gently stroked me where it gave the most pleasure. He caressed my breasts, leaning on his side twirling his fingers round the nipples till they ached and throbbed, causing them to harden for his lips to suck.

"Tell me how you feel, darling," he begged.

"If you don't fill me soon, I will die," I moaned.

He plunged into me and I lay there in an ecstacy of pleasure, my legs tightly clasped around him. I could smell the sweat from his body, while the hair on his chest scratched my breasts and we moved together in perfect harmony while the blood pounded in my head and I screamed, "Don't stop, don't stop, Raoul," terrified that he would finish before I could take my pleasure in full. We came together shuddering for an ecstatic moment in time.

When we awoke it was still dark, and Raoul began to caress me again, but I felt guilty for enjoying the night.

"I must get ready for the journey," I murmured, and after a lingering kiss, Raoul departed to make ready for our trip.

As I bathed and dressed, my thoughts were only of my baby son. I prayed that the waters would heal his leg. A surge of love went through me as I remembered his sweet face and how pleased he would be to see me. As for Fernando, I didn't give a fig for him, I told myself.

While I was watching the maid pack my clothes, I decided to tell my husband definitely that little Louis wasn't his. That way I would be rid of him, and have the child to myself. I knew I could never marry Raoul. Although he hardly even saw his wife any more, she still existed. I accepted this and anyway, I didn't really love him. It was just another affair. I arranged my coiffure in the dressing table mirror, and I smiled, thinking that although I had lost Fernando, little Louis was more precious to me than any man. I would devote my life to making him well and happy. Men had always caused problems for me. Then I remembered the night before. I could still feel Raoul's fingers on my breasts, and his maleness hard inside me. I looked at the maid to see if she could read my thoughts, and she did seem to be eyeing me strangely.

"Come along, girl we haven't got all day. I don't want that silver ball gown, only travelling gowns and day dresses. Well, perhaps the blue silk. Now, hurry!"

The girl smirked and did as she was told. Presently light appeared through the window, and I walked over to it briskly and looked out. All was grey and still. Excitement made my heart beat faster, knowing that I was going to meet my child. Even the thought of Fernando and de Villette was blotted out. They were welcome to each other. Only my son mattered to me.

Chapter 29

"This is getting to be a not unpleasant habit," Raoul laughed as we took our places in the coach.

I arranged my brown travelling dress neatly about me and smoothed my matching bonnet. "I really think you were most unwise to insist on accompanying me in my coach, Raoul. Nobody will believe your story of fear for my safety."

"After what happened the last time you travelled without me, I'm sure everyone was hoping that I would protect you."

"But insisting that my servant should travel in a separate coach could hardly be seen as necessary."

I heard the crack of the whips and the coach lurched forward as Raoul said lightly, "I promised her it would allay suspicion, then she and I could get together when we arrive at Bourbon."

I removed my shoe, and clonked him on the head. "You rogue! The poor thing must have fainted."

Raoul didn't seem to feel the shoe, just stretched his black clad legs and smiled broadly. "On the contrary, she fluttered her pale lashes, and held a wrinkled hand to her flat bosom. 'Oh, Monsieur Raoul,' he mimicked her high squeaky voice, 'You'll never change.'" Then he turned to me. "You may kiss me if you wish," he remarked lazily.

"You conceited fop!"

He opened one eye, and grinned. "Perhaps you need time to recover, you did almost devour me last night, you know."

I bristled at this, and drew myself up and opened my mouth to protest, when I saw by his laughing, slanting eyes that he was teasing me.

"Don't worry, sweeting, I'll explain to Fernando that it was I who did all the running," he joked.

"I don't care what you tell that Spaniard! I've finished with him for good," I said airily, and meant it.

"That's the best piece of news I've heard all day," he exclaimed with surprise. "I always knew you preferred me."

"That has nothing whatsoever to do with it," I shot at him.

"But you do, don't you? Why won't you admit it?"

"I'm sorry to disappoint you, but you are both so different that I can hardly think of you both as of the same species."

"I know what you mean." He stroked his thigh leisurely.

"You have no idea what I mean, so don't talk rubbish."

"There's no need to get worked up, you're not the first woman whose husband has left her for another."

"You know perfectly well Fernando has only taken little Louis for the healing waters," I spat at him, "And knowing Fernando as I do, he only took the old cow to spite me, hoping to make me jealous." I turned my head away from him and looked out of the window, fingering my smart brown bonnet with its gold buckle at the front.

"For someone who doesn't care, you're making enough fuss."

I stared at the trees shining in the summer sun, and turned back to him. He was smiling still.

"I didn't mean to upset you, sweeting. The wounds are raw, after all."

"It's none of your business, anyway. Let's talk about your wife and family," I told him innocently.

The smile faded and he clamped his mouth shut. "Don't be ridiculous!"

"No, I'm really interested, Raoul. How many children have you?"

"I have six still living, four girls and two boys. One the age of your son, a bright little fellow, and playful too."

"How long is it since you saw him?"

"Oh, quite eight months or more. But a soldier has to put duty before family."

"Doesn't your wife mind your devotion to your 'duty'?" I asked him even more sweetly, eyes rounded with interest. "After all, it's a long time for a woman to be on her own."

"Bettina knows I love her, and is content and busy enough attending to the children and the household to fill her mind with nonsense." He sat upright, loosening his silk cravat.

"Do you love her?" I asked with feigned concern.

"Well, it's a different kind of love than the love I have for you," he tucked his chin in, "More of a brotherly and sisterly love."

"Hmmmm—and six children..." I smiled, fluttering my lashes.

"You wouldn't understand. Ours was a marriage arranged by our families. We have the greatest respect for each other."

"I *am* glad. So nice to hear of a loving husband."

I gave him a grimace of admiration and turned to look out of the window once more.

"I suppose it must be, when you lack one yourself."

I spun around and slapped him with all my strength, but it stung my hand and there was no sign of it on his face. He laughed and brought a flask from his coat and held it out for me. I ignored him and sat there fuming as the coach jolted and surged in the heat of the day. The thought of the drink caused my mouth to go dry, but I couldn't tell him I'd changed my mind.

"Ah! that tastes good. You don't know what you're missing. Here!"

I allowed myself to be persuaded, but refused to meet his gaze. The drink was good, whatever it was. Brandy, I think. It certainly made me feel better, more at ease and looking forward even more to seeing my dearest child.

"Why don't we have some air in here, it's roasting?" I suggested.

"The windows are open, unless you want to go up on top.

I'm afraid it will be much hotter soon. Would you like me to draw the curtains and you can undress? I won't mind under the circumstances, and I'll explain to your husband that I tried to look away."

I removed my shoe and boxed him round the ears with it. "You go too far!" I screamed at him.

He grabbed both my wrists while I seethed, and my shoe dropped to the floor. "I couldn't go much further, could I?"

I kicked his shin with my shod foot and his face clouded with pain. He pushed me with one motion onto the floor, and clamped his feet on my back, forcing me to stay there while I kicked furiously.

"Let me up, you pig!" I choked from the dust all around me.

"Not until you apologize, and kiss my leg better, or better still, kiss my feet," he said pleasantly.

"You swine, wait till the King hears of this! Let me up at once!"

"The King will hear of a lot else besides," he assured me suavely, shifting one foot to the top of my head. My hat lay beside me, the buckle askew. My nose tickled from the carpet and caused me to sneeze.

"Oh dear, you're not taking a chill, I hope. Let me cover you with my coat." He removed his foot from my head and covered it carefully with his coat till I thought I would suffocate.

"Please, Raoul," I begged, "I can't breathe!"

"Are you going to kiss my feet?" he asked in a most reasonable tone.

"Kiss your ass!" I screamed into the carpet, all pretense of gentility forgotten. "Help me," I cried, but he pushed my face down with his boot and I resigned myself to stay there till we stopped, with the sweat trickling down my back. I refused to give in to him. But God help him when we reached our destination!

The heat was almost unbearable, but I forced myself to keep calm and think of little Louis and how thrilled he would be to see me. I had a beautiful doll wrapped carefully in my luggage that one of the servants had brought for me when I was ready to leave. It was an amazing replica of little Louis himself; the same black curls, and a blue dress made from scraps of one he had actually worn. I pictured how he would react when I gave it to him. Love and warmth filled my heart and blotted out my intense discomfort as I was jolted by the rumbling of the wheels beneath me and the swaying of the carriage. My last thought as I fell into a sweat-soaked sleep was of my son's little arms encircling my neck.

Chapter 30

Voices and noises of doors slamming and horses' rattling accoutrements woke me. My mouth tasted foul and I felt sticky and most uncomfortable. I sat up, wiped the sweat from my eyes with the back of my hand, and blinked. I was alone, someone was speaking to me from the open door.

"You look a fine sight, here."

Raoul threw me his handkerchief and turned on his heel while I threw it straight back at him and stood shakily. I tidied myself as best I could, and held my head high as my maid and a footman helped me down the step and into a pleasant looking inn.

I snatched a jug of ale from the table and drank from it, gasping after one deep swallow. I looked neither to right nor left, just followed my maid to the room allotted to me, and asked her to leave me alone after she had poured me some wine and loosened my clothes. After washing, I lay on the bed by the open window, and let the cool breeze dry the perspiration that continued to trickle from my hair. A growing hunger forced me to don clean clothes quickly, after calling the maid to assist me.

"Hurry! Hurry! That will do. I'm going down to eat. I'm

too hungry for a tray up here." How glad I was to have brought the blue silk. I felt quite cool now, and made my way down the winding crooked stairs to the dining room, where I was greeted by the stale smells of forgotten meals, followed by the maid who crimsoned at the sight of Raoul, spread eagled in a chair sipping wine, and surrounded by our retinue. She ambled over to join him, but noticing that I'd stopped at the other table away from the window, she came reluctantly back to me.

"It's much cooler by the window, My Lady."

"Yes," I said slowly and loudly for Raoul and all to hear, "But so much *cleaner* here. Do sit at the window if you wish, I have had enough wind for one day. Hot or cold."

Some of the men grinned, I noticed. She became flustered, looking from me to Raoul, not knowing quite what to do, her dry face flushed, and pale eyes glassy. I ate enough for two and drank till the terrible thirst I had abated. I wanted to take my revenge on Raoul, and made a quick plan in my mind.

"I think I'll retire now, and would like you to go to your room to sew a hem for me."

Her mouth drooped, but with only a furtive look towards Raoul, she followed me meekly.

"I don't like my room. You take it, and I'll take yours."

"But it's in the attic, My Lady."

"Never mind that."

She didn't need much persuading. "Now I want that hem first thing in the morning, so no stealing from your room to shirk your duty. It should take you all evening."

"Yes, My Lady," she sullenly replied.

I took pen and ink and made my way up the narrow, creaking stairs. I looked about me. I'd spent the night in worse rooms than this sloping chamber with its low walls and rickety bed. I sat on the only chair, and rested the two sheets of paper on the battered wood that served as a table. I wrote quickly:

Stay where you are, I will come to you at midnight.

Douse the candle and don't utter a sound lest your mistress hears. I love you.

Raoul.

Then I penned another:

You were right to chastize me. I am waiting for you to make amends. The maid has ears like a hawk. Don't make a sound.

Solange.

I leaned back, pleased with my work, then folded the notes and pushed the chair back. I opened the door and tip-toed down and put one note under the door of the room which was supposed to be mine, then found the inn wife and asked her to put the other note under Raoul's door, not forgetting to hand her a gold piece. She winked knowingly, and promised to do the errand at once. I chuckled and looked forward to an entertaining night.

I left my door ajar and listened for footsteps. I didn't have to wait long. I heard creaking stairs and then a faint knock. I counted ten, then took my candle down the few stairs and put my ear to the door of my old room. I could hear faint movements and put my eye to the key-hole and tried to see by holding the candle near. But the only thing I got for my trouble was nearly setting myself on fire. I sucked my thumb where the flame had caught it. There was no light in the room. I could hear the bed creak and smacking sounds. Everything was going according to plan. I ached with glee as I crept carefully back to the attic and stuffed my face into the pillow to muffle my laughter. I couldn't wait to see their faces in the morning.

Chapter 31

"Oh, Madame, it's the most beautiful morning. I've never known such a heavenly day!" It was the maid bringing breakfast. Her plain face was uplifted as if she'd had a visitation in the night, which, indeed, she had.

I smiled, pleased with my little joke, and wondered how much I could pry out of her. I stretched my arms wide and yawned. "Did you sleep well?" I asked innocently. Her face changed color before my eyes.

"Never better," she answered, her eyes glazing over, and stood lost in her thoughts.

"I noticed Monsieur Raoul eyeing you at dinner. I think he's in love with you. I was hoping that you two would get together in time."

"Oh, Madame," she held both hands clasped in front of her. "You are so clever! I can hardly believe it. You are quite right. I received this note." She pulled the familiar piece of paper from her bosom and handed it to me.

I pretended to show surprise. "Oh! I am so glad for you, you deserve a little pleasure."

She squinted and looked down at her large narrow feet. "Yes, at last love has come to me. I fell asleep in his arms. I have never been so happy. To think that at my age such a gentleman should be interested in me."

"Did he . . . you know?" I prompted.

She looked at me through imbecilic eyes, ringed with shadows. "Twice," she whispered, as tears of joy crept down the ugly cheeks. I was satisfied.

"Did he say when you were to meet again?" I asked nonchalantly as I sipped my wine.

"I'm afraid I fell asleep before he left. Do you think he will be insulted?" she asked, frantic with worry now.

"Oh, no, it was just the right thing to happen," I assured the dithering creature.

She almost collapsed with relief. "You know, Madame, forgive me if I'm speaking out of turn, but we all thought, well . . . er . . ."

"Go on," I encouraged. "You may speak freely."

"Well, My Lady, it had passed through my mind that perhaps you and Monsieur Raoul er . . ."

"Oh no," I laughed, "Whatever gave you that idea?"

"Well, that's all right then."

The naïve fool, I thought, but she mustn't have her heart broken. Last night must just be a beautiful memory for her to cherish.

"You know, perhaps I should explain the ways of gentlemen to you. Don't be surprised if he behaves as if he doesn't know you this morning. Although he desires you madly, he'll realize that last night must never be repeated. Imagine the disgrace if it were found out!"

Her face fell for an instant. "Oh, of course, I understand, I'm happy, My Lady. My life is complete." I choked on my wine. "Are you all right, My Lady?"

I coughed. "Thank you, yes."

"I'm afraid I have a confession to make, My Lady."

"What's that?"

"I have only finished half the hem of your gown. I'll do it now."

"Oh, is that all? I'll wear something else. Now hurry, I wish to leave very soon."

"Thank you, My Lady. I'll pack at once."

She hurried out, and I finished dressing, hardly able to wait to hear Raoul's side of the story.

I followed the maid down the stairs and we made our way to the coach. I gave Raoul a dazzling smile, and though he returned my greeting, he looked slightly puzzled, as, completely ignoring my maid's adoring glances, he helped me into the coach for the last part of our journey.

I waited until the bustle had died down, the luggage arranged, and the doors shut, then, hardly able to contain myself, I turned to him.

"I trust you had a good night?"

"How do you mean? You know what kind of a night I had. I can hardly walk after it. I've heard of still waters running deep, but you certainly let rip last night!" He yawned with obvious exhaustion.

I felt my jaw sag with disappointment. Could it be possible that that skinny old maid could have hidden talents? No, it just wasn't possible.

"Thank you for the best night of my life, sweeting, but now . . ." he stretched his arms again and yawned loudly and closed his eyes, "I've just got to get some rest. What a night!"

"Er, what exactly did you like about it?" I asked, devoured by curiosity.

"Oh, you were fantastic! I'll never forget it."

"Yes, but in what *way*?"

"You know, you don't need to ask, now please let me sleep, I'm only human."

I was furious! This wasn't working out at all as I had planned. Loud snoring came from his corner of the coach where he'd settled down his chin resting on his shoulder. The circles under his eyes were really black, he certainly was tired. I sat and wondered what on earth she'd done to him. What had a wreck like her to offer a young, healthy bedfellow? How dare he snore in my company! I edged up to him and nudged him in the ribs with my elbow, but he didn't move. I shook his arm roughly and he snuffled a bit, but didn't wake. Exasperated by now, I pinched his cheek hard, then shot back to the other side of the coach while he blinked.

"What is it? What is it?"

I feigned sleep, keeping one eye slightly open.

He curled up and was about to doze off again. "Er, Raoul."

"Mmmm".

"Tell me about last night."

"I'm tired."

"Just tell me quickly."

No answer. "Raoul, answer me at once."

"Go away."

"Wake up this instant, I say."

"Later!"

I was more inquisitive than ever before. It just didn't seem possible that my inexperienced maid could know something that I didn't. But I wasn't going to find out for quite some time, because he was snoring again.

At last we arrived at our destination, and I was so excited at the thought of seeing my little Louis, that I pushed Raoul to the back of my mind. As I alighted and made my way to the inn, I immediately planned my inquiry, and walking through the door I asked the Innkeeper, "Don Fernando and party, where are they, please?"

"They be gone this very mornin' Madame."

"Oh, no!" I sank into the nearest chair, my head in a turmoil. "Had they a child with them?"

"Oh, aye, a fine little lad," the small and shrivelled innkeeper replied, puckering his face in anxious speculation.

"Had he an iron on his leg?"

"Not that I could see, but I'll ask the maid. Charlotte! Charlotte!"

A maid put her head round the door, ears as big as an elephant's, eyes like freezing water.

"Did the little lad wear an iron?" he wheezed, and threw out his chest.

"No, no, both legs were unhampered."

So Fernando had refused to have those disfiguring supports on the child. I was relieved.

"Thank heaven for that, at least! Where were they headed?"

The lines about the small man's eyes and mouth creased tighter, he opened his mouth, then shut it for a moment while I waited anxiously.

"How could I tell?" he asked in a high-pitched voice.

"Well, think, man, think! You must remember some word, anything." He looked back at me vacantly. I could see I was wasting my time.

Raoul came in at last, still fatigued from his night of love.

"They've already left, and no one knows where they've gone. What shall I do?"

"Well, I'm not travelling any more today. I want a meal." I forgot my quarrel and game with Raoul. I had to. I needed his assistance.

Raoul lounged easily against the wall. "We must think carefully before making a move," he said lazily. "I can see no point in running helter skelter across the country. I say we go back tomorrow. All news ends up at Court."

My maid grinned foolishly up at him, then scuttled away to make my room ready. If she thought she was in for another entertaining night, she was very much mistaken. I'd soon put a stop to that. But there were more important things to worry about.

Raoul put an arm about my shoulders, "I'll find your son for you, Solange, don't worry. And in the meantime," he bent down and whispered in my ear, "As a special treat I'll do all those things you begged me for last night. I'm feeling rested now."

I restrained the urge to snap at him, but I wouldn't show my feelings.

"Was there a big woman with Don Fernando?" I asked the innkeeper who hovered about as Charlotte of the big ears brought food and wine for us.

"No, no," he flicked his meat-like hands together as

though on an imaginary towel. "Only the nurse and an elegant lady, plump and pretty."

"That will do," I snapped.

As I washed my hands and face, I thought about the journeys I had yet to take. They were a continuous nightmare, never ending. Shoddy inns were to be my home, it seemed. Where was Louis now, I wondered for the hundredth time? What small towns was he passing, what distant mountains?

My maid's smug face was in front of me, and I could no longer stand it. "I don't need you. After you've eaten, go to your bed and stay there. Eat in the kitchen!" Her nose turned red and shiny. "Oh, do stop snivelling, woman!"

She sniffed, "I'm sorry your son has left already, My Lady."

"Thank you."

"I'm sure it would do you more good to come down with me, My Lady. You'll only brood up here on your own."

I had a sudden thought. Sitting up quickly I said, "On one condition."

She grinned, showing yellowish teeth. "What is it? Anything I can do I'm sure."

I swung my legs off the bed and allowed her to attend me. "I want to know *exactly* what happened last night with Monsieur Raoul."

Instead of refusing as I imagined she would, a look of pride appeared on the dull face, and she was only too pleased to relate the details of her one night of love.

"Well, My Lady, I'd never been with a man before," she began.

"Don't stop dressing me while you're talking, woman."

"But I knew you were supposed to lie with your legs open. Anyway, he sent that note."

"Did he, indeed? Oh yes, you showed it to me."

"As soon as I got his note to say he was going to visit me, I undressed and lay on the bed, waiting."

"Yes, well go on."

She patted my hair into place.

"I waited a long time, but I didn't mind." She clasped both hands to her bosom and turned ecstatically glazed eyes to mine. "I never knew..."

"Yes? What didn't you know?"

"Well, er..."

I stamped my foot, impatient with her stumbling words.

"I can't say it."

"Right. Then you'll stay up here with me and eat, and you won't set eyes on him till morning, I'll see to that."

"I'll tell you," mumbled, looking down at her feet.

"Will you stop babbling woman, you're not a child!" I pulled her towards me and sat her on the bed, a trembling jelly of embarrassment. Then all in one breath she told me.

"I'd always been told you had to open your legs, but he turned me over and did it the other way."

I was silent for a moment. "Both times?"

"Yes, My Lady," she answered me. "Will that be all, My Lady?"

"I wonder..." I tapped her shoulder with my forefinger, wondering if it were possible.

"Yes, My Lady?"

"Never mind," I said jovially. "Come, let's to our dinner. I'm starved."

"Is it all right, then?"

"What? Ah, that! If it's all right with you, then that's all that matters."

She breathed a sigh of relief, and we made our way for the meal.

I ignored Raoul till after we'd eaten a hearty dinner, then glanced at him under my lashes and he came over to me from the other side of the table.

"Good evening, sweeting," he whispered, grinning from ear to ear. "I'm glad you are not too worried about your son, he won't be far away, that's for sure."

I stood and smiled at him. "I know Fernando wouldn't harm him." He linked arms with me and we walked slowly outside, much to the maid's surprise. "But I must find somebody from whom I can enquire about my son's treatment to relieve my mind, and it will be almost impossible to find anyone, till we catch up with the runaways."

He kicked a stone and we stopped under a large tree in full bloom, its branches shielding us from the inn.

"You can rely on me."

"That would be a help, thank you, Raoul. Tell me something." I leaned against the tree.

"Anything, sweeting."

"That manservant of yours."

"What about him?" Raoul looked into my eyes.

"I don't think he cares for the company of ladies, does he?"

He grinned down at me, his teeth shining in the dusk. "Not particularly, but he wouldn't refuse me a favour."

"You beast!" I thumped his shoulders, screaming curses at him. "How could you, the stupid old fool is sick with love for *you*!"

He laughed then, till the tears trickled out of the corners of his eyes, not seeming to feel my fists. "I had to teach you a lesson, sweeting."

"Let me go at once!" He obeyed me, but the look of mischief on his face made me smile, and soon I found I was joining him in his merry laughter.

"How did you know I was going to trick you?"

"Sit down, sweeting, the moon is nearly up, it's lovely out here."

He removed his velvet coat and spread it on the grass. We both sat, our backs against the tree, and watched the moon sliding into place.

"How did you know I'd changed rooms with my maid?"

"I know you, sweeting. You're far too stubborn a creature to surrender without a fight." He picked a blade of grass, and tickled my neck with it. "I wouldn't want to break the poor thing's heart. I'll send my man back again tonight."

"No, you mustn't! What about the older man with the beard? He looks as if he's lonely."

"You have a kind heart, sweeting. Very well, as you wish."

"And another thing."

"Mmmm?"

"Why were you so exhausted, you looked half dead this morning."

"Oh! I'd been up all night playing cards with the innkeeper."

"You . . . you . . ." but I couldn't say another word. He'd covered my mouth with his, and although I swore I wouldn't let this happen again, it seemed the natural thing to do out there in the moonlight, beneath the swaying branches.

"You've suffered too much, sweeting," he whispered hoarsely, "I'll always be near to take care of you from now on." I heard the rustle of my gown as he lifted it, and as I expected to feel him against me, he whispered, "Would you like me to arrange your maid's night of love, first?"

"No," I snapped peevishly, "You can do that later," but he was already on his feet.

"I won't be a moment, sweeting."

"But your coat." I pulled my gown over my legs.

"I'll be right back."

Closing my eyes, I saw little Louis' face in front of me, laughing, his dark eyes shining with contentment. And then, another picture came to give my heart a lurch; a little leg dragging along after its partner, forcing the first picture back, and I saw again the little chubby arms reach out for me. It was so real that I cried out, but just then Raoul returned, and his arms clasped me as we rolled on the grass in the velvet night, a bird call the only sound.

"You smell of wine, darling." I whispered. He just grunted and turned me over onto my stomach. The grass tickled me, but I loved the fresh earthy smell. He plunged into me, grunting. The weight of his body pushed me till the earth felt hard and I gasped as he took his pleasure, oblivious of my discomfort. I thought the plunging would never stop as it pushed harder and quicker. At last he gasped, and it was over. Then he slapped me hard on my buttocks.

"Ow! that hurt!" I turned over and dried the liquid that trickled down my legs with the skirt of my gown, but tripped on the hem.

"Oops, steady there, dearie!" A hand loosely held my arm as I steadied myself. A terrible realization came over me. I swayed at the shock and put my hands out to the tree for support.

"Who are you?" I sobbed, almost choking on the words.

"It's alright, dearie, I won't tell."

I felt myself slip to the ground. "I'll kill him!" I hissed, and clawed the grass.

"Oh, it wasn't as bad as all that," a simpering voice remarked, "Surely, dearie!"

It was Raoul's manservant, of course, the very one who had obliged my maid.

"Tell your master," I snarled, "That I won't rest till he is paid in full for this . . . this insult."

"There's no need to take that attitude, I'm sure," he pouted. "Only a little poke, I mean, joke."

I took several deep breaths, as the insulted servant made his way back to the inn, lisping his despair of 'never pleasing *some* people'.

I felt hopelessly lost and dirty. I'd thought Raoul my friend as well as lover. Now with the truth before me, I knew he was neither. I cried my loneliness into the dark night. If only I could find my son again I would devote myself to caring for him. Life was never secure for me. I seemed, as Madame de Maintenon had said, to invite trouble. Perhaps I'd been wrong thinking I was sending Raoul to the maid's bed. But surely that wasn't nearly as bad as what he'd done to me. And why had he needed to punish me this way? I couldn't understand it.

I crawled to my feet, and stumbled my way into the silent inn. Reaching my room, I fell on the bed and slept, fully dressed, determined to find out the truth.

Chapter 32

That night I was feverish, having nightmares of men with women's breasts, and Court ladies who lifted satin gowns to reveal male organs between silk garters. I saw a horse wearing a tasselled night cap, who winked at me and edged its head to one side, inviting me to follow it. Even the hunting dogs belonging to his Majesty, Bonne, Ponne and Nonne, had their black floppy ears jewelled with sapphires, and were part of the audience at a play attended by the Court.

On the stage I saw my son Louis and Don José. Don José had one leg, and Louis had a sword thrust through his middle. Don José pranced about the stage on his single leg, and Louis, with two perfect feet, showed his back to the audience where the point of the sword protruded.

I heard the Courtiers squeal their amazement at this brilliant trick. But then Fernando appeared, and clapped his hands. The stage darkened, and the curtains swayed, revealing Louis dragging an iron boot, larger than himself. The company jeered, pointing jewelled fingers at his foot, while the child cried and bent down, trying to lift the boot. Fernando watched from the side of the stage, arms folded, leaning lazily against a pillar, a satisfied smile playing about his sensuous mouth.

Suddenly, the stage became light, and an ivory-faced Madame de Maintenon appeared with Manoela, both wearing identical gowns of silver. There was no one else with them. They exchanged virginal looks while the audience yawned and began to drift out. Only Louis was left in the center of the stage, trying frantically to lift the iron boot so that he could join the others, but he was held fast, and tears poured down that angel face. All I could do was rave in my fever, knowing I was being held down.

For many weeks I knew nothing, but one day I woke, weak but clear-headed, and whispered, "Little Louis, where are you?"

My head ached with a dull thudding persistency, and my stomach contracted with anxiety. I tried to lift my head, but it was too painful, so I fell back against the pillow.

"There's a letter come for you," my maid quietly told me.

"Who is it from?"

"I don't know, but the messenger wore Madame de Maintenon's livery."

"Maybe it's about Louis." I forced myself up in the bed.

"No, you mustn't excite yourself, or you'll be ill again."

"I'll be ill if I don't read it. Give it to me at once!" My hands shook as I held the letter, causing the firm handwriting to swim before my eyes. "Read it to me, please. My bones seem to have turned to water."

The maid read:

Dearest Mama,

Madame de Maintenon is writing to you for me because my letters are not quite ready for words. I wish you a speedy recovery. I am in good health, and dearest Papa is very kind to me.

So Madame had adopted this method of letting me know that my darling was safe and well! How grateful I was!

My heart lifted to know he was well, but I felt a lurch at the mention of Fernando. As soon as I am strong, I told myself, *I'll deal with 'dearest Papa.'*

"Yes, read on, please."

She settled herself in the chair and continued:

I have a puppy dog, a present from his Majesty, and Madame de Maintenon says I mustn't tell you, but he wet my shoes this morning.

I smiled, imagining Madame de Maintenon choosing to write that down after all.

Our thoughts are all with you, dearest Mama, and we all wait in eagerness for your return.

All my kisses are here for you.

Your son,
Louis Fernando

I felt almost well again, knowing he was safe and happy.

"Are you all right, My Lady?"

"I'm feeling much better, and would like to dress and leave here at once."

"Oh, no. I dare not dress you. The physician from the Palace left strict instructions that, although you are much improved, rest is most important, and he won't hear of you leaving till the fall."

"God's teeth, woman, do as I say, or so help me, I'll have you dismissed!" She stood there, her dull face contorted, uncertain what to do. "Anyway, what ailed me?"

"They weren't sure, My Lady. One physician thought it was a brain fever."

"A brain fever! Bring me my mirror!"

"Now what would you be wanting with a mirror? Here, drink this mulled wine."

I shot her a glance that made her move on the instant, and was shocked to find, as I looked in the glass, that my hair had been cut. I fingered the tufts that were left with despair.

"It'll soon grow, if you obey the physician's orders, and eat to put some flesh on your bones."

I resolved to do as I was bade, and show them how quickly I could recover. A few days later I took my first tottering steps, and after that I progressed from day to day.

Surprisingly, I learned that Raoul had left taking his retainers with him when the physicians arrived, leaving only my maid, and I mentioned as much to her.

"You were too sick to be moved, My Lady. No one knew how long you would be forced to stay here. We are going for a short ride in the carriage today. I'll see if it's ready."

When the physician came again, he was so pleased with me that I begged him to say I was well enough to travel.

"Now, you must continue to rest, my dear. I'll make you a sleeping draught," he chuckled rather unpleasantly, then paused a moment whilst he sought my acceptance and thanks.

I'd penned a letter to Louis as soon as I felt able. The first time I tried to write, my hands were shaking. The quill felt clumsy in my fingers, but eventually I managed to write:

My dearest Louis Fernando,

Your beautiful letter helped me back to good health. I long to see you, and pray for you each night. I hope your shoes dried quickly! How kind of his Majesty to give you a pet of your own.

My dearest wishes to the King and Madame de Maintenon. Be a good boy, and do as you are told. I'm sure you are grown a great deal since the Summer, although I hope you will be pleased with the big doll I am keeping for you. Perhaps it can be dressed as a cavalry officer, if a doll seems to be rather babyish to you.

Soon I will return, when we will play all your favourite games. Be happy.

All my heart's love to you my darling son,

Your devoted

Mama

The effort of writing had exhausted me, but my heart felt light, knowing I would soon be reunited with my darling boy.

The next day we took our last walk before our journey home. Scuttling clouds moved quickly across the sky, and gently falling amber leaves sailed over us as we reached the big tree.

Beneath the boughs a carpet was forming, as each leaf

added to its thickness. I remembered the events of the night before I became ill, but was relieved to feel no emotion of any kind. The leaves made a crackling sound, as I pushed them with my foot, and I pulled my cloak more tightly round my shivering frame.

"It grows chilly, My Lady. The summer has gone for sure."

"And just as well, too," I answered.

On our return the innkeeper met us at the door, bowing obsequiously. "I've received word from Madame de Maintenon that you're not to worry about money. It's all being taken care of." He stepped back.

"I thank you for your attention," I told him.

"We give thanks to God I'm sure, My Lady, that you've recovered."

When I was settled by the fire in my chamber I turned to my maid. "Do you know that in all the time you've looked after me, I never asked your name?" She flushed. "I had other things on my mind, I'm afraid."

She gave the fire an extra hard poke. "It's Celia, M'Lady."

"Well then, Celia, I think it's high time I thanked you for looking after me. Would you like to keep that dress, and any of the others? In fact, when we return, I want you to have all the things we have here."

"Oh, My Lady!" she stroked the fine cloth of my rose-colored day dress.

"And here," I removed the bracelet, encrusted with rubies from my arm. "Hold out your hand!"

Her pale eyes opened wide, "Oh, My Lady, I couldn't!"

"Of course you could. Now, do as I say."

Still clutching the dress, she held out her bony arm, and I slipped the bracelet over her veined hand. "Fancy, a ruby bracelet and all those beautiful dresses!"

"You deserve them, Celia. I've been most unjust to you." Before she could protest, I shooed her away. "Now, I must sleep," and sleep I did.

It was several days before the coach arrived for our homeward journey, but although I was most impatient to be off, it gave me time to regain my strength completely. In my talks with Celia, we discussed little Louis, and she never tired of listening.

"I love children, My Lady, and Master Louis Fernando is the loveliest child."

I suddenly had a thought. "I want you to look after him when we return, Celia. I trust you. Would you like that?"

The watery eyes no longer seemed ugly, like those of a dead fish.

"Oh, My Lady, no one will care for him better than I."

"Then it's settled." I could never bring myself to confess to Celia the trick I'd played on her with Raoul, but I wanted to make up for it in my own way.

Being dressed and ready to leave at last, I helped to arrange my hair. "I'm so relieved it's grown enough to curl prettily."

"I never had pretty hair," Celia said, not unhappily. "Now I'm thirty, I'm quite resigned to being plain." I took a closer look at Celia. "I know I look much older, My Lady."

"I didn't mean to..."

"Even as a girl my skin was dry and mottled. They called me 'cabbage-face' at home."

"Oh, Celia!" I laughed, "Poor Celia, how awful for you!"

She held her bracelet up to the light, "Not any more, My Lady."

It gave me a warm feeling to know I had made her happy, and taking her arm I strode out to the waiting coach. The horses snorting in the cold morning air made a fine sight. The innkeeper stood, hands on hips, giving orders to his stable lad, and stood there, bowing, till we were out of sight.

"At last we are on our way home, Celia!" I sighed contentedly. "Give me the doll, please."

She handed me the beautiful life-like doll, the image of little Louis that the unknown girl in the Palace had given to me in the summer. I twisted the curls round my fingers and fluffed out the dress.

"She's very clever to get such a likeness, My Lady."

"Indeed she is, Celia. Do you know her well?"

"I've never seen her until the day we left."

"Well, I must thank her properly. She must have worked very hard, it's really the most glorious doll I've ever seen."

"I'll make enquiries, My Lady."

"Please do, Celia. Little Louis will certainly adore it." I lifted the doll's dress to admire the blue satin slippers, and felt a coldness clutch my heart. My back went stiff with fear, and I thought that I would collapse.

"I knew you should have rested a little longer." I heard Celia's worried voice as if from afar. I drank from the flask which she held to my lips, coughing as the fiery liquid ran down my throat. "You're very pale, My Lady. Shall I ask the coachman to turn back?"

"Look at the legs, Celia," I heard myself whisper.

"The legs, My Lady?"

"Look at the doll's legs and feet!"

She sucked in her breath. "Is this some cruel joke, do you think?"

"If it is, I must have a mortal enemy. If the child were to see it..." I was in a towering rage, and could easily have strangled the girl who had made it with my bare hands. One of the doll's legs was longer than the other and the foot hung crooked.

Celia shook her head forbodingly. "I'm afraid it's witchcraft, My Lady."

Chapter 33

If I thought I'd been frightened before, it was nothing compared to the dread I felt when Celia told me of her suspicions. The coach wheels squeaked, but to me it was a scream, every sound intensified, till I was shaking uncontrollably. I dropped the doll as if it were burning hot. Celia picked it up, and her eyes grew troubled as she examined the deformed foot.

"My Lady, one of the servants knows a witch who lives in a cave in one of the villages, and she told me that you can buy spells."

"But what has that to do with it? Who would want to buy a spell to hurt my child?" But even as I spoke, I could think of several. Celia removed the satin slipper, and revealed pins sticking into the doll's foot. A cold shiver crept up my neck to my head as I mouthed the dreaded words, "Black magic!"

The morning had darkened as if for rain. Dark clouds were scuddering across the grey sky. It was hard to believe how clear it had been on leaving the inn. Trees swished their branches backwards and forwards in time with the wind that had blown up, causing brown and rust-colored leaves to fly through the air.

"Does this mean that little Louis is in danger, Celia, or has the damage already been done?" I begged, frantically. She looked away from me, picking her grey wool dress into bunches. "Celia, for God's sake! Tell me, I must know." Grabbing her shoulders I shook her, forcing an answer from her.

Large drops of rain hit the windows as the day became darker. I shivered and felt my heart thud fast and loud, as if it would burst.

"I'm not sure, My Lady, but from what I've heard, anyone wanting to harm another seldom stops at injury. But there are ways of fighting it, I think."

"What ways?" I cried. "Tell me, at once!"

Celia's face screwed up in thought. "I don't know, only what I've heard here and there. There was talk that the King's ex-mistress Athénaïs, the Marquise de Montespan, had a Black Mass celebrated because she was desperate to take the place of his other mistress, Louise de la Valliere, and it worked, but that was a long time ago."

"Where is she now?"

"I'm not sure, My Lady. I think she retired to a convent."

"We must find her, and at once!"

"You would do better to consult Madame de Maintenon, I think, My Lady."

"What, Madame de Maintenon practices witchcraft?" It seemed beyond belief.

"Oh no, it was her, they said, who even the dreaded Abbé Guibourg couldn't work against. His powers failed in the end, and that was when Madame de Maintenon replaced Athénaïs in the King's affections."

"I've never heard this mentioned before. Are you sure it isn't just Court gossip?" My body ached from the tension of straining to catch every word above the noise of the wind which had whipped up to an alarming degree, causing the coach to sway precariously.

"The woman told me a lot more, My Lady, but I'm sure that Madame de Maintenon knows it all."Celia had that amazing habit of servants, who couldn't wait to tell you any trifling scandal, but as soon as they knew they held your undivided attention, sat back and waited for you to wheedle further information from them. Celia's moment of power had arrived, and I could see by the smug expression on her mottled face and her folded arms, that she intended to drag that moment out as long as possible.

I was in no mood for play-acting. "My son's life might well be in danger! I'm only going to ask you once, Celia," I said in a clear loud voice. "Either you tell me all you know at once, and I mean *all*, or I'll give orders to the outriders to prise it out of you. This is no trifling matter."

The complacent expression faded before my eyes, and turned to one of guilt. "I was going to tell you, anyway." She sounded hurt.

"Yes, well go on!"

"I heard that Athénaïs, the Marquise de Montespan, had children sacrificed on her naked body in Black Mass." Holding my breath, I felt sick to my soul. "There was an execution long before I came to the Palace. The beautiful Marquise de Brinvilliers, I think it was. Before she was put to death for poisoning many of her relatives, she said she wasn't the only one involved. There was an inquiry, ordered by the King, and they found a Satanic temple in La Voisin's house. Black candles, and a mattress on the altar."

"Well yes, get on," I whispered.

"There was a furnace behind it, and charred bones of children."

"That's enough! I can't believe it's true! How do you know your friend isn't making half of it up?" But I knew it probably was all too true. Vomit spewed from my mouth, while I retched, shivering and shaking in a cold sweat.

"Oh My Lady, you poor soul." Celia quickly tried to wipe the mess off the seat, and dabbed at my dress as best she could with her handkerchief, but the stench was terrible in the confined coach, and the handkerchief of little use. I felt too weak to do anything about it.

"Water!" I whispered, while I continued to throw up. She fumbled in the valise, and produced a flask. Holding my lolling head forward, she tipped the liquid for me to drink. I coughed as the water touched my throat, but at least it calmed my stomach, and I felt a little strength creep along my arms and legs.

"No more," I said, and pushing it away I raked at the damp hair that had fallen in my eyes. I was terrified for my son, and in all my wretchedness I prayed that I could save him from whoever was plotting against us. "Celia," I croaked.

"Yes, My Lady?" She turned from her task of mopping up the seat with a rag she'd found.

"We must make a list of all possible enemies. Who could be our enemies?"

"I can't think of anyone."

"But I can."

The wind had dropped as the day became ominously darker. Bird calls became louder and the trees seemed to stand out much more clearly than usual. I winced as there was a flash of light, and then thunder crashed around us. The coach slowed, creaking and shuddering to a stop.

"They must have decided to seek shelter." Celia's frightened voice came from her corner, where she crouched like a little mouse.

The door was opened by the drenched outrider, dripping rain as he leaned from his horse.

"I think it would be advisable, Madame, if we took shelter till the storm passes. The horses are nervous. With your permission, of course."

"Only for a very short period. It is most urgent that I reach the Palace today. By all means stop for a rest, but we mustn't delay."

"Very well, Madame, as you wish. There is an *auberge* quite near, but I suggest sheltering at the side of the road till the thunder passes us. It will only be a matter of minutes."

"Minutes, how many minutes might make the difference between life and death to my son?"

"I beg your pardon, Madame?" I looked up, startled. I hadn't realized that I'd spoken my thoughts aloud.

"I'm sure you'll do your utmost for all our safety. Do as you think fit, but please make all speed."

"Thank you, Madame."

He shut the window, and I picked up the doll from its corner, removed the pins, and stuck them in the red velvet upholstery. Placing the slipper back on the foot, my fingers cold and trembling, I wondered what Madame de Maintenon would say to me when I showed her this gruesome thing.

"Pray," she would certainly advise. Although I had to admit I didn't really place much hope in prayer any more, any hope, however small, must be used, I reasoned. The coach turned slightly, causing us to lurch against each other, and the doll fell, cracking its china head into ugly jagged lines. It stared up at us the brown glass eyes never wavering. The shattered porcelain face looked terrifying beneath its perfect silk black curls.

I let out a strangled cry. "Look, the wooden foot has dropped off! Put it together again, quickly, Celia, quickly!"

The sight that met the eyes of the men as they peered through the windows while the coach sheltered under a tree must have seemed ludicrous in the extreme; two grown women crying over a broken doll. Celia tried to replace the crudely-fashioned wooden foot, but the only way was by wrapping it and the leg together at the base with a ribbon I tore from my hat. The brown ribbon was an ugly bandage. I didn't care if the men did think we were demented. In my tortured mind, I imagined that our ministrations would mean that little Louis' foot would be healed and he would be safe.

Snatching the doll from Celia, I sang 'Rosas das Rosas', the lullaby Fernando had taught me in the days when life was full of happiness, as I nursed the doll like a baby in my arms. As I felt the tears trickle slowly down my cheeks, they splashed onto the cracked doll's pitiful face. I think it was then that my reason began to fail me.

"We must mend its face," I said.

"We will find a way, My Lady, I promise you," came Celia's troubled reply, as she tried to force a flask into my hand.

"Milk, thank you, Celia." I held a little to the doll's mouth, and tried to coax it to drink. "You must drink, Louis, to make you strong. Drink to please your dear Mama!"

Celia was looking at me strangely, while the thunder sounded fainter and fainter, as it travelled farther away. The coach moved on at a snail's pace, and turned into the road.

"We'll soon be home," I crooned to my baby, rocking him to the sway of the coach.

"Let me look after the doll, My Lady."

"Don't touch him!" I cringed back into my seat.

Celia's outstretched hands slowly fell to her lap, deep creases of concern on her face.

I clutched my baby closer, and covered him to the neck with my shawl.

"I knew it was too soon for you to travel! You're almost as sick as you were before."

"Sick? I'm not sick, my baby's sick. Use your eyes, woman."

"Now, My Lady, you know how Celia helped to make you well? I'll make the baby well, too. You trust me, don't you, My Lady?"

I could see the worried look in her eyes, and allowed her to prise my hands from the baby. "Make him better quickly, Celia, he's all I have," I whimpered.

"You have me, My Lady." I watched, fascinated, as she removed my shawl and completely rewrapped the baby, covering its face. "Trust me, My Lady." She held the bundle, watching me closely, then pushed it gently but firmly under the seat.

I made a movement as if to take it back. "No, *ducette*," Celia said firmly.

"*Ducette*?" I was Berthe's *ducette*! Why was Celia calling me "*ducette*"? I felt tired, trembling like a jelly, just as in the days when I lay love-sick, and Berthe had nursed me. But this weakness was much worse, different and strange somehow.

"You must believe me, My Lady, that your son is quite safe in the Palace. That doll is only wood and porcelain. It isn't long since we received that lovely letter about Master Louis."

We didn't speak for some time, while I pondered on her words.

"Take a drink to warm you. Here, the damp is chilling."

As I was encouraged, I drank deeply, and was only half aware of Celia kicking the doll farther back till it was out of sight.

"There! Isn't that better, *ducette*? I think I need a warming too." Celia took a few sips, and then put the flask back in its place in the valise. "The storm upset you. I loathe them myself, but it's over now. Look! There is a rainbow, isn't it lovely?"

I shuddered, but as I followed her gaze, felt much better. "Indeed there is, Celia, and the rain has stopped. Now, let me see the letter again."

She took it from my reticule, and handed it to me. I read it again, and a warm glow caused my heart to ache. Of course he was safe! The storm had upset me more than I'd realised. But there was something still niggling at the back of my mind. "Of course!"

"Of course what, *ducette*?"

"We mustn't forget the Black Magic!"

"It will be dealt with as soon as we are home, I promise."

"I think perhaps we should pray, Celia. I know Madame de Maintenon would advise it."

"A very good idea."

We knelt on the floor of the bumpy coach, our eyes closed, hands clasped in front of us, and recited our silent prayers.

We were interrupted when the coach ground to a halt, and the bundle rolled up to me. I felt strangely peaceful, and didn't prevent Celia from pushing it back again, and wedging it with the food basket.

"How tired I am of inns, Celia, although I'd love to rest my head."

The *auberge* looked much like all the others. On wobbly legs I was half carried by Celia and an outrider through the door, and passed the travellers supping their ale to a room on the floor above. It was larger than usual, and a wood fire crackled merrily in the grate.

"I really do think it would be wiser to stay the night, *ducette.* A warm bed is just what you need."

"I don't know," I yawned, and lifted my skirts high to feel the warmth from the fire on my chilled limbs.

Celia giggled like a girl, "That's more like it. Let me help you undress, then in you go!"

I didn't need telling twice. The huge bed did look inviting, plump and soft. Soon I was tucked up, and sipping delicious broth, while Celia drank hers by the fire. She lit the candle, removed the plates, then drew the flowered curtains.

"Now, straight to sleep."

"Thank you, Celia," I murmured, as I snuggled down, and fell into a dreamless slumber.

Chapter 34

Another morning in another inn, was my first thought on waking, and I swore it would be the last. The curtains were already open, and Celia had lit the fire. A steaming drink sat waiting on my bedside table. What a gem she'd turned into, I mused. Feeling much improved after breaking my fast, I hurried about my toilette, eager to be off, and my travels over at last. I hummed as I checked my appearance in the cracked mirror. My cheeks were no longer pink and my eyes seemed much larger than before. But I didn't care, even though my dress hung on my body. That would soon be taken care of. I hadn't noticed my appearance yesterday, but then I was too excited at the thought of returning home to care.

This leg of our journey was pleasant, past fields and narrow waters, and we made good time until we felt a sickening jolt, and I knew we'd lost a wheel.

"I could cry at having to endure another delay!" I snapped at Celia.

We were transferred to the luggage coach, and finally arrived, not in grand style, but my heart was light and full of joy as I ran all the way to my little Louis' nursery.

The stumbling Celia was weighed down with my hand luggage. I ignored the stares and remarks of everyone we passed. Let them call me a mad woman! I was mad with happiness, if that were possible.

Panting for breath, I passed the lackeys at the doors, and was met by incredulous looks from the women sitting around, embroidering or chatting. I hurried to the bedchamber, and flung the door wide.

I was unprepared for the sight that met my eyes; there were two people in the bed, Fernando and de Villette. As this fact dawned on my hurt brain slowly, I stood transfixed, watching fascinated as the nude bodies continued to sleep undisturbed.

Suddenly, my heart seemed to stop. Wedged between them was the naked body of my son! I blinked my eyes, refusing to accept what stared me in the face. Strangely enough, I didn't care that he was asleep between them. Corrupted he might be, but at least he was alive. The dark lashes touched the peach-like cheeks which had the lustre of health.

Celia stood like a statue at my side, not knowing how to react. I leaned over the sleeping bodies, and picked my son up in my arms, while Fernando snored on. De Villette lay there, her loose breasts pale, like turnips in the half lit room. The bulk of little Louis was heavy in my arms. Never had I loved him more than at that moment. He blinked his eyes open as I set him down, not forgetting to satisfy myself that his foot was still intact. A wave of nausea went over me as I looked, and thanked God that it seemed perfectly normal. Celia sprang to life, covering him with the shirt that had been discarded at the bottom of the bed.

I put two fingers in front of my mouth, "Sh!"

He gave a whoop of joy, and buried his head in my skirts, wrapping his arms about my hips. How he'd grown, I could hardly believe it!

"Mama, you're home!"

The shirt fell away from him, and Celia rushed forward to cover him again. I had my darling back with me, or rather I was back with my darling, dearest child! I'd forgotten how warm and fresh his skin smelt, and as I kissed the glossy, black curls, I trembled, remembering how I'd feared for him.

Something was pushing us. Little Louis disentangled himself, "Look, Mama, Look who's come to welcome you. It's my dog, Sonny."

The dog licked his master's hands with joy, and together they rolled about in the shirt, the dog pushing his head against his master each time he stopped the game, insisting on continuing the merry romp.

But Celia felt he should be dressed. While my son struggled in Celia's grasp, his nanny appeared and helped to dress him. Nanny persevered while arms and legs flailed about, until he was properly attired in blue velvet breeches and jacket. I'd only seen him in an infant's dress before. Pride welled up in me. He was a fine boy!

"How grown up you are, my darling!"

Sonny leaped about his master, brown coat shining, bushy tail wagging furiously.

Nanny showed no surprise at the figures in the bed, just sniffed her disapproval, and muttered under her breath to me, "Believe me, Donna Solange, I'm glad to see you returned safely to us. I only stayed for your sake, and the little master's, of course."

"I understand, Nanny, I'm very grateful." As indeed, I was.

"Forgive me, Donna Solange, but you don't look too well yet. Don't let this spectacle upset you."

"Thank you, Nanny, I won't."

She gripped little Louis' hand tightly, a 'no nonsense' expression on her disciplined face. Sonny sniffed at my shoes, then leaped over to his master, and followed Louis to the door. My heart felt heavy. The foot still dragged as before, but what was that, compared to the fears I'd had?

"We'll away to our walk," Nanny muttered, "Your dear Mama will rest in her *appartement* till she's had time to consider the situation."

Much emphasis was placed on the word 'situation'. Little

Louis' head was turned towards me while she marched him away. He mouthed a kiss to me, and I did the same.

I was happy at last, not minding about the yawning de Villette who sat up and gawped. Bleary, blood-shot eyes peered up at me, while she dug her elbow in my husband's ribs. His sallow skin looked even darker against the white body on either side of him; the woman's skin was tinged with blue. One of her fat legs covered Fernando's hairy one. She pulled a sheet from under her, and covered her sagging flesh.

"So, you're back, are you?" she drawled, and scratched her tousled hair.

Fernando grunted, but didn't move. De Villette dug her elbow in, harder this time, but I didn't wait to give them the pleasure of my company. I turned on my heel, and made my way to my appartements, Celia talking incessantly at my side of that fickle Don Fernando and that whore the Duchesse de Villette. "I always knew those foreigners had dreadful habits!"

I soon learned that dear Berthe had passed away in my absence, but I had little time to grieve. I had to write to Thérèse and tell her it was a peaceful end. How I wished my friend were here to help me! I had a task before me that needed strength and cunning, and prayed that I was strong enough to overcome the evil that threatened my son.

Celia dressed my hair in red ribbons, clustered on either side of my face. It was the first time I'd worn red since I'd left Spain. She held Don Fernando's rubies towards me as I examined myself in the mirror.

"I won't wear those, I hate them!"

"You need something round your neck, and I'll have to take that waist in more. Look how the gown hangs loose!"

I tossed the magnificent rubies aside, and tied a red ribbon round my neck. I applied rouge with abandon. My lips were the red of the rubies, and no longer looked pinched.

"Come, Celia, we must work fast. Have you managed to find the girl who gave us the doll yet?"

"She's nowhere to be found. I've asked in the kitchen. One of the stable boys is making enquiries, My Lady."

As she spoke, Tienne came smiling towards us. "Welcome home, Donna Solange!" How sick the title 'Donna' made me! But nothing could mar my joy at seeing my dear Tienne again. We embraced, and I marvelled at the handsome young man who stood before me, upright and strong of chin.

"I've a note for Celia," he said. She took it quickly, and scanned the contents, then handed it to me and read:

> "Tell your Mistress to take one hundred golden louis when the moon rises, to the cave outside the gates, forty paces and one to the left, then ninety paces forward. Come alone and disguised. Ignore these instructions at your peril."

I crushed it into my sleeve and shuddered.

"I'll go for you, My Lady," Celia offered.

"Go where?" Tienne wanted to know.

"I'll go alone, and now I must speak to Madame de Maintenon. Celia will tell you while I'm gone, Tienne, dear." I left him, looking perplexed.

In spite of feeling hungry, fear soon removed my appetite.

I asked for an audience with Madame de Maintenon, and was not disappointed. It gave me hope, remembering what Celia had told me. In spite of the Black Masses said against her, Madame de Maintenon had won the King's heart. I carried the crushed doll in a fur muff in front of me, and curtsied to Madame. I took strength from the sight of her tranquil face.

"I am glad to have you back amongst us, Solange. A little thinner, but well again, I am thankful to see." She held her cheek forward for me to kiss.

"Thank you, dear Madame, for that and for your letters."

"It was nothing, your son is a lovely child." She dismissed her ladies with a movement of her plump fingers. The lace on her grey hair was nun-like, and she seemed more tired than I remembered.

"It is a great compliment to know you take an interest in my son." I sat next to her where she had indicated, and sipped the wine which was offered me. I felt I might need more than wine before the night was out.

"Would you look at this awful doll Madame?"
"What doll?"
I held the fur muff towards her. "I have had a most frightening experience."
"In what way, child?"
"Perhaps you can help me to get to the bottom of something that I don't understand."
She held her glass in mid-air as I removed the doll. Her eyes seemed to lose their lustre, and I heard her suck in her breath.
"Where did it come from?" Before she touched it, she felt the cross at her throat, and I saw her close her eyes as if in prayer.
"How did it come into your possession? You must tell me when, and if the face was cracked when you found it. Was the bandage already on the ankle?"
I told her all I knew, and watched as she nodded her head slowly, several times, deep in thought. It seemed an eternity before she spoke again.
"I see." Then she held the doll carefully and examined the foot. "You say you removed the pins?"
"Yes." Although I knew the eyes were only glass, I was sure they could see. Madame pressed her forehead with two fingers, and sighed deeply. The room seemed to have gotten colder, and the heavy blue velvet drapes moved in a draught from the windows. Placing the doll carefully on the table, Madame frowned. It's glassy stare seemed to follow my movements. I drained my glass, and tucked my dress tightly round my legs.
"Show me the note!" she demanded. I did so. After reading it, Madame tore it up quickly, and said "Put it on the fire at once!"
"But I may forget the instructions."
"You are not to go." Madame's face was pale.
"But I must!"
"I forbid it, Solange!" Madame rose, walked determinedly to the fireplace and flung the pieces of paper onto the flames which licked at it hungrily, then died down again.

She sat in the big velvet chair by the fire, and held her hands out to its warmth. Her many rings flickered and dazzled in the glow. She sat there, debating to herself, even after I'd joined her opposite the fireplace. I hadn't realized how cold I was till I felt the heat seep into me. Staring at the exquisite lapis lazuli cup on the mantle, surmounted by Neptune in silver, I began to count the diamonds round the bottom.

"We will pray together," she said at last in a dull monotonous voice.

I came back to reality with a start. "The way you prayed to be the King's mistress, instead of the Marquise Athénaïs?"

"Who told you that?" Madame hissed angrily. The color had returned to her face, eyes flashing in rage. Her hand flew to her forehead, and she pressed hard, as if to ease a pain.

"I'm sorry, Madame, I've spoken out of turn, but I've been sick with worry for my child."

"Who told you that story?" she insisted, her voice raised in temper.

"So it isn't true? I'd hoped it was," I said dejectedly. Disappointment welled up in me, and I felt hopelessly afraid again.

"I was *never* the King's mistress," Madame stormed, keeping her voice level. "It has been my fortunate vocation in life to help His Majesty onto a path of righteousness and purity, for the sake of his soul. The fact that others have failed in the end to attain the opposite of my attentions, only goes to prove that prayer and a blameless life reap just rewards."

"I understand, Madame," I said in a respectful voice, and was sure I saw the familiar twinkle in her eyes as her lips twitched up the corners.

"I know you've been sorely worried, child, and so we will pray together again, and if we continue to do so, morning and night, you can be sure your prayers will be answered." She lifted her first finger with the large sapphire ring, and shook it at me. "But you must lead a blameless life from now on. I will see to it that Master Louis' leg is treated properly, and I will take sole charge and responsibility for his health."

"I would rather he didn't take the waters after all, Madame."

"Very well."

"Oh Madame, I feel as if a great burden has been lifted from my shoulders, and a weight from my heart! Thank you, dear Madame. I will do exactly as you say, but I want him to stay here with me, where I know he's safe."

She leaned back and fluffed her dark dress around her. "Good. Then let us pray."

I recited after her:

"Good St. Luke, our Lord's beloved physician, safeguard my child's body from all evil wishing."

I clasped my hands tight, and gnawed my knuckles in the intensity of my emotion. When we had finished I felt strangely at peace.

Madame opened her eyes and asked me, "Have you anything else to tell me?"

"I don't think so, Madame."

"What of your husband, Don Fernando?"

"I . . . I don't think . . ."

"Don't be afraid, child, you may tell me anything. I want to help you."

I swallowed, and explained the spectacle that met me on my return.

Madame frowned, "It's not unusual, I'm afraid."

"It's happened before, then?"

"It's quite common for the ladies of the Court to put the children in bed with them, but hardly usual for a child to join a lady and her paramour. I am most displeased. We must make sure that it isn't repeated, and I myself will instruct Master Louis in his devotions."

"Thank you, Madame," I answered, imagining little Louis' dismay at having to sit still for hours on end at such a tender age. "I'm very grateful for your help, dearest

Madame. I can't tell you how relieved I am feeling." I could relax at last, and I sank back into my chair enjoying the warmth.

"Isn't there something you've forgotten to tell me, Solange?"

I sat up with a start. "Do you mean about Monsieur Raoul?"

"I do *not* mean Monsieur Raoul, I've heard quite enough about that disreputable character."

"Then I'm not sure what you mean . . . oh, yes, I know. About Athénaïs and the Black Masses."

"What!" Madame got to her feet surprisingly quickly, her face masked in anger.

"But I thought you knew all about them. I'll tell you all I heard."

"I do not wish to hear! Only who gave you this . . . this information." Madame walked quickly towards the window, and I meekly followed. She spun round, and I could see she was seething at my news. Her mouth was clamped shut, causing her lips to wrinkle.

"I only heard the servants gossiping one day, long before I left for Spain, Madame. I can't remember who they were." (I didn't want to get Celia into trouble).

"Are you quite sure?" She screwed up her eyes, and peered into mine.

"I'll try to remember if it's important, Madame." This seemed the perfect answer, for she relaxed, and became more herself.

"We will speak of this matter another time. I'm feeling fatigued." The two fingers pressed again on the lined forehead.

"I am sorry to have taken up so much of your time, Madame." I curtisied. She nodded slowly, her mind miles away, it seemed. I glanced towards the shattered doll, lying spread-eagled where Madame had placed it. The glass eyes were watching me. "Shall I leave the doll here?"

"Yes, I will dispose of it."

I forced myself to look away from the stare, hoping never

to see it again. Madame had closed her eyes, so I tiptoed from the room to find little Louis with Tienne and Celia, chatting with the ladies.

Sonny frisked about, making himself a nuisance, much to Nanny's tut-tutting as the dog nearly tripped her up. Tienne caught her as she fell forward, her arms outstretched. A look of complete surprise was on her stern features. I couldn't help joining in the laughter.

To watch little Louis was my biggest pleasure. I'd almost forgotten the note and the doll, but Celia wouldn't let me. I kissed my little boy who flung himself into my arms, then Celia took me aside.

"Come and tell me what Madame de Maintenon said."

I was about to tell her I'd stay with my son for a while, but even as I opened my mouth, he was running away from me, full of mischief, after the dog who'd almost disappeared under an ebony and mother-of-pearl cabinet. Only a piece of frisky tail could be seen. I knew it would soon be his bedtime, and reluctantly pulled myself away from the happy scene.

After we had changed our costumes, we made our way to dine in the Grand Salon, pushing our way through the crowds.

"There's so much chattering and bustle that we can talk undisturbed if we keep our voices modulated, and our expressions gay, Celia." I nodded to right and left. It hardly seemed that I'd been away; there was the Duchesse de Seasti, fatter than ever. She caught my eye, and came waddling over.

"How lovely you look, Donna Solange! We all wondered where that husband of yours kept you hidden!"

"Just a little change of scene, Duchesse," I answered the chalk mask. Soon we were joined by several of my old acquaintances, but we made polite excuses, and took our places at table.

How gay everyone looked, beribboned and garlanded more elaborately than I remembered. The lackeys served us venison and sweetbreads, garnished in exquisite designs. Everything was piled high from gold platters. I tasted the fish which was placed before me. It was delicious!

As we ate, I informed Celia of my conversation with Madame, remembering to smile, and between courses, talk through closed teeth as I'd seen others do on several occasions, if they didn't wish to be overheard.

As I popped a succulent piece of *gateau* into my mouth, I noticed Fernando squeezing into a chair with de Villette opposite him. I was glad they were so far away, even though everyone would note our separation. It was one thing to be separated by leagues, but quite another to be at the same table without acknowledging each other.

I felt a lurch as I recalled how I'd once felt about him. Then our eyes met. Even from across the room, I could see him flush, then whisper across to de Villette who turned her elaborate *coiffe* in my direction and gave me a stony smile. I waved prettily. Fernando strode towards me, taking long, elegant steps. I had to admit he was by far the handsomest man at Court. How the cream silk ruffles at his throat became his dark complexion!

"Don't acknowledge him," I hissed to Celia from the corner of my mouth. He stood beside me as I drank my wine to the bottom of the goblet.

"I need to talk with you!" I could feel all eyes turned our way with interest. The noises of cutlery on gold plate, chatter and laughter drowned my whisper.

"Not any more." Aloud I raised my voice; "No, I really don't think I'd care to join your fat friend, I find her conversation decidedly dull."

There were appreciative titters across from me.

"We have matters to be discussed," he replied furiously.

"I'm sure we do," I hissed, but in a loud voice I answered, "As you have sworn you've finished with her, I suppose I could spare a word or two with you."

"I haven't dined yet, so . . ." he began.

"But I have." I smiled up to him, and allowed him to help me to my feet.

I gave Celia a sly wink, and linked my arm in my husband's. I told him under my breath, "If you glance in her direction, I'll kick you in the shins." We created quite a stir as we passed de Vilette. Without slowing our pace I said in a stage whisper, "What's that awful odour?" and wrinkled my nose. This was duly noted. I could hear the laughter long afterwards.

"That wasn't necessary!"

"Neither was your kidnapping of our son!"

"That has nothing to do with it!"

"I was worried and insulted!" We passed the huge displays of flowers in their golden urns, and then sat at a table, where we took wine together.

"I've missed you, Solange," he covered my small hand with his hairy, large one, causing my flesh to tingle. I drew my hand away.

"You knew I was ill, and never a word from you, as usual. I'll never forgive you for stealing my son!"

"*Our* son."

"Are you sure?" I asked sarcastically, eyeing him with disgust.

The muscles in his cheeks twitched as if I'd slapped him. "I love the boy, I know he's mine."

"Do you, indeed? Then you know more than I do."

He clenched his teeth. "We've no privacy here. I've a great deal to say to you."

"I'll enjoy listening. I've nothing else to do for an hour or so, and it may prove to be entertaining." I made my voice as casual as I knew how, drawling my words lazily. But all the while my heart was pounding. How I wished that I hated him! It would have made things so much simpler.

He flushed angrily. "Stop playing games, Solange."

"I was under the impression it was you playing games, not I."

"From what I've heard, you've done more than play. You're the talk of the Palace."

"Good, it's gratifying to be remembered!"

I allowed him to take my arm and escort me to our apartments. He walked so fast I had to run to keep up with him. Behind closed doors, he stood, arms akimbo, and glowered at me. I pretended not to notice, and regarded my reflection in the mirror.

"I wished to talk with you with good intentions, but you insist on making it impossible for me," he roared.

I spoke into the mirror, keeping my voice steady. "Aren't you forgetting that you removed *my* son without my permission, making me ill with worry? Because of you and your stupid ways, I've spent months of anguish. I could have died for all you cared, while you amused yourself with that old cow!"

He spun me round by the shoulders, and shook me till my teeth rattled, and bawled down at me, "The only reason I took Fernando was to get treatment for his leg! How was I to know his case wasn't suitable for the waters. I was told it was an Act of God, and rest would cure it."

"That isn't what Fagin said."

"He doesn't know everything, and neither do you. The foot is just the same."

"For your information, Madame de Maintenon is attending to it with much success."

"Be that as it may, and kindly do not address *my* son by *your* name. You may call him Louis. The 'Fernando' is optional. I will thank you to keep your hands to yourself, or I'll have you removed from this room. It would have suited you very well if I had died, wouldn't it? You could have claimed the child you profess to love as your own."

He placed his hands around my neck, his thumbs lightly pressing.

"If I wanted you dead, there are quicker ways, by far."

"Leave this room at once!"

"You can't make me. I will go when I have told you what I came to tell you."

"In that case, perhaps you would show some manners, and bring me a chair."

He removed his hands from my neck, and I swallowed in relief. There was no telling what he'd do in one of his rages. As I sat in the chair he brought me, I realized my legs were shaking. I must have been mad to agree to see him alone. The man was demented.

"Pour me a glass of wine, please." He seemed happy to do so, and poured one for himself as well. With his glass in one hand he leaned against the mantlepiece.

"If you will allow me to speak without interruption, I think you will understand that my actions are quite reasonable, under the circumstances."

"Hah!"

"Please, just let me explain."

"Explain away, let the charade begin." I settled myself comfortably, and sipped my wine.

"You won't even allow me the chance to speak. I am judged and condemned without trial."

"So, this is to be a trial, is it? And if you're proved guilty, what then? The guillotine?"

"Ah, but what if I can prove my innocence?"

"And why would you wish to do that?"

"I would have thought you knew that already. What do you expect me to do, lie down on the floor, and let you trample all over me?" He swung his glass out, and dregs of wine spun out, splattering the velvet-hung wall. He turned away from me and refilled his glass from the decanter at his elbow, and after a glance in my direction, replenished mine. Then he drew up a chair near mine, and ran a hand through his glossy hair which shone from the flickering candles.

"When I left you at my home in Spain, you knew I was summoned to do important work for France. I may never talk of it, even to you. I must ask you to trust me. His Majesty will vouch for the imperative task he set me. As you know the war continues, and at any time I may be called away again." As he spoke I noted the tired lines, etched in his face, and almost stretched my hand out to comfort him. How could I tell if he was lying? His story sounded true enough, so far. "I had only been here a very short time when you arrived with Raoul and our son. What was I to think? I don't want to drag up the past, that is best forgotten, and so I won't mention my Uncle, except to say . . . no, that is better left alone." He didn't look at me, but seemed to grow weary as he continued. "I was away from you a long time. A man gets very lonely, away from his loved ones. I admit I was jealous and angry to think of you, a woman amongst all those soldiers with only Raoul to protect you, knowing of his feelings for you. I have since come to know Raoul rather better. We are now good friends. The unfortunate timing of your arrival painted a picture at the worst possible time, I know. The Duchesse and I had more than our share of wine, I admit it. But when one knows one may be called away at any time, perhaps never to return, one tends to indulge oneself. Who knows, there may never be another chance." He smiled, revealing his gleaming teeth, and I couldn't help but return it. "'The cow' was always waiting, no matter what insults I heaped on her. I only had to be there, and she was happy. When I took Fernando . . ."

"Louis," I interrupted.

"Fernando Louis," he acquiesced.

"Louis Fernando," I insisted.

He bowed his head, mocking me. "As you wish. I was glad of her support. She has never meant anything to me, you know. I'm really rather sorry for her."

"Hah!"

"How would *you* like to look in the mirror and see that puffy face and spreading body?"

"You have a point there," I agreed, sliding my hand delicately over my slender waist.

"I suppose I was flattered by her attention at one time, but that was long before I fell in love with you."

In spite of myself I knew I was weakening. I certainly wanted to believe him. As our eyes met, I suddenly longed for him to hold me in his strong arms, and tell me that he loved me still. He was waiting for me to speak.

The clock chimed on the mantle, and I stood up from the chair. "What time is it?" The moment that almost had us reunited, was broken. "I must know the time."

Fernando left his chair, "Why must you know the time?

It's eleven o'clock. What's so important? Are you meeting someone?" His voice had suspicion in its enquiry.

I gasped my relief, and flopped back in the chair. "Perhaps it's my turn to talk, but whatever you say, I've quite made my mind up."

"You're leaving me, and taking the child?"

"No, nothing like that."

"Then what is it that you are so determined about?"

"When I was about to leave here to look for little Louis, one of the servants gave Celia, my maid, a doll." I noted his puzzled expression but continued. "We can't find the girl, but know that she is evil. The doll looked just like little Louis and had pins stuck in its foot. I sobbed as I remembered.

"Don't go on," he was beside me, his arms around my shaking shoulders. "Where is this . . . this doll now?"

"Madame de Maintenon has it. It dropped, and its face cracked . . . it was horrible," I sobbed.

"I'll find the girl, at once. What did she look like?"

"Celia saw her, I didn't, and anyway, somebody sent a note to me, advising me to come alone to a cave near the village at midnight."

"Ah, then it's witches' work for sure! I don't believe in their rubbish. They earn their bread by tricking and terrifying dull-witted people. Show me this note."

"Madame de Maintenon threw it on the fire."

"The best place for it."

I dried my eyes quickly. "I have to keep the rendezvous. I'm afraid if I don't pay, harm will befall my son."

"Nonsense!"

"I'm not prepared to take the smallest chance."

"If you've made up your mind, I'll come with you, and watch out for you."

"But I must take a purse of gold.

"What! Where on earth will you get a purse of gold so quickly? You must be mad to even think of it. You really are naïve, Solange." Fernando placed a hand on my chin, and spoke more kindly to me.

"I'll go with you and take some of my men. I'll finish that

witch once and for all, and put an end to this thieving and blackmail."

I dried my eyes daintily on my handkerchief, and sniffed. "It's a pity she wasn't burnt with the rest of them. Who knows how many of their brats are still alive, continuing their evil practices?"

"Is it true, then about Athénaïs and the Black Masses?"

"The foolish woman must have parted with a small fortune, imagining she could hold on to the King. She was no match for the pious Madame and her relentless prayers, although I fail to see how he can stand her sour face."

"She can be very soothing."

"Perhaps, but only to an old man, which his Majesty is."

"I trust Madame, she is a real friend to me. I'm going now. Will you please hand me my cloak?" He gathered it around my shoulders lingeringly, but I twisted away, and left him standing, his face clouded in dismay.

"I'll wait for you in the Marble Courtyard, if you insist on this useless errand."

"The instructions were for me to go *alone*."

"We'll keep out of sight and remember, no golden louis."

"I have very few at the moment . . . anyway, leave me now, I must hurry."

Celia appeared and covered my red cloak with her own black cloak and hood. It brought back memories of the night Thérèse had eloped to England. Who would have dreamed that only a few years later my life would take such turns?

"You're sad, My Lady?"

"Not really, Celia, I was just thinking of the time Berthe helped me dress my friend for her elopment. I remember she made her wear servant's shoes, because they were stronger. Berthe really was an angel, a mother to her."

"And you shall do the same." Before I could protest, she changed my red slippers for her old leather boots. "I'm relieved that Don Fernando will be nearby tonight. I've heard bloodcurdling tales of the witches' Sabbaths and Masses. Don't drink anything, nor let her take any of your hair!"

"Oh Celia, you do go on!"

The clock on my table showed a quarter to the hour. We hugged briefly, and with her whispered warnings echoing in my ears, I hurried to the Marble Courtyard, keeping my face hidden by the hood. I didn't want Madame to hear I'd left the Palace. She'd be sure to guess where I was going.

Chapter 35

Fernando was standing by his horse. Seven men surrounded him on horseback. As I approached, he stopped talking, and the men faced me in the moonlight, greeting me under their breath and bowing low. I remember wondering at Raoul being amongst them. I couldn't mistake those sparkling eyes.

"I'll lift you in front of me." Fernando held his arms out.

"No, I'll go on foot, someone may be watching. The witch must have spies at Court, else how could I have had word?"

"Perhaps you are right. I'll leave a trail for you, of rags tied to the trees as I go along. Here, take this lamp." He lowered his voice and bent over my hand, kissing it softly. The shaking of my body made the lamp flicker.

I shivered, perhaps from his lips, or the breeze pushing at my hood. Pulling it tighter round my face, I watched him mount his horse and quickly disappear into the night.

It was darker away from the Palace grounds, and the wind whipped at my skirts, but nothing would deter me from my task—there was too much at stake. In my heart I believed in the tales I had heard. They brought back snatches of gossip I'd heard at Clagny as a girl. Grandmère had a talisman, and told me to touch it from time to time. I remembered she kept it tucked in her bodice. I expect she died wearing it, only a piece of paper with crooked stars and words I don't remember, but she had treated it with respect. And after I'd touched it, I was made to close my eyes and imagine myself surrounded by an orange light, and yes, it was coming back to me now, my feet had to be bare, and I was made to stamp the bare earth three times after asking to be kept away from the 'evil eye', whatever that was. Afterwards she would encourage me to eat well, "To stop you floating on the astral." I used to quite enjoy those little rituals, and wished I'd payed more attention. Perhaps it would have helped me now. I lowered the lamp and followed the wind chasing ribbon rags of cloud that pointed to a turn on the muddy road.

The only sound was the wind moaning in the trees, until a fox's bark nearly made me die with fright. I was sorry I hadn't let Celia accompany me after all. My hands felt damp with fright, and I felt sure Fernando and Raoul had forgotten to tie those markers on the trees. My heart palpitated with fright, and I hurried on with irregular steps, not daring to look about me. I saw another white flicker to point my way as it began to rain, lightly at first, but then with a vengeance. The hem of my dress was caked with mud, and it dragged heavily around my legs. The turbulent wind blew the hair across my face, and as many times as I pushed it back into the hood, so the tireless wind blew it back again. I was sure I was lost, and even thought of turning back for Celia who knew the district far better than I.

"Fernando," I called, but my voice sounded like a wail, carried by the storm. Continuing walking without any clear conception of where I was, I became palsied with terror, convinced the men had been killed and I was soon to follow. The dim, yellow moon was covered by a lacy branch of a tree, and as I watched, a black cloud inched across it, leaving me in fearful darkness except for the feeble lamp I clutched in front of me. The rain stung my eyes as I ran, and looked in vain for where I should go. The wind tore at my clothes when

I stopped dead, stiffened with fear, and clenched my teeth till my jaw ached.

"You're late!"

"Who is it?" I gasped, cowering back from the darkness in front of me. Suddenly, a lamp was held high, casting its smoking light on an old crone who looked no more than a bundle of tattered rags.

"You'd best come out of the storm." I shrank away from the cracked rasp of a voice, no longer feeling the heavy rain. The hair hung in long matted locks over a ravaged face. The ageless eyes, devoid of expression, were fixed on me, and I knew that the creature could smell my fear.

A laugh pierced the air, shrill and loud. The witch turned and I stumbled after her searching frantically for signs of the men. Inarticulate words came as I forced myself after the demoniacal being, with an anxiety that amounted to agony. She led me into a passage that stank of urine and human excrement. My clothes were sodden, and I was cold. Something brushed against my leg, and I gave out a strangled cry.

"Ha, ha, ha, ha, ha," she laughed. "The cat won't harm you, will you, Asmodée? Not unless she doesn't like you. Ha, ha, ha."

We entered a cavern, the walls hewn from rock, with water dripping down. The flicker of candle flames gave a faint light. I stood there, half-conscious, so terrified that I was numb. There were several more black candles in pewter holders on a high altar, covered with a dusty cloth. A skull peered at me from two sightless eyes. I began to tremble as I saw, lying next to it, a large tapering knife, its handle shaped like the hilt of a sword. The cat slunk to the fire that crackled with twigs, warming the cauldron that hissed its smoke around the gruesome place, giving off odours of stale blood, and burning flesh, and others I couldn't identify.

A claw-like hand took my lamp and placed it on the floor. She sat on a three-legged stool at the side of the altar, and the cat sprang onto her shoulder. I shrank back, terrified that it would jump on me.

"Drink from the goblet by the skull, don't be afraid, it'll warm you." I shook my head. "Bring it here, I'll show you, ha, ha, ha, ha, ha."

I picked it up and noticed with horror the rope and bones beside it. I handed the goblet to her, and watched her drink deeply. My mouth felt full of dust and I forced myself to take a sip. It was bitter, but not too vile. The snake eyes followed my movements.

"Good, isn't it? Menstrual blood and cat piss, nothing like it! Ha, ha, ha, ha, ha." I gagged at the thought of what I'd just drunk, and held my stomach and my gut heaved. The room was swimming dizzily, and the cold floor came up to meet me.

When I came to, she was still sitting in the same position, the cat staring at me. My first thought was to run, but I knew I must nerve myself to do what I'd come for.

"Why did you send for me?" I pushed myself up by my elbows and propped myself against the clammy wall.

"Did you bring the gold?"

I pushed my hood off, and undid my cloak, and reached inside for the diamond that had been returned to me, and held it out to her. "I've brought something more valuable than gold."

The snake eyes glittered for a moment, then went dead again. The wrinkled claw snatched it from me, and in an instant it was hidden somewhere amongst her ragged garments. As she removed her hand an object fell out. I recognized it at once, and my breath caught in my throat. Lying there at our feet was an old satin slipper belonging to my son. I froze at the sight of it, but knew I mustn't panic if I wanted the truth.

"Now, I know how clever you are, and have paid you far more than you asked. I think it only right that you fulfill your part of the bargain."

The yellow eyes flicked over the slipper, and then back to me. "I made no bargains. The message I got was that you wanted the name of the person who gave you the doll. That's all I am prepared to do."

"Well, what is it?" I bent and picked up the pathetic little slipper and tucked it in my sleeve.

"It was a man who had me make the doll, and send it to you. Who handed it over isn't important, just the first person he saw."

"A man, what man?"

"Can't you guess?"

"I've not paid you to make me guess."

"True, he, he, he, he!" The noise echoed from the walls like an animal screeching over its prey.

"Well, who is this man?"

"Haven't you noticed a man's loving eye on the handsome, dark Spanish gentleman? He must think a great deal of him to buy a love potion, and go to the trouble of paying for the doll, and bring me the slipper and hair. My potions don't come cheap."

I knew instantly. It was Raoul she spoke of. I whispered his name in astonishment. Of the men, only he was at Fernando's side continually. That was why he was so loving to me one moment, and strangely cruel at others. He was in love with Fernando! I should have guessed.

"But why would he want to harm the child?"

"That isn't hard to fathom when you've helped as many schemers as I have. Get rid of the little lame brat, then the mother, and there is no one to keep his love from him."

I gasped aloud, "And I thought de Villette was after Fernando for herself!"

"She was, and the pretty fair gentleman used her as a convenient camouflage."

But surely it can't be hard for Monsieur Raoul to show his true feelings at Court. After all, it's nothing unusual, why does he keep them to himself?"

"Because the dark gentleman isn't interested in Monsieur Raoul."

"I understand."

"I've other things to do. You'll have to go."

"And you won't harm my son now?"

"I didn't say that."

"How can I be sure that you won't?"

"You can't."

"I'll do anything you ask me, if you promise not to harm him."

A flicker of avarice passed over her wizened countenance. "It won't be easy," she cackled.

"I'm ready."

"Can't imagine why a brat's worth all the trouble. There's many we've burnt here, and good riddance to the little bastards!"

Bile rose in my throat, and the stench from the contents of the cauldron stank in my nostrils. I shuddered. "Tell me what you want, and I'll go away."

"I want gold."

"That's impossible. I've already given you the diamond, which is worth more than many gold coins."

"I can't spend the diamond, and do you think I'm going to deck myself with it? That's my price, now leave me. I know there's more gold in the Palace than anywhere on earth."

"You've no idea what you're saying, it's out of the question." I panicked.

"You pretty ladies at Court know how to wheedle gold from the King. Now leave me, I say."

"Very well, I'll try."

"I want it by tomorrow and you must come yourself, your maid will not do. And tell the men I knew they were outside. I should punish you for bringing them. But if you get the gold, I'll take the matter lightly. Should you decide to get clever, I'll know, and you can guess the result. He, he, he, he, he!" I pulled my cloak on, and tied the hood. I couldn't wait to escape the stinking cave. "Asmodée will go looking for you, if you fail me," she cried after me.

I shuddered as I grabbed the lamp and groped my way out along the dark passage. Two pairs of eyes followed me. I could feel them on my back. The awful smells, putrid and sickening, clung to me long after I reached the fresh air.

Fernando was there waiting under a tree, alone. I could see him silhouetted on his horse in the dawn light. As soon as he caught sight of me, he cantered over, bent and lifted me up in front of him.

"Why didn't you come sooner? I've been frightened out of my wits. I thought you'd lose me."

The horse carried us towards the Palace in the cold, clear air.

"On the contrary, I was always nearby. I've only just sent the men back. You handled that well."

"How do you know?"

"I was in the passageway, ready if you needed me."

"If only I'd known!"

"If you had, it might have shown in your manner, and we would never have known the truth."

"You didn't suspect Raoul, then?"

"I knew he was fond of me, but not to such a degree. I'd always thought it was you he loved."

"Perhaps he loved us both."

"Perhaps, but is that reason enough to want the death of our innocent child? It could have turned into a tragedy."

"So you believe in witchcraft, after all?"

He clutched my waist tighter, and urged his horse faster. The wind licked my face, and I felt cleansed of the stink that I'd never wholly forget.

"I think the death of the witch will solve our problems. I'm not prepared to take a chance on a child's life."

"You can't have her killed, there are still things to be done. You heard what she said."

"It is impossible to get her gold. If she doesn't exist, there is nothing she can do."

We entered the Cour de Marbre that we'd left only a few hours earlier, and I realized sadly that now I knew there were people so evil that they'd stop at nothing to achieve their hearts' desires. I felt that what I had gone through would sour me for a long time.

Chapter 36

Fernando joined me in the bed chamber, after we had undressed in our separate ante-rooms. We had been apart a long time, and I for one felt by no means at ease with him. With my son's slipper hidden amongst my laces, I forced myself to speak of the gold. Between us we sat and schemed, but we couldn't think of a way to get so much gold within only a few hours. Then suddenly it came to me.

"I will go to his Majesty, and tell him the truth."

"You must be mad, Solange!" Fernando sprang to his feet. "Only mention witchcraft and he'll never listen to another word. His Majesty went to enormous trouble to have witchcraft stamped out. If it hadn't been for Athénaïs being mixed up in it, even our old crone would have been burnt, no doubt."

"There isn't time for anything else, unless . . ." I twisted a curl that had fallen onto my shoulder.

"Unless what? What mad scheme have you thought up now?"

"Unless I ask the King to let me borrow the gold for one day."

"And why would he do that, may I ask? What will be your reason?"

"I'll have to think of one. Do be quiet a moment, I'm concentrating! Order some hot chocolate."

"But..."

"Please, Fernando, I'm thinking."

He did so, and stalked around the room, convinced I was out of my wits, no doubt.

"I've got it!"

"Got what?"

The hot chocolate had arrived, and we drank cup after cup, while I told him of my simple plan. "It's my birthday tomorrow, or rather today. I'll have a party and ask his Majesty to let me possess the gold till it's over."

Fernando's firm eyebrows raised, dubiously. "He'll be sure to refuse such a stupid request."

"We shall see. I'll say I want to pretend it's mine."

"Ridiculous! You don't stand a chance."

Morning light was already creeping in through the curtains. I opened them myself, and looked out to a clean, new day. "I feel that all will go well. It has to. What will you do about Raoul?"

"Leave that to me, he won't be around much longer. If only he had made his love clear to me, we could have come to some arrangement. I could kill him with my bare hands, when I think what he tried to do. Did he think I'd love him better, with you and Louis Fernando gone? The man's a bigger fool than I suspected."

"I'm chilly, Fernando, I'm going to rest for an hour. His Majesty won't be up till it's time for the *levée*. I'll see him directly after. He won't refuse me." I slipped out of my dressing robe, and Fernando tucked the coverlet under my chin. "I'm sure I won't close my eyes, but I want to be refreshed for a long, hard day."

He bent and kissed my forehead tenderly, his warm lips caressing my flesh. I almost stretched my arms out to kiss him back, then he smiled gently. "You've been through a great deal, my lovely wife. Sleep well. All will go well, I'm sure, and then perhaps..." but he didn't finish the sentence.

"Now to deal with Raoul, but not before I take a look at my son."

His face softened, and I realized that he was truly fond of the child.

"You can't deal with Raoul in a dressing robe."

"Don't you think I must know something of such things, after the work I've been doing all this time? I would not have survived. Do give me some credit, please!"

I smiled to myself. It really was amazing, I thought, not for the first time, how like a little boy he was at times.

"Of course, forgive me, I must be more tired than I realized," I yawned.

When I awoke, I could hardly believe the happenings of the night, but then my hand felt for the diamond, and I knew it was no dream. It was impossible for me to sleep, so I rang for Celia, and asked her to dress me at once.

"But, My Lady, I've been waiting to hear!"

"Later, Celia, please. All is under control, but I have to see his Majesty soon, and I must look my best."

"After all I've been through with you," Celia whined, "And to think how I've never slept a wink, worried sick as I've been."

"Oh very well, Celia, you're quite right. Give me the rust-colored riding habit, now be quick, woman."

She dressed me, interrupting at almost every word I uttered till I refused to continue.

"I promise I won't stop you again, My Lady, please go on!" But when I came to the part about Raoul, she didn't seem to understand.

"Don't try to understand," I advised, "It's true, anyway . . . and Celia?"

"Yes, My Lady?" she stood in front of me, gazing down at her big feet.

"It wasn't Raoul you spent the night with in the inn."

The watery eyes met mine. "What do you mean?" she rasped.

"It was his manservant, I know for sure, do you

understand?"

"No, no I don't at all."

"Would you mind, dear, if we left the full explanation till after tonight? I must get to the *levée* early."

Before she had time to protest, I took a last fleeting look at myself in the mirror. Yes, the rust velvet was most becoming. I said quickly, "Celia, my crop." She ran for it, and I left her standing there, open-mouthed. I'm sure she was convinced I'd had a spell cast on me.

I had to be sure my son was in good health before I did anything, and made the long trip to the nurseries. I was shown into the bedchamber where little Louis was still asleep, surrounded by toys, one pink thumb firmly in his mouth. Nanny removed it very gently. The soft curls framed his rosy face, and I could smell the warm cleanliness of his skin. I smiled, and after thanking Nanny and her maids, quietly departed.

I couldn't get into the King's room while the levée was taking place, bustling with noblemen and all those privileged to witness the King's dressing and toilette, and the procession to Mass which followed. Only after calling to see Madame to pay my respects did I manage to come face to face with his Majesty.

"You look very pale, Solange," Madame remarked, "I hope you're not worried still about our little problem of yesterday."

"I think there are too many lilies and tuberoses in my room, Madame."

Madame lay on her day bed, the lines of her face blurred as if she had not long risen from sleep. "I told you not to worry! I suppose you've been without sleep!"

"Yes, I must admit I have, Madame."

"Now, this won't do, what is the point of my taking all this trouble on your account, if you don't benefit from it."

"I'm sure I'll be able to sleep after today, Madame. Did you destroy the doll?" I couldn't help asking.

"Indeed I did! Disgusting thing it was!" Her ladies fussed round her, arranging her coiffure. "That will do," she dismissed them. "I'm very tired today too, I didn't sleep well, I can't think why."

"I'm sorry if I tired you, Madame."

"It wasn't your fault, child."

"May I ask you a favor, Madame?" I said quickly.

"What is it?"

"It's my birthday today." Madame smiled.

"Look on the silver table." I turned my head, then in delight smiled.

"Oh, Madame, you remembered!"

On the silver table under the window, there was something silken that caught the light. I laid my crop on the chair nearby, and touched the gown, lifting it up, feeling the thick silk. I gasped, "It's the most beautiful gown I've ever seen!"

Madame beamed. The ivory satin glowed, and felt cool to my touch. Small diamonds and emeralds encircled the décolletage, and rich cream lace formed transparent sleeves. Emerald green leaves were embroidered on the skirt, and tiny bunches of ivory satin formed buds between them.

"I'm pleased you like it, child."

"Like it? I love it, and shall wear it this evening! You are too kind, Madame. Thank you for my lovely present. I was wondering if I might have a small party."

"Of course you may, child." Madame beamed her pleasure. "If you take a rest this afternoon. Don't you think a ride will be too tiring after a sleepless night?" She eyed my elegant habit.

"I thought the excursion might be good for me." I folded the dress carefully over the outstretched arms of the servant who had brought in the wine, and instructed her to have it laid out for me in my room. "Do you think it would be possible for me to speak to his Majesty this morning, Madame, after the *levée*?"

"His Majesty will be here in a moment, I believe. Why don't you forget about your ride, and join us in a glass of wine?"

I tried not to seem too relieved at this stroke of good

fortune. "I would be honoured, Madame." I sipped wine with Madame, chatting about little Louis' health and I frantically wracked my brain as to how I'd be able to speak to him alone about the delicate and unseemly request I had to make.

"You're miles away, child. You certainly need an afternoon's nap, and so do I." Madame yawned behind her hand, the fat fingers dented where the rings dug into her flesh.

We were joined by several of the King's gentlemen, fashionably attired in velvet coats and breeches, lace ruffles at their wrists and throats. Soon his Majesty appeared, and I swooped into a deep curtsey.

"Ah, Madame Solange, this is an early call. I am delighted to have you back in our Court. On your way to ride, I see? It looks a fine Autumn day, blustery and dry." He sat down near Madame.

"Good morning, Sire."

If it were not for the magnificence of their apparel, and the luxury of their surroundings to remind one of their eminence, one would have taken them for any old married couple, seeing them exchange contented, well-worn smiles.

"I am pleased to see your Majesty is in good health," I stammered, terrified that his sharp eyes would bore into my brain, and refuse what I now realized to be an impossible request before I had asked it. "Yes, I was thinking of riding this morning, your Majesty." I was shocked to see how old he looked in the harsh light from the window, the nose quite hooked and curved, and his jowls sagging.

As his gentlemen attended to his every need, I noted the intelligent black eyes hadn't lost any of their intensity. One elegant hand rested on his thigh, and he stretched one white stockinged leg while describing the antics of his dogs to Madame. I began to think my task was hopeless, until he stood to take his leave.

"By the way, I have a little something I think you'll like, Solange. Let us take a stroll, if Madame will forgive us."

Madame nodded her head graciously, and we took our

leave. I could hardly believe my good luck, as with my hand on the King's arm we entered another Salon. I felt sure he could hear my heart beating.

"I will not be needing you, now," his Majesty casually told his gentlemen, without a glance in their direction.

He turned to me, and stroked my neck tenderly. I felt hot suddenly, not quite knowing what to say. But after all he was still a man, and I supposed the best thing to do was to seem flattered.

"Now, tell me what you think of our Court since you were with us last?" I felt his warm breath on my face, and before I could answer, he'd buried his mouth in my neck, and pushed his hand beneath my skirt. I glanced quickly around us, and noted with relief that the gentlemen had departed. The perfume of his clothes, dry and heady, filled my nostrils, and then I felt his mouth on mine, surprisingly strong, his body hard-pressed against mine. It was not unpleasant.

"Happy Birthday, dear little Solange," he smiled to me.

I whispered, "Thank you, Sire," flustered and rather shy.

"Don't run away, my pet, come and tell me what you would like for a gift?" He sat and held his arms out to me, and I ran to him, and sat on his lap.

Although I didn't want to appear ungrateful, I'd rather have asked for the loan of the gold, and disappear quickly. But I knew by now that life wasn't quite so simple. One had to work for one's needs, one way or another.

"Well, I'm waiting, or will you leave the choice to me?" I felt his hand caress my breast through my habit.

"I only want to borrow something." He examined my face, and I flushed, feeling ungrateful for all he'd done for me, and knowing that I needed to trick him.

"You're hiding something. Do you want to tell me?" How could I try to charm gold from his coffers, when so many at Court had done so before? I couldn't read his eyes, they were so knowledgeable. What could I tell him that was different? How many had dared to borrow a King's ransom in gold?

"Don't put a furrow on your brow, or you'll ruin your pretty face." He set me on my feet, and led me to the chaise longue which was covered in green silk. "Let me look at you properly—gladden the eyes of an old man."

I stood before him, and he half lay on the chaise, one elegant leg hanging down. "Without your worldy goods" he teased, eyebrows raised in mock expectation. Instead of thinking of my son, and how perhaps a mating with the King might help my mission, I was shocked to realize that my only thought was whether I'd grown too thin during my illness to please him.

He was by far the most vibrant man I had ever known, despite his age. I felt his virility like invisible wires connecting him to me. Quickly as I could, I began to loosen my riding habit.

"Don't hurry, my pet, there's no rush." And so, to please him, I took my time. Feeling his eyes caressing me, I removed my coat first, and then my long skirt. I let them drop around me, and my body prickled as our eyes met. I removed the rest of my underthings slowly, and as teasingly as I could. An imperceptible veil had descended on his face. I was left in my stockings, garters and stays. Never lifting my eyes from his, I slid the yellow garter down my leg, and threw it to him, and he raised it to his lips. We both laughed, knowing that today was a good day, and we'd enjoy it. I tripped over to him, and removed his coat, and threw it as far as I could, we heard a crash as it knocked a small gold chair over.

I flung myself across his large body, and knew that I was pleasing him. He held me as if I were a flower, delicate and fragile. I loved the sensation of his beautiful silky clothes and didn't care that his jewels scratched my naked flesh, in fact I rather liked the feeling.

"There's something special about you," he said.

"Perhaps only because you have made me special, Sire!"

"Not yet," he smiled, and we laughed again. He brought his hand from behind the chaise, and held a glass to my lips. I drank it down, not having realized how thirsty I'd become. After he'd poured me a glass, we fell into each other's arms, and rolled off the chaise onto the rich Savonnerie carpet. I tickled his chest and arms, and soon we were giggling as though we were playing a game. His wig fell awry, and his clothes were in disarray.

"I think this appointment was overdue," he mocked as I straightened his wig. "You please me, my little white dove," and he squeezed my breast again before he stood and straightened his clothes.

I wondered if I dared ask him now! Of course, I'd picked the wrong moment, but I didn't want to ask him before, in case he thought it was a condition for our love-play. Not that anyone would dream of refusing the King. Anyway, who could resist such a handsome and virile man? He was still like a lion.

"We'll have to go riding again, soon!" He threw at me, and we laughed easily together. I was relieved that I had pleased him, he who had tasted all the pleasures, and those I'd never know of.

"You honour me, Sire," and I meant it. "Your Majesty?" I stood there, half dressed. "Would you grant me a small favor, just for one night?"

"Again? Already?" He chuckled, and I laughed till the tears flowed. We seemed to amuse each other so easily, it made my task almost a pleasure.

"Would you trust me to borrow a purse of gold, just for my birthday?"

He adjusted his wig in the long, gold mirror over the mantle, the flames from the fire flickering over him. "I think I can find something to please you more."

"No!" I replied, too quickly. "Er . . . that is exactly what I have in mind for my party this evening."

"That is a strange gift—a loan!" Was there a note of suspicion? I glanced up at him fleetingly. I couldn't look him straight in the eyes, so busied myself dressing, fussing with my skirt, fluffing it and twisting my body to get it falling just right.

"I have some work to attend to now." His brow was creased in thought. He seemed to have changed moods quickly. "I'll arrange for you to 'borrow'" (an eyebrow raised) "my gold, if that is what you desire most."

My heart leaped in my throat, but I couldn't speak. I'd expected to plead and beg and kiss his feet, anything he asked, but not have my request granted as if it were a mere trifle.

I flung myself at his feet, then looked up at him.

"This does seem to me to be a little demonstrative, even for the loan of a purse of gold, or do you intend to steal my gold after all?"

"Oh, no, believe me . . ." but I could see he was amusing himself, and using his own experienced acting ability on me. He lifted me up by the elbows, and kissed me lightly on top of my head.

"You are a precious girl, and I don't mind having a lovely girl play a little trick on me." I gasped, convinced he was playing with me, and about to have me arrested. "So, you grow pale, my little white dove. I'm quite used to intrigue and tricks. I think I know you well, Solange, you won't want me to think ill of you. So I leave you for the moment to your little game, and perhaps you will amuse me in the telling when you return my gold tomorrow?" He leaned back and pursed his lips, mocking me very slightly.

"Your Majesty," I trembled, not knowing what to say.

He placed a finger on my lips. "Tomorrow will do very well. Is it a pact?"

I let out my breath in relief, and clasped his hand tightly to my lips, and kissed it. I felt hot tears of relief. "Thank you," I whispered.

He fingered his chin, deep in thought, then led me by the elbow to a chair next to the upturned one, and waited till I had composed myself. With his own hands he poured wine for me, and as I sipped, I realized that I loved this great King in quite a different way from my love for my child or husband. I wanted to tell him, but what was the love of one subject, when he had the adulation of a nation?

He interrupted my thoughts, "Wait here a moment, little dove, you shall have your gold." A minute later his gentlemen returned to escort him away. I covered my face with my hands, and felt the hot tears slide through my fingers. I had not realized how much I had hoped he would do as I asked. I didn't even care if his men had been watching us make love, which I suspected they had.

I waited a long time before two lackeys entered, one holding a purse of gold on a velvet cushion in front of him.

Chapter 37

As I entered little Louis' nursery, he was playing with several of the children of the Court, miniatures of their elders, in their flowered dresses and little velvet suits.

"Mama!" He saw me at last. "Dearest Mama!"

All the children lined up, well-rehearsed, and as my little Louis lifted his hand, all in chorus, Nanny included with several of the ladies, wished me "Happy Birthday". It was such a thrill for me to see my little Louis in command of these Royal play-mates. I was choked with love, and could just manage to convey my thanks. Than a portrait of my son was pushed into my hands. I admired it through a blur of tears, and held him against me.

"It's the most beautiful birthday I've ever had, darling."

"I had to sit still for simply ages, Mama, didn't I, Ma'mselle?"

Ma'mselle nodded approvingly. "Indeed, you did, young man." The others crowded round me, and my arms were filled with tokens of their affection.

Soon they were playing again, the joy of giving forgotten. Happy screeches and shouting rent the air, as Ma'mselle warned, "One more minute, and then lessons begin."

Little Louis didn't seem to hear as he chased a pretty, plump doll of a girl, then pulled her dark brown ringlets. Was that a twinge of jealousy I felt as I watched her flutter long-lashed eyes at him? I was much too emotional today, I told myself. A night without sleep played funny tricks.

In spite of the excitement of the coming night, the party, and then the return visit to the witch, I managed to sleep after the *petit dejeuner.* I felt stronger and confident when Celia brought my my hot chocolate, then assisted the ladies with my ball gown. As my hair was being dressed into a high crown, Celia brought me a black box, old and costly-looking, of fine tooled leather. There was a note with it. I knew it was from Fernando, and opened it with the women fluttering round. I read to myself, feeling the return of the warm glow of love:—

To remind you of my jealous eye and heart on your Birthday, my beloved wife. If you wear my gift tonight, given with all of my undying love for you, I will know that you have forgiven your husband.

I stuffed the note down my bodice, and opened the box. There were gasps from the ladies.

"Who sent them?"

"My husband."

"Magnificent!"

"How fitting!"

Celia helped me to put the emerald earrings on. They hung like green tear-drops, surrounded by diamond stars, and seemed to make my eyes more luminous. I was pleased, and knew they had been carefully chosen. He must have known my gown had emerald leaves on it. I swung my head slowly in the mirror, and watched the stones flash their green light. I wore ivory-colored feathers in my hair, held with ribbons of emerald silk, and knew I looked my best.

Fernando escorted me in to dinner. He was waiting for me by the staircase. His eyes told me how pleased he was that I was wearing his beautiful earrings.

Fernando looked superb in cloth of silver, and bowed low over my hand, never taking his eyes from mine as he kissed it, lingeringly.

He whispered, "I've sent Raoul away with a flea in his ear. He'll not bother us again. I know the remorse he suffers will punish him enough."

I breathed a sigh of relief, and the old feeling came creeping back, causing my legs to tremble, and my eyes to sparkle, knowing that Fernando was satisfied that his punishment was just.

I was the guest of honor, and toasts were drunk to my health. I felt gay as the Courtiers crowded round me and even the Dauphin stopped for a chat, his full, healthy face relaxed above his large body. The light wig suited him, but he wasn't interested in gaining my affection and seemed oblivious of my charms, which rather annoyed me. But I had no time for reflections. Everyone else seemed to find me amusing. The noise of our revelry was almost deafening. We had to shout to be heard. It was a pity that Monsieur Phillipe couldn't be with us, he had loved a good party.

But there was no time to regret for long.

In the Salon d'Apollon, before the dancing, the gentleman opposite me threw a grape down my neckline, and even Fernando joined in, throwing grapes to the lady opposite him. I was glad she was only the fat Duchesse de Siesli, nevertheless. Soon there wasn't a bunch of grapes intact, in fact, scores were being kept—two points for a bull's eye, and three if the grape disappeared inside a dress.

Many a lackey was hit in the eye and stopped in the serving of refreshments as a flying grape hit him and slithered down his front. One of the servants wiped a smashed green grape from his straight nose where it had landed, never flinching. He continued serving the old Comte de Villette with chicken in wine sauce, and several grapes then hit him on his posterior. We were like children enjoying a harmless prank while the grown-ups were not watching. A cheer went up as Fernando scored eleven points—but he was cheating!

The heat from the chandeliers began to make me feel faint with all the exertion. De Villette had loosened her already gaping décolletáge as Fernando continued to score twelve, thirteen and fourteen points as the grapes continued to hit their target. I shot Fernando a devilish look, and he obliged by rubbing his hand over de Villette's middle, squashing the grapes to a gooey mash.

"The amorous imp," the ladies squeeled.

"What does he want with that Grandmère?" a beautifully gowned matron remarked.

"I do find a change for the worse can be quite invigorating," the Dauphin calmly remarked, as he pushed a whole bunch of black grapes down my beautiful gown, then bent to remove them with his thick lips, one by one.

Soon the ladies stood on the table, amongst the refreshments, causing the gold dishes to clatter to the floor. Goblets spilled, and food congealed. No one seemed to care, and the game continued with gusto. But, though the gentlemen called for more grapes to be brought, apparently we'd exhausted the supply. "Solange must invent the next game," the rotund Comte de Toulouse cried out in glee, as he ogled my bosom with the protruding eyes of a pug dog.

I was lifted onto the table by someone. So the next game was suggested by me. I must have had too much wine. I clapped my hands, and pushed a dish of glazed cherries and cakes to the floor with my foot. "I know, everyone!" All huddled closer, those who hadn't a place on the table trying to push us off, but we kicked out, and most of us managed to keep our privileged positions. "Another competition will be set up," I cried.

"Yes, a good idea," came from all sides. "Tell us, Solange, what shall it be?"

"Clear the table, everyone." Instead of allowing the lackeys to do so (it would have meant making room for them to squeeze through and no one was prepared to give up their place) we pushed the remaining food and wine onto the floor, or over the luckless people who squeezed forward to join in the fun. My green silk slippers were covered in jelly. As I kicked a mound of it away, some landed on the ugly Dauphine's full breasts as she knelt, about to climb onto the table. One of the large ladies, adorned in a severely-cut grey silk gown, began eating it, cheered by her friends.

I had never known such a party, we were uproariously gay. The ugly Dauphine was lifted onto the table as a reward, followed by her delighted friend, but of course, that meant two other large people were pushed off.

I held up my hand. "Quiet, everyone! Quiet please!" The voices lowered slightly, but then the laughter and stamping continued, as food was still being thrown, some hitting their targets on the ceiling. Tienne beamed up at the design which the pink and brown gateaux had made next to the ormolu chandelier as it came hurtling down, and caught a stony-faced footman on the top of his neat white wig, then dripped like thawing dirty snow onto his immaculate blue doublet. He stood there like a statue beside the double doors, and I wondered if he'd even noticed. This delighted everyone. "Bravo, bravo!" was echoed from the company.

I held up my hand again. "The competition!" There was a buzz of anticipation as they waited, eager to be on with the game. Fernando held an arm round my waist, and whispered in my ear, but I couldn't hear what he said. A roar went up. Everyone wanted to know what it was.

I shouted, "Quiet, I beg of you, or we'll not be able to begin."

I caught sight of de Villette, her eyes glazed and swivelling. As if in a trance, she looked ecstatically happy, propped against a silver table, adorned with a huge gold vase of pink tuberoses. I could see her goblet was held so loosely in her hand, that the wine dripped onto the floor. I began to laugh, and pointed. She looked so funny, with her *postiche* leaning dizzily to one side, that it reminded me of the time I'd pulled it loose, so long ago when I was unhappy.

She smiled an imbecilic grin of pleasure as fun was made of the spectacle. She even joined in the laughter, not caring, or perhaps not knowing, it was aimed at her.

"The competition" I managed to croak, and lifted a candelabra from the table, blew the candles out, and bent over to find a space on the table to bang it. Fernando moved a couple of inches, but it was impossible, for when I managed to lift it, the space was quickly filled with feet.

"Silence!" I shouted, and Fernando and several others followed suit. At last there was a semblance of order. The heat was stifling. I brushed a hand across my brow. "First of all, the ladies will remove their gowns, as it's so hot."

"Oohs" and delighted giggles met this suggestion, but no one obeyed. Then some of the gentlemen began to assist the ladies, and soon we were out of our gowns, which some were lucky enough to have collected by the servants, while others were trampled underfoot. Fernando threw mine to Tienne, who ran and handed it to an expressionless footman.

"Now," I shouted, "The gentlemen will remove their breeches." There were squeals of laughter, as the ladies assisted, more skillfully than could be imagined.

"The gentlemen will now be blindfolded by the ladies." This task took quite some time, as unsteady, but eager fingers tried to tie tiny handkerchiefs round large heads.

Fernando whispered, "Now we'll slip away."

"The ladies will throw their garters onto the table, and the gentlemen will pick one to find their love of the evening." All were delighted, and the scrambling began as soon as the ladies removed blue, red, yellow or green silk and lace garters, and threw them on the table.

I noticed one young beauty push her yellow garter onto the wrist of the man of her choice. She wasn't taking any chances!

We found our way down from the table, falling amongst the crumpled table linens and scurrying people. Fernando lifted me into the crowded mass of Courtiers, trampled food and clothes. No one seemed to notice or care, they were so busily engaged. The stony-faced footman opened the doors, and we were in the ante-room.

As if by pre-arrangement, our garments were hurriedly found by a slightly dizzy-looking Tienne who helped us put them on behind a tapestry screen.

"You remembered my instructions well," Fernando told him, as Tienne beamed.

"Tell Celia not to worry, and not a word to anyone else, Tienne, and no more wine this evening."

"I promise, Madame. Don Fernando has explained all to

me. I'll come with you if you wish," he offered hopefully, straightening his young back.

"You're a very brave young man," and I stretched to kiss his flushed cheek. "I wouldn't hear of it. You will watch over the nurseries for me. That is most important." Tienne pushed his chest out, and bowed his pleasure.

"I've just remembered, Fernando!"

"What is it?"

"His Majesty hasn't made an appearance."

"Perhaps it's just as well, the party's rather out of hand."

"I know he wouldn't miss my party, I should really wait for him."

"Tienne will take a message at once." He turned to Tienne. "Tell his Majesty that we will join him at his pleasure for a private celebration when we will have something to tell him of importance."

"I'll go at once!"

"No, wait, cherub," I put out a staying hand. "Tell him that I will return the gold as well."

Tienne looked slightly nonplussed, but made his way to deliver these words, a jaunty step in his walk.

I felt Fernando's eyes on me. "You love that boy as if he were your own."

"Tienne is like a brother to me. I love him dearly."

"He's a fine young man."

We clasped hands, and as we approached the guard room, Fernando's man appeared, and handed us our cloaks. Soon we were in the cold night air, and at once the merriment of the party was gone, and the job to be done weighed heavily on me.

Chapter 38

Sensing my apprehension, Fernando held me close to him. "I want you to let me go instead. You know it isn't necessary for you to take the gold."

I pulled away from him, and hurried over to the waiting horses, and after Fernando joined me, he lifted me up onto my horse. I dug my heels in the horse's sides, urging her to race into the night, remembering the direction of the day before.

I didn't give a backward glance, but knew the men and my husband were following. I could hear the horses' hoof beats in the distance. It was a clear night, as I remember, the moon full. It seemed no time before I came close to the figure leaning against the cave with Asmodée's bright eyes watching me. I slid down, and tied my horse to a scraggy tree.

"Good evening," I said politely.

"Have you brought it?"

"Of course."

"You can give it to me then."

I made to walk through the opening, but Asmodée sprang at me, and spat, causing me to leap back, shuddering. The witch followed me into the cave, just as Fernando rushed into the passage, and pushed me to one side. He seized the witch by her grey locks, and dropped her head back, exposing the dirty sinews of her neck.

The blade of his dagger glinted, as he slashed her throat, and I screamed to see the dark blood ooze after the knife. I was horrified to see the evil black cat stretch up, and lick the blood as it dripped.

I had to cling hard to my senses. As the witch lay slumped against the wall of the passage, I heard Fernando's voice,

"We've got to get the diamond back!"

Feeling deadly faint, I tottered forward, "I can't touch her. I'd feel unclean forever."

With an exclamation Fernando dropped to his knees, and rummaged in the dirt-stiff rags. After what seemed an interminable time, he pulled out the diamond, which flashed clearly in that midden of a cave. Pushing it into my pocket, he half-dragged, half-carried me out into the clean air.

I removed my hood, and placed the chain round my neck. Everything had happened so quickly. I hardly realized that my deepest fears were gone. It was enough to know that the witch was dead, and could do no more harm. My son could grow up safely and get stronger each day.

Instead of riding back quickly, Fernando and I lingered. "I didn't need the gold, Fernando. To think what a performance I had to put on in order to get it!"

"What performance?"

"Oh, you know."

"No, I don't know."

I made my voice sound casual, "I practically had to beg his Majesty."

"Oh!"

"Come on, it's cold." We urged our horses on, and presently the lights of the Palace met us, and we rode down the empty lanes, and through the Park to the Marble Courtyard, ghostly in the early morning light.

"You know, there was no gold in the purse," Fernando confessed. "I discussed the plan with his Majesty last night, and we thought it safer not to tell you!"

"Oh my God, what if she'd found out?"

Fernando clasped me about the waist, and lifted me down beside him, and held me close. "There wasn't time, I made sure of that."

I rested my head against his shoulder, and knew that I was trembling. "Do you think little Louis will be safe now?"

"I know he will, don't worry any more."

"And his leg?"

"We'll make sure he is given every assistance to make it right again."

We walked on air into the Palace, passing Courtiers sleeping propped against walls and statues, their wigs at rakish angles, their spoiled garments looking garish in the morning light.

"I still can't get used to people sleeping in crevices when they have beds and homes to go to."

"We are honoured to have rooms here."

"We are, indeed."

The servants were all asleep as we made our way to bed. I dreaded having to face the King tomorrow, and wished it had been I, not Fernando, who had hatched the plot with him. Worse still was the fear of Fernando hearing of my coupling with his Majesty, for there were few secrets here.

I lay in Fernando's arms, and instantly fell asleep, in spite of my misgivings, which had diminished now that my little Louis was safe.

But the new day that had been upon us before we slept blossomed all too soon, and as I blinked my eyes, and was about to step from the bed, I felt my hand grasped.

"Not so quickly, wife!"

I turned to face my husband. "I didn't know you were awake."

He grinned, revealing those gleaming teeth. "We have a rendezvous with the King, have you forgotten? It must be mid-day." I tried to pull my hand away. The grin broadened.

"You have a duty here, first."

"I must see little Louis before I see the King, Fernando. I must go!"

He pulled me to him, and as soon as our lips met, nothing could have persuaded me to go. His arms felt so strong as he turned me over, and traced his lips down my body, and then he ripped my nightgown in two. His body felt firm and smooth, his long legs hairy against mine.

"Did you miss me all the time I was away, dearest?" he whispered.

"I didn't dare answer, but thought it safer to cover his mouth with kisses, and pursed my lips up to his, but he persisted, "Not until you tell me."

"Don't kiss me, then," I pouted.

"Did you miss me?" he insisted.

"You know I did, Fernando, what a question," I said lightly.

"Swear it on our son's life!"

I pulled away from him and snarled, "Don't you *ever* ask me to swear that, after all I've been through! Get away from me, always thinking of yourself. How much I missed you, indeed." I sprang from the bed, and flung my robe around me. "When I was waiting in Burgos perhaps, or whilst I was kept prisoner in the Pyrenees; or maybe while I was following my son to wherever I heard he'd been kidnapped, do you think I missed you then? Hah!" I stamped my foot, then rang for my maid.

He lay there, scowling, while I flounced after pink-faced Celia to my dressing room.

Chapter 39

After I was gowned, and had broken my fast, I made my way to the Grande Appartements to keep my appointment with the King. I knew little Louis would be out for his walk at such an hour.

Tienne accompanied me as usual.

"How strange it seems, cherub, that you are now taller than I."

This caused him to hold his head high with pride. "Hadn't you noticed before?"

"I suppose I did. When I think how tiny you were when I first came to the Court, it makes me feel I'm getting old."

"We're nearer the same age now, whereas before I was but a child." He gave a casual lift to his hand, to emphasize the point.

"And your courtly manners are showing," I teased.

He bowed, and lisped in a small voice, "Your servant, Ma'mselle," an eager expression, as of a child, lit his cheeky face.

"That is exactly what you said to me the first day we met."

"I know," he smiled.

We stood inside the ante room, and I squeezed his hand.

Bontemps showed me to the King's bedroom. He was taking some light refreshment after his afternoon nap. A fire was leaping in the fireplace, and his Majesty sat in front of a silver table, sipping from a goblet, surrounded by courtiers and advisers, chatting and laughing.

A lackey held a chair at the table for me, and several gentlemen bowed acknowledging my presence.

"You are late for our rendezvous," his Majesty remarked rather icily, and eyed me with a face darker than Fernando's in one of his sulks. I began to tremble as I heard the chatter cease, and we were surrounded by curious eavesdroppers.

I looked down at my lilac-clad arms, and felt my hands tremble. I should have known better than to forget my promise to his Majesty. I looked up at him quickly, about to beg his forgiveness on my bended knees, if necessary. He was stroking his chin, and eyeing me quizzically. Then his face broke into a slow smile, "A glass for Donna Solange."

A goblet was whisked in front of me. I sat down, too nonlussed to speak. "Drink with me," his Majesty invited. I felt disappointment around me; they had hoped for fireworks at least. "You may leave us," his Majesty commanded.

Several of the gentlemen lingered, I thought, hoping to be included in our conversation. One icy stare from his Majesty, and they quickly found the door.

I took a long drink of wine, and as I placed the goblet back on the table, I was surprised to see Fernando enter and bow low. He wore his purple velvet coat, and seemed quite composed.

"Don Fernando."

"Your Majesty?"

"Go next door to the 'Bull's-eye Chamber' and bring me the box from the table inlaid with Florentine pietra dura mosaic."

Fernando bowed to the King and walked away, his eyes reluctant to leave mine. I seized the opportunity whilst he was away, and said hurriedly, "There is something I have been trying to ask you all the years I've been at Court, your Majesty."

He placed a finger in front of my lips to silence me. "Not now!"

Fernando returned, and handed him the black velvet box. With a flourish of his wrist, the King flung its contents on to the silver table in front of us. Our eyes goggled at the diamonds blazing like a handful of rainbows that tumbled and glittered before us. I gasped.

"They're all there but one," the King said knowingly, holding me with his eyes. I put out a cautious finger and touched a hard, cold gem. "Have you guessed my meaning?"

Knowledge flooded over me. My hand crept up and pulled the little linen bag containing my own treasured jewel from between my breasts.

The King leaned back on his pillow, and half shut his eyes. "I had a dear friend, Cardinal Mazarin. He and my mother taught me nearly everything I know, and the courtiers flattered me and likened me to the sun, and so I chose it as my symbol. When Mazarin died, he bequeathed his eighteen perfectly matched diamonds to me. They are known as 'Les Mazarins', and here are seventeen of them." He swept his hand over the shimmering heap.

"Nearly twenty-two, or was it twenty-four, years ago, on the way to Versailles, I saw a girl. She was like sunlight . . ." His voice sounded far away. "She was only a peasant, but her beauty was dazzling. Her hair was curled in tendrils, and caught the light of the sun. She ensnared my heart."

"My mother, Sire?" I breathed.

"Yes," he whispered, his small, brilliant eyes staring into space. "Your pretty face puzzled me for a long time, like the memory of a dream. Then I remembered."

I realized that it was true, that the great Louis did indeed give the impression of knowing everything. I took my diamond—the diamond that the Sun King had given my Mother—from its linen shroud. I stretched out my hand, and moved to place the gem amongst the others, but he took my wrist, and with his other hand, closed my fingers around it. I felt the facets against my palm as he drew my hand to his lips, and then held it to his cheek.

"This is the only Mazarin missing from the eighteen, and you must keep it, Solange. It will be a keepsake when you are living in Spain again. I should have known when you first came to our Court that you were my Sun Princess. And now you know the answer to the question you wished to ask, it seems to me."

"Yes," I whispered, "I've learned a lot of things, but that was the most important. I had no idea of the answer, Sire."

"And neither had I, till last night when Fernando told me of your troubles, and of the huge cushion-shaped diamond he wanted to retrieve for you. I knew it had to be my Mazarin. It was unlike me to split a complete set of jewels, but your Mother was a precious girl."

"Thank you, Sire."

"And now I know your husband wants you to return to Spain with him. I have need of him there."

I glanced at Fernando, and noted the look of pride in his face as he looked at me. "Say you will, Princess Solange," he teased. I smiled, realizing I hadn't lied to his Mother, the Iron Butterfly; after all, I really was a Princess. Could it be possible that I had an inkling of the truth all along, even as we had disported ourselves on my birthday? Who knows?

I came back to the present with a start. His Majesty was asking me a question. "You may leave your delightful son here, if you wish. We have all grown quite attached to him, and that way we will be sure of your speedy return."

Before I could answer that I wouldn't hear of it, Fernando spoke for us both, "Our son must travel with us, your Majesty, but we are deeply honoured by your proposal. My Father, Don Miguel will be waiting to see his grandson again. With your permission, of course, when he is older we will be honoured if you would have him as a page for the Royal household."

"Of course. In that case," his Majesty shrugged and smiled, "Shall we say that you will return with my grandson before his eighth birthday, my daughter?"

I felt myself blush at the compliment of his Majesty's acknowledgement, and turned to Fernando who held my hand in his.

"I think we can safely promise that."

We took our leave of my father, the King, and spent one last night in the Palace before our journey to Fernando's home. As we lay clasped in each others arms, I felt it wasn't enough for Fernando to call little Louis his son. I pulled away from him, and looked hard into his eyes, darker than ever in the light of the single candle.

"Do you really accept Louis Fernando as your true son? I must know."

He frowned, returning my stare. "Isn't it enough to know we truly love each other?" I leaned over him, my hair brushing his face, and heard his husky whisper coming through my hair. "I'll tell you this, *ma cherie*, our next child will certainly be mine!"

I smiled and licked my finger, and pinched out the flame of the candle.

the trade

william h. hallahan

'Puts William Hallahan up above Le Carré, Deighton and Co.'
The Bookseller

Journalist Bernie Parker didn't make a lot of sense that day. His words needed a bit of explanation. But Bernie is in no position to do that right now because he's just stopped several bullets outside a Paris metro. Bernie is dead. And no one knows what his last words mean.

The least Colin Thomas owes his late friend is a reason. As an international arms dealer scoring off the hotter edges of the cold war he has contacts. Contacts that lead him back to a ruthless and uninhibited woman and to the centre of a devastating plan to change the face of Europe – even if it means starting World War 3 – even if it means starting the countdown to doomsday . . .

ADVENTURE THRILLER 0 7221 4215 3 £1.75